NOON: 22nd CENTURY

Night on Mars

Suddenly the red-brown sand under the crawler treads gave way. Pyotr Alekseevich Novago threw her into reverse. "Jump!" he shouted to Mandel. The crawler shuddered, throwing up clouds of sand and dust, and started to turn stern up. Novago switched off the engine and scrambled out of the crawler. He landed on all fours, and, without standing up, scurried off to one side. The sand slid and sank underneath him, but Novago managed to reach firm ground. He sat down, tucking his legs under him.

He saw Mandel, who was kneeling at the opposite edge of the crater, and the stern of the crawler, shrouded in steam and sticking up out of the sand on the bottom of the newly formed crater. Theoretically it was impossible for something like this to happen to a Lizard model. Here on Mars, at least. A Lizard was a light, fast machine—a five-seat open platform mounted on four autonomous caterpillar-tracked chassis. But here it was, slowly slipping into a black pit, at the bottom of which sparkled the treasure of deep-buried water. Steam was gushing up from the water.

"A cavity," Novago said hoarsely. "This wasn't our day, it seems."

Mandel, his face covered up to the eyes by his oxygen mask, turned to Novago. "No, it sure wasn't," he agreed.

There was absolutely no wind. Puffs of steam from the crater rose vertically into the violet-black sky sprinkled with bright stars. The sun hung low in the west—a small bright disk over the dunes. Black shadows stretched from the dunes to a reddish valley. It was completely still—the only sound was the rustling of the sand flowing into the crater.

"Well, all right," Mandel said as he got up. "What'll we do? We can't drag it out." He nodded in the direction of the cavity. "Or can we?"

Novago shook his head. "No, Lazar, we can't pull it out."

There was a long, slurping sound, the stern of the crawler disappeared, and on the black surface of the water a few bubbles swelled up and burst.

"You're probably right—we can't pull it out," said Mandel. "So we'll have to walk, Pyotr. But it's no big deal—thirty kilometers. We should get there in five hours or so."

Novago looked at the black water. A delicate pattern of ice was already forming on it.

Mandel glanced at his watch. "It's eighteen-twenty now. We should be there by midnight."

"Midnight," Novago said dubiously. "Right at midnight."

There are thirty kilometers left, he thought. *Of which we'll have to cover twenty in the dark. Of course we do have infrared glasses, but it's still a bum deal. Something like this would have to happen. . . . In the crawler we would've arrived before dark. Maybe we should go back to the base and get another crawler? But the base is forty kilometers away, and all the crawlers are out, and we'd get to the settlement tomorrow morning, which would be too late. Damn, what a mess this has turned out to be!*

"Never mind, Pyotr," Mandel said, and slapped himself on the thigh, where under his coat a pistol hung in its holster. "Let's get a move on."

"Where are the instruments?" Novago asked.

Mandel looked about. "I threw them off," he said. "Aha! Here they are." He took a few steps and picked up a small valise. "Here they are," he repeated, brushing sand off the valise with the fur sleeve of his coat. "Shall we go?"

"Let's go," said Novago.

They crossed the valley, scrambled up a dune, and started down again. The going was easy. Even the one-hundred-and-eighty-pound Novago, together with oxygen tanks, heating system, fur clothing, and lead-soled boots, weighed less than ninety pounds here. Small, lean Mandel walked as if he were out for a stroll, casually swinging the valise. The sand was firm, caked together. Walking on it left almost no footprints.

"I'm really going to get it from Ivanenko about the crawler," Novago said after a long silence.

"What are you talking about?" objected Mandel. "How could you have known that there was a cavity there? And anyhow, we discovered water."

"The fact is the water discovered us," Novago said. "And I'll catch it for the crawler all the same. You know old Ivanenko— 'Thank you for the water, but I'll never trust you with a crawler again.'"

Mandel laughed. "Never mind, it'll blow over. It won't even be all that hard to tow out the crawler—look, what a beauty!"

On the crest of a nearby dune, with its fearsome triangular head turned toward them, sat a mimicrodon—a seven-foot lizard, brick red in imitation of the color of the sand. Mandel threw a pebble at it, but missed. The lizard crouched there with its legs spread, unmoving, like a piece of stone.

"Proud, beautiful, and imperturbable," said Mandel.

"Irina says that there are a lot of them around the settlements," said Novago. "She feeds them."

By unspoken agreement they increased their pace.

The dunes came to an end. Now they were walking over a level salt flat. Their lead soles slapped resoundingly against the congealed sand. Great patches of salt glittered in the rays of the white setting sun. Around the patches, spheres of cactus bristling with long needles showed yellow. There were a lot of these strange, rootless, leafless, stemless plants on the flat.

"Poor Slavin," said Mandel. "He's worrying, no doubt."

"Me too," Novago muttered.

"Well, you and I are doctors," Mandel said.

"So we're doctors. You're a surgeon and I'm an internist. I've performed a delivery exactly once in my life, and that was ten years ago in the best clinic in Archangel, with a full professor standing behind my back."

"Never mind," said Mandel. "I've done several deliveries. Everything will be O.K."

A prickly sphere appeared at Mandel's feet. Mandel kicked it skillfully. The ball described a long, gentle arc in the air, then started rolling, bouncing up and down and breaking off needles.

"It's a kick, and the ball slowly rolls off," Mandel said. "It's something else that's bothering me: how will the child develop under conditions of reduced gravity?"

"That's the one thing *not* bothering me," Novago said firmly. "I've already spoken with Ivanenko. We can set up a centrifuge."

Mandel thought a moment. "It's an idea," he said.

As they were skirting the last salt patch, there was a shrill whistle, and a sphere ten paces from Novago rushed high into the sky and, trailing a whitish tail of moist air behind it, flew over the doctors and fell into the center of the salt patch.

"Damn!" shouted Novago.

Mandel laughed.

"What an abomination!" Novago complained. "Every time I go by a salt patch, one of these damn—"

He ran up to the nearest sphere and kicked it clumsily. The sphere clung with its needles to the bottom of his coat.

"Damn!" Novago snapped again. With great difficulty, as he walked, he tore the sphere first off the coat, then off his gloves.

The sphere fell onto the sand. It was supremely indifferent. So it would lie, entirely motionless, sucking in and compressing the rarified Martian air, until suddenly it let it all out at once with a deafening whistle, and shot like a rocket for thirty or forty feet.

Mandel suddenly stopped, looked at the sun, and brought his watch up before his eyes. "Nineteen thirty-five hours," he muttered. "Half an hour and the sun will set."

"What did you say, Lazar?" Novago asked. He stopped too and looked at Mandel.

"The bleating of the kid lures the tiger," Mandel said. "Don't talk so loudly when it's almost sunset."

Novago looked around. The sun was already very low. Behind, in the valley, the shining salt patches had already winked out. The dunes were dark. The sky in the east had grown as black as India ink.

"Right," said Novago, looking back. "No sense in talking loud. They say *it* has very good hearing."

Mandel blinked his frost-covered eyelashes, bent down, and drew his warm pistol from its holster. He drew the bolt back with a click and shoved the pistol into the top of his right boot. Novago got out his pistol too, and inserted it into the top of his left boot.

"You shoot left-handed?" Mandel asked.

"Yes," Novago answered.

"Good," said Mandel.

"They say it helps."

They looked at each other, but by now it was impossible to make out anything above the masks and below the fur trim of the hoods.

"Let's go," said Mandel.

"Let's go, Lazar. Only now we should walk single file."

"Okay," Mandel agreed cheerfully. "Dibs on going first."

And they went on: Mandel first with the valise in his left hand, and Novago five paces behind him. *It's getting dark really fast,* Novago thought. *Twenty kilometers left. Well, maybe a little less. Twenty kilometers through the desert in total darkness . . . and any second it could jump us. From behind that dune, for instance. Or from that one, farther on.* Novago shivered. *We should have left this morning. But how could we know that there was a cavity on the route? Amazingly bad luck. But still, we should have left this morning. Or even yesterday, with the rover taking the diapers and equipment to the settlement. Or no, Mandel did an operation yesterday. . . . It's getting darker and darker. No doubt Mark is already fretting. Running to the tower again and again to see whether the long-awaited doctors are coming. But the long-awaited doctors are slogging through the sand in the desert at night. Irina tries to calm him down, but of course she's worried herself. It's their first child, and the first child born on Mars, the first Martian. She's a very healthy and steady woman. A wonderful woman! But in their place I wouldn't have had a child. Well, it will all work out. But if only we hadn't been delayed. . . .*

Novago looked steadily to the right, at the gray crest of the dunes. Mandel was also looking to the right. Consequently, at first they didn't notice the Pathfinders. The Pathfinders were also a pair, and they came up from the left.

"Hey there!" shouted the taller of the two.

The other, short, almost square, slung his carbine over his shoulder and waved.

"Whew!" Novago said with relief. "It's Opanasenko and Morgan, the Canadian. Hey, comrades!" he shouted joyfully.

"Fancy meeting you here!" said the lanky Humphrey Morgan as he came up. "Good evening, doctor," he said as he shook Mandel's hand. "Good evening, doctor," he repeated as he shook Novago's.

"Hello, comrades," boomed Opanasenko. "Fancy meeting you here."

Before Novago could answer, Morgan said unexpectedly, "Thank you—it's all healed," and again stretched out his long arm to Mandel.

"What?" asked the perplexed Mandel. "I'm glad, whatever it is."

"Oh, no, he's still in camp," said Morgan. "But he's almost well too."

"Why are you talking so strangely, Humphrey?" inquired Mandel, confused.

Opanasenko grabbed Morgan by the edge of his hood, drew him close, and shouted in his ear, "You've got everything wrong, Humphrey! You lose!"

Turning to the doctors, he explained that an hour before the Canadian had accidentally broken the diaphragms in his headphones, and now couldn't hear, although he maintained that he could get along fine in the Martian atmosphere without the help of acoustic equipment. "He claims that he knows what people will say to him anyway. We made a bet, and he's lost. Now he has to clean my carbine five times."

Morgan laughed and said that the girl Galya at the base had nothing to do with anything. Opanasenko waved his hand hopelessly and asked, "You're headed for the settlement, the biostation, I assume?"

"Yes," said Novago. "To the Slavins."

"Say, that's right," said Opanasenko. "They'll really be wanting to see you. But why are you on foot?"

"What a pain in the neck!" said Morgan guiltily. "I can't hear a blessed thing."

Opanasenko again drew him over and shouted, "Hold on, Humphrey! I'll tell you later!"

"Fine," Morgan said in English. He walked off a few paces, looked around, and unslung his carbine. The Pathfinders had heavy double-barreled semiautomatics with magazines of twenty-five explosive bullets.

"Our crawler sank on us," Novago said.

"Where?" Opanasenko quickly asked. "In a cavity?"

"Right. On the route, about forty kilometers out."

"A cavity!" Opanasenko said joyously. "Do you hear, Humphrey? Another cavity!"

Humphrey Morgan stood with his back to them and turned his head within his hood, scanning the dark dunes.

"Okay," said Opanasenko. "We'll save that for later. So the crawler sank on you and you decided to go on foot? Are you armed?"

Mandel slapped his leg. "I've got this," he said.

"Ri-ight," said Opanasenko. "We'll have to go with you. Humphrey! Damn—he can't hear."

"Hold it," said Mandel. "Why all the fuss?"

"*It* is around here somewhere," said Opanasenko. "We've seen tracks."

Mandel and Novago exchanged glances.

"Of course you know best, Fedor," Novago said indecisively, "but I had supposed. . . . After all, we *are* armed."

"Madmen," Opanasenko said with conviction. "You people at the base are, forgive me, simpletons. We warn you, we explain to you, and look what happens. At night. Through the desert. With *pistols.* What's the matter—wasn't Khlebnikov enough?"

Mandel shrugged. "I had thought that under the circumstances —" he began, but Morgan broke in, "Quiet!" and Opanasenko instantly unslung his carbine and took a position next to the Canadian.

Novago quietly let out a breath and slipped the pistol from his boot.

The sun was almost gone—a narrow yellow-green stripe shone over the black serrated silhouettes of the dunes. The whole sky had turned black, and there was a vast multitude of stars. Starlight glinted off the barrels of the carbines, and the doctors could see the barrels slowly moving right and left.

"My mistake—sorry," Humphrey said, and they immediately started forward.

Opanasenko shouted in Morgan's ear, "Humphrey, they're going to Irina Slavina at the biostation! They need an escort!"

"Fine. I'll go," said Morgan.

"We're going together!" shouted Opanasenko.

"Fine. We'll go together."

The doctors were still holding the pistols in their hands. Morgan turned to them, took a good look, and exclaimed, "Hey, no! Put them away."

"Yes, please," said Opanasenko. "Don't even think of shooting. And put on your glasses."

The Pathfinders were already wearing infrared glasses. Mandel shamefacedly shoved the pistol into the deep pocket of his coat and transferred the valise to his right hand. Novago hesitated a moment, then put his pistol back into the top of his left boot.

"Let's go," said Opanasenko. "We won't take you by the regular route—we'll go cross-country, through the excavations. It's faster."

Now Opanasenko, with the carbine under his arm, was walking in front and to the right of Mandel. Behind and to the right of Novago paced Morgan. His carbine hung on a long strap over his shoulder. Opanasenko walked quickly, cutting sharply to the west.

Through the infrared glasses the dunes looked black and white, and the sky empty and gray. It was like a drawing in lead pencil. The desert quickly fell behind, and the drawing showed less and less contrast, as if obscured by a cloud of smoke.

"Why are you so happy about our cavity, Fedor?" asked Mandel. "The water?"

"Well, what do you think?" Opanasenko said without turning around. "Water in the first place, and, second, one cavity we found turned out to be lined with flagstones."

"Yes," said Mandel. "Of course."

"You'll find a whole crawler in *our* cavity," Novago muttered darkly.

Opanasenko suddenly made a sharp turn, and skirted round a level sandy area. At its edge stood a pole with a drooping flag.

"Quicksand," Morgan said from behind. "Very dangerous."

Quicksand was real trouble. A month ago, a special detachment of volunteer scouts had been organized to locate and mark all the quicksand patches in the vicinity of the base.

"But as I recall, Hasegawa proved that the appearance of those stone slabs could also be explained by natural forces," said Mandel.

"Yes," said Opanasenko, "that's just the point."

"Have you found anything lately?" asked Novago.

"No. They discovered oil in the east, and they found some very interesting fossils. But nothing in our line."

They walked silently for some time. Then Mandel said thoughtfully, "It could be there's nothing strange in that. Archaeologists on Earth deal with the remains of cultures that are at most hundreds of thousands of years old. But here they're tens of millions. On the contrary, it would be strange if—"

"Well, we're not complaining much," Opanasenko interrupted. "After all, we got such a fat tidbit right off—two artificial satellites. We didn't even have to dig. But then," he added after a pause, "looking is just as interesting as finding."

"Especially since the area you've already gone over is so small," said Mandel.

He stumbled and almost fell. Morgan said in an undertone, "Doctor Novago, Doctor Mandel, I suspect you're talking all the time. You shouldn't do that right now. Ask Fedor if you don't believe me."

"Humphrey's right," Opanasenko said guiltily. "We'd better keep quiet."

They passed over the ridge of dunes and started down into a valley, where patches of salt glimmered weakly under the stars.

Here we go again, thought Novago. *Those cactuses.* He had never chanced to see them at night. They radiated a bright, steady infralight. Spots of light were scattered over the whole valley. *Very pretty!* thought Novago. *Maybe they don't go off at night. That would be a pleasant surprise. My nerves are on edge as it is: Opanasenko said that* it *is out here somewhere. It* is *out here somewhere. . . .* Novago tried to imagine what it would have been like for them now without the escort, without these calm men with their heavy, deadly guns at the ready. A belated chill of fear ran over his skin, as if the outside cold had penetrated his clothing and had touched his bare body. Amid the dunes at night with just those little pistols. . . . He wondered whether Mandel knew how to shoot. He must—he had worked for several years at Arctic stations. But all the same. . . . *You didn't even think to get a rifle at the base, idiot!* Novago told himself. *We'd be in fine shape now without the Pathfinders. Of course, there was no time to think of rifles. And even now I should think about something else—about what will happen when we get to the biostation. That's more important. Right now that's the most important thing period, the most important thing of all.*

It *always attacks from the right,* thought Mandel. *Everyone says it attacks only from the right. No one knows why. And no one knows why it attacks at all. It's as though for the past million years it had done nothing except to attack from the right those people who were careless enough to set off from the base on foot at night. You can understand why it's the ones away from the base. You can imagine why it's at night. But why people, and why from the right? Could there really have been Martian bipeds who were more vulnerable on the right than on the left? Then where are they? In five years of colonization on Mars we haven't encountered one animal here bigger than a mimicrodon. At least until* it *appeared, two months ago. Eight attacks in two months. And no one here has got a good look at it—it attacks only at night. I wonder what it is. Khlebnikov had his right lung ripped out—they had to give him an artificial lung and two ribs. Judging by the wound,* it *has an unusually complex mouth mechanism. At least eight maxillae with incisor blades sharp as razors. Khlebnikov remembers only a long shining body with straight hair. It jumped him from behind a dune maybe thirty paces away.* Mandel glanced quickly to both sides. *There the two of us would be, walking along. I wonder, does Novago know how to shoot? Probably—for a long time he worked with the geologists in the taiga. He had a good idea there about the centrifuge. Seven or eight hours a day of normal weight should be quite enough for the little guy. Though come to think of it, why should it be a boy? What if it's a girl? All the better—girls can stand variations from the norm better.*

They had left the valley and the salt patches behind. To the right stretched long narrow trenches, and pyramidlike piles of

sand. In one of the trenches stood an excavator, its bucket drooping despondently.

We should get the excavator out of here, Opanasenko thought. *What
is it standing around here for? Soon the storm season starts. Maybe I'll
take it myself on the way back. Too bad it's so slow—less than a kilometer
an hour on the dunes. Otherwise it would be just the thing. My legs ache.
Morgan and I have covered around fifty kilometers today. They'll be
worried at the camp. Well, we'll send a radiogram from the biostation.
There must really be an uproar at the biostation by now! Poor Slavin.
But still, it's great. There'll be a kid on Mars! So someday there'll be people
who will say, "I was born on Mars." If only we're not too late.* Opanasenko started walking faster. *And these doctors! Doctors think rules are
made for other people. Good thing we met them. It's clear that at the base
they have no idea of what the desert is like at night. It would be a good
idea to organize a patrol, or even better, a full-scale hunt. Use every
crawler and rover the base has.*

Humphrey Morgan, immersed in silence, walked with his
hands resting on his carbine. He looked steadily to the right. He
thought about how at the camp everyone must be asleep already
except for the night watch, who would be worrying about his and
Opanasenko's absence; about how tomorrow they would have to
transfer a group to Quadrant E-11; about how he would now
have to clean Fedor's gun five evenings in a row; about how he
would have to get his headphones fixed. Then he thought that the
doctors were men with courage, and that Irina Slavina also had
courage. Then he remembered Galya, the radio operator at the
base. Whenever they met, he thought regretfully, she always
asked him about Hasegawa. The Japanese was an okay guy, but
lately he had been showing up a lot at the base too. Of course,
there was no denying that Hasegawa was smart. He was the first
one to come up with the idea that hunting for the "flying leech"
(*sora-tobu hiru*) could have a direct relation to the Pathfinders'
mission, because they might put humans onto the trail of Martian
bipeds. . . . Oh, those bipeds! Building two gigantic satellites and
then not leaving anything else behind!

Opanasenko stopped suddenly and raised his arm. Everyone
halted, and Humphrey Morgan threw up his carbine and turned
sharply to the right.

"What's happening?" Novago asked, trying to speak calmly.

He very much wanted to get out his pistol, but he felt too embarrassed.

"*It* is here," Opanasenko said softly. He waved to Morgan.

Morgan came running up, and they bent down, examining the sand. Through the firm sand ran a broad shallow rut, as if a bag with something heavy in it had been dragged over the sand. The rut began five paces to the right and ended fifteen paces to the left.

"That's it," said Opanasenko. "*It* has tracked us down and is stalking us."

He stepped across the rut, and they moved on. Novago noticed that Mandel had again transferred his valise to his left hand, and had stuck the right into his coat pocket. Novago smiled, but he felt uneasy. He had tasted fear.

"Well," Mandel said in an unnaturally cheerful voice, "since *it*'s already tracked us down, let's start talking."

"All right," said Opanasenko. "And when it springs, fall face down."

"What for?" asked Mandel, offended.

"It doesn't touch anyone who's lying on the ground," Opanasenko explained.

"Oh, yes, right."

"There's only one minor detail," muttered Novago. "Knowing when it'll spring."

"You'll notice," said Opanasenko. "We'll start firing."

"I wonder," said Mandel. "Does *it* attack mimicrodons? You know, when they stand straight up? On the tail and hind legs. . . . Hey!" he exclaimed. "Maybe *it* takes us for mimicrodons?"

"There's no point in tracking and attacking mimicrodons only from the right," Opanasenko said with some irritation. "You can just walk up and eat them—head first or tail first, as you please."

Fifteen minutes later they again crossed a rut and after another ten minutes, still another. Mandel grew silent. Now he would not take his right hand out of his pocket.

"*It* will spring in five minutes or so," Opanasenko said in a strained voice. "Now it's to the right of us."

"I wonder," Mandel said quietly. "If we walked backward would it still spring from the right?"

"Be quiet, Lazar," Novago said through his teeth.

It sprang after three minutes. Morgan shot first. Novago's ears rang. He saw the double flash of the shots; the traces, straight as an arrow, of the two streams of fire; and the white stars of the explosions on the crest of the dune. A second later Opanasenko opened fire. *Pow-pow, pow-pow-pow!* thundered the carbine shots, and he could hear the bullets tear into the sand with a muffled *whump*. For an instant it seemed to Novago that he could see a snarling muzzle and bulging eyes, but the stars of explosions and the streams of fire had already moved far to one side, and he realized that he had been mistaken. Something long and gray rushed low over the dunes, crossing the fading threads of gunfire, and only then did Novago throw himself face down on the sand.

Crack! Crack! Crack! Mandel was up on one knee and, holding the pistol in his outstretched hand, was methodically ravaging an area somewhere between Morgan's and Opanasenko's lines of fire. *Pow-pow-pow! Pow-pow-pow!* thundered the carbines. Now the Pathfinders were firing by turns. Novago saw the tall Morgan scramble over the dune on all fours and fall, saw his shoulders tremble with the shots. Opanasenko fired kneeling, and time after time white flashes lit up his huge black glasses and the black muzzle of his oxygen mask.

Then silence returned.

"We beat it off," said Opanasenko, getting up and brushing sand from his knees. "That's how it always is—if you open fire in time, *it* jumps to the side and clears out."

"I hit it once," Humphrey Morgan said loudly. They could hear the metallic ring as he pulled out an empty clip.

"You got a good look at it?" asked Opanasenko. "Oh, right, he can't hear."

Novago, grunting, got up and looked at Mandel. Mandel had turned up the bottom of his coat and was cramming his pistol into its holster. Novago began, "You know, Lazar. . . ."

Mandel coughed guiltily. "I think I missed," he said. "*It* moves with exceptional speed."

"I'm very glad you missed," Novago said crossly. "Think of who you might have hit!"

"But did you see it, Pyotr?" Mandel asked. He rubbed his fur-gloved hands nervously. "Did you get a good look at it?"

"Gray and long like a hungry pike."

"It has no extremities!" Mandel said excitedly. "I saw quite distinctly that it has no extremities! I don't think it even has eyes!"

The Pathfinders walked over to the doctors.

"In all this commotion," said Opanasenko, "it would be very easy to conclude it has none. It's much harder to tell that it does have them." He laughed. "Well, all right, comrades. The main thing is that we beat off the attack."

"I'm going to look for the carcass," Morgan said unexpectedly. "I hit it once."

"Oh, no, you're not," said Novago quickly.

"No," said Opanasenko. He drew Morgan over and shouted, "No, Humphrey! No time! We'll look together tomorrow on the way back!"

Mandel looked at his watch. "Ugh!" he said. "It's already ten-fifteen. How much farther, Fedor?"

"Ten kilometers, no more. We'll be there by midnight."

"Wonderful," said Mandel. "But where's my valise?" He turned around. "Ah, here it is."

"We'll walk the same way as before," said Opanasenko. "You people to the left. It could be that *it* isn't alone here."

"There's nothing to be afraid of now," Novago muttered. "Lazar's clip is empty."

They set out as before. Novago was five paces behind Mandel. In front and to the right was Opanasenko, his carbine under his arm, and behind and to the right walked Morgan with his carbine hanging from his shoulder.

Opanasenko walked quickly. It was impossible to go on this way, he thought. Whether Morgan had killed that one monster or not, the day after tomorrow they would have to go to the base and organize a hunt. Using all the crawlers and rovers, with rifles, dynamite, and rockets. An argument to use with the unconvinced Ivanenko popped into his head, and he smiled. He would say to Ivanenko, "We have children on Mars now, so it's time to rid the planet of these monsters."

What a night! thought Novago. *It's no worse than the times I got lost in the taiga. But the most important part hasn't even begun yet, and it won't finish before five in the morning. Tomorrow at five, or, say, six o'clock the little guy will already be yelling over the whole planet. If only Mandel doesn't let us down. No, Mandel won't do that. Mark Slavin the proud papa can rest easy. In a few months all of us at the base will be taking the little guy in our arms and inquiring with monotonous regularity, "Well, who is this little fellow here, hey? Is it an itty bitty baby?" Only we've got to think out that business about the centrifuge very carefully. We'll have to get them to send us a good pediatrician from Earth. The little guy has to have a pediatrician. Too bad the next ships won't arrive for another year.*

Novago never doubted that the child would be a little guy, and not a little girl. He liked boy babies. He would carry it in his arms, inquiring from time to time, "Is it an itty bitty baby?"

Almost the Same

THEY were sitting in the corridor on the windowsill opposite the door—they were about to be called in. Sergei Kondratev swung his feet, while Panin, twisting his short neck around, looked out the window at the park. There, in the volleyball court, the girls from the Remote Control Division were jumping up and down near the net. His chin resting on his hands, Sergei Kondratev looked at the door, at the shining black plate that read "Large Centrifuge." In the Advanced School of Cosmonautics there were four divisions. Three of them had training halls, with plates with the same words hanging at the door. It always made you nervous waiting till they called you into the Large Centrifuge. Take Panin, for example. He was obviously gawking at the girls in order not to show how nervous he was. And Panin just had the most ordinary conditioning scheduled for today.

"They play a good game," Panin said in his bass voice.

"Right," Sergei said without turning around.

"Number four does a great pass."

"Yeah," said Sergei. He shrugged. He had a great pass too, but he didn't turn around.

Panin looked at Sergei, glanced at the door, and then said, "They're going to carry you out of here today."

Sergei remained silent.

"Feet first," said Panin.

"Sure thing," said Sergei holding himself back. "No chance of them carrying you, though."

"Calm down, superjock," said Panin. "A true superjock is always calm, cool, ready for anything."

"I am calm," said Sergei.

"You? Calm?" Panin said, poking him in the chest with his finger. "You're vibrating, shaking like a smallfry at a launch. It's disgusting, seeing the way you tremble."

"So don't look," Sergei advised him. "Look at the girls instead. Great passing ability, and all that."

"You haven't got the right attitude," Panin said, and looked through the window. "They're fantastic girls! They play an amazing game!"

"So look," said Sergei. "And try not to let your teeth chatter."

"Whose teeth are chattering?" Panin asked in amazement.

"Yours."

Sergei remained silent.

"It's all right for *my* teeth to chatter," Panin said after thinking it over. "*I'm* not a jock." He sighed, looked at the door and said, "But I wish they'd call us in and—" He broke off.

From the left, at the end of the corridor, appeared Grigory Bystrov, a second-year cadet who was class representative. He was wearing a test suit. He walked slowly, running his finger along the wall, his face pensive. He stopped in front of Kondratev and Panin and said, "Hello, guys." His voice was sad.

Sergei nodded. Panin condescended to say, "Hello, Grigory. Do you start vibrating before you ride the Centrifuge, Grigory?"

"Yeah," Grigory answered. "A little."

"Well," Panin said to Sergei. "So Grigory vibrates just a little. But then of course he's still a smallfry."

"Smallfry" was what they called underclassmen at the school.

Grigory sighed and sat down on the windowsill too. "Sergei," he said, "Are you really making your first try at eight Gs today?"

"Yeah," said Sergei. He had not the least desire to talk, but he didn't want to offend Grigory. "If they let me, of course," he added.

"Probably they will," Grigory said.

"Think of it, eight Gs!" Panin said flippantly.

"Have you tried pulling eight yourself?" Grigory asked with interest.

"No," said Panin. "But then I'm not a jock."

"But maybe you will try?" said Sergei. "Right now, together with me."

"I'm a simple man, a guileless man," Panin answered. "There is a norm. The norm is five gravities. My simple, uncomplicated organism cannot bear anything exceeding the norm. My organism tried six once, and got carried out at six minutes some seconds. With me along."

"Who got carried out?" asked Grigory, confused.

"My organism," Panin explained.

"Oh," said Grigory with a weak smile. "And I haven't even pulled five yet."

"You don't have to pull five in the second year," said Sergei. He jumped off the windowsill and started doing knee-bends alternately on right and left legs.

"Well, I'm off," Grigory said, and jumped off the windowsill too.

"What happened, Great Leader?" Panin asked him. "Why such melancholy?"

"Someone played a joke on Kopylov," Grigory answered sadly.

"Again?" said Panin. "What kind of joke?"

Second-year cadet Valentin Kopylov was famous throughout the division for his devotion to computer technology. Recently a very good new LIANTO waveguide computer had been installed in the division, and Valentin spent all his free time at its side. He would have spent his nights there too, but at night LIANTO did calculations for the diplomats, and Valentin was heartlessly shown the door.

"One of our people programmed a love letter," Grigory said.

"Now on the last cycle LIANTO prints, 'Kopylov fills my life with blisses / So from LIANTO, love and kisses.' In simple letter code."

" 'Love and kisses,' " said Sergei, massaging his shoulders. "Some poets. They should be put out of their misery."

"Just think," said Panin. "One of the current smallfry has gotten all jolly."

"And witty," said Sergei.

"What are you telling me for?" said Grigory. "Go tell those idiots. 'Love and kisses,' indeed! Last night Kan was running a calculation, and instead of an answer, *zap!*—'Love and kisses.' Now he's called me on the carpet."

Todor Kan, Iron Kan, was the head of the Navigation Division.

"Wow!" said Panin. "You're going to have an interesting half hour, Great Leader. Iron Kan is a very lively conversationalist."

"Iron Kan is a lover of literature," Sergei said. "He won't tolerate a class representative with such rotten versifiers for classmates."

"I'm a simple man, a guileless man . . ." Panin began. At that moment the door opened slightly and the trainer stuck his head through.

"Panin, Kondratev, get ready," he said.

Panin stopped short and straightened out his jacket. "Let's go," he said.

Kondratev nodded to Grigory and followed on Panin's heels into the training hall. The hall was enormous, and in the middle of it sparkled a thirteen-foot double arm resting on a fat cubical base—the Large Centrifuge. The arm was turning. The gondolas on its ends, thrown outward by centrifugal force, lay almost horizontal. There were no windows in the gondolas; observation of the cadets was carried out from inside the base with the help of a system of mirrors. By the wall several cadets were resting on a vaulting box. Craning their necks, they followed the hurtling gondolas.

"Four Gs," said Panin, looking at the gondolas.

"Five," said Kondratev. "Who's in there now?"

"Nguyen and Gurgenidze," the trainer said.

He brought two acceleration suits, helped Kondratev and

Panin to put them on, and laced them up. The acceleration suits looked like silkworm cocoons.

"Wait," the trainer said, and went over to the base.

Once a week every cadet rode the centrifuge, getting acceleration conditioning. One hour once a week for the whole five years. You had to sit there and stick it out, and listen to your bones creak, and feel the broad straps dig through the thick cloth of the suit into your soft body, feel your face droop, feel how hard it was to blink, because your eyelids were so heavy. And while this was going on you had to solve boring problems, or else assemble standard computer subprograms, and this wasn't at all easy, even though the problems and the subprograms were ones you had had your first year. Some cadets could pull seven gravities, while others couldn't manage even three—they couldn't cope with vision blackouts. They were transferred to the Remote Control Division.

The arm turned more slowly, and the gondolas hung more nearly vertical. From one of them crawled skinny, dark Nguyen Phu Dat. He stopped, hanging onto the open door, rocking. Gurgenidze tumbled clumsily from the other gondola. The cadets on the vaulting box jumped to their feet, but the trainer had already helped him up, and he sat down on the floor, propping himself up with his arms.

"Step lively now, Gurgenidze," one of the cadets shouted loudly.

Everyone laughed. Everyone except Panin.

"Never mind, guys," Gurgenidze said hoarsely, and got up. "Nothing to it!" He contorted his face horribly, stretching the numbed muscles of his cheeks. "Nothing to it!" he repeated.

"Boy, they sure are going to carry you out today, superjock!" Panin said, softly but very energetically.

Kondratev made as if he were not listening. *If they do carry me out,* he thought, *that will be the end. They can't do it. They mustn't.* "He's on the chubby side, Gurgenidze is," he said aloud. "The heavy ones don't take acceleration well."

"He'll thin down," Panin said cheerfully. "If he wants to, he'll thin down."

Panin had lost fifteen pounds before he had managed to endure the five gravities established as the norm. It was an excruciating process. But he did not at all want to get sent to Remote Control. He wanted to be a navigator.

A hatch opened in the base. Out crawled an instructor in a white coat, who took the sheets of paper with Nguyen and Gurgenidze's answers.

"Are Kondratev and Panin ready?" he asked.

"Ready," said the trainer.

The instructor glanced cursorily over the sheets of paper. "Right," he said. "Nguyen and Gurgenidze can go. You've passed."

"Hey, great!" Gurgenidze said. He immediately began to look better. "You mean I passed too?"

"You too," said the instructor.

Gurgenidze suddenly hiccuped resoundingly. Everyone laughed again, even Panin, and Gurgenidze was very embarrassed. Even Nguyen Phu Dat laughed, loosening the lacing of his suit at the waist. He obviously felt wonderful.

The instructor said, "Panin and Kondratev, into the gondolas."

"Sir—" began Sergei.

The instructor's face took on a preoccupied look. "Oh, I forgot. I'm very sorry, Sergei, but the doctor has forbidden you to try accelerations above the norm. Temporarily."

"What?" Sergei asked with fright.

"You're forbidden."

"But I've already pulled seven Gs."

"I'm very sorry, Sergei," the instructor repeated.

"It's some sort of mistake. It's got to be."

The instructor shrugged.

"I can't have this," Sergei said in despair. "I'll get out of shape." He looked at Panin. Panin was looking at the floor. Sergei once again faced the instructor. "It's the end of everything for me."

"It's only temporary," said the instructor.

"How long is temporary?"

"Until further notice. Maybe two months, no longer. It happens sometimes. In the meantime you'll be training at five Gs. You'll catch up later."

"Never mind, Sergei," Panin said in his bass. "Take a little rest from your multigravities."

"I would still like to ask—" Sergei began in a repulsively ingratiating voice that he had never used before in his life.

The instructor frowned. "We're wasting time, Kondratev," he said. "Get into the gondola."

"Yes, sir," Sergei said softly, and crawled into the gondola.

He seated himself in the couch, fastened himself in with the broad straps, and began to wait. In front of the couch was a mirror, and in it he saw his gloomy, angry face. *It would be better if they did carry me out,* he thought. *Now my muscles will get soft and I'll have to start all over. Now when will I ever get to ten Gs? Or even eight? They all think I'm some sort of jock,* he thought venemously. *The doctor too. Maybe I should tell him?* He imagined that he was telling the doctor why he had to have all this and that the doctor looked at him with cheery, faded eyes and said, "Moderation, Sergei, moderation."

"Overcautious old bird," Sergei said aloud. He meant the doctor, but suddenly he realized that the instructor might hear him over the speaking tube and take it personally. "Well, all right," he said loudly.

The gondola rocked smoothly. The conditioning session had begun.

When they had left the training hall, Panin quickly started massaging the bags under his eyes. Like all the cadets inclined to stoutness, he always got bags under his eyes after the Large Centrifuge. Panin worried a good deal about his appearance. He was handsome and was used to being admired. Consequently, right after the Large Centrifuge he immediately set to work on the bags.

"You never get this crud," he said to Sergei.

Sergei remained silent.

"You have a very efficient physique, superjock. Like a roach."

"I wish I had your problems," Sergei said.

"They told you it's only temporary, worrywort."

"That's what they told Galtsev, and then they switched him over to Remote Control."

"Oh, well," Panin said judiciously, "so this wasn't the job he was cut out for."

Sergei clenched his teeth.

"Oh, agony!" said Panin. "They won't let him pull eight Gs. Now take me, I'm a simple man, a guileless man. . . ."

Sergei stopped. "You listen," he said. "Bykov brought the *Takhmasib* back from Jupiter only by going to twelve gravities. Maybe you didn't know that?"

"I know it," said Panin.

"And Yusupov died because he couldn't take eight. You know that too?"

"Yusupov was a test navigator," Panin said, "so he doesn't count here. And Bykov, I'll have you know, did not have one hour of acceleration conditioning in his entire life."

"Are you sure?" Sergei asked angrily.

"Well, maybe he did have conditioning, but he didn't go try and rupture himself like you, superjock."

"Do you really think I'm a jock?" Sergei asked.

Panin looked at him in puzzlement. "Well, I'm not saying there's anything wrong with it. It's a very useful thing out there, of course."

"Okay," said Sergei. "Let's go over to the park. We have a chance to loosen up."

They started down the corridor. Panin, still massaging the bags under his eyes, glanced through every window.

"The girls are still playing," he said. He stopped at a window and stuck out his neck. "Ha! There she is!"

"Who?" asked Sergei.

"I don't know her name."

"Impossible."

"No, really—I danced with her day before yesterday. But I have no idea what her name is."

Sergei looked out the window too.

"That one," said Panin. "With the bandaged knee."

Sergei caught sight of the girl with the bandaged knee. "I see her," he said. "Let's go."

"Very nice-looking," said Panin. "Very. And smart."

"Come on, come on," said Sergei. He took Panin by the elbow and dragged him along.

"Where's the fire?" Panin asked in surprise.

They walked past empty classrooms and glanced into the

simulator room. The simulator room was fitted out like the navigation deck of a real interplanetary photon ship, except that on the control board was mounted the big white cube of the stochastic computer in the place of the video screen. The computer was the source of navigation problems. When turned on, it randomly supplied input for the board's indicators. The cadet then had to set up a system of course commands optimally responding to the conditions of the problem.

Right now, a whole gaggle of obvious smallfry was crowded in front of the control board. They shouted to one another, waved back and forth, and shoved each other. Then suddenly it became quiet, and the clicking of the keys on the board could be heard. Someone was entering a command. The agonizing silence was broken by the buzz of the computer, and on the board a red light went on—an incorrect solution. The smallfry let out a roar. They dragged somebody out of the control seat and shoved him away. The disheveled unfortunate shouted loudly, "I told you so!"

"Why are you so sweaty?" Panin asked him with disdain.

"Because I'm so mad," said the smallfry.

The computer buzzed again, and again the red light on the control board went on.

"I told you so!" the same smallfry yelled.

"Now then," Panin said, and shouldered his way through the crowd.

All the smallfry quieted down. Sergei saw Panin bend over the board, then the keys clattered quickly and surely, the computer began to hum, and a green light appeared on the board. The smallfry groaned.

"Well, so that's Panin," someone said.

"That's Panin for you," the sweaty smallfry said to Sergei reproachfully.

"Smooth plasma," said Panin, extracting himself from the crowd. "Carry on. Let's go, Sergei."

Then they glanced into the computer room. People were studying there, but beside the graceful gray casing of LIANTO squatted three technicians, rummaging through circuit diagrams. The sad second-year cadet, Grigory Bystrov, was there as well.

"From LIANTO, love and kisses," Panin said. "It seems that Bystrov is still alive. Curious."

He looked at Sergei and slapped him on the back. A respectable echo rang down the corridor. "Buck up," Panin said.

"Cut it out," said Sergei.

They descended the staircase, passed through the lobby with the big bronze bust of Tsiolkovsky, and went out into the park.

By the entrance a second-year man was watering the flowers with a hose. As he passed him, Panin declaimed, with exaggerated gestures, "Kopylov fills my life with blisses/So from LIANTO, love and kisses." The second-year man smiled with embarrassment and glanced at a window on the second floor.

They walked along a narrow lane planted with bird-cherry bushes. Panin was about to begin a loud song, but a group of girls in shorts and T-shirts came out from around a bend, walking towards them. The girls were coming back from the volleyball court. In front, with the ball under her arm, walked Katya. *That's just what I needed*, thought Sergei. *Now she'll stare at me out of those round eyes. And she'll start the thousand-words-with-a-glance routine.* He even stopped for a second. He had a fierce desire to jump through the bird-cherry bushes and crawl away somewhere. He glanced sidelong at Panin.

Panin smiled pleasantly, straightened his shoulders, and said in a velvet voice, "Hello, girls!"

The Remote Control Division vouchsafed him closed-mouthed smiles. Katya had eyes only for Sergei.

Oh, lord, he thought, and said, "Hi, Katya."

"Hi, Sergei," said Katya. She lowered her head and walked on. Panin stopped.

"Well, what's your problem?" Sergei asked.

"It's *her,*" said Panin.

Sergei looked back. Katya was standing there, arranging her tousled hair and looking at him. Her right knee was wrapped in a dusty bandage. They looked at each other for several seconds —Katya's eyes opened wide. Sergei bit his lip, turned, and went on without waiting for Panin. Panin caught up with him.

"Such beautiful eyes," he said.

"Sheep's eyes," said Sergei.

"Sheep yourself," Panin snapped. "She's a very, very beautiful girl. Hold it," he said. "How come she knows you?"

Sergei didn't answer, and Panin kept silent.

In the center of the park was a broad meadow with thick soft grass. Here the cadets usually crammed before theory exams and rested after acceleration conditioning, and here couples met on summer nights. At present the place was occupied by the fifth-year men of the Navigation Division. Most of them were under a white awning, where a game of four-dimensional chess was in progress. This highly intellectual game, in which the board and pieces had four spatial dimensions and existed only in the imaginations of the players, had been introduced to the school several years before by Zhilin, the same Zhilin who was now engineer on the trans-Martian voyager *Takhmasib*. The senior classmen were quite fond of the game, but by no means could everyone play it. On the other hand, anyone who felt like it could kibitz. The shouts of the kibitzers filled the entire park.

"Should've moved the pawn to E-one-delta-H."

"Then you lose the fourth knight."

"So? The pawns move into the bishops' volume—"

"What bishops' volume? Where do you get bishops' volume? You've got the ninth move down wrong!"

"Listen, guys, take old Sasha away and tie him to a tree. And leave him there."

Someone, probably one of the players, yelled excitedly, "Shut up! I can't think!"

"Let's go watch," said Panin. He was a great fan of four-dimensional chess.

"I don't want to," said Sergei. He stepped over Gurgenidze, who was lying on Malyshev and twisting his arm up toward his neck. Malyshev was still struggling, but it was clear who had won. Sergei walked a few paces away from them and collapsed on the grass, stretching out full length. It was a little painful to stretch muscles after acceleration, but it was very helpful, and Sergei did a neck bridge, then a handstand, then another neck bridge, and finally lay down on his back and gazed at the sky. Panin sat down beside him and listened to the shouts of the kibitzers while he chewed on a stem of grass.

Maybe I should go see Kan? Sergei thought. *Go to him and say, "Comrade Kan, what do you think about interstellar travel?"* No—not like that. *"Comrade Kan, I want to conquer the universe."* Damn—what nonsense! Sergei turned over on his stomach and propped himself up on his elbows.

Gurgenidze and Malyshev had quit fighting, and they sat down near Panin. Malyshev caught his breath and asked, "What was on the SV yesterday?"

"*Blue Fields,*" Panin said. "Relayed from Argentina."

"So how was it?" asked Gurgenidze.

"They should've kept it," said Panin.

"Oh," said Malyshev. "Is that where he keeps dropping the refrigerator?"

"The vacuum cleaner," Panin corrected.

"Then I've seen it," said Malyshev. "Why didn't you like it? It's not a bad film. The music is good, and it has a good odor scale. Remember, when they're by the sea?"

"Maybe," said Panin. "Only the olfactor on my set's broken. It reeks of smoked fish all the time. It was really something when they went into the florist shop and smelled the roses."

Gurgenidze laughed. "Why don't you fix it?"

Malyshev said thoughtfully, "It would be something if they could figure out a way to broadcast tactile sensations in movies. Imagine—somebody is kissing somebody on the screen, and you feel like you're getting slapped in the face. . . ."

"I can imagine," said Panin. "That's already happened to me. Without any movie."

And then I'd pick my crew, Sergei thought. *Even now I could pick good guys for this. Mamedov, Petrov, Zavialov from Engineering. Briushkov from the third year can pull twelve gravities. He didn't even need conditioning—he has some special sort of middle ear. But of course he's a smallfry and doesn't understand anything yet.* Sergei remembered how, when Panin had asked him what the point of it was, Briushkov had puffed up self-importantly and said, "You try it, like me." *A smallfry, and too little to eat at that—a minnow smallfry. Yes, anyway, all of them are jocks, the smallfry and the final-year men. Maybe Valentin Petrov. . . .*

Sergei turned over on his back again. *Valentin Petrov.* Transactions of the Academy of Nonclassical Mechanics, *Volume Seven. Valentin Petrov eats and sleeps with that book. And of course other people read it too. They're always reading it! There are three copies in the library, all of them thumbed to pieces, and most of the time they're all checked out. So I'm not alone? Does that mean other people too are interested in "The Behavior of Pi-Quanta in Accelerators" and that they're drawing conclusions too? I should take Petrov aside,* Sergei thought, *and have a talk with him.*

"Well, what are you staring at me for?" said Panin. "Guys, how come he's staring at me? I'm terrified."

Sergei only now realized that he was up on all fours, and looking straight into Panin's face.

"Ah, the foreshortening!" said Gurgenidze. "I could use you as a model for 'Reverie.' "

Sergei got up and looked around the meadow. Petrov wasn't in sight. He lay back down and pressed his cheek against the grass.

"Sergei," called Malyshev, "what's your analysis of all this?"

"Of all what?" Sergei asked into the grass.

"The nationalization of *United Rocket Construction.*" He gave the name in English.

" 'Approve Mr. Hopkins' present action. Expect more same spirit. Stop, Kondratev,' " said Sergei. "Send the telegram collect, payment through the Soviet State Bank."

United Rocket has good engineers. We have good engineers too. And this is the time for all of them to get together and build ramscoops. It's all up to the engineers now—we'll do our part. We're ready. Sergei imagined squadrons of gigantic starships at the launch, and then in deep space, at the edge of the light barrier, accelerating at ten or twelve gravities, devouring diffuse matter, tons of interstellar dust and gas.... Enormous accelerations, powerful artificial-gravity fields. ... The special theory of relativity was no longer any good—it would end up standing on its head. Decades would pass on the starship, and only months on Earth. And so what if there was no theory—instead there were pi-quanta at superaccelerations, pi-quanta accelerated to near-light velocities, pi-quanta that aged ten, a hundred times more rapidly than was laid down by classical theory. To circumnavigate the entire visible universe in ten or fifteen subjective years and return to Earth a year after takeoff. Overcome space, break the chains of time, make his generation a gift of alien worlds—except that that damned doctor had taken him off acceleration indefinitely, damn him to hell!

"There he lies," said Panin. "Only he's depressed."

"He's in a bad way," said Gurgenidze.

"They won't let him train," Panin explained.

Sergei raised up his head and saw that Tanya Gorbunova, a second-year cadet from the Remote Control Division, had walked over to him.

"Are you really depressed, Sergei?" she asked.

"Yes," said Sergei. He remembered that Tanya and Katya were friends, and he began to feel uneasy.

"Sit down by us, Tanya old girl," said Malyshev.

"No," said Tanya. "I have to have a talk with Sergei."

"Ah," said Malyshev.

Gurgenidze shouted, "Hey, guys, let's go get the kibitzers!"

They got up and left, and Tanya sat down next to Sergei. She was thin, with lively eyes, and it was remarkably pleasant to look at her, even if she was Katya's friend.

"Why are you mad at Katya?" she asked.

"I'm not," Sergei said gloomily.

"Don't lie," said Tanya. "You're mad at her."

Sergei shook his head and began to look off to the side.

"So you don't love her."

"Listen, Tanya," said Sergei, "do you love your Malyshev?"

"I do."

"Well, there you are. If you had a fight, I'd try to get you back together."

"You mean you had a fight?" said Tanya.

Sergei was silent.

"Look, Sergei, if Misha and I have a fight, then of course we make up. Ourselves. But you—"

"We're not going to make up," said Sergei.

"So you did have a fight."

"We're not going to make up," Sergei said distinctly, and looked straight into Tanya's lively eyes.

"But Katya doesn't even know you and she have had a fight. She doesn't understand anything, and I feel just terrible about her."

"Well, what do you want me to do, Tanya? Look at my side of it. The same thing has happened to you, I'll bet."

"It happened once," Tanya agreed. "Only I told him right away."

"There, you see!" Sergei said happily. "And how did he take it?"

Tanya shrugged. "I don't know," she said. "But he survived."

She got up, brushed off her skirt, and asked, "They're really not going to let you pull Gs?"

"Really," Sergei said, getting up. "Look, it's all right for you —you're a girl—but how am I going to tell her something like that?"

"You'd better tell her."

She turned and walked toward the four-dimensional chess fans, where Misha Malyshev was shouting something about mindless cretins. Sergei called after her, "Tanya. . . ." She stopped and turned around. "I don't know—maybe this will all blow over. Right now I haven't got my head together."

He knew it wouldn't blow over. And he knew that Tanya realized this. But Tanya smiled and nodded.

After everything that had happened, Sergei wasn't a bit hungry. He reluctantly dipped his cookies into strong, sweet tea, and listened as Panin, Malyshev, and Gurgenidze discussed the menu. Then they set to eating, and for a few minutes silence reigned at the table. They could hear someone at the next table assert, "These days you can't write like Hemingway. You've got to write concisely, provide maximum information. Hemingway lacks precision."

"And a good thing, too! Precision belongs in technical encyclopedias."

"In encyclopedias? Take Strogov's *Road of Roads*. Have you read it?"

" 'Precision, precision'!" said someone's bass. "You yourself don't even know what——"

Panin put down his fork, looked at Malyshev, and said, "Now tell us about the insides of a whale."

Before school, Malyshev had worked in a whale-butchering complex.

"Hold it, hold it," said Gurgenidze.

"I should tell you instead about how they catch cuttlefish off Miao-lieh Tao," Malyshev proposed.

"Cut it out!" Sergei said irritably.

Everyone looked at him and fell silent. Then Panin said, "This can't go on, Sergei. Get a grip on yourself."

Gurgenidze got up and said, "Right! Time for a little snort."

He went over to the buffet, came back with a decanter of tomato juice, and said excitedly, "Hey, guys, Phu Dat says that on the seventeenth Liakhov is leaving for Interstellar One."

Sergei at once lifted up his head. "When exactly?"

"The seventeenth," Gurgenidze repeated. "On the *Lightning.*"

The photon ship *Khius-Lightning* was the first manned ram-scoop in the world. It had been two years in construction, and for the last three years the best spacemen had been testing it within the System.

This is it, it's begun, thought Sergei. He asked, "Do you know the range?"

"Phu Dat says one and a half light-months."

"Comrade spacemen!" said Malyshev. "We must drink to the occasion." He ceremoniously poured the tomato juice into their tumblers. "Let us raise our glasses," he said.

"Don't forget the salt," said Panin.

All four clinked glasses and drank. *It's begun, it's begun,* thought Sergei.

"I've seen the *Khius-Lightning,*" said Malyshev. "Last year, when I was interning on the *Astericus.* It's enormous."

"The diameter of the mirror is seven hundred meters," Gurgenidze said. "Not all that large. But on the other hand the span of the scoop is—get this—six kilometers. And the length from edge to edge is almost eight kilometers."

Mass, one thousand sixteen metric tons, Sergei recalled mechanically. *Average thrust, eighteen megasangers. Cruising speed, eighty megameters per second. Maximum rated acceleration, six G's. Too little. Maximum rated intake, fifteen wahrs. . . . Too little, too little.*

"Navigators," Malyshev said dreamily, "that's our craft. We'll ship out on ones like that."

"Over the sun from Earth to Pluto!" Gurgenidze said.

Someone at the other end of the hall shouted in a ringing tenor, "Comrades! Did you hear? On the seventeenth the *Lightning* is leaving for Interstellar One!"

Noise broke out all over the hall. Three cadets from the Command Division got up from the next table and rapidly took to voice.

"The aces are right on course," said Malyshev, following them with his eyes.

"I'm a simple man, a guileless man," Panin said suddenly,

pouring tomato juice into his glass. "And what I still can't understand is who needs these stars, anyhow?"

"What do you mean, who needs them?" Gurgenidze asked in surprise.

"Well, the moon is a launching pad and observatory. Venus is for actinides. Mars is for purple cabbage, the atmosphere project, colonization. Wonderful. But what are the stars good for?"

"Do you mean to say you don't know why Liakhov is going to Interstellar?" Malyshev asked.

"A freak!" said Gurgenidze. "A victim of mutation."

"Listen," Panin continued. "I've been thinking about it for a long time. Here we are, interstellar spacers, and we go off to UV Ceti. Two and a half parsecs."

"Two point four," said Sergei, looking into his glass.

"We travel," Panin continued. "We travel a long time. Let's even say there are planets there. We land, we do research, see the seven sails, as my grandfather says."

"*My* grandfather has better taste," Gurgenidze put in.

"Then we start back. We're old and stiff, and arguing all the time. Or at least Sergei isn't talking to anyone. And we're already pushing sixty. Meanwhile on Earth, thanks to Einstein, a hundred and fifty years have gone by. Some bunch of very young-looking citizens meets us, and at first everything is very nice: Music, flowers, and shish kebab. But then I want to go see my home town, Vologda. And it turns out nobody lives there any more. You see, it's a museum."

"The Boris Panin Memorial Museum-City," said Malyshev. "Chock full of memorial plaques."

"Right," Panin continued. "Chock full. Anyhow, you can't live in Vologda, but on the other hand—and will you like that 'other hand'?—there's a monument there. A monument to me. I look at myself and inquire why there are horns growing out of my head. I don't understand the answer. It's clear only that they aren't horns. They explain to me that a hundred and fifty years ago I wore a helmet like that. 'No,' I say, 'I never had any such helmet.' 'Oh, how interesting!' says the curator of the museum-city, and he starts making notes. 'We must inform the Central Bureau for Eternal Memory of this immediately,' he says. And the words

'Eternal Memory' have unpleasant connotations for me. But how can I explain this to the curator?"

"You're getting carried away," said Malyshev. "Get back to the point."

"Anyhow, I begin to understand that I've ended up in another alien world. We deliver a report on the results of our expedition, but it gets a curious reception. You see, the results have only a narrow historical interest. Everything has already been known for fifty years, because human beings have been to UV Ceti— that's where we went, isn't it?—twenty times by now. And anyhow, they've built three artificial planets the size of Earth there. They can make trips like that in two months. You see, they have discovered some new property of space-time which we don't yet understand and which they call, say, trimpazation. Finally they show us the *News of the Day* film clip covering the installation of our ship in the Archaeological Museum. We look, we listen. . . ."

"How you do get carried away!" said Malyshev.

"I'm a simple man," Panin said threateningly. "Now and again my imagination runs free."

"I don't like the way you're talking," Sergei said quietly.

Panin immediately became serious. "All right," he said, also quietly. "Then tell me where I'm wrong. Tell me what we need the stars for."

"Wait," said Malyshev. "There are two questions here. The first is, what use are the stars?"

"Right, what?" asked Panin.

"The second question is, granting that they do have some use, can we exploit it in the present generation? Right?"

"Right," said Panin. He was not smiling any longer, and he looked steadily at Sergei. Sergei remained silent.

"I'll answer the first question," said Malyshev. "Do you want to know what's going on in the system of UV Ceti?"

"All right, I want to," said Panin. "What of it?"

"Well, I myself want to very much. And if I go on wanting for my whole life, and if I go on trying to find out, then before my death—untimely, I hope—I will thank the nonexistent God for creating the stars and filling up my life."

"Ah!" said Gurgenidze. "How beautiful!"

"You see," said Malyshev, "we're talking about human beings."

"So?" asked Panin, turning red.

"That's all," said Malyshev. "First a creature said, 'I want to eat.' He wasn't yet human at that point. But then he said 'I want to know.' Then he was a human being."

"This human being of yours," Panin said angrily, "still has no clear idea of what's under his feet, and he's already snatching at the stars."

"That's why he's a human being," Malyshev answered. "That's the way he is. Look, don't go against the laws of nature. It doesn't depend on you. There's a law: the aspiration to find out in order to live inevitably turns into the aspiration to live in order to find out. You, you're just afraid of acceleration."

"All right," said Panin. "So I'll become a teacher. I'll plumb the depths of children's souls for the sake of everyone. But for whose sake are you going to find out about the stars?"

"That's the second question," Malyshev began, but here Gurgenidze jumped up and started yelling, with eyes flashing, "You want to wait until they invent your trimpazation? So wait! *I* don't want to wait! I'm going to the stars!"

"Bah," said Panin. "Quiet down."

"Don't worry," Sergei said without raising his eyes. "They won't send you on a starship."

"And why not?" inquired Panin.

"Who needs you?" shouted Gurgenidze. "Go sit on the Moon run!"

"They'll pity your youth," said Sergei. "As for whose sake will we find out about the stars . . . for our own, for everyone's. Even for yours. But you won't take part in it. You'll make your discoveries in the newspapers. You're afraid of acceleration."

"Hold on, guys," Malyshev said anxiously. "This is a purely theoretical discussion."

But Sergei knew that another moment and he would start swearing and would try to prove that he wasn't a jock. He got up and quickly left the dining hall.

"Had enough?" Gurgenidze said to Panin.

"Well," said Panin, "in a situation like this, in order to remain a human being, you've got to act like an animal."

He grabbed Gurgenidze by the neck and bent him in two. There no longer was anyone in the dining hall, except for the three aces from the Command Division, who were clinking glasses of tomato juice by the counter. They were drinking to Liakhov, to Interstellar One.

Sergei Kondratev went straight to the videophone. *First I've got to straighten things out,* he thought. *Katya first. Oh, what a mess it's all turned out to be! Poor Katya. Poor me, for that matter.*

He took the receiver off the cradle and stopped, trying to remember the number for Katya's room. And suddenly he dialed the number for Valentin Petrov. Until the last moment he was thinking about how he had to talk with Katya right away, so he was silent for a second or two, looking at the lean face of Petrov which had appeared on the screen. Petrov too was silent, arching his sparse eyebrows. Sergei said, "Are you busy?"

"Not particularly," said Petrov.

"I have something to talk about. I'll come over right away."

"Do you need Volume Seven?" Petrov said, squinting. "Come on over. I'll call someone else. Maybe we should invite Kan?"

"No," said Sergei. "It's too early. Just ourselves for now."

PART TWO: *Homecoming*

3

Old-timer

When his assistant returned, the traffic controller was standing as before in front of the screen, with his head bent and his arms thrust into his pockets almost up to the elbows. A bright white dot was crawling slowly within the depths of the coordinate-gridded screen.

"Where is he now?" the assistant asked.

The controller did not turn around. "Over Africa," he growled. "At nine megameters."

"Nine——" said the assistant. "And the velocity?"

"Almost circular." The controller turned around. "Well, what do you think? And what else is out there?"

"You'd better calm down," said the assistant. "What can you do from here? . . . He grazed the Big Mirror."

The controller exhaled noisily and, without taking his hands out of his pockets, sat down on the arm of a chair. "Madman," he muttered.

"So what's gotten you so worked up?" the assistant asked uncertainly. "Something's happened. His controls are malfunctioning."

They fell silent. The white dot kept crawling, cutting slantwise across the screen.

"Where did he get the gall to enter the station zone with malfunctioning controls?" the controller said. "And why doesn't he give his call sign?"

"He *is* transmitting something."

"It's not a call sign—it's gibberish."

"It's still a call sign," the assistant said quietly. "All the same, it's on a fixed frequency."

" 'Frequency, frequency,' " the controller said through his teeth.

The assistant bent toward the screen, peering myopically at the figures on the coordinate grid. Then he looked at the clock and said, "He's passing Station Gamma now. Let's see who it is."

The controller laughed gloomily. *What else can I do?* he thought. *I think we've done everything we can. All flights have been stopped. All touchdowns have been forbidden. All near-Earth stations have been alerted. Turnen is getting the emergency robots ready.*

The controller fumbled at the microphone on his chest and said, "Turnen, what's happening with the robots?"

Turnen answered unhurriedly: "I'm planning on launching the robots in five or six minutes. After they're launched, I'll tell you more."

"Turnen," said the controller, "I'm begging you, don't dawdle —hurry it up a little."

"I never dawdle," Turnen answered with dignity. "But it's senseless to hurry when you don't have to. I will not delay takeoff by one extra second."

"Please, Turnen," said the controller, "please."

"Station Gamma," said the assistant. "I'm giving maximum magnification."

The screen blinked, and the coordinate grid disappeared. In the black emptiness appeared a strange construction like a distorted garden summerhouse with absurdly massive columns. The controller gave a drawn-out whistle and jumped up. This was the last thing he had expected. "A nuclear rocket!" he shouted in astonishment. "How? From where?"

"Ye-es," the assistant said indecisively. "Really . . . can't understand it. . . ."

The incredible structure, with its five fat pillarlike tubes sticking out from under a dome, was slowly turning. A violet radiance trembled under the dome—the pillars looked black against its background. The controller slowly lowered himself down onto the arm of the chair. Of course—it was a nuclear rocket, an interplanetary ship. Photon drive, two-layer parabolic reflector of mesomatter, hydrogen engines. A century and a half ago there had been many such ships. They had been built for the conquest of the planets. Solid, leisurely machines with a fivefold safety margin. They had served long and well, but the last of them had been scrapped long ago—long, long ago.

"Really . . ." muttered the assistant. "Amazing! Where have I seen something like that? . . . Greenhouses!" he shouted.

From left to right, a wide gray shadow quickly crossed the screen. "Greenhouses," the assistant whispered.

The controller narrowed his eyes. *A thousand metric tons,* he thought. *A thousand tons and speed like that. . . . To bits . . . to dust . . . the robots! Where the hell are the robots?*

The assistant said hoarsely, "He got through. . . . Can it really be? He got through!"

The controller opened his eyes wide again. "Where are the robots?" he yelled.

A green light flared up on the selector board by the wall, and a calm male voice said, "This is D-P. Slavin calling Main Control. Request permission for touchdown at Base Pi-X Seventeen."

The controller, flushing red, started to open his mouth, but did not make it. Several voices at once thundered through the hall:

"Go back!"

"D-P, permission denied."

"Captain Slavin, go back!"

"Captain Slavin, this is Main Control. Immediately assume any orbit in Zone Four. Do not touch down. Do not approach. Wait."

"Roger, wilco," Slavin responded in confusion. "Enter Zone Four and wait."

The controller, suddenly remembering, closed his mouth. He could hear a woman's voice at the selector board, arguing with someone, "Explain to him what's going on. Explain it, for pity's sake." Then the green light on the selector board went out again, and all the noise ceased.

The display on the screen faded. Once again the coordinate grid appeared, and once again a bright glimmering spark crawled within the depths of the screen.

Turnen's voice rang out: "Emergency officer to control. The robots have launched."

At the same second, in the lower right corner of the screen appeared two more bright points. The controller rubbed his hands nervously, as though he felt chilly. "Thank you, Turnen," he muttered. "Thank you very much."

The two bright dots—the emergency robots—crawled across the screen. The distance between them and the nuclear craft gradually decreased.

The controller looked at the glimmering point crawling between the precise lines, and thought that the old-timer was just entering Zone Two, which was thick with orbital hangars and fueling stations; that his daughter worked on one of those stations; that the mirror of the Orbiting Observatory's Big Reflector had been smashed; that the ship moved as if blind, and it either did not hear signals or did not understand them; that every second it risked destruction by plowing into any of the numerous heavy structures or by ending up in the launching zone of the D-ships. He thought that it would be very hard to stop the blind and senseless motion of the ship, because it kept changing velocity in a wild and disorderly fashion; and that the robots could end up ramming through it, even though Turnen must be directing them himself.

"Station Delta," said the assistant. "Maximum magnification."

On the black screen, once again the image of the ungainly hulk appeared. The flashes of plasma under the dome grew uneven, arhythmical, and it seemed as if the monster were advancing convulsively on fat black legs. The dim outlines of the emergency robots appeared alongside. The robots approached carefully, springing back at every jerk of the nuclear rocket.

The controller and his assistant were all eyes. Stretching his neck as far as it would go, the controller whispered, "Come on, Turnen. . . . Come on . . . come on, old buddy. . . . Come on."

The robots moved quickly and surely. From both sides, titanic tentacles stretched out toward the nuclear rocket and seized hold of the widely spaced pillar-tubes. One of the tentacles missed, ended up under the dome, and vanished into dust beneath the force of the plasma. ("Ouch!" the assistant said in a whisper.) A third robot dropped down from somewhere above, and latched onto the dome with magnetic suckers. The nuclear rocket moved slowly downward. The flickering radiance below its dome went out.

"Ooh!" the controller muttered, and wiped his face with his sleeve.

The assistant laughed nervously. "Like giant squids and a whale," he said. "Where does it go now?"

The controller inquired into his microphone, "Turnen, where are you taking it?"

"To our rocket field," Turnen said unhurriedly. He was gasping slightly.

The controller suddenly imagined Turnen's round face, shiny with sweat, lit up by the screen. "Thank you, Turnen," he said with feeling. He turned to the assistant. "Give the all-clear. Correct the schedule and have them get back to work."

"And what are you going to do?" the assistant asked plaintively.

"I'm going to fly there."

The assistant also wanted to be there, but he only said, "I wonder whether the Cosmonautical Museum is missing any ships." The matter was coming to a more or less happy ending, and he was now in a fairly good mood. "What a watch!" he said. "All day I've been quaking in my boots."

The controller clicked a few keys, and a rolling plain appeared on the screen. The wind drove broken white clouds about the sky, and it formed ripples on dark puddles between the sparsely vegetated hummocks. Ducks splashed about in a large pond. *Spaceships haven't taken off from there in a long time*, thought the assistant.

"I'd still like to know who it is," the controller said between his teeth.

"You'll find out soon enough," the assistant said enviously.

The ducks unexpectedly took to the air and darted forward in a sparse flock, beating their wings as hard as they could. The clouds began to whirl into a funnel, and a tornado of water and steam began to rise from the middle of the plain. The hills disappeared, the pond disappeared, and scrawny uprooted bushes rushed off into the clouds of turbulent haze. Something dark and enormous showed for an instant in the spreading mist, something flared with a scarlet glow, and they saw a hill in the foreground tremble, distend, and slowly flop over, like a layer of turf under the share of a powerful plow.

"My God!" said the assistant, his eyes glued to the screen. But by now he could see nothing except the fast-spreading white and gray clouds of steam.

By the time the helicopter had landed, a hundred yards from the edge of the enormous crater, the steam had dispersed. In the center of the crater the nuclear vessel lay on its side, the thick posts of its reactor rings jutting stupidly and helplessly into the air. The steel-blue hulks of the emergency robots, half-buried in hot mud, lay nearby. One of them slowly drew its mechanical paws back under its armor.

Hot air shimmered over the crater.

"Doesn't look good," someone muttered as they were getting out of the helicopter.

Overhead, rotors softly whirred—more helicopters rushed through the air and landed close by.

"Let's go," said the controller, and everyone straggled out after him.

They went down into the crater. Their feet sank up to the ankles in the hot slush. They did not see the man at first, but when they did see him, they all stopped at once.

He was lying face down with his arms spread out and his face buried in the damp ground, pressing his whole body into the soil and trembling as if from severe cold. He wore a strange suit, crumpled and seemingly chewed up, of unusual cut and color. The man himself was red-haired, vividly red-haired, and he did not hear their footsteps. When they ran up to him, he raised his head, and everyone saw his face, blue-white and dirty, slashed across the lips by an unhealed scab. The man must have been crying, for his deepset blue eyes sparkled, and there was mad joy and suffering in those eyes. They picked him up, grasping him under his arms. Then he spoke.

"Doctor," he said faintly and unclearly—the scab crossing his lips hindered his speech.

At first no one understood him—it was only after several seconds that they realized he was asking for a medic.

"Doctor, hurry. Sergei Kondratev is in bad shape." He shifted his wide-open eyes from one face to another and suddenly smiled. "Hello, great-great-grandchildren."

The tension of the smile made the wound on his face open up, and thick red drops hung on his lips. Everyone had the impression that the man had not smiled for a long time. People in white coats hurried down into the crater.

"Doctor," the redhead repeated, and collapsed, his dirty blue-white face slumping back.

The Conspirators

THE four inhabitants of Room 18 were widely renowned within the confines of the Anyudin School, and this was only natural. Such talents as consummate skill in the imitation of the howl of the giant crayspider of the planet Pandora, the ability to discourse freely upon ten methods of fuel economy in interstellar travel, and the capacity to execute eleven knee-bends in a row on one leg could not go unnoticed, and not one of these talents was foreign to the inhabitants of Room 18.

The history of Room 18 begins at a point in time when the companions were only three in number and still lacked both their own room and their own teacher. Even in those days Genka Komov, better known as the Captain, exercised unlimited authority over Pol Gnedykh and Aleksandr Kostylin. Pol Gnedykh, familiarly known as Polly or Lieber Polly, was famous as an individual of great cleverness of mind, an individual capable of anything. Aleksandr Kostylin was of unquestionable good nature, and covered himself with glory in battles associated with the application not so much of intelligence as of physical force. He could not endure being called Kostyl for short (and understandably so, for "kostyl" means "crutch"), but he willingly answered to the nickname of Lin. Captain Genka, who had mastered to perfection the popular-science book *The Road to Space*, who knew many various useful things, and who was, to all appearances, easily capable of repairing a photon reflector without so much as changing the spacecraft's course, indefatigably led Lin and Polly toward reknown. Thus, for example, wide celebrity resulted from the tests of a new type of rocket fuel that were conducted under his direction in the school park. A fountain of dense smoke flew up higher than the tallest trees, while the crash of the explosion could be heard by all who were on the school grounds at the right moment. It was an unforgettable feat, and long afterward Lin still sported a long scar on his back, and went shirtless whenever possible in order that this scar should be exposed to the gaze of envious eyes. This too was the threesome that revived the pastime of ancient African tribes by swinging from trees on long ropes simulating lianas—simulating them inadequately, as experience demonstrated. Moreover, it was they who introduced the practice of welding together the plastic of which clothing is made, and they repeatedly utilized this ability to temper the unbearable pride of the older comrades who were permitted to go swimming with face masks and even aqualungs. However, while all these feats covered the threesome with glory, they did not bring the desired satisfaction, and so the Captain decided to participate in the Young Cosmonauts' Club, which held forth the brilliant prospect of riding the acceleration centrifuge and perhaps even of winning one's way at last to the mysterious cosmonautical simulator.

It was with great amazement that the Captain discovered in the club one Mikhail Sidorov, known for various reasons also as Athos. To the Captain, Athos initially appeared to be an arrogant and empty-headed individual, but the first serious conversation with him demonstrated that in his personal qualities he undoubtedly surpassed one Walter Saronian, who was at that time on reasonably affable terms with the threesome, and who occupied the fourth bunk in the just-assigned Room 18.

The historic conversation proceeded in approximately this wise:

"What do you think about nuclear drive?" Genka inquired.

"Old hat," quoth Athos shortly.

"I agree," the Captain said, and he looked at Athos with interest. "And photon-annihilation drive?"

"So-so," said Athos, shaking his head sadly.

Genka then put to him the premier question: which system seemed more promising, the gravigen or the gravshield?

"I acknowledge only the D-principle," Athos declared haughtily.

"Hmm," said Genka. "Okay, let's go to Eighteen—I'll introduce you to the crew."

"You mean your crummy roommates?" Athos-Sidorov winced, but he went.

A week later, unable to endure intimidation and open violence, and with the teacher's permission, Walter Saronian fled Room 18; Athos established himself in his place. After that the D-principle and the idea of intergalactic travel reigned in the minds and hearts of Room 18 firmly and to all appearances for good. Thus was formed the crew of the superstarship *Galaktion:* Genka, captain; Athos-Sidorov, navigator and cyberneticist; Lieber Polly, computerman; Sashka Lin, engineer and hunter. The crew moved forward with bright hopes and extremely specific plans. The master blueprints of the superstarship *Galaktion* were drawn up; regulations were worked out; and a top-secret sign (a special way of holding the fingers of the right hand) by which the crew members might recognize one another was put into effect. The threat of imminent invasion hung over the galaxies Andromeda, Messier 33, and others. So went the year.

Lin, engineer and hunter, delivered the first blow. With his characteristic thoughtlessness, he had asked his father (on leave from an orbital weightless casting factory) how old you had to be to be a spaceman. The answer was so horrifying that Room 18 refused to believe him. The resourceful Polly induced his kid brother to ask the same question of one of the teachers. The answer was identical. The conquest of galaxies must be put off for an essentially infinite period—about ten years. A short era of disarray ensued, for the news brought to naught the carefully elaborated Operation Flowering Lilac, according to which the full complement of Room 18 would stow away on an interplanetary tanker bound for Pluto. The Captain had counted on revealing himself a week after takeoff and thus automatically merging his crew with that of the tanker.

The next blow was less unexpected, but much heavier for all of that. During this era of confusion the crew of the *Galaktion* somehow all at once became conscious of the fact—which they had been taught much earlier—that, strange as it might seem, the most honored professionals in the world were not spacemen, not undersea workers, and not even those mysterious subduers of monsters, the zoopsychologists, but doctors and teachers. In particular, it turned out that the World Council was sixty percent composed of teachers and doctors. That there were never enough teachers, while the world was rolling in spacemen. That without doctors, deep-sea workers would be in real trouble, but not vice versa. These devastating facts, as well as many others of the same ilk, were brought home to the consciousness of the crew in a horrifyingly prosaic fashion: on the most ordinary televised economics lesson; and, most frightful of all, the allegations were not disputed in the least degree by their teacher.

The third and final blow brought on genuine doubts. Engineer Lin was apprehended by the Captain in the act of reading *Childhood Catarrhal Diseases,* and in response to a sharp attack he insolently declared that in future he planned on bringing some concrete benefit to people, not merely the dubious data resultant from a life spent in outer space. The Captain and the navigator were obliged to bring to bear the most extreme measures of persuasion, under the pressure of which the recreant acknowledged that he would never make a children's doctor anyhow, while in the capacity of ship's engineer or, in a pinch, of hunter, he had a chance of winning himself eternal glory. Lieber Polly sat in the corner and kept silent for the duration of the inquiry, but from that time on he made it a rule, when under the least pressure, to blackmail the crew with venomous but incoherent threats such as, "I'll go be a laryngologist" or "Ask Teacher who's right." Lin, on hearing these challenges, breathed heavily with envy. Doubt was dividing the crew of the *Galaktion.* Doubt assailed the soul even of the Captain.

Help arrived from the Outside World. A group of scientists who had been working on Venus completed, and proposed for the consideration of the World Council, a practical plan to precipitate out the atmospheric cover of Venus, with the aim of the eventual colonization of the planet. The World Council examined the plan and approved it. Now the turn had come of the wastes of Venus—the great fearsome planet was to be made into a second Earth. The adult world set to work. They built new machines and accumulated energy; the population of Venus skyrocketed. And in Room 18 of the Anyudin School, the captain of the *Galaktion*, under the curious gaze of his crew, worked feverishly on the plan of Operation October, which promised an unprecedented sweep of ideas, and a way out of the current serious crisis.

The plan was finished three hours after the publication of the World Council's appeal, and was presented for the crew's inspection. The October plan was striking in its brevity and in its information density:

1. Within six weeks, master the industrial and technological specifications of standard atmospherogenic assemblies.

2. Upon expiry of the above-mentioned period, early in the morning —so as not to disturb the housefather—run away from school and proceed to the Anyudin rocket station, and in the inevitable confusion attendant upon a landing, sneak into the cargo hold of some vessel on a near-Earth run and hide until touchdown;

3. Then see.

The plan was greeted with exclamations of "Zow-zow-zow!" and approved, with three votes for and one abstention. The abstention was the noble Athos-Sidorov. Gazing at the far horizon, he spoke with unusual scorn of "crummy atmosphere plants" and of "wild goose chases," and averred that only the feelings of comradeship and mutual assistance prevented him from subjecting the plan to sharp criticism. However, he was prepared to withhold all objections, and he even undertook to think out certain aspects of their departure, provided than no one should look upon this as consent to the abandonment of the D-principle for the sake of a bunch of cruddy-smelling precipitators. The Captain made no comment but gave the order to set to work. The crew set to work.

In Room 18 of the Anyudin School, a geography lesson was in progress. On the screen of the teaching stereovision, a scorching cloud over Parícutin blazed with lightning, hissing lapilli flashed past, and the red tongue of a lava stream, like an arrowhead, thrust out of the crater. The topic was the science of volcanology, volcanoes in general and unsubdued volcanoes in particular. The tidy domes of the Chipo-Chipo volcanological station showed white through the gray magma that was piling up and that would harden only God knew when. In front of the stereovision sat Lin, his eyes glued to the screen and feverishly biting the nails of his right and left hands by turns. He was running late. He had spent the morning and half the afternoon on the playground, verifying a proposition expressed by his teacher the day before: that the ratio of the maximum height of a jump to the maximum length of a jump is approximately one to four. Lin had high-jumped and broad-jumped until he started seeing spots before his eyes. Then he obliged some little kids to concern themselves with the matter, and he tired them out completely, but the resultant data indicated that the teacher's proposition was close to the truth. Now Lin was making up for what he had missed, and was watching the lessons the rest of the crew had already learned that morning.

Captain Genka, at his desk by the transparent outside wall of the room, was carefully copying the diagram for a medium-power two-phase oxygen installation. Lieber Polly was lying on his bed (an activity that was not encouraged during the daytime), pretending to read a fat book in a cheerless jacket—*Introduction to the Operation of Atmospherogenic Assemblies*. Navigator Athos-Sidorov stood by his desk and thought. This was his favorite pastime. Simultaneously he observed with contemptuous interest the instinctive reactions of Lin, who was enthralled by geography.

Beyond the transparent wall, under a kindly sun, the sand showed yellow and the slender pines rustled. The diving tower, with its long springboards, jutted over the lake.

The instructor's voice began to tell how the volcano Stromboli had been extinguished, and Lin forgot himself completely. Now he was biting his nails on both hands at the same time, and the noble nerves of Athos could stand no more. "Lin," he said, "stop that gnawing!"

Without turning around, Lin shrugged in vexation.

"He's hungry!" declared Pol, coming to life. He sat up on the bed in order to elaborate upon this theme, but here the Captain slowly turned his large-browed head and glared at him.

"What are you looking at me for?" asked Pol. "I'm reading, I'm reading. 'The output of the AGK-ii is sixteen cubic meters of ozonized oxygen per hour. The stra-ti-fi-ca-tion method permits—' "

"Read to yourself!" Athos advised.

"Well, I don't think he's bothering you," the Captain said in an iron voice.

"You think he isn't, and I think he is," said Athos-Sidorov.

Their glances met. Pol watched the development of the incident with enjoyment. He was sick to the nth degree of the *Introduction to.*

"Have it your way," said the Captain. "But I'm not figuring on doing everyone's work myself. And you're not doing anything, Athos. You're as much use as a fifth wheel."

The navigator smiled scornfully and did not deem it necessary to answer. At that moment the screen went out, and Lin turned around with a creak of his chair.

"Guys!" he said. "Zow! Guys! Let's go there."

"Let's go!" Pol shouted, and jumped up.

"Where is there?" the Captain asked ominously.

"To Parícutin! To Mount Pelée! To—"

"Hold it!" yelled the Captain. "You're a bunch of lousy traitors! I'm sick and tired of messing around with you! I'm going by myself. You can take off for wherever you feel like. Is that clear?"

"Phooey!" said Athos elegantly.

"Phooey yourself, you understand? You approved the plan, you shouted 'zow-zow,' but what are you doing now? Well, I'm just plain sick and tired of messing around with you. I'll make a deal with Natasha or with that idiot Walter, you hear? You can go fly a kite. I've had it with you, and that's final!"

The Captain turned his back and wrathfully resumed copying the blueprint. A heavy silence ensued. Polly quietly lay back down and resumed studying the *Introduction to* furiously. Athos compressed his lips, and the ponderous Lin got up and started pacing the room with his hands in his pockets. "Genka," he said indecisively. "Captain, you—cut—this out. What do you want to—"

"You take off for your Mount Pelée," the Captain muttered. "For your Parícutin. We'll manage."

"Captain . . . what are you saying? You can't tell Walter, Genka!"

"Just watch me. I'll tell him all right. He may be an idiot, but he's no traitor."

Lin increased his pace to a run without taking his hands out of his pockets. "What would you go and do that for, Captain? Look, Polly is already grinding."

" 'Polly, Polly'! Polly is full of hot air. And I've just plain had it with Athos. Think of it—navigator of the *Galaktion!* The blow-hard!"

Lin turned to Athos. "You're right. Athos, something . . . it's not right, you know. We're all trying."

Athos studied the forested horizon. "What are you all jabber-ing for?" he inquired politely. "If I said I'd go, I'll go. I don't think I've ever lied to anyone yet. And I've never let anyone down, either."

"Cut it out," Lin said fiercely. "The Captain's right. You're just loafing, being a pig."

Athos turned and narrowed his eyes. "So tell me, o Great Worker," he said, "why is a Diehard inferior to an AGK-7 under conditions of nitrogen surplus?"

"Huh?" Lin said distractedly, and looked at the Captain. The Captain barely raised his head.

"What are the nine steps in operating an Eisenbaum?" asked Athos. "Who invented oxytane? You don't know, you grind! Or in what year? You don't know that either?"

That was Athos—a great man despite his numerous failings. A reverent silence settled over the room, except for Pol Gnedykh's angry leafing of the pages of the *Introduction*.

"Who cares who invented what?" Lin muttered uncertainly, and stared helplessly at the Captain.

The Captain got up, went over to Athos, and poked him in the stomach with his fist. "Good man, Athos," he declared. "I was a fool to think you were loafing."

"Loafing!" Athos said, and poked the Captain in the side. He had accepted the apology.

"Zow! Guys!" proclaimed the Captain. "Set your course by Athos. Feeders on cycle, spacers! Stand by for Legen accelerations. Watch the reflector. Dust flow to the left! Zow!"

"Zow-zow-zow!" roared the crew of the *Galaktion.*

The Captain turned to Lin. "Engineer Lin," he said, "do you have any questions on geography?"

"Nope," the engineer reported in turn.

"What else do we have today?"

"Algebra and work," said Athos.

"Ri-ight! So let's start with a fight. The first pair'll be Athos versus Lin. Polly, go sit down. Your legs are tired."

Athos started getting ready for the fight. "Don't forget to hide the materials," he said. "They're scattered all over—Teacher'll see them."

"Okay. We're leaving tomorrow anyhow."

Pol sat down on the bed and laid aside his book. "It doesn't say here who invented oxytane."

"Albert Jenkins," the Captain said without having to think. "In seventy-two."

Teacher Tenin arrived at Room 18, as always, at 4:00 P.M. There was no one in the room, but water was flowing copiously in the shower, and he could hear snorting, slapping, and exultant cries of "zow-zow-zow!" The crew of the *Galaktion* was washing up after their exertions in the workshops.

The teacher paced the room. Much here was familiar and usual. Lin, as always, had scattered his clothes over the whole room. One of his slippers lay on Athos's desk, undoubtedly representing a yacht. The mast was made out of a pencil; the sail, of a sock. This, of course, was Pol's work. In this regard Lin would mutter angrily, "You think that's pretty smart, huh, Polly?" The transparency system for the walls and ceiling was out of order —Athos had done that. The controls were by the head of his bed, and as he went to sleep, he would play with them. He would lie there pressing keys, and at one moment the room would become quite dark, and in the next the night sky and moon over the park would appear. Usually the controls were broken, if no one had stopped Athos in time. Athos today was doomed to fix the transparency system.

Lin's desk was chaos. Lin's desk was always chaos, and there was nothing to be done about it. This was simply one of those cases where the teacher's contrivances and the entire powerful apparatus of child psychology were helpless.

As a rule, everything new in the room was linked with the Captain. Today there were diagrams on his desk that had not been there before. It was something new, and consequently something that required some thinking. Teacher Tenin very much liked new things. He sat down at the Captain's desk and began to look over the diagrams.

From the shower room came:

"Add a little more cold, Polly!"

"Don't! It's cold already! I'm freezing!"

"Hold onto him, Lin. It'll toughen him up."

"Athos, hand me the scraper."

"Where's the soap, guys?"

Someone fell onto the floor with a crash. A yelp: "What idiot threw the soap under my feet?"

Laughter, cries of "Zow!"

"Very clever! Boy, will I get you!"

"Back! Pull in your manipulators, you!"

The teacher looked the diagrams over and replaced them. *The plot thickens*, he thought. *Now an oxygen concentrator. The boys are really taken up with Venus.* He got up and looked under Pol's pillow. There lay the *Introduction to*. It had been thoroughly leafed through. The teacher flipped thoughtfully through the pages and put the book back. *Even Pol*, he thought. *Curious.*

Then he saw that the boxing gloves that had been lying on Lin's desk day in and day out, regularly and unvaryingly for the last two years, were missing. Over the Captain's bed, the photograph of Gorbovsky in a vacuum suit was gone, and Pol's desktop was empty.

Teacher Tenin understood everything. He realized that they wanted to run away, and he knew where they wanted to run to. He even knew when they wanted to go. The photograph was missing, and therefore it was in the Captain's knapsack. Therefore the knapsack was already packed. Therefore they were leaving tomorrow morning, early. The Captain always liked to do a thorough job, and not put off until tomorrow what he could do today. (On the other hand, Pol's knapsack couldn't be ready yet —Pol preferred to do everything the day after tomorrow.) So they were going tomorrow, out through the window so as not to disturb the housefather. They had a great dislike of disturbing housefathers. And who did not?

The teacher glanced under a bed. The Captain's knapsack was made up with enviable neatness. Pol's lay under his bed. Pol's favorite shirt—red stripes and no collar—stuck out from the knapsack. In the cabinet reposed a ladder skillfully woven from sheets, undoubtedly Athos's creation.

So . . . that meant there was some thinking to be done. Teacher Tenin grew gloomy and cheerful simultaneously.

Pol, wearing only shorts, came tearing out of the shower room, saw the teacher, and turned a cartwheel.

"Not bad, Pol!" the teacher exclaimed. "Only keep your legs straight."

"Zow!" Pol yelped, and cartwheeled the other way. "Teacher, spacemen! Teacher's here!"

They always forgot to say hello.

The crew of the *Galaktion* darted into the room and got stuck in the doorway. Teacher Tenin looked at them and thought . . . nothing. He loved them very much. He always loved them. All of them. All those he brought up and launched into the wide world. There were many of them, and these were the best of all. Because they were now. They were standing at attention and looking at him just the way he liked. Almost.

"K-T-T-U-S-T-X-D," signaled the teacher. This meant, "Calling crew of *Galaktion*. Have good visual contact. Is there dust on course?"

"T-T-Q-U-Z-C," the crew answered discordantly. They also had good visual contact, and there was almost no dust on the course.

"Suit up!" the teacher commanded, and stared at his chronometer.

Without saying anything more, the crew rushed to suit up.

"Where's my other sock?" Lin yelled, and then he saw the yacht. "You think that's clever, Polly?" he muttered.

The suiting-up lasted thirty-nine and some tenths seconds,

Lin finishing last. "You pig, Polly," he grumbled. "Wise guy!"

Then everyone sat down at random, and the teacher said, "Literature, geography, algebra, and work. Right?"

"And a little phys ed too," added Athos.

"Undoubtedly," said the teacher. "That's clear from your swollen nose. And speaking of phys ed, Pol is still bending his legs. Alexandr, you show him how."

"Okay," Lin said with satisfaction. "But he's a little slow, Teacher."

Pol answered quickly, "Better a somewhat sluggish knee / Than a head full of stupidity."

"C plus." The teacher shook his head. "Not too elegant, but the idea is clear. In thirty years maybe you'll learn to be witty, Pol, but when it happens don't abuse your power."

"I'll try not to," Pol said modestly.

C plus wasn't so bad, but Lin sat there red and sulky. By evening he would have thought up a rejoinder.

"Let's talk about literature," Teacher Tenin proposed. "Captain Komov, how is your composition feeling today?"

"I wrote about Gorbovsky," the Captain said, and fished in his desk.

"A fine topic!" said the teacher. "I hope you've been equal to it."

"He's not equal to anything," Athos declared. "He thinks that the important thing about Gorbovsky is the know-how."

"And what do you think?"

"I think that the main thing about Gorbovsky is the daring, the courage."

"I would suppose you're wrong, Navigator," said the teacher. "There are very many daring people. And among spacemen you won't find any cowards. The cowards simply die out. But the Assaultmen, especially ones like Gorbovsky, are unique. I ask you to believe me because I know, and you don't, not yet. But you'll find out, Navigator. And what did you write?"

"I wrote about Doctor Mboga," said Athos.

"Where did you find out about him?"

"I gave him a book about flying leeches," Pol explained.

"Wonderful, boys! Have you all read the book?"

"Yes," said Lin.

"Who didn't like it?"

"We all liked it," Pol said with pride. "I dug it out of the library."

He of course had forgotten that the teacher had recommended that book to him. He always forgot such details—he very much liked to "discover" books. And he liked everyone to know about this. He liked publicity.

"Good for you, Pol!" said the teacher. "And you, of course, wrote about Doctor Mboga too?"

"I wrote a poem!"

"Oho, Pol! And aren't you afraid?"

"What is there to be afraid of?" Pol said blithely. "I read it to Athos. The only things he complained about were trivia. And just a little bit."

The teacher looked doubtfully at Athos. "Hmm. As far as I know Navigator Sidorov, he is rarely distracted by trivia. We'll see, we'll see. And you, Alexandr?"

Lin silently thrust a thick composition book at the teacher. A monstrous smudge spread over the cover. "Zvantsev," he explained. "The oceanographer."

"Who is that?" Pol asked jealously.

Lin looked at him with shocked contempt and remained silent. Pol was mortified. It was unbearable. It was awful. He had never so much as heard of Zvantsev the oceanographer.

"Well, great," the teacher said, and gathered up the composition books. "I'll read them and think about them. We'll talk about them tomorrow."

He immediately regretted saying that. The Captain was so visibly discomfited by the word "tomorrow." To lie, to dissemble, ran very much against the grain of the boy. There was no need to torture them—he would have to be more careful in his choice of words. After all, they were not planning anything bad. They were not even in any danger—they would get no farther than Anyudin. But they would have to come back, and that would really hurt. The whole school would laugh at them. Kids were sometimes malicious, especially in cases like this, where their comrades imagined that they could do something that others couldn't. He thought of the great scoffers in Rooms 20 and 72, and about the jolly smallfry who would jump with a whoop upon the captive crew of the *Galaktion* and tear them limb from limb.

"Speaking of algebra," he said. (The crew smiled. They very much liked that "speaking of." It seemed to them so enthrallingly illogical.) "In my day one very quaint instructor gave the lectures on the history of mathematics. He would stand by the board"— the teacher started to demonstrate—"and begin, 'Even the ancient Greeks knew that $(a+b)^2$ equals a^2 plus $2ab$ plus—'" The teacher looked at his imaginary notes. "'Plus ... uhhh ... b^2.'"

The crew broke out into laughter. The seasoned spacemen looked at Teacher. They were in raptures. They thought this man was great and simple, like the world.

"But now look at what curious things sometimes happen with $(a+b)^2$," the teacher said, and sat down. Everyone crowded around him.

There began that without which the crew could no longer live and the teacher would not want to—the adventures of numbers in space and time. A mistake in a coefficient threw a ship off course and plunged it into a black abyss from which there would be no return for the man who had put a plus instead of a minus before the radical; a cumbersome, horrible-looking polynomial broke up into astonishingly simple factors, and Lin yelped in distress, "Where were my eyes? How simple!"; there resounded the strange, solemn-funny stanzas of Cardano, who had described in verse his method of solving cubic equations; the incredibly mysterious story of Fermat's Last Theorem rose up from the depths of history. . . .

Then the teacher said, "Fine, boys. Now you can see: if you can reduce all of your problems in life to polynomials, they'll be solved. At least approximately."

"I wish I *could* reduce them to polynomials," burst out Pol, who had suddenly remembered that tomorrow he wouldn't be here, that he had to leave Teacher, perhaps forever.

"I read you, Comrade Computerman," the teacher said affectionately. "The most difficult part is putting the question properly. Six centuries of mathematical development will do the rest for you. And sometimes you can get along even without the mathematics." He was silent for a moment. "Well, boys, shall we have a four-one fight?"

"Zow!" the crew exploded, and dashed out of the room, because for the game four-one you needed room, and soft ground underfoot. Four-one was an exacting game, demanding great intelligence and an excellent knowledge of the ancient holds of the *sambo* system of combat. The crew worked up a sweat, and Teacher threw off his jacket and collected himself a few scratches. Then they all sat under a pine on the sand and rested.

"On Pandora a scratch like that would call for an emergency alarm," the teacher informed them, looking at his palm. "They'd put me in isolation in the med section, and would drown me in virophages."

"But what if a crayspider bit off your hand?" Pol asked with sweet horror.

The teacher looked at him. "A crayspider doesn't bite like that," he said. "It couldn't get a hand into its mouth. Anyway, now Professor Karpenko is working on an interesting little thing which makes virophages look like kid games. Have you heard about bioblockading?"

"Tell us!" The crew were all ears.

Teacher started to tell them about bioblockading. The crew listened with such fascination that Tenin felt sorry that the world was so enormous, and that he couldn't tell them right now about everything known and unknown. They listened without stirring, hanging on his every word. And everything was very fine, but he knew that the ladder made from sheets was waiting in the cabinet, and he knew that the Captain—at least the Captain!—knew this too. *How to stop them?* Tenin thought. *How?* There were many ways, but none of them were any good, because he had not only to stop them, but to make them understand why they must stop themselves. There was also one good way. One, at least. But for that he would need a night, and a few books on the regeneration of atmospheres, and the complete plan of the Venus project, and two tablets of sporamine in order to last it out. The boys couldn't leave that night. And not that evening either—the Captain was intelligent and saw a good deal. He saw that Teacher was onto something, and maybe onto everything. *So I'll do without night,* thought the teacher. *But give me just four or five hours. I've got to hold them back, keep them busy, for that long. How?*

"Speaking of love of neighbor," he said—and the crew once more rejoiced in that "speaking of"—"what do you call a person who picks on those weaker than himself?"

"A parasite," Lin said quickly. He could not express himself more strongly.

"The three worst things are a coward, a liar, and a bully," recited Athos. "Why do you ask, Teacher? We never have been, and we never will be."

"I know. But in the school it happens . . . sometimes."

"Who?" Pol jumped up. "Tell us, who?"

The teacher hesitated. Actually, what he planned to do was foolish. To involve the boys in such a matter meant risking a good deal. They were hot-headed and could ruin everything. And Teacher Schein would be justified in saying something not very pleasant regarding Teacher Tenin. But he had to stop them and. . . .

"Walter Saronian," the teacher said slowly. "But this is hearsay, boys. Everything has to be carefully verified." He looked at them. Poor Walter! Knots of tension moved across the Captain's cheeks. Lin was terrible to behold.

"We'll check it out," Pol said, his eyes narrowing meanly. "We'll be very careful."

Athos exchanged glances with the Captain. Poor Walter!

"Let's talk about volcanoes," proposed the teacher. And he thought, *It will be a little hard to talk about volcanoes. But I think I've hit on the natural thing to hold them back until dark. Poor Walter! Yes, they'll verify everything very carefully, because the Captain doesn't like to make mistakes. Then they'll go looking for Walter. All that will take a lot of time. It's hard to find a twelve-year-old after supper in a park that occupies four hundred hectares. They won't leave until late evening. I've won my five hours, and . . . oh, my poor head! How are you going to cram in four books and a six-hundred-page plan?*

And Teacher Tenin started telling them how in eighty-two he had happened to take part in the extinguishing of the volcano Stromboli.

They caught up with Walter Saronian in the park, by the pond. This was in one of the park's most remote corners, where not every smallfry would venture, and therefore only a few knew about the pond's existence. It was spring-fed, with dark deep water in which, fins moving, large yellow fish rested between the long green water-lily stems stretching up from the bottom. The local hunters called the fish *bliamb,* and shot them with homemade underwater rifles.

Walter Saronian was stark naked except for a face mask. In his hands was an air pistol that shot jagged-edged darts, and on his feet were red and blue swim fins. He stood in a haughty pose, drying off, with his mask pushed up on his forehead.

"We'll get him wet for a start," whispered Pol.

The Captain nodded. Polly rustled the bushes and gave a quiet, low-pitched cough. Walter did exactly what any of them would have done in his place. He pulled the mask over his face and, wasting no time, dove without the least splash into the water. Slow ripples swept over the dark surface, and the water-lily leaves placidly rose and sunk a few times.

"Pretty well done," Lin remarked, and all four emerged from the bushes and stood on the bank, looking into the dark water.

"He dives better than I do," said the objective Pol, "but I wouldn't want to trade places with him now."

They sat down on the bank. The waves dispersed, and the water-lily leaves grew still. The low sun shone through the pines. It was a bit close, and quiet.

"Who's going to do the talking?" inquired Athos.

"I am," Lin eagerly suggested.

"Let me," said Pol. "You can follow it up."

The gloomy Captain nodded. He did not like any of this. Night was approaching, and nothing was ready yet. They wouldn't manage to get away today, that was for sure. Then he remembered Teacher's kind eyes, and all desire to leave evaporated. Teacher had once told him, "All the worst in a human being begins with a lie."

"There he is!" Lin said in a low tone. "Swimming."

They sat in a semicircle by the water and waited. Walter swam beautifully and easily—he no longer had the pistol.

"Hi, Eighteen," he said as he was climbing out of the water. "You really snuck up on me." He stopped knee-deep in the water and started to dry himself with his hands.

Pol went first. "Happy sixteenth birthday," he said warmly.

Walter took off his mask and opened his eyes wide. "What?" he said.

"Happy sixteenth birthday, old buddy," Pol said still more affectionately.

"Somehow I don't quite understand you, Polly." Walter smiled uncomfortably. "You always say such clever things."

"Right," agreed the objective Pol. "I'm smarter than you. Besides, I read a whole lot more. And so?"

"And so what?"

"You didn't say thank you," Athos explained, taking up the lead. "We came to say happy birthday."

"What is this, guys?" Walter shifted his gaze from one to another, trying to make out what they wanted. His conscience was not clear, and he began to be wary. "What birthday? My birthday was a month ago, and I turned twelve, not sixteen."

"What?" Polly was very much surprised. "Then I don't understand what this face mask is doing here."

"And the fins," said Athos.

"And the pistol you hid on the other bank," said Lin, joining in again.

"Twelve-year-olds can't swim underwater by themselves," the Captain said angrily.

"Well, well!" Walter swelled up with contempt. "So you're going to tell my teacher?"

"What a nasty little boy!" exclaimed Pol, turning toward the Captain. The Captain did not deny it. "He means that *he* would rat if he caught me like that. Eh? So he's not just a rulebreaker, he's a——"

"Rules, rules," muttered Walter. "Haven't you ever gone hunting under water? Just think, I shot a bunch of *bliamb*."

"Yes, we've gone hunting," said Athos. "But always the four of us. Never alone. And we always tell Teacher about it. And he trusts us."

"You lie to your teacher," said Pol. "That means you could lie to anyone, Walter. But I like the way you're trying to make excuses."

The Captain narrowed his eyes. The good old formula—it cut him to pieces now: "Lie to teacher, lie to anyone." *It was stupid getting involved this way with Walter. Perfectly stupid. We have no right. . . .*

Walter was very uncomfortable. He said plaintively, "Let me get dressed, guys. It's cold. And . . . it's none of your business. It's my business, and my teacher's. Isn't that right, Captain?"

The Captain parted his lips. "He's right, Polly. And he's already softened up—he's making up excuses."

Pol pompously agreed: "Oh, yes, he's ready. His conscience is flickering. This was a psychological study, Walter. I really like studies in psychology."

"You and your bunch can clear out!" Walter muttered, and tried to get to his clothes.

"Quiet!" said Athos. "Don't be in such a hurry. That was the pre-am-ble. And now the amble begins."

"Let me," said the mighty Lin, standing up.

"No, no, Lin," said Pol. "Don't. It's vulgar. He won't understand."

"He'll understand," Lin promised. "He'll understand me all right."

Walter jumped nimbly into the water. "Four against one!" he shouted. "Conscience? Screw you!"

Pol jumped up and down with rage. "Four against one!" he yelled. "That smallfry Valka was four times weaker than you. No, five times, six times! But you knocked the daylights out of him, you lousy pig! You could've found Lin or the Captain if your paws were itching!"

Walter was pale. He had fastened his face mask, but he had not pulled it down, and now he was looking around distractedly, seeking a way out. He was cold. And he understood.

"Shame on you, Walter!" said the majestic Athos. "I think you're a coward. Shame on you. Come on out. You can fight us one at a time."

Walter hesitated, then came out. He knew what it was to fight Room 18, but still he came out and took up a stance. He felt that he had to settle up, and he realized that this was the best way to do it. Athos pulled his shirt over his head unhurriedly.

"Hold it!" yelled Pol. "It'll leave bruises! And we have something else to do!"

"Let me do it," requested the mighty Lin. "I'll be quick."

"No!" Pol quickly started undressing. "Walter! Do you know what the worst thing in the world is? I'll remind you—to be a coward, a liar, or a bully. You're not a coward, thank God, but you've forgotten the rest of it. And I want you to remember for a long time. I'm coming in, Walter. Repeat the magic words."

He gathered up Walter's clothes, which were lying in the bushes, and jumped into the water.

Walter watched him helplessly, and Athos started bounding

exultantly along the shore. "Polly!" he shouted. "Polly, you're a genius! Walter, how come you're not saying anything? Say it, say it, gorilla: a liar, a coward, or a bully."

The Captain gloomily kept track of Polly, who was dog-paddling, making a tremendous noise, and leaving a foamy trail behind him. Yes, Polly was as clever as ever. The opposite shore was overgrown with stinging nettles, and Walter could search there naked for his pants and such. In the dark, for the sun was setting. *That's just what he needs. But who's going to punish us? We're no angels ourselves—we're liars. That's not much better than being a bully.*

Polly came back. Gasping and spitting, he climbed onto the bank and immediately said, "There you are, Walter. Go and get dressed, gorilla. I don't swim as well as you, and I don't dive as well, but I wouldn't like to trade places with you now!"

Walter did not look at him. He silently pulled the mask over his face and got into the warm, steaming water. Before him was the bank with the stinging nettles.

"Remember!" Pol shouted after him. "A coward, a liar, or a bully. A bully, Walter! There's nothing worse than that. The nettles'll help out your bad memory."

"Right," said Athos. "Get dressed, Lieber Polly. You'll catch cold."

They could hear Walter on the opposite shore, hissing with pain through his teeth as he pushed through the thickets.

When they got back home to Room 18, it was already late evening—after Walter's chastisement, Lin had proposed that they play Pandora to relax, and Pandora was played with great gusto. Athos, Lin, and the Captain were hunters, and Polly the giant crayspider, while the park was the Pandoran jungle—impenetrable, marshy, and terrifying. The moon, which showed up at just the right time, played EN 9, one of Pandora's suns. They played until the giant crayspider, leaping from a tree onto Lin the hunter, tore his superdurable tetraconethylene pants down their entire length. Then they had to go home. They did not want to disturb the housefather, and the Captain was about to propose that they go in through the garbage chute (a magnificent idea that flashed like lightning through his gloomy ruminations), but then decided to take advantage of a humble workshop window.

They came into Room 18 noisily, discussing on the run the dazzling prospects opening up in connection with the idea of the garbage chute, and then they saw Teacher sitting at Athos's desk with a book in his hands.

"I ripped my pants," Pol said in confusion. Naturally he forgot to say good evening.

"Really!" exclaimed the teacher. "Tetraconethylene?"

"Uh-huh." Pol basked in his glory.

Lin grew green with envy.

"But boys," said the teacher, "I don't know how to mend them!"

The crew began to yell with triumph. They all knew how. They all thirsted to demonstrate, to talk and to do the repair.

"Go ahead," the teacher agreed. "But Navigator Sidorov will fix not the pants, but the transparancy system. Fate is cruel to him."

"Great galaxies!" said Athos. He could hardly reconcile himself to it.

Everyone got busy, including the Captain. For some reason he felt happy. *We won't leave tomorrow,* he thought. *We'll stay a little longer and make plans.* The idea of running away no longer seemed so attractive to him, but he could not very well let six weeks of study go for nothing.

"There are remarkable and interesting problems," Teacher told them, deftly wielding the high-frequency nozzle. "There are problems as great as the world. But there are also problems that are small but extremely interesting. A few days back I was reading an old, old book—very interesting. One thing it said was that up to that time the problem of ignis fatuus had never been solved —you know, the will-o'-the-wisp, in swamps? It was clear that it was some sort of chemiluminescent substance, but what? Phosphorus trisulphide, for example? I linked up with the Informatoreum, and what do you think? That riddle isn't solved even today!"

"Why not?"

"The fact is that it's very hard to catch this ignis fatuus. Like Truth, it flickers in the distance and refuses to be apprehended.

Lepelier tried to construct a cybernetic system to hunt it down, but nothing came of it."

Teacher Tenin's head ached unbearably. He felt awful. In the past four hours he had read and mastered four books on atmosphere regeneration, and had memorized the Venus plan. He had been forced to resort to the hypnoteacher for this, and after the hypnoteacher it was absolutely essential to lie down and sleep it off. But he couldn't. Perhaps he should not have overloaded his brain that way, but the teacher did not want to take chances. He had to know ten times more about Venus and about the project than the four of them put together. Otherwise his plan wasn't worth wasting time on.

Waiting for the moment to turn to the attack, he told them about the search for ignis fatuus, and he saw their childish eyes open wide, and saw the flame of great imagination writhe and flare in them, and as always it felt surprisingly gladdening and good to see this, even though his head was splitting into pieces.

But the boys were already sloshing through a marsh, wearing real, entrancing swamp boots, and around them were night, darkness, fog, and mysterious thickets; and from the depths of the swamp rushed clouds of repulsive exhalations, and it was very dangerous and frightening, but you mustn't be afraid. In front flickered the bluish tongues of ignis fatuus, whose secret—as was now clear—it was vital to discover, and on the chest of each of the hunters hung a miniaturized control for the trusty agile cybers who were stumbling through the quagmire. And these cybers had to be invented quickly, immediately, or else the last swamps would be drained and everyone would be left looking like fools.

By the time that the pants and the transparency system had been put into shape, no one cared any more about either. Pol was musing on a poem to be called "Will o' the Wisp," and while pulling on his pants he uttered the first line to flow out of him: "Mark! In the dark — The swampfire's glimmering spark!" The Captain and Athos, independently of each other, cogitated upon the design of a swamp cyber suitable for rapid locomotion through marshy regions, and reacting to chemiluminescence. Lin simply sat with his mouth open and thought, *Where were my eyes? How about that!* He firmly resolved to devote the rest of his life to swamps.

The teacher thought, *It's time. Just so I don't force them to lie or dissemble. Forward, Tenin!* And he began, "Speaking of diagrams, Captain Komov, what is this misshapen thing?" He tapped the diagram of the extractor with his finger. "You distress me, lad. The idea is good, but the execution is highly unsuccessful."

The Captain flared up and rushed into battle.

At midnight Teacher Tenin came out into the park and stopped by his pterocar. The enormous flat block of the school lay before him. All the windows on the first floor were dark, but above, some lights were still on. There was light in Room 20, where the five noted scoffers must be having a discussion with their teacher Sergei Tomakov, a former doctor. There was light in Room 107, where shadows were moving and it was clear that somebody was hitting somebody else over the head with a pillow, and intended to go on hitting him until the inaudible and invisible stream of infrarays forced even the most restless to go to sleep, which would happen in two minutes. There was light in many of the rooms of the oldest pupils—they were working on problems a little more important than ignis fatuus or how to put back together a torn pair of tetraconethylene pants. And there was light in Room 18.

The teacher got into the pterocar and began to watch the familiar window. His head raged on. He wanted to lie down and close his eyes, and put something cold and heavy on his forehead. *Well, my boys,* he thought. *Have I really stopped you? Oh, how hard it is, what a burden. And I'm not always sure whether I'm right, but in the end I've always turned out to be. And how remarkable that is, and how wonderful, and I couldn't live without it.*

The light in Room 18 went out. So he could go to sleep. He felt sleepy, but also sorry. *I probably didn't tell them everything I could have and should have. No, I did too. I wish it were morning! I feel bored without them, and lonely. Crummy little kids!* Teacher Tenin smiled and turned on the engine. He wished it were morning.

In Room 18, courageously fighting off sleep, the Captain was delivering a speech. The crew kept silent.

"Disgraceful! Showed up everyone! You lousy spongers! You miserable collection of slowboats and ignoramuses! What have you been doing for forty days? You, Lin? Shame on you! Not one intelligent answer."

Athos, playing with the transparency controls, muttered, "Cut the nagging, Captain! You're one to talk—out of five questions you missed four. And on the fifth—"

"What do you mean, out of five—"

"Don't argue, Captain, I counted."

If Athos said he had counted, that was it. Good grief, how disgraceful! The Captain screwed his eyes up to the point where he saw spots before his eyes. Operation October had failed. Had collapsed disgracefully. You couldn't storm Venus with this bunch of ignoramuses. No one had understood anything or learned anything. How much there was to cram about atmospheric assemblies, damn it all! *We're not ready to go anywhere. The great colonists from Room 18—ha!*

But Walter had really gotten his. Should they hand out some more? No, that was enough. And enough of all this nonsense in general. It was time to think about ignis fatuus.

. . . The Captain was sloshing through the swamp, together with Athos and Lin and Polly, who was wearing tattered pants. Amid the hazy exhalations flashed the quick-moving cybers, which they still had to invent.

Chronicle

NOVOSIBIRSK, 8 OCTOBER 2021. It was announced here today that the commission of the USCR Academy of Sciences studying the results of the *Taimyr-Ermak* expedition has finished its work.

As is well known, in pursuance of the international program of research into deep space and into the possibility of interstellar travel, in 2017 the Academy of Sciences of the USCR sent into deep space an expedition consisting of the two first-line interplanetary craft *Taimyr* and *Ermak*. The expedition departed November 7, 2017, from the international spaceport Pluto-2, in the direction of the constellation Lyra. The crew of the spaceship *Taimyr* consisted of captain and expedition head A. E. Zhukov, engineers K. I. Falin and G. A. Pollack, navigator S. I. Kondratev, cyberneticist P. Koenig, and physician E. M. Slavin. The spaceship *Ermak* served as an unmanned data collector.

The purpose of the expedition was to attempt to approach the light barrier (an absolute velocity of 300 thousand kilometers per second), and to perform research in proximity to the light barrier into the characteristics of space-time under arbitrary changes of velocity.

On 16 May 2020, the unmanned craft *Ermak* was detected and intercepted near the planet Pluto on its return orbit, and was brought to the international spaceport Pluto-2. The spaceship *Taimyr* did not appear on its planned return orbit.

A study of the data obtained by the spacecraft *Ermak* has demonstrated, in part, the following:

a) On the 327th day, subjective time, the *Taimyr-Ermak* expedition attained a velocity of 0.957 absolute relative to the sun, and turned to the execution of the research program;

b) The expedition obtained, and the receiving devices on the *Ermak* recorded, extremely valuable data relating to the behavior of space-time under conditions of arbitrary changes of velocity in proximity to the light barrier;

c) On the 342nd day, subjective time, the *Taimyr* initiated planned maneuvers bringing its distance from the *Ermak* up to 900 million kilometers. At 13 hours 09 minutes 11.2 seconds of the 344th day, subjective time, the tracking equipment on the *Ermak* detected, at the location of the *Taimyr*, a bright flash, after which the data flow from the *Taimyr* to the *Ermak* ceased, and was not resumed.

On the basis of the above-mentioned information, the commission has been obliged to conclude that the first-line interplanetary craft *Taimyr* has been lost with all hands (Aleksei Eduardovich Zhukov, Konstantin Ivanovich Falin, George Allen Pollack, Sergei Ivanovich Kondratev, Peter Koenig, and Evgeny Markovich Slavin) as a result of a serious accident. The cause and nature of the accident remain undetermined.

—*Bulletin of the International Scientific Data Center*, No. 237 (9 October 2021).

Two from the Taimyr

After his midday meal, Sergei Kondratev took a little nap. When he woke up, Evgeny Slavin came in. Evgeny's red hair lit up the walls—they turned pink, as at sunset. Evgeny smelled pleasantly but powerfully of an unfamiliar cologne.

"Hello, Sergei old man!" he shouted from the threshold.

And immediately someone said, "Please, talk a little more quietly."

Evgeny nodded readily toward the corridor, walked over to the bed on tiptoe, and sat so that Kondratev could see him without turning his head. His face was joyful, exultant. Kondratev could no longer remember when he had last seen him like that. And he saw the long reddish scar on Evgeny's face for the first time.

"Hello, Evgeny," Kondratev said.

Evgeny's head of flaming hair suddenly blurred. Kondratev squinted and sobbed. "Oh, for God's sake," he muttered angrily.

"Sorry about that. I've gone all to pieces here. Well, how are you doing?"

"All right, quite all right," Evgeny said in a choked-up voice. "Everything is simply amazing! The main thing is that they've brought you through. I was really worried about you, Sergei. Especially at first. All by myself, the depression, the homesickness! I rush off to see you and they won't let me in. I swear at them, and it makes no dent at all. I start talking, arguing, trying to prove that I'm a doctor myself . . . though what kind of a doctor am I now, anyhow?"

"All right, I believe you, I believe you," Kondratev said affectionately.

"And suddenly today Protos himself calls me. You're really on the mend, Sergei! In ten days or so I'll be teaching you how to drive a pterocar. I've already ordered you one."

"Oh?" said Kondratev. He had a spinal column broken in four places and a torn diaphragm, and his neck had parted from his skull. In his delirium he kept imagining himself as a rag doll that had been flattened under the caterpillar track of a truck. But you could depend on Protos. The doctor was a ruddy fat man, around fifty years old (or a hundred—who could tell these days?), very taciturn and very kind. He came every morning and every evening, sat down beside the bed, and breathed out so comfortably that Kondratev at once would begin to feel better. And he was, of course, a superb doctor, if up to now he had kept alive a rag doll flattened by a truck.

"Well, what the hell," said Kondratev. "Could be."

"Hey!" Evgeny shouted enthusiastically. "In ten days you'll be driving a pterocar for me. Protos is a magician, and I say that as a former doctor!"

"Yes," said Kondratev. "Protos is a very good man."

"A brilliant doctor! When I found out what he was working on, I realized that I would have to change professions. So I'm changing professions, Sergei! I'm going to be a writer!"

"So," said Kondratev. "You mean the writers haven't gotten any better?"

"Well, you see," said Evgeny, "one thing is clear: they're all modernists, and I'll be the only classicist. Like Trediakovsky the poet in the eighteenth century."

Kondratev looked at Evgeny out of half-opened eyes. Evgeny certainly was not wasting time. Dressed in the height of fashion, no doubt—shorts and a loose soft jacket with short sleeves and an open collar. Not one single seam, everything in soft, bright colors. The hair given a light, casual trim. Smooth-shaven and cologned. He was even trying to enunciate the way the great-grandchildren did—firmly and resonantly, and without gesticulation. And the pterocar . . . and only a few weeks had gone by. "Evgeny, I've forgotten again what year it is here," Kondratev said.

"Two thousand one hundred and nineteen," Evgeny answered ceremoniously. "They just say 'one nineteen.' "

"Well then, Evgeny," Kondratev said very seriously. "How are redheads doing? Have they survived into the twenty-second century or have they all died out?"

Evgeny answered just as ceremoniously, "Yesterday I had the honor of conversing with the secretary of the Northwest Asian Economic Council: a most intelligent man, and quite infrared."

They laughed and looked at each other. Then Kondratev asked, "Listen, Evgeny, where did you get that slash across your face?"

"That?" Evgeny fingered the scar. "You mean you can still see it?" he asked, distressed.

"Well, naturally," said Kondratev. "Red on white."

"I got that the same time you got smashed up. But they promised it would go away soon. Disappear without a trace. And I believe it, because they can do anything."

"Who are 'they'?" Kondratev asked gravely.

"What do you mean who? People—Earthlings."

"You mean 'we'?"

Evgeny was silent a moment. "Of course," he said uncertainly. " 'We.' In one sense of the word." He stopped smiling and looked at Kondratev attentively. "Sergei," he said softly, "does it hurt a lot, Sergei?"

Kondratev smiled weakly and said with his eyes, No, not much. But it was still good that Evgeny had asked. "Sergei, does it hurt a lot, Sergei?"—those were good words, and he had said them well. He had said them exactly as he had on the unlucky day when the *Taimyr* had buried itself in the shifting dust of a nameless planet and Kondratev, during a sortie, had hurt his leg.

That had hurt a lot, although, of course, not like now. Evgeny had thrown away his movie camera and had crawled along the crumbling slope of a dune, dragging Kondratev after him and swearing furiously. And then, when at last they had managed to scramble onto the crest of the dune, Evgeny had felt Kondratev's leg through the fabric of the spacesuit and had suddenly asked quietly, "Sergei, does it hurt a lot, Sergei?" Over the pale blue desert a hot white disk crawled into the violet sky, static hissed annoyingly in the headphones, and they sat a long time waiting for the return of the cyberscout. The cyberscout never did return —probably it had sunk into the dust—and finally they had started crawling back to the *Taimyr*. . . .

"What do you want to write about?" Kondratev asked. "About our trip?"

Evgeny began to speak with animation about sections and chapters, but Kondratev was no longer listening. He looked at the ceiling and thought, *It hurts, it hurts, it hurts.* And as always when the pain became unendurable, an oval hatch opened in the ceiling, and a rough gray tube with tiny winking green openings slid out noiselessly. The tube came down steadily until it had almost touched Kondratev's chest, and then stopped. Then a quiet vibrating rumble began.

"Wh-what's that?" Evgeny asked, jumping up.

Kondratev remained silent, his eyes closed, delightedly feeling the mad pain subside, disappear.

"Perhaps I had better leave?" Evgeny said, looking around.

The pain had gone. The tube retracted noiselessly upward, and the hatch in the ceiling closed.

"No," said Kondratev. "That's just treatment. Sit down, Evgeny." He tried to remember what Evgeny had been talking about. Yes—a fictionalized sketch to be called *Across the Light Barrier.* About the flight of the *Taimyr*. About the attempt to slip through the light barrier. About the accident that had brought the *Taimyr* across a century.

"Listen, Evgeny," Kondratev said. "Do they understand what happened to us?"

"Yes, of course," said Evgeny.

"Well?"

"Hmm," said Evgeny. "They understand, of course. But that

doesn't help us any. I for one can't understand what they understand."

"But still?"

"I told them everything, and they said, 'Ah, yes: Sigma deritrinitation.' "

"What?" said Kondratev.

"De-ri-tri-ni-ta-tion. With a sigma in front."

"Trimpazation," Kondratev muttered. "Did they happen to say anything else?"

"They told me straight out, 'Your *Taimyr* came right up to the light barrier under Legen acceleration and sigma-deritrinitated the space-time continuum.' They said that we shouldn't have resorted to Legen accelerations."

"Right," said Kondratev. "So then we shouldn't have resorted, but the fact remains that we did resort. Deri— teri— What's that word?"

"Deritrinitation. That's the third time I've told you. To put it briefly, so far as I understand it, any body approaching the light barrier under certain conditions distorts the form of worldlines extremely strongly, and pierces Riemann space, so to speak. Well . . . that's about what Bykov Junior had predicted in our day."

"Uh-huh," said Kondratev.

"They call this penetration 'deritrinitation.' All their long-range ships work on that principle. D-ships."

"Uh-huh," Kondratev said again.

"Under deritrinitation, those same Legen accelerations are especially hazardous. I didn't understand at all where they come from or what they consist of. Some sort of local vibrational field, plasmatic hypertransition, or something. The fact remains that under Legen interference extraordinarily strong distortions of time scale are inevitable. That's what happened to us in the *Taimyr*."

"Deritrinitation," Kondratev said sadly, and closed his eyes. They fell silent. *It's a bum deal,* Kondratev thought. *D-ships, Deritrinitation. We'll never get through it all. Plus a broken back.*

Evgeny stroked Kondratev's cheek and said, "Never mind, Sergei. I think we'll understand in time. Of course, we'll have to learn an awful lot."

"Relearn," Kondratev whispered without opening his eyes.

"Don't deceive yourself, Evgeny. Relearn. Relearn everything from the very beginning."

"So all right, I'm willing," Evgeny said brightly. "The main thing is to want to."

" 'I want to' means 'I can'?" Kondratev inquired bitterly.

"That's it."

"That saying was invented by people who could even when they didn't want to. Iron men."

"Well," said Evgeny, "you're not made of paper either. A couple weeks back I met a certain young woman. . . ."

"Oh?" said Kondratev. Evgeny very much liked meeting young women.

"She's a linguist. Smart. A wonderful, amazing person."

"Of course," said Kondratev.

"Let me talk, Sergei. I understand everything. You're afraid. But here there's no need to be lonely. There are no lonely people here. Get well soon, Navigator. You're turning sour."

Kondratev was silent a while, and then asked, "Evgeny, do me a favor and go over to the window."

Evgeny got up and, walking noiselessly, went over to the enormous—wall-high—blue window. Kondratev could see nothing out the window except sky. At night the window was a blue-black abyss studded with piercing stars, and once or twice the navigator had seen a reddish glow blaze up—blaze up and quickly die out.

"I've arrived," said Evgeny.

"What's there?"

"A balcony."

"And farther?"

"Below the balcony is a pad," Evgeny said, and looked back at Kondratev.

Kondratev frowned. Even old Evgeny was no help. Kondratev was as alone as could be. So far he knew nothing. Not a thing. He didn't even know what sort of floor there was in his room, because footsteps made no sound on it. Last evening the navigator had tried to sit up and look the room over, and had immediately fainted. He had not tried again, because he could not stand being unconscious.

"This building where you are is a nursing home for serious

cases," said Evgeny. "The building has sixteen stories, and your room—"

"Ward," muttered Kondratev.

"—and your room is on the ninth floor. There's a balcony. Outside are mountains—the Urals—and a pine forest. From here I can see, first, another nursing home like this one. It's about fifteen kilometers away. Farther in the same direction is Sverdlovsk. It's ninety kilometers off. Second, I see a landing pad for pterocars. They're really wonderful machines! There are four of them there now. So. What else? Third, a plaza with flowers and a fountain. Near the fountain there's a child. By all appearances, he's thinking about how much he would like to run away into the forest."

"Is he a serious case too?" the navigator asked with interest.

"It's possible. Though it doesn't look like it. So. He's not going to manage his getaway, because a certain barefoot woman has caught him. I am already acquainted with the woman because she works here. A very charming individual. She's around twenty. Recently she asked me whether I had happened to know Norbert Wiener and Anton Makarenko. Now she's dragging the serious case off, and, I think, edifying him en route. And here another pterocar is landing. Or no, it's not a pterocar. You should ask the doctor for a stereovision, Sergei."

"I did," the navigator said gloomily. "He won't let me have one."

"Why not?"

"How should I know?"

Evgeny turned toward the bed. "All this is sound and fury, signifying nothing," he said. "You'll see everything, learn everything, and stop feeling strange. Don't be so impressionable. Do you remember Koenig?"

"Yes?"

"Remember when I told him about your broken leg, and he shouted out loud in his magnificent accent, 'Ach, how impressionable I am! Ach!'"

Kondratev smiled.

"And the next morning I came to see you," Evgeny continued, "and asked how things were, and you answered with a touch of spite that you had spent 'a variegated night.'"

"I remember," said Kondratev. "And I've spent many variegated nights right here. And there are a lot of them coming up."

"Ach, how impressionable I am!" Evgeny quickly shouted.

Kondratev closed his eyes again and lay silent for some time. "Listen, Evgeny," he said without opening his eyes. "What did they say to you on the subject of your skill in piloting spaceships?"

Evgeny laughed merrily. "It was a great big scolding, although very polite. It seems I smashed through some enormous telescope, but I didn't even notice at the time. The head of the observatory almost slugged me, but his upbringing wouldn't permit it."

Kondratev opened his eyes. "Well?" he said.

"But later, when they learned I wasn't a pilot, it all cleared up. They even congratulated me. The observatory head, in an access of good feeling, even invited me to help with the rebuilding of the telescope."

"Well?" said Kondratev.

Evgeny sighed. "Nothing came of it. The doctors wouldn't let me."

The door opened a bit, and a dark girl wearing a white coat tightly belted at the waist looked into the room. She looked sternly at the patient, then at the visitor, and said, "It's time, Comrade Slavin."

"I'm just leaving," said Evgeny.

The girl nodded and closed the door. Kondratev said sadly, "Well, here you are leaving me."

"But not for long!" exclaimed Evgeny. "And don't go sour, I beg you. You'll be flying again, you'll make a first-class D-spacer."

"D-spacer. . . ." The navigator smiled crookedly. "Okay, be on your way. They are now going to feed the D-spacer his porridge. With a baby spoon."

Evgeny got up. "I'll be seeing you, Sergei," he said, carefully shaking Kondratev's hand, which lay on top of the sheet. "Get well. And remember that the new world is a very good world."

"Be seeing you, classicist," said Kondratev. "Come again. And bring your intelligent young lady. What's her name?"

"Sheila," said Evgeny. "Sheila Kadar."

He went out. He went out into an unknown and alien world, under a limitless sky, into the green of endless gardens. Into a world where, probably, glass superhighways ran arrow-straight to the horizon, where slender buildings threw delicate shadows across the plazas. Where cars darted without drivers or passengers, or with people dressed in strange clothing—calm, intelligent, benevolent, always very busy and very pleased to be so. Evgeny had gone out to wander over a planet both like and unlike the Earth they had abandoned so long ago and so recently. He would wander with his Sheila Kadar and soon would write his book, and the book would, of course, be very good, because Evgeny was quite capable of writing a good, intelligent book.

Kondratev opened his eyes. Next to the bed sat fat, ruddy Doctor Protos, watching him silently. Doctor Protos smiled, nodded, and said quietly, "Everything will be all right, Sergei."

7

The Moving Roads

"PERHAPS you'll spend the evening with us after all?" Evgeny said indecisively.

"Yes," said Sheila. "Let's stay together. Where will you go by yourself with such a sad expression on your face?"

Kondratev shook his head. "No, thank you," he said. "I'd rather be alone." Sheila smiled at him warmly and a little sadly, and Evgeny bit his lip and looked past Kondratev.

"Don't worry about me," Kondratev said. "It bothers me when people worry about me. See you." He stepped away from the pterocar and waved.

"Let him go," said Evgeny. "It'll be all right. Let him walk by himself. Have a good walk, Sergei—and you know where to find us."

He offhandedly touched the keyboard on the control panel with his fingertips. He did not even look at the controls. His left arm lay behind Sheila's back. He was magnificent. He didn't even slam the door shut. He winked to Kondratev and jackrabbitted the pterocar from the spot in such a manner that the door slammed itself shut. The pterocar shot up into the sky and sailed off on its wings. Kondratev made his way toward the escalator.

Okay, he thought, *let's plunge into life. Old Evgeny says it's impossible to get lost in this city. Let's find out.*

The escalator moved noiselessly. It was empty. Kondratev looked up. Overhead was a translucent roof. On it lay the shadows of pterocars and helicopters, belonging, no doubt, to the building's inhabitants. Every roof in the city was a landing pad, it seemed. Kondratev looked down. Below was a wide, bright lobby. Its floor was smooth and sparkling, like ice.

Two young girls ran past Kondratev, clicking their heels in a staccato on the steps. One of them, small, wearing a white blouse and a vivid blue skirt, glanced at his face as she ran past. She had a freckled nose and a lock of hair across her forehead. Something about Kondratev struck her. She stopped a moment, grabbing the railing so as not to fall. Then she caught up to her friend, and they ran farther, but below, already in the lobby, both of them looked back. *So,* thought Kondratev, *it begins. Here comes the elephant parading through the streets.*

He descended to the lobby (the girls were already gone) and tested the floor with his foot to see whether it was slippery. It wasn't. Alongside the lobby doors were enormous windows, and through one of them he could see that there was a great deal of greenery outside. Kondratev had already noticed this when flying over in the pterocar. The city was buried in greenery. Verdure filled up all the spaces between roofs. Kondratev walked around the lobby, and stood for a moment in front of a coat rack on which a solitary violet raincoat hung. After looking around cautiously, he felt the material, and then headed toward the doorway. On the steps of the porch he stopped. There was no street.

A trampled-down path stretched directly from the porch into thick, high grass. In ten paces it disappeared amid thickets of bushes. After the bushes came a forest—tall straight pines alternating with squat oaks, obviously very old. The clean light-blue walls of buildings extended to the right and to the left. "Not bad!" Kondratev said, and sniffed the air.

The air was very good. Kondratev put his hands behind his

back and set off resolutely down the path. It led him to a fairly wide sandy walk. Kondratev hesitated, then turned right. There were many people on the walk. He even tensed up, expecting that at the sight of him the great-great-grandchildren would break off conversation, turn away from urgent problems, stop short, and start staring at him. Maybe even start asking him questions. But nothing of the sort occurred. Some elderly great-great-grand-child, overtaking him from behind, bumped into him clumsily and said, "Excuse me, please. No, I wasn't talking to you, dear." Kondratev smiled to be on the safe side.

"Has something happened?" He heard a faint feminine voice, coming, it seemed, from inside the elderly great-great-grand-child.

"No," said the other great-great-grandchild, nodding benevo-lently toward Kondratev. "I've accidentally pushed a young man here."

"Oh," said the woman's voice. "Then do some more listening. I said that I would have nothing to do with the plan and that you would be against it too." The elderly great-great-grandchild moved off, and the woman's voice gradually faded out.

Great-great-grandchildren overtook Kondratev from behind, and came toward him from the front. Many smiled at him, some-times even nodding. But no one stared and no one was crawling with questions. True, for some time a dark-eyed lad with his hands in his pockets described a complicated trajectory around Kondratev, but at the very moment when Kondratev at last took pity and decided to nod toward him, the boy, in obvious despair, had dropped behind. Kondratev felt more at ease and started looking and listening.

Generally, the great-great-grandchildren seemed to be very ordinary people. Young and old, short and tall, homely and beau-tiful. Men and women. There was no one senile or sickly. And there were no children. The great-great-grandchildren on this green street behaved quite calmly and unconstrainedly, as if they were at home, with old friends. You couldn't say that they all radiated joy and happiness. Kondratev saw worried and tired faces, and more rarely even gloomy ones. One young fellow sat by the side of the walk among dandelions, picking them one after another and blowing on them fiercely. It was obvious that his thoughts were wandering somewhere far away, and that these thoughts were anything but happy.

The great-great-grandchildren dressed simply and quite variously. The older men wore long pants and soft jackets with open collars; the women wore slacks or long elegant dresses. The young men and girls almost all wore loose shorts and white or colored smocks. Of course you also encountered women of fashion sporting purple or gold cloaks, thrown over short bright ... shirts, Kondratev decided. These fashion plates were looked at.

It was quiet in the city, or at least there were no mechanical sounds. Kondratev heard only voices and, sometimes, from somewhere, music. The treetops rustled too, and very occasionally there came the soft *"fr-r-r-r"* of a pterocar flying past. Obviously most aircraft usually traveled at high altitudes. In short, nothing here was entirely alien to Kondratev, although it was very strange to be walking down paths and sandy walks, with clothes brushing against the branches of bushes, in the middle of an enormous city. The suburban parks of a hundred years earlier had been almost the same. Kondratev could have felt entirely at home here, if only he did not feel so useless, undoubtedly more useless than any of these gold and purple fashion plates with their short hems.

He overtook a man and woman walking arm in arm. The man was saying, "At this point the violin comes in—*tra-la-la-la-a*—and then the delicate and tender thread of the choriole—*di-i-da-da-da ... di-i-i.*" His rendition was piercing but not very musical. The woman looked at him with some doubt.

By the wayside two middle-aged men stood silently. One suddenly said gloomily, "All the same, she had no call to tell the boy about that."

"Too late now," answered the other, and they again fell silent.

A threesome—a pale girl, a giant elderly black, and a pensive fellow who was smiling absentmindedly—walked slowly toward Kondratev. The girl was talking, abruptly waving about her clenched fist. "The question has to be resolved another way. As an artist, either you're a writer or a sensationalist. There is no third possibility. But he plays games with spatial relationships. That's craft, not art. He's just an uncaring, self-satisfied hack."

"Masha, Masha!" the black droned reproachfully.

The young fellow kept smiling absentmindedly.

Kondratev turned onto a side path, passed a hedge mottled with big blue and yellow flowers, and stopped dead. Before him was a moving road.

Kondratev had already heard about the amazing moving roads. Their construction had begun long ago and now they extended between many cities, forming an uninterrupted ramifying transcontinental system from the Pyrenees to the Tien Shan, and south across the plains of China to Hanoi, and in the Americas from Port Yukon to Tierra del Fuego. Evgeny had told improbable tales about the roads. He said that they did not use energy and need not fear time; if they were destroyed, they would restore themselves; they climbed mountains with ease and threw themselves across abysses on bridges. According to Evgeny, these roads would move as long as the sun shone and Earth was intact. And Evgeny also had said that the moving road was not actually a road, but a flow of something halfway between the animate and inanimate. A fourth kingdom.

A few steps away from Kondratev the road flowed in six even gray streams, the strips of the Big Road. The strips moved at various speeds and were separated from each other and from the outside grass by two-inch-high white barriers. On the strips people were standing, walking, sitting. Kondratev approached and placed one leg indecisively on the barrier. And then, bending and listening, he heard the voice of the Big Road: squeaking, crackling, rustling.

The surface of the road was soft like warm asphalt. He stood for a while, and then transferred to the next strip.

The road flowed down a hill, and Kondratev could see it stretch all the way out to the deep-blue horizon. It sparkled in the sun like a tarred highway.

Kondratev began to look at the rooftops sailing by over the crowns of the pines. On one roof there sparkled an enormous structure made from several huge square mirrors strung on a light openwork frame. On all the roofs sat pterocars—red, green, gold, gray. Hundreds of pterocars and helicopters hung over the city. With a faint whistling sound, eclipsing the sun for a long time, a triangular airship floated along the road, and then disappeared behind the forest. The outlines of some sort of structure

—not exactly masts, not exactly stereovision towers—showed far off in the foggy haze. The road flowed evenly, without jolts; the green bushes and brown pine trunks ran merrily backward; great glass buildings, bright cottages, open verandas under sparkling multicolored awnings appeared and disappeared in the spaces between the branches.

Kondratev suddenly realized that the road was taking him to the outskirts of Sverdlovsk. *Well, let it,* he thought. *Fine.* This road must be able to take you anywhere you liked—Siberia, India, Vietnam. He sat down and clasped his knees with his arms. It wasn't particularly soft seating, but it wasn't hard either. In front of Kondratev three lads sat tailor-fashion, bending over multicolored squares of some sort. They must be solving a problem in geometry. Or perhaps they were playing a game. *What are these roads good for?* Kondratev thought. It wasn't likely that anyone would take it into his head to ride this way to Vietnam or India. Too little speed. And too hard a seat. After all, there were stratoplanes, the enormous triangular airships, pterocars—what good was a road? And what it must have cost! He began to recall how they had built roads a century ago—not moving ones, either, but the most ordinary sort, and not especially good ones at that. The enormous semiautomatic road layers, the stench of tar, the heat, and the sweaty, tired people inside dust-powdered cabs. And of course enormously greater heaps of labor and thought had been hammered into the Big Road than into the Trans-Gobi Highway. And evidently all so that you could get on wherever you liked, sit wherever you liked, and poke along without worrying about anything, picking camomile flowers along the way. It was strange, incomprehensible, irrational. . . .

The stories of glass above the pine tops suddenly came to an end. Ahead rose a gigantic block of gray granite. Kondratev stood up. On top of the block, with an arm stretched out over the city, straining ever forward, stood Lenin, just as he had stood, and must still be standing now, in the square in front of Finland Station in Leningrad. Lenin held his arm out over this city and over this world, this shining and wonderful world that he had seen two centuries before. Kondratev stood and watched the enormous monument retreat into the bluish haze over the glass roofs.

The pines grew lower and denser. For a moment a broad clearing opened up alongside the road. A group of people in coveralls were fiddling with some complicated mechanism. The road slipped under a narrow semicircular bow bridge and ran past a sign with an arrow which said, MATROSOVO—15 KM, YELLOW FACTORY—6 KM, and something else which Kondratev did not have time to read. He looked around and saw that there were few people left on the ribbons of road. The ribbons running the opposite way were almost empty. *Matrosovo must be a housing development. But what about Yellow Factory?* Through the pine trunks flashed a long veranda with tables. People at the tables sat eating and drinking. Kondratev felt hungry, but after hesitating, he decided to hold off for a bit. *On the way back,* he thought. He was very happy to feel strong, healthy hunger, and to know that he could satisfy it at any moment.

The pines thinned out, and from somewhere a broad superhighway turned up, sparkling in the rays of the evening sun. Along the superhighway whizzed a series of monstrous vehicles —on two, three, even eight undercarriages, or without an undercarriage altogether—bluntnosed, with enormous, boxcar-sized trailers covered with bright-colored plastic. The vehicles were moving toward him, toward the city. Evidently somewhere nearby the superhighway dived underground and disappeared into multileveled tunnels. Looking closely, Kondratev noticed that the vehicles did not have cabs—there was no place for a driver. The machines moved in an unbroken stream, buzzing modestly, maintaining a distance of two or three yards between each other. Through the spaces between, Kondratev saw several of the same sort of vehicle going the other way. Then thickets once again densely lined the road, and the superhighway disappeared from view.

"Yesterday a truck jumped off the road," someone said behind Kondratev's back.

"That's because they took off the power monitor. They're digging new levels."

"I don't like these rhinos."

"Never mind—soon we'll finish the conveyer, and then we can close the whole highway."

"It's about time."

Another veranda with tables appeared ahead.

"Leshka! Leshka!" people at one of the tables shouted, and waved.

A fellow and a young woman in front of Kondratev waved back, transferred to the slow belt, and jumped onto the grass opposite the veranda. A few other people jumped off here too. Kondratev was about to do the same, but he noticed a post with the sign, YELLOW FACTORY—1 KM, and he stayed on.

He jumped off at a turn. Between the tree trunks a narrow trampled path leading up the side of a large hill could be seen. At the top of the hill the outlines of small structures stood out distinctly against the background of sunset. Kondratev moved unhurriedly along the path, feeling the springy ground under his feet with pleasure. *It must get muddy when it rains,* he thought. On the way he bent down and picked a large white flower from the grass. Small ants ran over the flower's petals. Kondratev threw the flower away and walked more quickly. A few minutes later he came out onto the top of the hill and stopped at the edge of a gigantic basin that seemed to stretch to the very horizon.

The contrast between the peaceful soft greenery under the dark-blue evening sky and what opened before him in the basin was so striking that Kondratev took a step backward. At the bottom of the basin seethed hell. Real hell, with ominous blue-white flashes, swirling orange smoke, and bubbling viscous liquid, red hot. There something slowly swelled and puffed up, like a purulent boil, then burst, splashing and spilling shreds of orange flame; it clouded over with varicolored smoke, threw off steam, flame, and a hail of sparks, and once again slowly swelled and puffed up. In the vortices of raging matter many-forked lightnings flashed; monsterous indistinct forms appeared and disappeared within a second; whirlwinds twisted; blue and pink ghosts danced. For a long time Kondratev watched this extraordinary spectacle, spellbound. Then he came a little more to his senses and began to notice something else.

Hell was noiseless and bounded with strict geometry. The mighty dance of flame and smoke produced not one sound; not one tongue of flame, not one puff of smoke went beyond a certain limit, and, looking closely, Kondratev discovered that the whole vast expanse of hell stretching to the far horizon was enclosed by a barely noticeable transparent covering, the edges of which merged into the concrete—if it was concrete—that paved the bottom of the basin. Then Kondratev saw that the covering had two and even, it seemed, three layers, because from time to time flat reflections flashed in the air under the covering, probably images of sparks on the outer surface of an inner layer. The basin was deep; its round, even walls, lined with smooth gray material, plunged into the depths for hundreds of meters. The "roof" of the invisible covering soared over the bottom of the basin to a height of no less than fifty. Evidently this was the Yellow Factory of which the signs warned. Kondratev sat down on the grass, lay his arms on his knees, and began to look through the covering.

The sun set, and multicolored reflections began to leap along the gray slopes of the basin. Kondratev very soon noticed that chaos did not reign unchecked in the raging, hellish kitchen. Certain regular, distinct shadows appeared now and then in the smoke and flame, sometimes unmoving, sometimes rushing head-long. It was very difficult to get a proper look at them, but once the smoke suddenly cleared for several instants, and Kondratev got a fairly clear view of a complicated machine like a daddy longlegs. The machine jumped in place, as if trying to extricate its legs from some viscous fiery mass, or else it kneaded that flaming mass with its long sparkling articulations. Then some-thing flashed under it, and again it was covered by clouds of orange smoke.

Over Kondratev's head a small helicopter sputtered by. Kon-dratev raised his head and watched it. The helicopter flew over the covering, then suddenly turned sharply to the side and crashed down like a stone. Kondratev gave a cry, but the helicop-ter was already sitting on the "roof" of the covering. It seemed simply to be hanging motionless above the tongues of flame. A minute black figure got out of the helicopter, bent over, resting its hands on its knees, and looked down into hell.

"Tell them I'll be back tomorrow morning!" shouted someone behind Kondratev's back.

The navigator turned around. Nearby, buried in luxuriant lilac bushes, stood two neat one-story houses with large lit-up windows. The windows were half hidden in the bushes, and the lilac branches, swaying in the wind, stood out against a back-

ground of bright blue rectangles in delicate openwork silhouettes. He could hear someone's steps. Then the steps stopped
for a second, and the same voice shouted, "And ask your mother
to tell Ahmed."

The windows in one of the houses went dark. From the other
house came the strains of a sad melody. Grasshoppers chirred in
the grass, and he could hear the drowsy chirping of birds. *Anyhow, I have nothing to do at this factory*, thought Kondratev.

He got up and headed back. He floundered for a few minutes
in the bushes, looking for the path, then found it and started
walking among the pines. The path showed dull white under the
stars. In a few more minutes Kondratev saw a bluish light in
front of him—the gas lamps on the signpost—and almost at a run
he came out to the moving road. It was empty.

Kondratev, jumping like a hare and shouting "Hup! Hup!,"
ran over to the strip moving in the direction of the city. The
ribbons shone gently underfoot, and to the right and left the dark
masses of bushes and trees rushed backward. Far in front of him
in the sky was a bluish glow—the city. Kondratev suddenly felt
fiercely hungry.

He got off at a veranda with tables, the one near the sign that
said YELLOW FACTORY—1 KM. From the veranda came
light, noise, and appetizing smells; and all the tables were taken.
Looks like the whole world eats supper here, Kondratev thought with
disappointment, but all the same he went up the steps and
stopped at the threshold. The great-great-grandchildren were
drinking, eating, laughing, talking, shouting, and even singing.

A long-legged great-great-grandchild from the nearest table
tugged at Kondratev's sleeve. "Sit down, sit down, comrade," he
said, getting up.

"Thank you," muttered Kondratev, "But what about you?"

"Never mind! I've eaten, don't worry."

Kondratev sat down uneasily, resting his hands on his knees.
The person opposite him, an enormous dark-faced man who had
been eating something very appetizing from a bowl, looked up
at him suddenly and asked indistinctly, "Well, what's going on
over there? They drawing it out?"

"Drawing what out?" asked Kondratev.

Everyone at the table looked at him.

The dark man, distorting his face, swallowed and said, "You from Anyudin?"

"No," said Kondratev.

A thickset youth sitting on the left said happily, "I know who you are! You're Navigator Kondratev from the *Taimyr*!"

Everyone became more lively. The dark-faced man immediately raised his right hand and introduced himself. "I am yclept Ioann Moskvichev. Or Ivan, as we say today."

A young woman, sitting at the right, said, "Elena Zavadskaya."

The thickset youth, shuffling his feet under the table, said, "Basevich. Meteorologist. Aleksandr."

A small pale girl, squeezed in between the meteorologist and Ivan Moskvichev, gaily chirped that she was Marina.

Ex-Navigator Kondratev rose and bowed.

"I didn't recognize you at first either," declared the dark-faced Moskvichev. "You've gotten a lot better. We people here have been sitting and waiting. We've got nothing left to do but sit and eat sacivi. This afternoon they offered us twelve places on a food tanker—they thought we wouldn't take them. Like idiots we started drawing straws, and in the meantime they loaded a group from Vorkuta onto the tanker. Really great guys! Ten people barely squeezed into the twelve places, and the other five were left here." He laughed unexpectedly. "And we sit eating sacivi. . . . By the way, would you like a helping? Or have you already eaten?"

"No, I haven't," said Kondratev.

Moskvichev rose from the table. "Then I'll bring you some."

"Please," Kondratev said gratefully.

Ivan Moskvichev went off, pushing his way through the tables.

"Have some wine," Zavadskaya said, pushing a glass over to Kondratev.

"Thank you, but I don't drink," Kondratev said automatically. But then he remembered that he wasn't a spacer, and never again would be one. "Excuse me. On second thought, I will, with pleasure."

The wine was aromatic, light, good. *Nectar*, thought Kondratev. *The gods drink nectar. And eat sacivi. I haven't tried sacivi in a long time.*

"Are you traveling with us?" squeaked Marina.

"I don't know," said Kondratev. "Maybe. Where are you going?"

The great-great-grandchildren looked at each other. "We're going to Venus," said Aleksandr. "You see, Moskvichev has got the urge to turn Venus into a second Earth."

Kondratev put down his glass. "Venus?" he asked mistrustfully. He himself remembered what Venus was like. "Has your Moskvichev ever been on Venus?"

"He works there," said Zavadskaya, "but that's not the point. What is important is that he hasn't supplied the transportation. We've been waiting for three days."

Kondratev remembered how he had once orbited Venus in a first-line interplanetary ship for thirty-three days and had decided not to land. "Yes," he said. "That's terrible, waiting so long."

Then he looked with horror at small pale Marina and imagined her on Venus. *Radioactive deserts,* he thought. *Black storms.*

Moskvichev returned and crashed a tray covered with plates onto the table. Among the plates stuck out a pot-bellied bottle with a long neck. "Here," he said. "Eat, Comrade Kondratev. Here is the sacivi itself—you recognize it? Here, if you like, is the sauce. Drink this. . . . here's ice. . . . Pegov is talking to Anyudin again, and they promise a ship tomorrow at six."

"Yesterday they promised us a ship 'tomorrow at six' too," said Aleksandr.

"Well, now it's for sure. The starship pilots are coming back. D-ships aren't your piddling food tankers. Six hundred people a flight, and the day after tomorrow we'll be there."

Kondratev took a sip from his wineglass and started in on the food. His table companions were arguing. Evidently except for Moskvichev they were all new volunteers, and they were all going to Venus. Moskvichev exemplified the present Venusian population, oppressed by the severe natural conditions. For him everything was perfectly clear. As a Venusian he gave Earth seventeen percent of its energy, eighty-five percent of its rare metals, and lived like a dog, that is, did not see the blue sky for months at a time, and waited for weeks his turn to lie for a while on greenhouse grass. Working under these conditions was of course intolerably difficult; Kondratev was in full agreement.

The volunteers also agreed, and they were setting off for Venus with great eagerness, but by this means they pursued quite various ends. Thus squeaky Marina, who turned out to be some sort of heavy-systems operator, was going to Venus because on Earth her heavy-systems work had ceased expanding. She did not want to go on moving houses from place to place or digging basins for factories any more. She yearned to build cities on swamps, and for ferocious storms, for underground explosions. And for people to say afterward, "Marina Chernyak built these cities!" There was nothing to be said against her plans. Kondratev was in full agreement with Marina too, although he would have preferred letting her grow a bit more and, by means of specialized physical training, making her more of a match for swamps, storms, and underground explosions.

Aleksandr the meteorologist was in love with Marina Chernyak, but it wasn't only that. When Marina had asked him for the third time to cut the comedy, he became very judicious and proved logically that for terrestrials there were only two ways out: since the work on Venus was so hard, we had either to abandon it entirely, or to improve the working conditions. Could we, however, desert a place where we had once set foot? No, we could not! Because there was the Great Mission of Humanity, and there was the Hour of the Earthman, with all the consequences flowing therefrom. Kondratev agreed even with this, although he strongly suspected that Aleksandr was continuing to exercise his wit.

But Elena Zavadskaya was going to Venus with the most unexpected intentions. In the first place, she turned out to be a member of the World Council. She was categorically opposed to the conditions under which Moskvichev and twenty thousand of his comrades worked. She was also categorically opposed to cities on swamps, to underground explosions, and to new graves over which the black winds would sing the legends of heroes. In short, she was going to Venus in order to study the local conditions carefully and to take necessary measures toward Venus's decolonization. She conceived the Earthman's mission to be the establishment of automatic factories on alien planets. Moskvichev knew all this. Zavadskaya hung over him like the sword of Damocles, threatening all his plans. But besides that, Zavadskaya was an embryomechanical surgeon. She could work without a clinic, under any conditions, up to her waist in a swamp, and there were still very few such surgeons on Earth. On Venus they were irreplaceable. So Moskvichev held his tongue, evidently hoping that eventually everything would work out somehow. Kondratev, coming to the conclusion that Zavadskaya's method was irrefutable, got up and quietly went out onto the porch.

The night was moonless and clear. Above the dark, huge, formless forest, bright white Venus hung low. Kondratev looked at it a long time and thought, *Maybe I should have a try there? It wouldn't matter as what—ditchdigger, a leader of some sort, demolition man. It can't be that I'm no good for anything at all.*

"Are you looking at it?" came a voice out of the darkness. "I am too. I'm waiting until it sets, and then I'll go to bed." The voice was calm and tired. "I think and think, you know. Planting gardens on Venus . . . drilling into the moon with an enormous auger. In the last analysis, that's the meaning of our existence, expending energy. And, as much as possible, in such a way that it'll be interesting to you and useful to somebody else. And it's gotten rather difficult to expend energy on Earth. We have everything, we're too powerful. A contradiction, if you like. Of course, even today there are many people who work at full output—researchers, teachers, doctors in preventive medicine, people in the arts. Agrotechnicians, waste-disposal specialists. And there always will be a lot of them. But what about the rest? Engineers, machine operators, doctors in curative medicine. Of course some go in for art, but the majority look in art not for escape but for inspiration. Judge for yourself—wonderful young guys. There's too little room for them! They have to blow things up, remake things, build things. And not build just a house, but at least a world—Venus today, Mars tomorrow, something else the day after tomorrow. The interplanetary expansion of the human race is beginning—like the discharge of some giant electric potential. Do you agree with me, comrade?"

"I agree with you too," said Kondratev.

8

Cornucopia

EVGENY and Sheila were working. Evgeny was sitting at a table, reading Harding's *Philosophy of Speed*. The table was piled high with books, microbook tapes, albums, and files of old newspapers. On the floor, among scattered microbook cases, sat a portable access board for the Informatoreum. Evgeny read quickly, fidgeting with impatience and making frequent notations on a scratch pad. Sheila was sitting in a deep armchair, with her legs crossed, reading Evgeny's manuscript. The room was bright and nearly quiet—colored shadows flashed by on the stereovision screen, and the tender strains of an ancient South American melody could barely be heard.

"This is an amazing book," said Evgeny. "I can't even slow down. How did he do it?"

"Harding?" Sheila said absently. "Yes, Harding is a great craftsman."

"How does he do it? I don't understand what his secret is."

"I don't know, dear," Sheila said without taking her eyes off the manuscript. "No one knows. He himself doesn't know."

"You get an amazing feel of the rhythm of the thought and the rhythm of the words. Who is he?" Evgeny looked at the preface. "Professor of structural linguistics. Aha. That explains it."

"That explains nothing," said Sheila. "I'm a structural linguist too."

Evgeny glanced at her, and then immersed himself again in his reading. The twilight was thickening outside the open window. Tiny lightning-bug sparks flashed in the dark bushes. Late birds called to one another sleepily.

Sheila gathered up the pages. "Wonderful people!" she said loudly. "Such daring!"

"Really?" Evgeny exclaimed happily, turning toward her.

"Did you people really endure all that?" Sheila looked at Evgeny with eyes wide. "You went through all that and still remained human. You didn't die of fear. You didn't go crazy from loneliness. Honestly, Evgeny, sometimes I think you really are a hundred years older than I."

"Precisely," said Evgeny.

He got up, crossed the room, and sat down by Sheila's feet. She ran her fingers through his red hair, and he pressed his cheek to her knee.

"You know what was the most frightening part of all?" he said. "After the second ether bridge. When Sergei lifted me out of the acceleration cradle and I started to go to the control room, and he wouldn't let me."

"You didn't write about that," said Sheila.

"Falin and Pollack were still in the control room," said Evgeny. "Dead," he added after a silence.

Sheila stroked his head silently.

"You know," he said, "in a certain sense ancestors are always richer than descendants. Richer in dreams. The ancestors dream about things that will be mere routine for the descendants. Oh, Sheila, that was a dream—to get to the stars! We had given everything for that dream. But you flit off to the stars the way we flew home to Mother for summer vacation. You people are poor, poor!"

"Each age has its dream," said Sheila. "Your dream took man

to the stars, while ours is returning him to Earth. But it will be a completely different person."

"I don't understand," said Evgeny.

"We ourselves don't understand it properly yet. It *is* a dream, after all. *Homo omnipotens.* Master of every atom in the universe. Nature has too many laws. We discover them and use them, but still they get in our way. You can't break a law of nature. You can only obey it. And that's very boring, when you stop to think about it. But *Homo omnipotens* will just change the laws he doesn't like. Just up and change them."

Evgeny said, "In the old days such people were called magicians. And they chiefly inhabited fairy tales."

"*Homo omnipotens* will inhabit the universe. The way you and I do this room."

"No," said Evgeny. "That I don't understand. That is somehow beyond me. Probably I'm a very prosaic thinker. Somebody even told me yesterday that I was boring to talk to. And I didn't take offense. I really don't understand everything yet."

"Who was it that said you were boring?" Sheila asked angrily.

"Well, somebody. It doesn't matter—I really wasn't up to my usual form. I was in a great hurry to get home."

Sheila took him by the ears and looked him straight in the eyes. "The person who said that to you," she muttered, "is a jackass and an ingrate. You should have looked down your nose at him and said, 'I gave you the road to the stars, and my father gave you the road to everything you have today.' "

Evgeny grinned. "Well, people forget that. Ingratitude to ancestors is the ordinary thing. Take my great-grandfather. He died in the siege of Leningrad, and I don't even remember his name."

"Well, you should," said Sheila.

"Sheila, my dear, Sheila, my sweet," Evgeny said lightly, "the reason descendants are forgetful is that ancestors aren't touchy. Take me for example—the first person ever born on Mars. Who knows about that?" He took her in his arms and started to kiss her. There was a knock at the door and Evgeny said with annoyance, "Wouldn't you know it!"

"Come in!" called Sheila.

The door opened a bit, and the voice of their neighbor Yurii the waste-disposal engineer asked, "Am I interrupting something?"

"Come in, Yurii, come on in," said Sheila.

"Well, if I'm interrupting, I've already interrupted," Yurii said, and came in. "Let's go into the garden," he requested.

"What is there new to see in the garden?" asked Evgeny, surprised. "Let's watch stereovision instead."

"I have a stereovision set of my own at home," said Yurii. "Come on, Evgeny, tell Sheila and me something about Louis Pasteur."

"Which disposal station do you work at?" Evgeny asked in turn.

"Disposal station? What's that?"

"Just a disposal station. They bring all sorts of garbage, slop, and process it, and dump it. Into the sewer."

"Ah!" the waste-disposal engineer cried happily. "I've just remembered. Disposal towers. But there haven't been any disposal towers on the Planet for a long time, Evgeny!"

"Well, I was born a full century and a half after Pasteur," said Evgeny.

"All right, then tell us about Doctor Morganau."

"Doctor Morganau, as I understand it, was born a year after the takeoff of the *Taimyr*," Evgeny replied tiredly.

"In short, let's go into the garden," said Yurii. "Sheila, bring him."

They went out into the garden and sat on a bench under an apple tree. It was quite dark, and the trees in the garden looked black. Sheila shivered a bit from the chill, and Evgeny dashed back into the house for her jacket. For some time everyone was silent. Then a large apple broke off a branch and hit the ground with a muffled thunk.

"Apples still fall," said Evgeny. "But somehow I don't see any Newtons."

"Polymaths, you mean?" Sheila asked seriously.

"Yes," said Evgeny, who had only wanted to make a joke.

"In the first place, today we're all polymaths," Yurii said with unexpected warmth. "From your antediluvian perspective, of course. Because there is no biologist who does not know mathematics and physics, and a linguist like Sheila, for example, would be in real trouble without psychophysics and the theory of historical procession. But I know what you mean! There are, you say, no Newtons! Show me, you say, an encyclopedic mind! Everyone works in a narrow field, you say. When it comes down to the wire, Sheila is still only a linguist, and I'm still only a waste-disposal specialist, and Okada is still only an oceanographer. Why not, you say, all of them at once, in one person?"

"Help!" shouted Evgeny. "I didn't want to upset anybody. I was just joking."

"Well, do you know, Evgeny, about what we call the 'narrow problem'? You chew it over all your life and there's still no end in sight. It's a tangle of the most unexpected complications. Take that same apple, for instance. Why was it that that apple in particular fell? Why at that particular moment? The mechanics of the contact of the apple with the ground. The process of the transference of momentum. The conditions of the fall. A quantum-mechanical picture of the fall. Finally, how, given the existence of the fall, to get some use out of it?"

"The last part is simple," Evgeny said soothingly. He bent over, groped on the ground, and picked up the apple. "I'll eat it."

"It's still unclear whether that would be the optimum utilization," Yurii said irritably.

"Then *I'll* eat it," said Sheila, grabbing the apple away from Evgeny.

"And anyhow, about use," Evgeny said. "You, Yurii, like to talk about optimum use all the time. Meanwhile, unimaginably complicated litter robots, gardener robots, moth-and-caterpillar-eating robots, and ham-and-cheese-sandwich-making robots are running all over the place. That's crazy. It's even worse than killing flies with a sledge hammer, as we said in my day. It's building single-occupant studio apartments for ants. It's sybaritism of the first water."

"Evgeny!" protested Sheila.

Yurii laughed gaily. "It's not sybaritism at all," he said. "Quite the opposite. It's the liberation of thought, it's comfort, it's economy. After all, who wants to pick up trash? And even if you did find some such garbage fancier, he'd still work more slowly and less thoroughly than the cybers. And then these robots are by no means as difficult to produce as you think. It's true that they were a bit hard to invent. They were difficult to perfect. But as soon as they had reached mass production, they were much less trouble to make than ... uh ... what did they call shoes in your day? Buskins?"

"Shoes," Evgeny said briefly.

"And the main thing is that nowadays no one makes single-purpose machines. So you're quite wrong to distinguish between litter robots and gardener robots in the first place. They're the same gadget."

"Well, pardon me," said Evgeny, "but I've seen them. Litter robots have these scoop things, and vacuum cleaners. And gardener robots—"

"It's just a question of changing their manipulator attachments. And even that isn't the point. The point is that all these robots, and all sorts of everyday machines and appliances in general, are magnificent ozonizers. They eat garbage, dry twigs and leaves, the grease from dirty dishes, and all that stuff serves them as fuel. You've got to understand, Evgeny, these aren't the crude mechanisms of your time. In essence, they're quasi-organisms. And in the process of their quasi-life they also ozonize and vitaminize the air, and saturate it with light ions. These are good little soldiers in the enormous, glorious army of waste disposal."

"I surrender," said Evgeny.

"Modern waste disposal, Evgeny, isn't disposal towers. We don't simply annihilate garbage, and we don't pile up disgusting dumps on the seabed. We turn garbage into fresh air and sunlight."

"I surrender, I surrender," said Evgeny. "Long live waste-disposal specialists! Convert me into sunlight."

Yurii stretched with pleasure. "It's nice to meet someone who doesn't know anything. The best recreation of all is to blab on about things everybody knows."

"Well, I'm sick of being the man people recreate on," said Evgeny.

Sheila took his hand, and he fell silent.

The thin squeal of a radiophone sounded.

"It's mine," Yurii whispered, and then said, "Hello."

"Where are you?" inquired an angry voice.

"In the garden with Slavin and Sheila. I'm sitting and recreating."

"Have you thought of anything?"

"No."

"What a guy! He's sitting and recreating! I'm going out of my mind, and he's recreating! Comrade Slavin, Sheila, throw him out!"

"I'm going, I'm going, you don't have to shout!" said Yurii, getting up.

"Get right to a screen. And listen to this: now I'm completely sure that the benzene processes are not the answer."

"What did I tell you!" shouted Yurii, and with much crackling he crawled through the bushes toward his own cottage.

Sheila and Evgeny went back inside.

"Shall we go have supper?" Evgeny asked.

"I'm not hungry."

"That's how it always is! You fill up on apples and then you're not hungry."

"Don't growl at me!" said Sheila.

Evgeny started hugging her.

"I'm frozen," she said plaintively.

"That's because you're hungry," Evgeny declared. "I'm a little frozen too, and I don't at all feel like going to a restaurant. Is it really impossible to organize life so as to have supper at home?"

"Anything is possible," said Sheila. "But what's the point of it? Who eats at home?"

"I eat at home."

"Evgeny, dear," said Sheila, "would you like for us to move to the city? There's the delivery line there, and you could eat at home all you wanted."

"I don't want to live in the city," Evgeny said stubbornly. "I want to live out in the open air."

Sheila looked at him thoughtfully for some time. "Would you like me to drop by the restaurant right now and bring supper home? It will only take a couple of minutes. . . . Or maybe we could go together? Sit for a while and chat a bit with the guys?"

"I want just the two of us," said Evgeny. Nonetheless he fetched his jacket and started putting it on. "You know, Sheila, I have an idea," he said suddenly, and stuck his hand into his pocket. "Just listen to this."

"What?" asked Sheila.

"An advertisement. Somehow it ended up in my pocket. Listen. 'The Krasnoyarsk Appliance Factory . . .' Well, we can skip that. Here. 'The Universal Kitchen Machine, Model UKM-207, the Krasnoyarsk, is simple to operate and features a cybernetic brain rated for sixteen interchangeable programs. The UKM-207 includes a device for the trimming, peeling, and washing of raw or semiprepared foods, and an automatic dishwasher. The UKM-207 can prepare simultaneously two different three-course dinners, including first courses of various borschts, bouillons, *okroshki,* and other soups."

"Evgeny!" Sheila laughed. "That's a machine for restaurants and dining halls."

"So?"

Sheila tried to explain. "Imagine a new housing development. Or a temporary settlement, a camp. The delivery line is far away. And there's no link with Home Delivery—supply for the whole place is centralized. So they need a UKM."

Evgeny was very disappointed. "So they wouldn't give us one like that?" he asked, downcast.

"Well, they would, of course, but . . . but, you see, that's pure sybaritism."

"Sheila, sweetling! Sheila, dearest! May I order a machine like that? It's not going to hurt anybody! And then we wouldn't be forced to go anywhere in the evenings."

"Have it your way," Sheila said briefly. "But we're still having supper in the restaurant today."

They left—Evgeny following her docilely.

Early in the morning, Evgeny Slavin was awakened by the snorting of a heavy-duty helicopter. He jumped out of bed and ran to the window. He was just in time to see a dark blue helicopter fusilage with HOME DELIVERY printed on it in large white letters. The helicopter passed over the garden and disappeared behind the treetops, which were sparkling with dew and full of the chatter of birds. A large yellow box stood on the garden path by the porch. An emerald-green gardener robot stomped uncertainly around the box on its L-shaped legs.

"I'll get you, waste-disposer!" yelled Evgeny, and he started climbing through the window. "Sheila! Sheila dear! It's come!"

The gardener robot dashed off into the bushes. Evgeny ran up to the box and walked all the way around it without touching it.

"It's here!" he said, deeply moved. "Great lads, Home Delivery. Krasnoyarsk," he read off the side of the box. "It's here."

Sheila came out onto the porch, wrapping her bathrobe round her. "What a wonderful morning!" she said, yawning sweetly. "What are you making so much noise for? You'll wake up Yurii."

Evgeny looked toward the garden, where, behind the trees, he could see the white walls of Yurii's cottage. Something over there suddenly gave a crash, and they heard indistinct exclamations. "He's awake already," said Evgeny. "Give me a hand, Sheila, eh?"

Sheila came down from the porch. "What's that?" she asked. Near the box lay a large paper bag with a colorful label with pictures of various foods.

"That?" Evgeny stared absently at the colorful label. "That must be the raw ingredients and the semiprepared foods."

Sheila said with a sigh, "Well, okay. Let's pick up your toy."

The box was light, and they dragged it inside without difficulty. Only at this point did Evgeny realize that the cottage did not have a kitchen. *What do I do now?* he thought.

"Well, what are we going to do with it?" asked Sheila.

By dint of superhuman mental effort Evgeny instantly pounced upon the necessary solution. "Into the bathroom with it," he said lightly. "Where else?"

They put the box in the bathroom, and Evgeny ran back for the bag. When he returned, Sheila was doing her exercises. Evgeny started singing off key, "Monday roast beef, Tuesday string beans . . ." and tore the side off the box. The Krasnoyarsk, Model UKM-207, looked very inspiring. Much more inspiring than Evgeny had expected.

"Well?" asked Sheila.

"Now we'll get down to it," Evgeny said briskly. "I'll fix you a meal right off."

"I'd advise you to call for an instructor."

"Nonsense. I'll figure this machine out myself. After all, it said 'simple to operate.' "

The machine, enclosed in a smooth plastic housing, sparkled proudly amid piles of crumpled paper.

"It's all very simple," declared Evgeny. "Here are four buttons. It's perfectly clear that they correspond to the soup course, the main course, the dessert course, and. . . ."

". . . the after-dessert course," Sheila put in helpfully.

"Exactly, the after-dessert course," Evgeny affirmed. "Tea, for instance. Or cocoa."

He squatted down and opened a lid that said "Control System." "It's spaghetti inside," he muttered, "spaghetti. God help us if it ever breaks down." He stood up. "Now I know what the fourth button is for—slicing bread."

"An interesting conclusion," Sheila said thoughtfully. "Did it occur to you that the four buttons might correspond to the four elements of Empedocles? Earth, air, fire, and water."

Evgeny smiled reluctantly.

"Or the four arithmetic operations," Sheila added.

"All right," Evgeny said, and started unloading the bag. "Talk is talk, but I want goulash. You still don't know how I cook goulash, Sheila. Here's the meat, here's the potatoes . . . right . . . parsley . . . onion . . . I want goulash! Followed by cybernetic dishwashing! So the grease on the dishes turns into air and sunlight!"

Sheila went into the living room and brought back a chair. Evgeny, holding a piece of meat in one hand and four large potatoes in the other, was standing indecisively in front of the machine. Sheila put the chair beside the washbasin, and sat down comfortably.

Addressing no one in particular, Evgeny said, "I would be much obliged if somebody would tell me where the raw food goes in."

Sheila said, "I saw a cyberkitchen two years ago. It wasn't at all like this one, but I remember it had a sort of opening for the raw food on the right."

"I thought so!" Evgeny shouted happily. "There are two openings here. So the one on the right is for raw food, and the one on the left is for cooked dinners."

"Evgeny, dear," said Sheila, "you know, we should really go to a restaurant."

He did not answer. He put the meat and potatoes into the opening on the right, and set off, cord in hand, for the wall socket. "Turn it on," he said from a distance.

"How?" said Sheila.

"Push the button."

"Which one?"

"The second, dear. I'm making goulash."

"We should go to a restaurant," Sheila repeated, getting up reluctantly.

The machine responded to the push of the button with a muffled roar. A white light on its front panel went on, and Sheila, looking into the opening at the right, saw that there was nothing there. "It seems to have taken the meat," she said with surprise. This was more than she had expected.

"There, you see!" said Evgeny proudly. He stood up and admired his machine, listening to it hum and click. Then the white light went out and a red one came on. The machine stopped humming.

"That's it, Sheila my sweet," Evgeny said with a wink. He bent down and got the dishes out of the bag. They were light and shiny. He took two, put them in the opening on the left, then stepped back a step and and folded his arms across his chest. He and Sheila were silent for a minute.

Finally Sheila, shifting her eyes in puzzlement from Evgeny to the machine and back, asked, "Just what exactly are you waiting for?"

Uncertainty appeared in Evgeny's eyes. If the goulash were ready, he realized, it should have appeared in the opening on the left whether or not there were dishes there. He stuck his head into the opening on the left and saw that the dishes were still empty.

"Where's the goulash?" he asked distractedly.

Sheila did not know where the goulash was. "There are levers of some sort over here," she said.

On the upper part of the machine there were indeed levers of some sort. Sheila grabbed them with both hands and pulled toward herself. Out of the machine came a white box, and a strange odor spread through the room.

"What's inside?" asked Evgeny.

"Look for yourself," Sheila answered. She stood up, holding the box in her hands and, squinting, examined its contents. "Your UKM has converted the meat into air and sunlight. Maybe the instructions were here?"

Evgeny looked into the box and gave a cry. There lay a packet of some sort of thin sheets—red, speckled with white spots. A stench rose up from them. "What's this?" he asked with irritation, taking the top sheet with both hands. It fell apart, and the pieces dropped onto the floor, jangling like tin cans.

"Wonderful goulash," said Sheila. "Tinkling goulash, yet. A fifth element. I wonder what it tastes like."

Evgeny, turning beet red, stuck a piece of "goulash" in his mouth.

"What a daredevil!" Sheila said enviously. "My hero!"

Evgeny silently put down the bag of groceries. Sheila looked to see where to get rid of the mess, and dumped the contents of the machine's box onto the pile of packing paper. The odor got stronger.

Evgeny got out a loaf of bread. "Which button did you push?" he asked sternly.

"The second from the top," Sheila answered timidly, and immediately got the feeling that she had pushed the second from the bottom.

"I'm sure you must have pushed the fourth button," declared Evgeny. He stuck the loaf decisively into the opening on the right. "That's the bread-slicing button!"

Sheila started to ask how that could explain the strange metamorphoses undergone by the meat and potatoes, but Evgeny shoved her away from the machine and pushed the fourth button. A sort of clank sounded, and they could hear frequent muffled blows.

"You see," said Evgeny with a sigh of relief, "it's cutting the bread. I wish I knew just what was going on inside right now." He imagined what was going on inside right now, and shuddered. "But for some reason the light hasn't come on," he said.

The machine knocked and whinnied. The noise continued a fairly long time, and Evgeny started looking to see what to push to make it stop. But then the machine gave a pleasant-sounding ring, and the red light began blinking, while the machine continued to hum and knock. Evgeny looked at his watch and said, "I'd always thought that slicing bread was easier than cooking goulash."

"Let's go to a restaurant," Sheila said timidly.

Evgeny was silent. After three minutes he walked around the machine and then looked inside. He saw absolutely nothing there which could serve as food for thought. Nothing that could serve as food period, for that matter. He straightened up and met his wife's eyes. In answer to her inquiring glance he shook his head. "Everything's fine there." He risked nothing in making that declaration. There were two buttons yet to be investigated, and also a quantity of possible permutations and combinations of the four.

"Couldn't you stop it?" he asked Sheila.

Sheila shrugged, and for some time they continued to stand expectantly, watching the machine's blinking lights—the red one and the white by turns.

Then Sheila stretched out an arm and touched the uppermost button with her finger. There was a ring, and the machine stopped. The room became quiet.

"Good work!" Evgeny exclaimed in spite of himself.

Through the window they could hear grasshoppers chirring and the wind stirring the bushes.

"Where's the box?" Evgeny asked apprehensively.

Sheila looked around. The box was on the floor by the dishes. "So?" she asked.

"We didn't put the box back, and now I don't know where the sliced bread is."

Evgeny walked around the machine and looked into both openings—the one on the right and the one on the left. There was no bread. He looked with trepidation into the deep black slit in the machine where the box had been. The machine responded to his threatening glare with a red light. He clenched his teeth, narrowed his eyes, and stuck his arm into the slot.

It was hot inside the machine. He felt some sort of smooth surfaces, obviously not the bread. He withdrew his arm and shrugged. "No bread."

Sheila bent over and looked under the machine. "There's some sort of hose down here," she said.

"Hose?" he asked with horror.

"No, no—it's not the bread. It doesn't look in the least like bread. It's a real hose." She brought a long corrugated tube with a shiny ring on the end out from under the machine. "You haven't hooked the UKM up to the water, stupid. Think of it—no water! No wonder the goulash came out like that."

"Uh, yes," said Evgeny, casting a glance at the remains of the goulash. "There certainly isn't much water in it. But still, where's the bread?"

"What does it matter?" said Sheila gaily. "A mere side issue. Bread isn't the main problem. Observe as I attach the hose to the faucet."

"Maybe it's not worth the bother?" Evgeny said warily.

"Nonsense. Research is research. We'll make stew. There are vegetables in the bag."

The machine, roused into action by the top button, worked for about a minute this time. "The stew can't really drop out into the box too, can it?" Evgeny muttered uncertainly, fingering the levers.

"Let's give it a try," said Sheila.

The box was filled to the top with odorless pink goop.

"Borscht," Evgeny said sadly. "Ukrainian style. It's like—"

"I see for myself. Good heavens, the shame of it! I'm embarrassed even to call for an instructor. Maybe Yurii? . . ."

"Right," Evgeny said mournfully. "A waste-disposal specialist is just what we need here. I'll go call him over." He was desperately hungry.

"Come in!" shouted Yurii's voice.

Evgeny went in and stopped in the doorway, stricken.

"I hope you haven't brought your charming spouse along," said Yurii. "I'm not dressed."

He was wearing a clumsily ironed shirt. His tanned bare legs stuck out from underneath it. Strange machine parts and pieces of paper were strewn over the floor throughout the room. He was sitting on the floor, holding in his hands a box with rays of light streaming from little openings.

"What's that?" asked Evgeny.

"A tester," Yurii answered tiredly.

"No, no, all this!"

Yurii looked around. "That's a UWM-16. Universal Washing Machine with semicybernetic control. Washes, irons, and sews on buttons. Watch it! Don't step on anything."

Evgeny looked under his feet and saw a pile of black rags lying in a puddle of water. Steam was rising from the rags.

"Those are my pants," Yurii explained.

"So your machine isn't working either?" asked Evgeny. The hope of receiving advice, and dinner, evaporated.

"It's in perfect shape," Yurii said angrily. "I dismantled it down to the last screw, and figured out its principle of operation. Here's the output mechanism. Here's the analyser. I didn't dismantle that—it's working as it is. Here's the transporting mechanism and the heat-regulating system. Granted I haven't found the sewing device yet, but the machine is in perfect shape. I think the trouble is that for some reason it has twelve programming keys, while in the brochure it said four."

"Four?" asked Evgeny.

"Four," answered Yurii, absently scratching his knee. "But why did you say 'your machine'? Do you have a washing machine too? I just got mine an hour ago. Home Delivery."

"Four!" Evgeny repeated in delight. "Four, not twelve. . . . Tell me, Yurii, have you tried putting meat into it?"

Homecoming

9

SERGEI Kondratev returned home at noon. He had spent all morning at the Minor Informatoreum—he was looking for a profession. It was cool, quiet, and very lonely at home. Kondratev walked through all the rooms, drank some Narzan water, stood up in front of his empty desk, and set to thinking how he could kill the afternoon. Out the window the sun shone bright, some sort of bird was chirping, and a metallic rattle and clicking came from the lilac bushes. Obviously one of the efficient multilegged horrors which deprived an honest man of the opportunity to work at, say, gardening, was puttering around out there.

The ex-navigator sighed and closed the window. Should he go see Evgeny? No, he would be sure not to catch him at home. Evgeny had loaded himself down with the latest model dictaphones and was rushing all over the Urals; he had thirty-three things to worry about, not counting the little ones. "Insufficiency of knowledge," he would declare, "must be made up through excess of energy." Sheila was a wonderful person who understood everything, but she was never home except when Evgeny was. The navigator dragged himself to the dining room and drank another glass of mineral water. Perhaps he should eat dinner? Not a bad idea—he could dine carefully and tastefully. Except he wasn't hungry.

He went over to the delivery line cube, tapped out a number at random, and waited curiously to see what he would get. A green light flashed on over the cube—the order had been filled. With a certain wariness, the navigator opened the lid. At the bottom of the spacious cube-shaped box lay a paper plate. The navigator took it and set it on the table. On the plate were two large fresh-salted cucumbers. If only they had had cucumbers like that on the *Taimyr*, toward the end of the second year. . . . Maybe he should go see Protos? Protos was one in a million. But of course he was very busy, kindly old Protos. All the good people were busy with something.

The navigator absently picked a cucumber up off the plate and ate it. Then he ate the other one and put the plate in the garbage chute. *I could go out and hang around with the volunteers for a while again*, he thought. *Or go to Valparaiso. I've never been to Valparaiso.*

The navigator's ruminations were interrupted by the song of the door signal. The navigator was glad—he did not get many visitors. Evidently the great-great-grandchildren, out of false modesty, had not wanted to bother him. The whole week that he had been living here, he had only been visited once, by his neighbor, a sprightly eighty-year-old woman with an old-fashioned bun of black hair. She had introduced herself as the senior technician at a bread factory, and in the course of two hours she had patiently taught him how to punch the numbers on the control panel of the delivery line. They had somehow not gotten into a serious conversation, although she was doubtless an excellent person. And a few times some very young great-great grandchildren, quite clearly innocent of any feeling of false modesty, had arrived uninvited. These visitations were dictated by purely selfish considerations. One individual had evidently come to read the navigator his ode "On the Return of the *Taimyr*," of which the navigator had understood only individual words (*Taimyr*, *kosmos*), since it was in Swahili. Another was working on a biography of Edgar Allan Poe, and without any particular hope he asked for any little-known facts about the life of the great American writer. Kondratev told him the conjectures about meetings between Poe and Aleksandr Pushkin, and advised him to apply to Evgeny Slavin. Other boys and girls appeared for what Kondratev in the terminology of the twenty-first century would have called autograph hunting. But even the young autograph hunters were better than nothing, and consequently the song of the door signal gladdened Kondratev's heart.

Kondratev went out into the entryway and shouted, "Come in!" A tall man entered, wearing a full-cut gray jacket and long blue sweatsuit-style pants. He quietly closed the door behind him and, inclining his head a bit, started looking the navigator over. His physiognomy seemed to Kondratev to bear a very lively resemblance to the photographs he had once seen of the stone idols of Easter Island—narrow, long, with a high narrow forehead and powerful brows, deep-sunk eyes, and a long, sharply curved nose. His face was dark, but fair white skin showed unexpectedly from his open collar. This man bore little resemblance to an autograph hunter.

"You wish to see me?" Kondratev asked hopefully.

"Yes," the stranger said quietly. "I do."

"Then come on in," said Kondratev. He was moved, and a little disappointed, by the sad tone of the stranger. *Looks like an autograph hunter after all,* he thought. *But I must receive him a little more warmly.*

"Thank you," the stranger said still more quietly. Stooping a little, he walked past the navigator and stopped in the middle of the living room.

"Please, have a seat," said Kondratev.

The stranger was standing silently, looking fixedly at the couch. Kondratev, with some worry, looked at the couch too. It was a wonderful folding couch, broad, noiseless, and soft, with a springy light green cover that was porous like a sponge.

"My name is Gorbovsky," the stranger said quietly, without taking his eyes off the couch. "Leonid Andreevich Gorbovsky. I came to have a talk with you, spacer to spacer."

"What's happened?" Kondratev asked in fright. "Did something happen to the *Taimyr*? And sit down, please!"

Gorbovsky continued to stand. "To the *Taimyr?* Not at all. Or rather, I don't know," he said. "But then the *Taimyr* is in the Cosmonautical Museum. What could happen to it there?"

"Of course," said Kondratev, smiling. "After all, it won't likely be going anywhere."

"Nowhere at all," Gorbovsky agreed, and also smiled. His smile, like that of many homely people, was kind and somehow childlike.

"What are we standing for?" Kondratev exclaimed brightly. "Let's sit down."

"You.... I'll tell you what, Navigator Kondratev," Gorbovsky said suddenly. "Could I perhaps lie down?"

Kondratev choked. "P-please do," he muttered. "Don't you feel well?"

Gorbovsky was already lying on the couch. "Ah, Comrade Kondratev!" he said. "You're like the rest. Why does a man have to be feeling bad to want to lie down? In classical times practically everyone used to lie down—even at meals."

Kondratev, without turning around, groped for the back of his chair and sat down.

"Even in those days," Gorbovsky continued, "they had a multistage proverb the essence of which was, 'Why sit when you can lie down?' I'm just back from a flight. You yourself know, Navigator Kondratev—what sort of sofas do they have on shipboard? Disgustingly hard contrivances. And is it only on ships? Those unspeakable benches in stadiums and parks! The folding, or rather self-collapsing, chairs in restaurants! Or those ghastly rocks at the seaside! No, Comrade Kondratev, any way you like, the art of creating really comfortable things to lie on has been irretrievably lost in our stern era of embryomechanics and the D-principle."

You don't say! thought Kondratev. The problem of things to lie on presented itself to him in an entirely new light. "You know," he said, "I started out at a time when what they called 'private companies' and 'monopolies' were still in business in North America. And the one that survived the longest was a small company that made a fabulous fortune on mattresses. It put out some sort of special silk mattress—not many of them, but frightfully expensive. They say billionaires used to fight over those mattresses. They were splendid things. On one of them your arm would never get pins and needles."

"And the secret of them perished along with imperialism?" Gorbovsky asked.

"Probably," Kondratev answered. "I shipped out on the *Taimyr* and never heard any more about it."

They were silent a while. Kondratev was enjoying himself. Protos and Evgeny were splendid conversationalists too, but Protos liked to talk about liver operations, and Evgeny was usually teaching Kondratev how to drive a pterocar, or scolding him for his social inertia.

"And why?" said Gorbovsky. "We have splendid things to lie down on too. But no one is interested in them. Except me." He turned onto his side, rested his cheek on a fist and suddenly said, "Ah, Sergei old fellow! Why did you land on Blue Sands?"

The navigator choked again. The planet Blue Sands hung before his eyes with horrifying vividness. Child of an alien sun. Itself very alien. It was covered with oceans of fine blue dust and in these oceans were tides, ferocious gales and typhoons, and even, it seemed, some sort of life. Round-dances of green flame whirled around the buried *Taimyr*, blue dunes shouted and howled in various voices, dust clouds crawled across the whitish sky like giant amoebas. And human beings had not solved a single one of Blue Sands' mysteries. The navigator had broken his leg on the first sortie, they had lost every last cyberscout, and then in the middle of a total calm a real storm had set in, and good old Koenig, who had not had time to get back to the ship, was thrown along with the hoist against the reactor ring, was crushed, was flattened, was carried hundreds of miles into the desert, where among the blue waves gigantic rifts showered billions of tons of dust into the incomprehensible depths of the planet.

"Well, wouldn't you have landed?" Kondratev said hoarsely.

Gorbovsky was silent.

"You're in fine shape today on your D-ships. One sun today, tomorrow another, a third the day after tomorrow. But for me, for us, this was the first alien sun, the first really alien planet, do you understand? We had gotten there by a miracle. I couldn't refuse to land, because otherwise . . . what would it all be for then?" Kondratev stopped. *Nerves*, he thought. *Got to be calmer. It's all behind me now.*

Gorbovsky said thoughtfully, "The first one to land on Blue Sands after you must have been me. I started down in the landing boat and began with the pole. Ah, Sergei, what a time that was! For half a month I went around and around. Twelve probing runs! And all the machines we lost there! A quintessentially rabid atmosphere, Sergei. And you threw yourselves at her from the equator. Without reconnaissance. And in a decrepit old Tortoise. Yes."

Gorbovsky put his hands behind his head and stared at the ceiling. Kondratev could not figure out whether he was approving or condemning their action. "I couldn't do anything else, Comrade Gorbovsky," he said. "I repeat, that was the first alien sun. Try to put yourself in my place. It's hard to think of an analogy you might understand."

"Yes," said Gorbovsky. "No doubt. Still, it was very audacious."

Again, Kondratev did not know whether he was approving or condemning. Gorbovsky sneezed deafeningly and quickly sat up, taking his feet off the couch. "Pardon me," he said, and sneezed again. "I've caught another cold. I lie one night on the shore, and I've got a cold."

"On the shore?"

"Well, of course, Sergei. There's a meadow, grass, and you watch the fish swimming to the factories—" Gorbovsky sneezed again. "Pardon me. . . . And the moonlight on the water—'the road to happiness,' you know?"

"Moonlight on the water . . ." Kondratev said dreamily.

"You don't have to tell me! I'm from Torzhok myself. We have a river there—small, but very clean. And water lilies in the fish farms. Ah, marvelous!"

"I understand," Kondratev said, smiling. "In my time we called that 'pining for blue sky.'"

"We still call it that. But by the sea. . . . So yesterday evening I was sitting by the sea at night, a wonderful moon, and girls singing somewhere, and suddenly out of the water, slowly, slowly, comes some bunch or other wearing horned suits."

"Who!"

"Sportsmen." Gorbovsky waved his arm and lay back down. "I come home a lot nowadays. I go to Venus and back, ferrying volunteers. Great people, the volunteers. Only they're noisy, they eat a godawful lot, and they all, you know, are rushing off to some suicidal great deed."

Kondratev asked with interest, "What do you think about the project, Leonid?"

"The plan is all right," Gorbovsky said. "I was the one who made it up, after all. Not by myself, but I took part. When I was young I had a great deal to do with Venus. It's a mean planet. But of course you know that yourself."

"It must be very boring to haul volunteers on a D-ship," said Kondratev.

"Yes, of course, the real missions of D-ships are a little different. Take me, for example, with my *Tariel*. When all this is over, I'm going to EN 17—that's on the frontier, twelve parsecs out. There's a planet Vladislava there, with two alien artificial satellites. We're going to look for a city there. It's very interesting, looking for alien cities, Sergei."

"What do you mean 'alien'?"

"Alien . . . you know, Sergei, as a spacer, you would probably be interested in what we are doing now. I made up a little lecture especially for you, and if you like, I'll give it to you now. Okay?"

"It sounds fascinating." Kondratev leaned back in the chair. "Please."

Gorbovsky stared at the ceiling and began, "Depending on tastes and inclinations, our spacers are usually working on one of three problems, but I myself am personally interested in a fourth. Many consider it too specialized, too hopeless, but in my view a man with imagination can easily find a calling in it. Even so, there are people who assert that under no circumstances will it repay the fuel expenditure. This is what the snobs and the utilitarians say. We reply that—"

"Excuse me," Kondratev interrupted. "What exactly does this fourth problem consist of? And the first three, while you're at it."

Gorbovsky was silent for a while, looking at Kondratev and blinking. "Yes," he said finally. "The lecture didn't come out right, it seems. I started with the middle. The first three problems —planetological, astrophysical, and cosmogonic research. Then verification and further elaboration of the D-principle, *id est*, taking a brand new D-ship and driving it up against the light barrier until you can't stand any more. And finally, attempts to establish contact with other civilizations in space—very cautious attempts, so far. My own favorite problem is connected with nonhuman civilizations too. Only we aren't looking for contacts, but for traces. Traces of the visits of alien space travelers to various worlds. Some people maintain that under no circumstances can this mission be justified. Or did I already say that?"

"You did," said Kondratev. "But what sort of traces do you mean?"

"You see, Sergei, any civilization must leave a great number of remains. Take us, the human race. How do we treat a new planet? We place artificial satellites around it, and a long chain of radio buoys stretches from there to the Sun—two or three buoys a light-year—beacons, universal direction-finders. . . , If we manage to land on the planet, we build bases, science cities. And we don't exactly take everything along when we leave! Other civilizations must do likewise."

"And have you found anything?" asked Kondratev.

"Well, of course! Phobos and Deimos—you must know about that; the underground city on Mars; the artificial satellites around Vladislava . . . very interesting satellites. Yes . . . that's more or less what we do, Sergei."

"Interesting," said Kondratev. "But I still would have chosen research into the D-principle."

"Well, that depends on tastes and inclinations. And anyhow, now we're all ferrying volunteers. Even proud researchers of the D-principle. Now we're like the streetcar coachmen of your time."

"There weren't any streetcars left by my time," Kondratev said with a sigh. "And streetcars were driven not by coachmen, but by . . . they called it something else. Listen, Leonid, have you had dinner?"

Gorbovsky sneezed, excused himself, and sat up. "Hold it, Sergei," he said, extracting an enormous multicolored handkerchief from his pocket. "Hold it. Have I told you what I came for?"

"To talk spacer to spacer."

"Right. But I didn't say anything more? No?"

"No. Right away you got very interested in the couch."

"Aha." Gorbovsky blew his nose thoughtfully. "Do you by any chance know Zvantsev the oceanographer?"

"The only person I know is Protos the doctor," Kondratev said sadly. "And now I've just met you."

"Wonderful. You know Protos, Protos knows Zvantsev well, and I know both Protos and Zvantsev well. Anyhow, Zvantsev is dropping by shortly. Nikolai Zvantsev."

"Wonderful," Kondratev said slowly. He realized there was an ulterior motive lurking around here somewhere.

They heard the song of the door signal. "It's him," Gorbovsky said, and lay down again.

Zvantsev the oceanographer was enormously tall and extremely broad-shouldered. He had a broad copper-colored face, close-cropped thick dark hair, large steel-blue eyes, and a small straight mouth. He silently shook Kondratev's hand, cast a sidelong glance at Gorbovsky, and sat down.

"Excuse me," said Kondratev, "I'll go order dinner. What would you like, Comrade Zvantsev?"

"I like everything," said Zvantsev. "And he likes everything."

"Yes, I like everything," said Gorbovsky. "Only please, not oatmeal kissel."

"Right," Kondratev said, and went into the dining room.

"And not cauliflower!" Gorbovsky shouted.

As he punched out the numbers by the delivery-line cube, Kondratev thought, *They had some reason for coming. They're intelligent people, so they didn't come out of simple curiousity—they came to help me. They're energetic and active people, so they scarcely dropped by to console me. But how do they plan on helping? I need only one thing.* . . . Kondratev narrowed his eyes and stood still for a moment, with his hand braced against the lid of the delivery cube. From the living room came:

"You're lying around again, Leonid. There's something of the mimicrodon in you."

"Lolling is an absolute necessity," Gorbovsky said with deep conviction. "It's philosophically unassailable. Useless motions of the arms and legs steadily increase the entropy of the universe. I would like to say to the world, 'People! Lie around more! Beware the heat death!' "

"I'm surprised you haven't yet taken up crawling."

"I thought about it. Too much friction. From the entropic

point of view, locomotion in the vertical position is more advantageous."

"Blatherer," said Zvantsev. "Get up, and now!"

Kondratev opened the lid and set the table. "Dinner is served!" he shouted in a violently cheerful voice. He felt as if he were facing an exam.

There was noise of horseplay in the living room, and Gorbovsky answered, "I'm being brought."

He appeared in the dining room, however, in a vertical position.

"You must excuse him, Comrade Kondratev," said Zvantsev, who appeared close behind. "He's always lying around. First in the grass, and later, without even cleaning himself up, he lies on the couch!"

"Where's the grass stain? Where?" Gorbovsky shouted, and began looking himself over.

With difficulty, Kondratev smiled.

"I'll tell you what," Zvantsev said as he sat down at the table. "I see by your face, Sergei, that preambles are superfluous. Gorbovsky and I came to recruit you for work."

"Thank you," Kondratev said softly.

"I am an oceanographer and am working in an organization called the Oceanic Guard. We cultivate plankton—for protein— and herd whales—for meat, fat, hides, chemicals. Doctor Protos has told us that you are forbidden to go offplanet. And we always need people. Especially now, when many are leaving us for the Venus project. I'm inviting you to join us."

There was a moment of silence. Gorbovsky, not looking at anyone, assiduously ate his soup. Zvantsev also began eating. Kondratev crumbled his bread. "Are you sure I'll be up to it?" he asked.

"I'm sure," said Zvantsev. "We have many former spacemen."

"I'm about as former as you can get," said Kondratev. "You don't have any others like me."

"Give Sergei a little more detail about what he could end up doing," said Gorbovsky.

"You could be a supervisor on a laminaria plantation," said Zvantsev. "You could guard the plankton plantations. There's patrol work, but for that you need special qualifications—that will come with time. Best of all, there's whale herding. Get into whale herding, Sergei." He laid down his knife and fork. "You can't imagine how fine that is!"

Gorbovsky looked at him with curiosity.

"Early, early in the morning . . . quiet ocean . . . reddish sky in the east. You rise up to the surface, throw open the hatch, climb out onto the turret and wait and wait. The water below your legs is green, clear; up from the deep rises a jellyfish—it turns over and goes off under the minisub. . . . A big fish swims lazily past. . . . It's really fine!"

Kondratev looked at his dreamy, satisfied face, and suddenly, so unbearably that he even stopped breathing, he wanted to be on the ocean, in the salt air, instantly.

"And when the whales move to new pasture!" Zvantsev continued. "Do you know how it looks? In front and in back go the old males, two or three to a herd—they're enormous, bluish-black, and they surge forward so evenly that it seems that they're not moving, it's the water rushing past them. They go in front, and the young ones and pregnant females after them. We've got the old males tamed—they'll lead wherever we want, but they need help. Especially when young males are growing up in the herd—they always try to split it up and take part off with them. That's where we have our work. This is where the real business begins. Or all of a sudden grampuses attack."

He suddenly came to himself again and looked at Kondratev with a completely sober glance. "To put it briefly, the job has everything. Wide-open spaces, and depths, and being useful to people, and having good comrades—and adventures, if you especially want that."

"Yes," Kondratev said with feeling.

Zvantsev smiled.

"He's ready," said Gorbovsky. "Well, that's a spacer for you. Like you, I want to be on the turret . . . and with the jellyfish . . ."

"That's how it is," Zvantsev said in a businesslike manner. "I'll take you to Vladivostok. The course in the training school there begins in two days. Have you finished eating?"

"Yes," said Kondratev. *Work,* he thought. *Here it is—real work!*

"Then let's be on our way," said Zvantsev, rising.

"Where?"

"To the airport."

"Right now?"

"Well, of course right now. What is there to wait for?"

"Nothing," Kondratev said confusedly. "Only . . ." He recollected himself and quickly began clearing away the dishes.

Gorbovsky helped him while finishing a banana. "You go on," he said, "and I'll stay here. I'll lie down and read a bit. I have a flight at twenty-one thirty."

They went out into the living room, and the navigator looked around. The thought came distinctly that wherever he would go on this planet, he would find at his disposal the same sort of quiet little house, and kind neighbors, and books, and a garden out the window. "Let's go," he said. "Goodbye, Leonid. Thank you for everything."

Gorbovsky had already oozed onto the couch. "Goodbye, Sergei," he said. "We'll be seeing a good deal of each other."

PART THREE: **The Planet with All the Conveniences**

Languor of the Spirit

WHEN Pol Gnedykh appeared on the streets of the Volga-Unicorn Farm early one morning, people stared after him. Pol was deliberately unshaven and barefoot. On his shoulder he carried a many-branched stick, with a dusty pair of shoes tied with twine dangling from the end. Starting near the latticed tower of the microweather installation, a litter robot began dogging his footsteps. From behind the openwork fence of one of the cottages came the laughter of many voices, and a pretty girl standing on a porch with a towel in her hand inquired of the whole street, "Hail pilgrim! Returning from some holy shrine?" Immediately, from the other side of the street came a question, "Don't we have any opium for the masses?" The venture was working out gloriously well. Pol assumed a dignified air and began to sing loudly:

> Oh, what a hero I,
> Who cold or frost fear not!

Hung from a stick
For a thousand kliks
Of barefoot track,
Or stuck in a sack
Or wrapped in a pack
For the cobbler man
To fix if he can
My shoes
Ta-ra-ta-ta
I've brought.

Into the astounded silence came a frightened voice: "What is he?" Then Pol stopped, shoved the robot with his foot, and asked into space, "Does anyone know where I can find Aleksandr Kostylin?"

Several voices vied with each other to explain that Kostylin must be in the laboratory now, right over in that building.

"On thy left," a single voice added after a short pause.

Pol politely thanked them and continued on. The lab building was low, round, light blue. A towheaded, freckled youth in a white lab coat stood in the doorway, leaning against the doorpost, with his arms folded across his chest. Pol went up the steps and stopped. The towhead looked at him placidly.

"Can I see Kostylin?" Pol asked.

The youth ran his eyes over Pol, looked over Pol's shoulder at the shoes, looked at the litter robot, which was rocking on the step below Pol, its manipulators gaping greedily, and then turning his head slightly, he called softly, "Sasha, hey Sasha! Come out here a minute. Some castaway is here to see you."

"Have him come in," a familiar bass rumbled from the depths of the laboratory.

The towheaded youth looked Pol over again. "He can't," he said, "he's highly septic."

"So disinfect him," came the voice from the laboratory. "I'll be happy to wait."

"You'll have a long wait——" the youth began.

And here Pol appealed plaintively, "Zow, Lin! It's me, Polly!"

Something in the laboratory fell with a crash; out from the doorway, as if from a subway tunnel, came a whiff of cold air, the towheaded youth stepped aside, and on the threshold appeared

Aleksandr Kostylin, enormous, broad, in a gigantic white coat. His hands, with fingers spread wide, were thickly smeared with something, and he carried them off to the side, like a surgeon during an operation. "Zow, Polly!" he yelled, and the litter robot, driven out of its cybernetic mind, rolled down off the porch and rushed headlong through the street.

Pol threw down his stick and, forgetful of self, darted into the embrace of the white coat. His bones crunched. *What a way to go,* he thought, and croaked, "Mercy . . . Lin . . . friend. . . ."

"Polly—Little Polly!" Kostylin cooed in his bass, squeezing Pol with his elbows. "It's really great to see you here!"

Pol fought like a lion, and at last managed to free himself. The towheaded youth, who had been following the reunion with fright, sighed with relief, picked up the stick with the shoes, and gave it to Pol.

"So how are you?" asked Kostylin, smiling the whole width of his face.

"All right, thanks," said Pol. "I'm alive."

"As you can see, we till the soil here," Kostylin said. "Feeding all you parasites."

"You look very impressive," said Pol.

Kostylin glanced at his hands. "Yes," he said, "I forgot." He turned to the towhead. "Fedor, finish up by yourself. You can see that Polly has come for a visit. Little Lieber Polly."

"Maybe we should just chuck it?" said Fedor. "I mean, it's clear it's not going to work."

"No, we've got to finish," said Kostylin. "You finish up, will you please?"

"Okay," Fedor said reluctantly, and went off into the laboratory.

Kostylin grabbed Pol by the shoulder and held him off at arm's length to look him over. "Haven't grown a bit," he said tenderly. "Have you been getting bad feed? Hold it. . . ." He frowned worriedly. "What happened, your pterocar crack up? What kind of a getup is that?"

Pol grinned with pleasure. "No," he said. "I'm playing pilgrim. I've walked all the way from the Big Road."

"Wow!" Kostylin's face showed the customary respect. "Almost three hundred kilometers. How was it?"

"Wonderful," said Pol. "If only there'd been someplace to take a bath. And change clothes."

Kostylin smiled happily and dragged Pol from the porch. "Let's go," he said. "Now you can have everything. A bath, and milk . . ."

He walked in the middle of the street, dragging the stumbling Pol after him, and passed sentence while waving the stick with the shoes: ". . . and a clean shirt . . . and some decent pants . . . and a massage . . . and an ion shower . . . and two or three lashes for not writing . . . and hello from Athos . . . and two letters from Teacher."

"That's great!" exclaimed Pol. "That's great!"

"Yes, yes, you'll have the works. And how about ignis fatuus? You remember ignis fatuus? And how I almost got married? And how I missed you!"

The workday was beginning on the farm. The street was full of people, men and girls, dressed colorfully and simply. The people made way for Kostylin and Pol. The two could hear cries:

"They're bringing the Pilgrim!"

"Vivisect it—it's sick!"

"Some new hybrid?"

"Sasha, wait, let us have a look."

Through the crowd spread a rumor that during the night, near Kostylin's laboratory, a second *Taimyr* had landed.

"Eighteenth century," someone stated. "They're handing out the crew to researchers in comparative anatomy."

Kostylin waved the stick, and Pol gaily bared his teeth. "I love attention," he said.

Voices among the crowd sang, "O, what a hero I, / Who cold or frost fear not!"

Pol the Pilgrim sat on a broad wooden bench at a broad wooden table amid currant bushes. The morning sun pleasantly warmed his antiseptically clean back. Pol luxuriated. In his hand he had an enormous mug of cranberry juice. Kostylin, also shirtless and with wet hair, sat opposite and looked at him affectionately.

"I always believed that Athos was a great man," said Pol, making sweeping motions with the mug. "He had the clearest head, and he knew best of any of us what he wanted."

"Oh, no," Kostylin said warmly. "The Captain saw his goal best of any of us. And he moved straight toward it."

Pol took a sip from the mug and thought. "Maybe," he said. "The Captain wanted to be a spacer, and he became a spacer."

"Uh-huh," said Kostylin, "and Athos is still more of a biologist than a spacer."

"But what a biologist!" Pol raised a finger. "Honestly, I brag about having been friends with him in school."

"Me too," Kostylin agreed. "But you wait five years or so, and we'll be bragging about being friends with the Captain."

"Right," said Pol. "And here I drift around like a bit of foil in the wind. I want to try everything. Now, you were just scolding me for not writing." He put down his mug with a sigh. "I can't write when I'm busy with something. Writing is boring then. When you're working on a subject, writing is boring, because everything is ahead of you. And when you finish, it's boring because it's all behind you. . . . And then you don't know what's ahead. You know, Lin, everything has really been working out stupidly for me. Here I work four years on theoretical servomechanics. One girl and I solved Chebotarev's Problem—you remember, Teacher told us about it? We solve it, build two very good regulators , . . and I fall in love with the girl. And then everything ended and . . . everything ended."

"You haven't gotten married?" Kostylin asked sympathetically.

"That's not the point. It was just that when other people work, they always get new ideas of some sort, but I didn't. The work was finished, and it didn't interest me any more. In these ten years I've gone through four specialties. And again I'm out of ideas. So I thought to myself, I'll go find old Lin."

"Quite right!" Kostylin said in his deep voice. "I'll give you twenty ideas!"

"So give," Pol said sluggishly. He grew gloomy and buried his nose in the mug.

Kostylin looked at him with thoughtful interest. "Couldn't you get into endocrinology?" he proposed.

"Could be endocrinology," said Pol. "Even if it is a hard word. And anyhow, all these ideas are utter languor of the spirit."

Kostylin said suddenly, and without obvious relevance to what had gone before, "I'm getting married soon."

"Wonderful!" Pol said sadly. "Just don't tell me all about your happy love in X thousand boring words." He became more lively. "Happy love is inherently boring anyhow," he declared. "Even the ancients understood that. No real craftsman has been attracted by the theme of happy love. For great works, unhappy love was always an end in itself, but happy love is at best background."

Kostylin assented reluctantly.

"True depth of feeling is characteristic only of unrequited love," Pol continued with inspiration. "Unhappy love makes a person active, churns him up, but happy love calms him down, spiritually castrates him."

"Cheer up, Polly," said Kostylin. "It will all pass. The good thing about unhappy love is that it is usually short-lived. Let me pour you some more juice."

"No, Lin," said Pol, "I think this is long-lived. After all, two years have already gone by. She probably doesn't even remember me, and I . . ." He looked at Kostylin. "Excuse me, Lin. I know it isn't very nice when someone cries all over your shoulder. Only this is all so interminable. I sure as hell wasn't lucky in love."

Kostylin nodded helplessly. "Would you like me to put you in touch with Teacher?" he asked uncertainly.

Pol shook his head and said, "No. I don't want to talk to Teacher when I'm like this. I'd feel like a fool."

"Mmm, yes," Kostylin said, and thought, *What's true is true. Teacher can't stand unhappy people.* He looked at Pol suspiciously. Could clever Polly be playing the unfortunate? He had a good appetite—it was a pleasure to watch him eating. And he loved attention, as always. "Do you remember Operation October?" Lin asked.

"Of course!" Pol once again came to life. "Do you remember how the plan failed?"

"Well—how should I put it? . . . We were too young."

"Good heavens!" said Pol. He grew more cheerful. "Teacher sicked us on Walter on purpose! And then he smashed us in the examination—"

"What examination?"

"Zow, Lin!" Pol shouted delightedly. "The Captain was right —you're the only one who never figured it out!"

Kostylin slowly came to the realization. "Yes, of course," he said. "But what do you mean, I never figured it out? I just forgot. And do you remember how the Captain tested us for acceleration?"

"That was when you ate all that chocolate to see if you could handle the extra weight?" Pol said wickedly.

"And do you remember how we tested the rocket fuel?" Kostylin recollected hurriedly.

"Yeah," Pol said dreamily. "Boy, did it thunder!"

"I have the scar to this day," Kostylin said with pride. "Here —feel it." He turned his back to Pol.

Pol felt it with pleasure. "We were good kids," he said. "Glorious. Do you remember when on parade we turned into a herd of crayspiders?"

"Uff, it was noisy!"

They were sweet memories. Pol suddenly jumped up and with unusual animation imitated a crayspider. The surroundings filled with the repulsive gnashing howl of the multilegged monster that stole through the jungles of fearsome Pandora. And as if in reply, a deep roaring sigh came from afar. Pol froze in fright. "What's that?" he asked.

Kostylin laughed. "Some spider you make! That's cattle!"

"What sort of cattle?" Pol asked in indignation.

"Beef cattle," Lin explained. "Astonishingly good either grilled or roasted."

"Listen, Lin," said Pol, "those are worthy opponents. I want a look at them. And anyhow, I want to see what you do around here."

Kostylin's face filled with boredom. "Forget it, Polly," he said. "Cattle are cattle. Let's sit here a little longer. I'll get you some more juice. All right?"

But it was too late. Pol had filled with energy. "The unknown is calling us! Forward, on to the beef cattle, who throw down the gauntlet to crayspiders! Where's my shirt? Didn't some pedigreed bull promise me a clean shirt?"

"Polly, Polly," Kostylin exhorted, "you've got cattle on the brain! Let's go to the lab instead."

"I'm septic," Pol declared. "I don't want to go to the lab. I want to go to the cattle."

"They'll butt you," Kostylin said, and stopped short. That had been a mistake.

"Really?" Polly said with quiet rapture. "A shirt. Red. I'll get a bullfight going."

Kostylin slapped his hands on his thighs in despair. "Look what I get stuck with! A craymatador!"

He got up and headed for the building. As he walked past Pol, Pol stood on tiptoes, bent over, and did a semiveronica with great elegance. Lin began to bellow, and butted him in the stomach.

When he saw the cattle, Pol immediately realized that there would be no bullfight. Under the bright, hot sky, enormous spotted hulks moved slowly in a row through thick, succulent, man-high grass stretching out to the horizon. The line ate its way into the soft green plain—and behind it was left black steaming ground bare of a single blade of grass. A steady electric odor hung over the plain—there was the smell of ozone, warm black soil, grass, and fresh manure.

"Zow!" Pol whispered, and sat down on a hummock.

The line of cattle moved past him. The school where Pol had studied was in a grain district and Pol knew little about cattle raising, and had long forgotten what little he had learned. He had never had occasion to think about beef cattle, either. He simply ate beef. And now, with a rumble and ceaseless crackling, a herd of beef on the hoof, crunching, tramping, and masticating, went past him with heart-rending sighs. From time to time some enormous brown dribbling muzzle, smeared with green, stuck up from the grass and let out an indistinct deep roar.

Then Pol noticed the cybers. They walked a bit ahead of the line—brisk, flat machines on broad soft caterpillar treads. Now and again they stopped and dug into the ground, lagged behind, and then rushed forward. There were few of them, perhaps fifteen in all. They rushed along the line with frightening speed, throwing moist black clods out from under their treads in fan-shaped showers.

Suddenly a dark cloud covered the sun. A heavy, warm rain began. Pol looked back at the village, at the white cottages scattered over the dark green of gardens. It seemed to him that the paraboloid grids of the weather condensers, on the openwork tower of the microweather station, were staring straight at him. The rain passed quickly; the cloud moved along after the herd. Dim silhouettes that had unexpectedly appeared on the horizon caught Pol's attention, but here he started getting bitten. They were nasty-looking insects, small, gray, winged. Pol realized that these were flies. Perhaps even dung-covered ones. Once he had figured this out, Pol jumped up and rushed briskly back to the village. The flies did not pursue him.

Pol crossed a stream, stopped on the bank, and debated for some time whether or not to go swimming. Deciding it wasn't worth it, he began climbing the path to the village. As he walked, he thought, *It was right that I got the rain dumped on me. And the flies know who to land on. . . . It's what I get for being a parasite. Everybody works like human beings. The Captain is up in space . . . Athos catches fleas on blue stars . . . Lin, the lucky man, cures cattle. Why am I like this? Why should I, an honest, hard-working man, feel like a parasite?* He shuffled down the path and thought about how good it had been the night when he latched onto the solution of Chebotarev's Problem, and had dragged Lida from her bed and made her verify it. When everything had turned out right, she even kissed him on the cheek. Pol touched his cheek and sighed. It would be great to bury himself now in some really good problem like Fermat's Theorem! But there was nothing in his head but ringing emptiness and some idiotic voice that affirmed, "If we find a square root . . ."

On the edge of the village Pol stopped again. Under a spreading cherry tree, a one-seater pterocar was resting on its wing. Near the pterocar squatted a boy of about fifteen, with a sorrowful expression. In front of him, buzzing monotonously, a long-legged litter robot rolled through the grass. Evidently all was not well with the litter robot.

Pol's shadow fell over the boy, and the boy raised his head and then got up. "I landed the pterocar on him," he said with an unusually familiar guilty look.

"And now you're repenting, huh?" Pol asked as a teacher might.

"I didn't do it on purpose," the boy said angrily.

For some time they watched silently the evolutions of the squashed robot. Then Pol squatted down decisively. "Well, let's see what we've got here," he said, and took the robot by a manipulator. The robot let out a squeal.

"Does it hurt?" Pol sang tenderly, easing his fingers into the regulatory system. "Did im hurt ims paw? Poor baby hurt ims paw."

The robot squealed again, shuddered, and was quiet. The boy sighed with relief and squatted down too. "That's it," he muttered. "Boy, was it yelling when I got out of the pterocar!"

"Of course we yelled, we did," cooed Pol, unscrewing the armor. "We've got ourselves a good acoustics system, a loud-mouthed one. It's an itty bitty AKU-6, it is, with longitudinal vibration . . . molecular-notchedy-watchty, it is . . . ye-es." Pol took off the armor plate and carefully laid it on the grass. "And what is your name?"

"Fedor," said the boy, "Fedor Skvortsov." He watched Pol's deft hands enviously.

"Well, Uncle Fedor, the litter robot is as strong as three bears," Pol communicated, extracting the regulator block from the depths of the robot. "I already know one Fedor here. A likable fellow, freckled. A very, very aseptic young man. Are you related to him?"

"No," the boy said cheerfully. "I'm here for practical training. Are you a cyberneticist?"

"We're passing through, we are," Pol said, "in search of ideas. Do you-ums have any sparey-wary ideas?"

"I . . . my . . . in the laboratory we get a lot of ideas, and nothing ever works out."

"I understand," muttered Pol, digging into the regulator block. "A flock of ideas rush every whichway up into the air. At this point the hunter runs out and shoots the crayspider. . . ."

"You've been on Pandora?" the boy asked with envy.

Pol looked around furtively, then let out the yelp of a crayspider that is overtaking its prey.

"Great!"

Pol put the litter robot back together, whispered to it through its steel-blue back, and the robot rolled into the direct sunlight to accumulate energy.

"Marvelous!" Pol said, wiping his hands on his pants. "Now let's see what shape the pterocar's in."

"No, please," Fedor said quickly. "I'll do it myself, honest."

"By yourself, then," said Pol. "In that case I'll go wash my hands. Who's your teacher?"

"My teacher is Nikolai Kuzmich Belka, the oceanographer," the boy said, bristling.

Pol did not risk anything witty, and silently clapped the boy on the shoulder and went on his way. He felt much better. He had already gone two blocks into the village when a familiar pterocar darted by with a whoosh and a boy's voice, intolerably out of tune, imitated the yelp of a crayspider that is overtaking its prey.

Lost in thought, Pol ran into a two-headed calf. It shied off to the side and stared at Pol with both pairs of eyes. Then it lowered its left head to the grass under its feet and turned the right to a lilac branch hanging over the road. Here it was flicked with a switch, and it ran on, kicking. The two-headed calf was being herded by a very attractive suntanned girl who wore a colorful peasant dress and a tilted straw hat. Pol muttered crazily, "And everywhere that Mary went, her, uh, calf was sure to go."

"What?" asked the girl, stopping.

No, she wasn't just attractive. She was plain beautiful. So beautiful she couldn't fail to be smart, so smart she couldn't fail to be nice, so nice. . . . Pol suddenly wanted to be tall and broad-shouldered, with an unfurrowed brow and steely calm eyes. His thoughts darted in a zigzag. *If nothing else, I have to be witty.* He said, "My name is Pol."

The girl answered, "I'm Irina. Did you say something to me, Pol?"

Pol broke out in a sweat. The girl waited, looking impatiently after the calf, which was moving off. The thoughts in Pol's head darted in three layers. *Let us find the square root . . . Cupid fires from a double-barreled carbine. . . . Now she'll think I'm a stutterer. Aha! A stutterer—that was a thought.*

"Y-you're in a h-hurry, I see," he said, stuttering with all his might. "I'll l-look you up th-this evening, if I m-may. Th-this evening."

"Of course." The girl was obviously pleased.

"T-till evening," Pol said, and went on. *I talked a little,* he thought. *We had a little c-conversation. I'm a veritable skyrocket of wit.* He pictured himself at the moment of that conversation, and even moaned nasally at his awkwardness.

Somewhere nearby a loudspeaker boomed: "Will all unoccupied anesthesia specialists please stop by Laboratory Three? Potenko calling. We've got an idea. Will all unoccupied anesthesia specialists please stop by Laboratory Three? And don't come crashing into the main building like last time. Laboratory Three. Laboratory Three."

Why aren't I a specialist in anesthesia? thought Pol. *After all, I wouldn't dream of crashing into the main building.* Two fair maidens in shorts rushed past, down the middle of the street, their elbows pressed to their sides. Probably specialists.

It was quiet and empty in the village. A lonely litter robot languished in the sun at a perfectly clean intersection. Out of pity, Pol threw it a handful of leaves. The robot immediately came to life and set to work. *I haven't met so many litter robots in any city,* thought Pol. *But then, on a stock farm anything can happen.*

A solid thunder of hoofs sounded from behind. Pol turned around in fright, and four horses galloped headlong past him, flanks foaming. On the lead horse, crouched over the mane, was a fellow in white shorts, tanned almost black and glossy with sweat. The other steeds were riderless. Near a low building twenty yards from Pol, at full gallop, the fellow jumped from the horse right onto the steps of the porch. He whistled piercingly and disappeared into the door. The horses, snorting and twisting their necks, described a semicircle and came back to the porch. Pol did not even have time to be properly envious. Three boys and a girl ran out of the low building, leaped onto the horses, and rushed back past Pol at the same mad gait. They were already turning the corner when the fellow in the white shorts jumped out onto the porch and shouted after them, "Take the samples right to the station. Aleshka!"

There was no longer anyone on the street. The fellow stood there a little while, wiped his forehead, and returned to the building. Pol sighed and went on.

He stopped and listened at the threshold to Kostylin's laboratory. The sounds that reached him seemed strange: A muffled blow. A heavy sigh. Something sliding. A bored voice said, "Right." Silence. Again a muffled blow. Pol looked around at the sun-flooded laboratory square. Kostylin's voice said, "Liar. Hold it." A muffled blow. Pol went into the entryway and saw a white door with a sign, SURGICAL LABORATORY. Behind the door the bored voice said, "Why do we always take the thigh? We could take the back." Kostylin's bass answered, "The Siberians tried that—it didn't work." Again a muffled blow.

Pol went up to the door. It opened noiselessly. There was a lot of light in the laboratory, and along the walls shined strange-looking installations frosted with white. The broad panes set in the wall showed dark. Pol asked, "Can someone septic come in?"

No one answered. There were about ten people in the laboratory. They all looked gloomy and pensive. Three sat together, silent, on a large low bench. They looked at Pol without any expression. Two others sat with their backs to the door, by the far wall, with their heads together, reading something. The rest were gathered together in a semicircle in a corner. In the center of the semicircle, his face to the wall, towered Kostylin. He was covering his eyes with his right hand. His left hand was pushed through under his right arm. Freckled Fedor, who was also standing in the semicircle, slapped him on the left palm. The semicircle stirred, and thrust forward fists with thumbs up. Kostylin silently turned and pointed to a person, who silently shook his head, and Kostylin took up his former pose.

"So can someone septic come in?" Pol asked again. "Or is this a bad time?"

"The Pilgrim," one of the people sitting on the bench said in a bored voice. "Come on in, Pilgrim. We're all septic here."

Pol went in. The man with the bored voice said into space, "Peasants, I propose we look over the analyses one more time. Maybe there's still not enough protein."

"There's even more protein than we calculated," said one of the players of this strange game. An oppressive silence reigned; only the blows rang out, and somebody said from time to time, "Liar, you guessed wrong."

Hah, thought Pol. *All is not for the best in the surgical laboratory.* Kostylin suddenly pushed the players apart and walked out into the middle of the room. "A proposal," he said briskly. Everyone, even the ones poring over their notes, turned toward him. "Let's go swimming."

"Let's go," the man with the bored voice said decisively. "We've got to think it all out from the beginning."

No one responded further to the proposal. The surgeons spread out over the room and were quiet once again.

Kostylin went up to Pol and grasped him by the shoulders. "Let's go, Polly," he said sadly. "Let's go, boy. We won't be downhearted, right?"

"Of course not, Lin," said Pol. "If it doesn't work today, it'll work day after tomorrow."

They went out onto the sunny street. "Don't hold back, Lin," said Pol. "Don't be afraid to cry a little on my shoulder. Don't hold back."

There were about one hundred thousand stock-raising farms on the Planet. There were farms that raised cattle, farms that raised pigs, farms that raised elephants, antelope, goats, llamas, sheep. In the middle stream of the Nile there were two farms which were trying to raise hippopotamuses.

On the Planet there were about two hundred thousand grain farms growing rye, wheat, corn, buckwheat, millet, oats, rice, kaoliang. There were specialized farms like Volga-Unicorn, and broad-based ones. Together they provided the foundation for abundance—giant, very highly automated complexes producing foodstuffs: everything from pigs and potatoes to oysters and mangoes. No accidental mishap, no catastrophe, could now threaten the Planet with crop failure and famine. The system for ample production, established once and for all, was maintained completely automatically and had developed so swiftly that it had been necessary to take special precautions against overproduction. Just as there had never been a breathing problem, now mankind had no problem eating.

By evening Pol already had an idea, though only the most general, of what the livestock farmers did. The Volga Farm was one of the few thousand stock farms in the temperate zone. Evidently here you could busy yourself with practical genetics, embryomechanical veterinary science, the production side of economic statistics, zoopsychology, or agrological cybernetics. Pol also encountered here one soil scientist who was evidently loafing—he drank milk fresh from the cow, and courted a pretty zoopsychologist all out, continually striving to entice her off to the swamps of the Amazon, where there was still something for a self-respecting soil scientist to do.

There were about sixty thousand head in the Volga-Unicorn herd. Pol very much liked the herd's total autonomy—around the clock cybers and autovets cared for the cattle as a group, and each individually. The herd, in its turn, around the clock, served, on the one hand, the delivery-line processing complex and, on the other, the ever-growing scientific demands of the stock-raisers. For example, you could get in touch with the dispatch office and demand of the cowherd on duty an animal seven hundred twenty-two days old, of such-and-such a color and with such-and-such parameters, descended from the pedigreed bull Mikolaj II. In half an hour the designated animal, accompanied by a manure-smeared cyber, would be waiting for you in the receiving compartment of, say, the genetics lab.

Moreover, the genetics lab conducted the most insane experiments and functioned as the continual source of a certain friction between the farm and the processing complex. The processing workers, humble but ferocious guardians of world gastronomy, would be driven to a frenzy by the discovery in the regular cattle consignment of a monstrous beast reminiscent in appearance, and, more important, in flavor, of Pacific crab. A representative of the complex would quickly appear on the farm. He would immediately go to the genetics lab and demand to see "the creator of this unappetizing joke." All one hundred eighty staff members of the genetics lab (not counting schoolchildren doing field work) would invariably step forward to claim the title of creator. The representative of the complex would, with restraint, recall that the farm and the complex were responsible for the uninterrupted supply to the delivery line of all forms of beef, and not of frog's legs or canned jellyfish. The one hundred eighty progressively inclined geneticists would object as one man to this narrow approach to the supply problem. To them, the geneticists, it seemed strange that such an experienced and knowledgeable worker as so-and-so should hold such conservative views and should attach no significance to advertising, which, as everyone knew, existed to alter and perfect the taste of the populace. The processing representative would remind them that not one new food product could be introduced into the distribution network without the approbation of the Public Health Academy. (Shouts from the crowd of geneticists: "The great heroes saving us from indigestion!" "The Appendix-Lovers' Society!") The processing representative would spread his hands and indicate by his entire appearance that he was helpless. The shouts would turn into a muted growl and soon die out: the authority of the Public Health Academy was enormous. Then the geneticists would take the processing representative through the laboratories to show him "a little something new." The processing representative would go pale, and assert with oaths that "all this" was completely inedible. In response the geneticists would give him a formal tasting consisting of meat that did not need spices, meat that did not need salt, meat that melted in the mouth like ice cream, special meat for cosmonauts and nuclear technicians, special meat for expectant mothers, meat that could be eaten raw. The processing representative would taste, and then shout in ecstacy, "This is good! This is great!" and would demand amid oaths that all this should get through the experimental stage within the next year. Completely pacified, he would take his leave and depart, and within a month it would all start over again.

The information gathered during the day encouraged Pol, and inspired him with a certainty that there was something to do here. *For a start I'll join the cyberneticists. I'll herd cattle,* thought Pol, sitting on the open veranda of the cafe and looking absentmindedly at a glass of carbonated sour milk. *I'll send half the litter robots into the fields. Let them catch flies. Evenings I'll work with the geneticists. It'll be neat if Irina turns out to be a geneticist. Of course they'd attach me to her. Every morning I'd send her a cyber with a bouquet of flowers. Every evening too.* Pol finished the milk and looked down at the black field across the river. Young grass already showed faint green there. *Very clever!* thought Pol. *Tomorrow the cybers will turn the herd around and drive it back. There we have it, shuttle pasture. But it's all just routine—I see no new principles. Irina and I will develop cattle that eat dirt. Like earthworms. That will be something! If only the Public Health Academy . . .*

A large company, arguing noisily about the meaning of life, tumbled onto the veranda, and immediately began moving tables around. Someone muttered, "A person dies, and he doesn't care whether he has successors or not, descendants or not."

"It doesn't matter to Mikolaj II the bull, but—"

"Stuff the bull! You don't care either! You're gone, dissolved, disappeared. You don't exist, understand?"

"Hold on, guys. There is a certain logic in that, of course. Only the living are interested in the meaning of life."

"I wonder where you would be if your ancestors had thought like that. You'd still be making furrows with a wooden plow."

"Nonsense! What has the meaning of life got to do with anything here? It's simply the law of the development of productive forces."

"What's a law got to do with it?"

"The fact that productive forces keep developing whether you like it or not. After the plow came the tractor, after the tractor, the cyber—"

"Okay, leave our ancestors out of it. But do you mean there were people for whom the meaning of life consisted in inventing the tractor?"

"Why are you talking nonsense? Why do you always talk nonsense? The question is not what any given person lives for but what the human race lives for! You don't understand a thing, and—"

"You're the one who doesn't understand a thing!"

"Listen to me! Everybody listen! Peasants! I'll explain everything to you— Ow!"

"Let him talk! Let him talk!"

"This is a complex question. There are as many people arguing about the meaning of their existence as there are people in—"

"Shorter!"

"—in existence. First, ancestors don't have anything to do with it. A person is given life independently of whether he wants it or—"

"Shorter!"

"Well, then explain it yourself."

"Right, Alan, make it shorter."

"Shorter? Here you go: Life is interesting, ergo we live. And as for those who don't find it interesting, well, right in Snegirevo there's a fertilizer factory."

" 'Ataway, Allan!"

"No, guys. There's also a certain logic to this."

"It's cracker-barrel philosophy! What does 'interesting' or 'uninteresting' mean? What do we exist for? That's the question!"

"So what does displacement of the perihelion exist for? Or Newton's law?"

" 'What for' is the stupidest question there is. What does the sun rise in the east for?"

"Bah! One fool brings that question up to lead a thousand sages astray."

"Fool? I'm as much a fool as you are sages."

"Forget the whole thing! Let's talk about love instead!"

" 'What is this thing called love?' "

"What does love exist for—there's the question! Well, Zhora?"

"You know, peasants, pretend somebody is looking at you in a laboratory—people are just people. As to how philosophy begins . . . love, life. . . ."

Pol took his chair and squeezed into the company. They recognized him.

"Ah! The Pilgrim! Pilgrim, what is love?"

"Love," said Pol, "is a characteristic property of highly organized matter."

"What's the 'organized' for and what's the matter for—there's the question!"

"So then will you—"

"Pilgrim, know any new jokes?"

"Yes," said Pol, "but not any good ones."

"We aren't very good ourselves."

"Have him tell one. Tell me a joke and I'll tell you who you are."

Pol began, "A certain cyberneticist—" (laughter) "—invented a prognosticator, a machine that could foretell the future—a great, huge complex a hundred stories tall. For a start he asked the prognosticator the question, 'What will I be doing in three hours?' The prognosticator hummed away until morning, and then answered, 'You'll be sitting here waiting for me to answer your question.' "

"Ye-es," someone said.

"What do you mean 'ye-es'?" Pol said coolly. "You asked for it yourselves."

"Hey peasants, why are all these cyberjokes so dumb?"

"Not just 'why' but to what end, what for? There's the real question!"

"Pilgrim! What's your name, Pilgrim?"

"Pol," Pol muttered.

Irina came onto the veranda. She was more beautiful than the girls sitting at the table. She was so beautiful that Pol stopped listening. She smiled, said something, waved to someone, and sat down next to long-nosed Zhora. Zhora immediately bent over to her and asked her something, probably "what for?" Pol exhaled and noticed that his neighbor on the right was crying on his shoulder: "We simply can't do it—we haven't learned how. There's no way Aleksandr can get that through his head. Such things can't be done in bursts."

Pol finally recognized his neighbor—it was Vasya, the man with the bored voice, the same Vasya they had gone swimming with at noon.

"Such things can't be done in bursts. We aren't even adjusting Nature—we're smashing her to pieces."

"Ah . . . just what is the topic here?" Pol asked cautiously. He had absolutely no idea when and from where Vasya had appeared.

"I was saying," Vasya repeated patiently, "that a living organism that does not change its genetics outlives its time."

Pol's eyes were glued to Irina. Long-nosed Zhora was pouring her champagne. Irina was saying something rapidly, tapping the glass with dark fingers.

Vasya said, "Aha! You've fallen in love with Irina! Such a pity."

"With what Irina?" muttered Pol.

"That girl there—Irina Egorovna. She worked for us in general biology."

Pol felt as if he had fallen on his face. "What do you mean 'worked'?"

"As I was saying, it's a pity," Vasya said calmly. "She's leaving in a few days."

Pol saw only her profile, lit up by the sun. "For where?" he asked.

"The Far East."

"Pour me some wine, Vasya," said Pol. Suddenly his throat had become dry.

"Are you going to work here?" asked Vasya. "Aleksandr said you had a good head on your shoulders."

"A good head," muttered Pol. "A lofty unfurrowed brow and steely-calm eyes."

Vasya started to laugh. "Don't go pine away," he said. "We must both be all of twenty-five."

"No," said Pol, shaking his head in despair. "What is there to hold me here? Of course I'm not staying here. . . . I'll go to the Far East."

A heavy hand came to rest on his shoulder, and Kostylin's powerful bass inquired, "Just who is going to the Far East? Huh?"

"Lin, listen, Lin," Pol said plaintively. "How come I never have any luck?"

"Irina," said Vasya, getting up.

Lin sat down in his place and drew over to himself a plate of cold meat. His face looked tired.

Pol looked at him with fear and hope, just as in the old days when their neighbors on the floor would arrange a school-wide manhunt to catch the clever Lieber Polly and teach him not to be quite so clever.

Kostylin wolfed down an enormous piece of meat and said in a bass that overcame the noise on the veranda, "Peasants! The new catalogue of publications in Russian has arrived. If you want it, ask at the club."

Everyone turned toward him.

"What have they got?"

"Is there any Mironov, Aleksandr?"

"Yes," said Kostylin.

"How about *The Iron Tower?*"

"Yes. I already ordered it."

"*Pure as Snow?*"

"Yes. Look, there are eighty-six titles—I can't remember everything."

The veranda began to empty quickly. Allan left. Vasya left. Irina left with long-nosed Zhora. She didn't know anything. She hadn't even noticed. And, of course, she didn't understand. Nor would she remember. *She'll remember Zhora. She'll remember the two-headed calf. But she won't remember me.*

Kostylin said, "Unhappy love churns a person up. But it's short-lived, Polly. You stay here. I'll look after you."

"Maybe I'll go to the Far East anyhow," said Pol.

"What for? You'll only bother her and get underfoot. I know Irina and I know you. You're fifty years stupider than her Prince Charming."

"Still. . . ."

"No," said Kostylin. "Stay with me. Really, has your old buddy Lin ever led you astray?"

Pol gave in. He patted Kostylin's immense back affectionately, got up, and went over to the railing. The sun had set, and a warm pellucid dusk had settled over the farm. Somewhere nearby a piano was playing and two voices were singing beautifully in harmony. *Eh*, thought Pol. He bent over the railing and quietly let out the yelp of a giant crayspider that has just lost its trail.

The Assaultmen

THE satellite was enormous. It was a torus a mile and a quarter in diameter, divided inside into numerous chambers by massive bulkheads. The corridor rings were empty and bright, and the triangular hatchways leading into the bright empty rooms stood wide open. The satellite had been abandoned an improbably long time ago, perhaps even millions of years earlier, but the rough yellow floor was clean, and August Bader had said that he hadn't seen even one speck of dust here.

Bader walked in front, as befitted the discoverer and master. Gorbovsky and Falkenstein could see his big protruding ears, and the blondish tuft of hair on the top of his head.

"I had expected to see signs of neglect here," Bader said unhurriedly. He spoke in Russian, painstakingly enunciating each syllable. "This satellite interested us most of all. That was ten years ago. I saw that the outer hatches were open. I said to myself, 'August, you will see a picture of horrifying disaster and destruction.' I told my wife to stay on the ship. I was afraid of finding dead bodies here, you see." He stopped before some sort of hatch, and Gorbovsky almost ran into him. Falkenstein, who had fallen a bit behind, caught up to them and stopped alongside, knitting his brows.

"*Aber* here it was empty," said Bader. "It was light here, very clean, and completely empty. Please, look around." He made a smooth gesture with his arm. "I am inclined to think that this was the traffic control room of the satellite."

They pushed through to a chamber with a dome-shaped ceiling, and with a low semicircular stand in the middle. The walls were bright yellow, translucent, and they shone from within. Gorbovsky touched the wall. It was smooth and cool.

"Like amber," he said. "Feel it, Mark."

Falkenstein felt it and nodded.

"Everything had been dismantled," said Bader, "but in the walls and bulkheads, and also even in the toroid covering of the satellite, remain light sources as yet hidden from us. I am inclined to think—"

"We know," Falkenstein said quickly.

"Oh?" Bader looked at Gorbovsky. "But what have you read? You, Mark, and you, Leonid."

"We've read your series of articles, August," said Gorbovsky. " 'The Artificial Satellites of Vladislava.' "

Bader inclined his head. " 'The Artificial Satellites of Nonterrestrial Origin of the Planet Vladislava of the Star EN 17,' " he corrected. "Yes. In that case, of course, I can omit an exposition of my ideas on the question of the light sources."

Falkenstein walked along the wall, examining it. "Strange material," he said from a distance. "Metaloplast, probably. But I never saw metaloplast like this."

"It's not metaloplast," said Bader. "Don't forget where you are. You, Mark, and you, Leonid."

"We won't forget," said Gorbovsky. "We've been on Phobos, and there, it's an entirely different material, actually."

Phobos, a satellite of Mars, had for a long time been considered a natural one. But it had turned out to be a two-and-a-half-mile torus covered with a metal antimeteorite net. The thick net had been eaten away by meteorite corrosion, and torn through in places. But the satellite itself was intact. Its exterior hatches were open, and the gigantic doughnut was just as empty as this one. By the wear on the antimeteorite net they had calculated that the satellite had been placed in orbit around Mars at least ten million years before.

"Oh, Phobos!" Bader shook his head. "Phobos is one thing, Leonid. Vladislava is something else entirely."

"Why?" Falkenstein inquired as he came up. He disagreed.

"For example, because between the Sun, or Phobos, and Vladislava where we are now, there are two and a half million astronomical units."

"We covered that distance in half a year," Falkenstein argued. "They could do the same. And the satellites of Vladislava and Phobos have much in common."

"That remains to be proven," said Bader.

Grinning lazily, Gorbovsky said, "That's just what we're trying to do."

Bader pondered for some time and then announced, "Phobos and Earth's satellites also have much in common."

It was an answer in Bader's style—very weighty and off target by half a meter.

"Well, all right," said Gorbovsky. "What else is there besides the traffic-control room?"

"On this satellite," Bader said pompously, "there are one hundred sixty chambers ranging in size from fifteen to five hundred square meters. We can look at them all. But they're empty."

"If they're empty," Falkenstein said, "we'd be better off getting back to the *Tariel.*"

Bader looked at him and once again turned to Gorbovsky. "We call this satellite Vladya. As you know, Vladislava has another satellite, also artificial, and also of nonterrestrial origin. It is smaller in size. We call it Slava. Do you get it? The planet is called Vladislava. It is only natural to call its two satellites Vladya and Slava. Right?"

"Yes, of course," said Gorbovsky. This elegant reasoning was familiar to him. This was the third time he had heard it. "It was very clever of you to suggest that, August. Vladya and Slava. Vladislava. Wonderful."

"You people on Earth," Bader continued unhurriedly, "call

these satellites Y-1 and Y-2, corresponding respectively to Vladya and Slava. But as for us, we do it differently. We call them Vladya and Slava."

He looked sternly at Falkenstein. Falkenstein bit his lip to keep from smiling. As far as Falkenstein knew, "we" was Bader himself, and only Bader.

"As for the composition of this yellow material, which is by no means metaloplast, and which I call amberine—"

"A very good name," Falkenstein put in.

"Yes, not bad. . . . Well, its composition is as yet unknown. It remains a mystery."

A silence set in. Gorbovsky looked absently about the room. He tried to imagine the beings who had built this satellite and then had worked here at a time so long past. They were another race. They had come to the Solar System and had departed, leaving to Mars the abandoned space laboratories and a large city near the northern icecap. The satellites were empty, and the city was empty—there remained only strange buildings which extended for many levels below the ground. Then—or perhaps earlier—they had come to the EN 17 system, had constructed two artificial satellites around Vladislava, and then had left there as well. And here, on Vladislava, there ought to be an abandoned city as well. Where had they come from, and why? Where had they gone and why? The whys were clear. They were of course great explorers—the Assaultmen of another world.

"Now," said Bader, "we will go and examine the chamber in which I found the object which I arbitrarily call a button."

"Still there?" asked Falkenstein, coming to life.

"Who?" asked Bader.

"The object."

"The button," Bader said weightily, "at the present time is to be found on Earth, in the keeping of the Commission for Research of the Evidence of the Activity of Extraterrestrial Intelligence in Outer Space."

"Ah," said Falkenstein. "The Pathfinders have it. But I collected material about Vladislava, and no one showed me this button of yours."

Bader tugged his chin. "I sent it with Captain Anton Bykov half a subjective year ago."

They had passed Bykov en route. He should be arriving at Earth seven months after the takeoff of the *Tariel* for EN 17. "So," Gorbovsky said. "In that case we will have to postpone inspection of the button."

"But we can look at the chamber where I found it," Bader said. "There is a possibility, Leonid, that in the hypothetical city on the surface of the planet Vladislava you will find analogous objects." He climbed through the hatch.

Falkenstein said through his teeth, "I've had it with him, Leonid."

"Patience," said Gorbovsky.

The chamber where Bader had found the button turned out to be a third of a mile off. Bader pointed to the place where the button had lain and related in detail how he had found the button. (He had stepped on it and squashed it.) In Bader's opinion, the button was a battery, which originally had been spherical in shape. It was made of silvery translucent material, very soft. Its diameter was thirty eight point one six millimeters . . . density . . . weight . . . distance from the nearest wall. . . .

In the room opposite, on the other side of the corridor, two young fellows in blue work jackets sat amid instruments arranged on the floor. As they worked, they glanced over at Gorbovsky and Falkenstein, and conversed in low tones.

"Assaultmen. Docked yesterday."

"Um-hum. The tall one there is Gorbovsky."

"I know."

"And the other one, with the blond hair?"

"Mark Falkenstein. Navigator."

"Ah. I've heard of him."

"They're beginning tomorrow."

Bader at last finished his explanations and asked whether they had understood everything. "Everything," Gorbovsky said, and he heard laughter in the room opposite.

"Now we will go back home," Bader said.

They emerged into the corridor, and Gorbovsky nodded to the fellows in blue. They got up and bowed, smiling. "Good luck," one said. The other smiled silently, turning a skein of multicolored wiring in his hands.

"Thanks," Gorbovsky said.

Falkenstein also said, "Thanks."

After he had gone a hundred paces or so, Gorbovsky turned around. The two fellows in blue jackets were standing in the corridor watching them.

In the Baderian Empire (as jokers called the whole system of artificial and natural satellites of Vladislava—observatories, workshops, repair stations, chlorella plantations in black tanks, greenhouses, plant nurseries, glassed-in recreational gardens, and the empty tori of nonterrestrial origin), time was calculated in thirty-hour cycles. At the end of the third cycle after the D-ship *Tariel*, a giant almost four miles in length that from a distance looked like a sparkling flower, had assumed a meridional orbit around Vladislava, Gorbovsky undertook the first search run. D-ships are not suited for landings on massive planets, especially planets with atmospheres, and especially planets with wild atmospheres. The ships are too fragile for this. Auxiliary boats with either atomic-impulse or photon drive, steady, lightweight, intrasystem craft with a variable center of gravity, carry out such landings. A regular starship carries one such boat, but an Assault ship, two to four. The *Tariel* had two photon boats on board, and Gorbovsky made the first attempt to sound Vladislava's atmosphere in one of them. "To see whether it's worth it," Gorbovsky said to Bader.

Bader visited the *Tariel* personally. He did a lot of nodding and saying "ah, yes," and now, when Gorbovsky had cast off from the *Tariel*, he sat on a stool to one side of the observation board, and began to wait patiently.

All the Assaultmen had gathered by the screen and were watching the indistinct flashes on the gray oscillograph screen— the traces of the signal impulses sent by the telemetry on the boat. There were three Assaultmen in addition to Bader. They kept silent and thought about Gorbovsky, each in his own way.

Falkenstein thought about the fact that Gorbovsky would return in an hour. Falkenstein could not stand uncertainty, and he wished that Gorbovsky had already returned, even though he knew that the first search run always comes out all right, especially with Gorbovsky piloting the Assault boat. Falkenstein remembered his first meeting with Gorbovsky. Falkenstein had just returned from a jaunt to Neptune—had returned without losses, was proud of this, and was boasting dreadfully. That was on Chi Fei, the circumlunar satellite from which all photon ships usually took off. Gorbovsky had come over to him in the mess-room and had said, "Excuse me—you wouldn't happen to be Mark Falkenstein?" Falkenstein had nodded and said, "What can I do for you?" Gorbovsky had a very sad expression. He sat down alongside, twitched his long nose and asked plaintively, "Listen, Mark, do you know where I can get a harp around here?" "Here" was a distance of one hundred ninety thousand miles from Earth, at a starship base. Falkenstein choked on his soup. Gorbovsky looked him over with curiosity, then introduced himself and said, "Calm down, Mark; it's not urgent. Actually, what I want to know is at what rate did you enter Neptune's exosphere?" That was Gorbovsky's way—to go up to somebody, especially a stranger, and ask a question like that to see how the victim would handle it.

The biologist Percy Dickson—black, overgrown, with curly hair—also thought about Gorbovsky. Dickson worked in space psychology and human space physiology. He was old, he knew a great deal, and he had carried out on himself and others a heap of insane experiments. He had come to the conclusion that a person who has been in space all in all for more than twenty years grows unused to Earth and ceases to consider it home. Remaining an Earthman, he ceases to be a man of Earth. Percy Dickson himself had become one such, and he could not understand why Gorbovsky, who had covered fifty parsecs and had touched on a dozen moons and planets, now and then would suddenly raise his eyes high and said with a sigh, "Oh, to be in a meadow! On the grass. Just to lie there. And with a stream."

Ryu Waseda, atmosphere physicist, thought about Gorbovsky too. He thought about his parting words, "I'll go see whether it's worth it." Waseda greatly feared that Gorbovsky, on returning, would say, "It's not worth it." That had happened several times. Waseda studied wild atmospheres and was Gorbovsky's eternal debtor, and it seemed to him that he was sending Gorbovsky off to his death every time. Once Waseda had told Gorbovsky about this. Gorbovsky had answered seriously, "You know, Ryu, there hasn't been a time yet when I haven't come back."

Professor and Assaultman August Johann Bader, general

plenipotentiary of the Cosmonautical Council, director of the far-space starship base and laboratory Vladislava (EN 17), also thought about Gorbovsky. For some reason he remembered how Gorbovsky had said good-by to his mother fifteen years before, on Chi Fei. Gorbovsky and Bader were going to Transpluto. That was a very sad moment—taking leave of relatives before a space flight. It seemed to Bader that Gorbovsky had said good-by to his mother very brusquely. Bader, as ship's captain—he had been captain of the ship then—had considered it his duty to provide inspiration for Gorbovsky. "In such a sad moment as this," he had said sternly but softly, "your heart must beat in unison with that of your mother. The sublime virtue of every human being consists in. . . ," Gorbovsky had listened silently, and when Bader finished his reprimand, had said in a strange voice, "August, do you have a mama?" Yes, that was how he said it! "Mama." Not mother, not *Mutter*, but mama.

"He's come out on the other side," said Waseda.

Falkenstein looked at the screen. The splotches of dark spots had disappeared. He looked at Bader. Bader sat there gripping the seat of his stool, looking nauseated. He raised his eyes to Falkenstein's and gave a labored smile. "It is one thing," he said, enunciating with effort, "when it's you yourself. *Aber* it is quite another when it is someone else."

Falkenstein turned around. In his opinion it did not matter in the least who was doing it. He got up and went into the corridor. By the airlock hatch he caught sight of an unfamiliar young man with a tanned, clean-shaven face and a gleaming, clean-shaven skull. Falkenstein stopped and looked him over from head to toe and back. "Who are you?" he asked ungraciously. Meeting an unfamiliar person on the *Tariel* was the last thing he had expected.

The young man grinned a bit crookedly. "My name is Sidorov," he said. "I'm a biologist and I want to see Comrade Gorbovsky."

"Gorbovsky's on a search run," said Falkenstein. "How did you get on board?"

"Director Bader brought me—"

"Ah . . ," said Falkenstein. Bader had arrived on board two hours before.

"—and probably forgot about me."

"It figures," said Falkenstein. "That's quite natural for Director Bader. He's quite excitable."

"I understand." Sidorov looked at the toes of his shoes and said, "I had wanted to talk with Comrade Gorbovsky."

"You'll have to wait a little," Falkenstein said. "He'll be back soon. Come on, I'll take you to the wardroom." He took Sidorov to the wardroom, laid a bundle of the latest Earth magazines in front of him, and returned to the control room. The Assaultmen were smiling. Bader was wiping sweat from his forehead and smiling too. The flashes of dark could again be seen on the screen.

"He's coming back," said Dickson. "He said one turn is enough for the first time."

"Of course it's enough," said Falkenstein.

"Quite enough," said Waseda.

In a quarter-hour Gorbovsky scrambled out of the airlock, unfastening his pilot's coverall as he walked. He seemed abstracted, and looked over their heads.

"Well?" Waseda asked impatiently.

"Everything's all right," said Gorbovsky. He stopped in the middle of the corridor and started climbing out of his flight suit. He freed one leg, stepped on a sleeve, and almost fell. "That is to say, everything's all right, but nothing's any good."

"What is it, exactly?" inquired Falkenstein.

"I'm hungry," Gorbovsky declared. He finally got out of the flight suit and headed for the wardroom, dragging the suit along the deck by a sleeve. "Stupid planet!" he snapped.

Falkenstein took the suit from him and walked alongside.

"Stupid planet," repeated Gorbovsky, staring over their heads.

"It is quite a difficult planet for landings," Bader affirmed, enunciating distinctly.

"Let me have something to eat," said Gorbovsky.

In the wardroom he collapsed onto the sofa with satisfied moaning. As he entered, Sidorov jumped to his feet.

"Sit down, sit down," Gorbovsky said graciously.

"So what happened?" asked Falkenstein.

"Nothing in particular," said Gorbovsky. "Our boats are no good for landing."

"Why not?"

"I don't know. Photon craft are no good for landing. The

tuning of the magnetic traps in the reactor is always breaking down."

"Atmospheric magnetic fields," Waseda, the atmosphere physicist, said, and wrung his hands, making an audible rubbing sound.

"Perhaps," said Gorbovsky.

"Ah, well," Bader said unhurriedly. "I'll give you an impulse rocket. Or an ion craft."

"Do that, August," said Gorbovsky. "Please give us an ion craft or an impulse rocket. And somebody get me something to eat."

"Good lord," said Falkenstein. "I can't even remember the last time I flew an impulse rocket."

"Never mind," said Gorbovsky. "It'll come back. Listen," he said affectionately. "Are they going to feed me today?"

"Right away," said Falkenstein. He excused himself to Sidorov, took the magazines off the table, and covered it with a chlorovinyl tablecloth. Then he placed bread, butter, milk, and kasha on the table.

"The table is laid, sir," he said.

Gorbovsky got up from the sofa reluctantly. "You've always got to get up when you have to do something," he said. He sat down at the table, took a cup of milk with both hands, and drank it in one gulp. Then he drew a plate of kasha toward him with both hands and picked up a fork. Only when he picked up the fork did it become clear why he had used both hands for the cup and the plate. His hands were trembling. His hands were trembling so badly that he missed twice when he tried to take a bit of butter on the end of his knife.

Craning his neck, Bader looked at Gorbovsky's hands. "I'll try to give you my very best impulse rocket, Leonid," he said in a weak voice. "My very best."

"Do that, August," said Gorbovsky. "Your very best. And who is this young man?"

"This is Sidorov," Falkenstein explained. "He wanted to talk with you."

Sidorov stood up again. Gorbovsky looked benevolently up at him and said, "Please, sit down."

"Oh," said Bader. "I completely forgot. Forgive me. Leonid, comrades, allow me to introduce—"

"I'm Sidorov," said Sidorov, grinning uncomfortably because everyone was looking at him. "Mikhail. Biologist."

"*Welcome*, Mikhail Sidorov," Percy Dickson said in English.

"Okay," said Gorbovsky. "I'll finish eating in a minute, Comrade Sidorov, and then we'll go to my cabin. There's a sofa there. There's a sofa here too," he said, lowering his voice to a conspiratorial whisper, "but Bader is sprawled out all over it, and he's the director."

"Don't even think of taking him," Falkenstein said in Japanese. "I don't like him."

"Why not?" asked Gorbovsky.

Gorbovsky was taking his ease on the couch, and Falkenstein and Sidorov were sitting by the table. On the table lay shiny skeins of videotape.

"I advise against it," said Falkenstein.

Gorbovsky put his hands behind his head.

"I don't have any relatives," Sidorov said. Gorbovsky looked at him sympathetically. "No one to cry over me."

"Why 'cry'?" asked Gorbovsky.

Sidorov frowned. "I mean that I know what I'm getting into. I need data. They're waiting up for me on Earth. I've been sitting here over Vladislava for a year already. A year gone almost for nothing."

"Yes, that's annoying," Gorbovsky said.

Sidorov linked his fingers together. "Very annoying, sir. I thought there would be a landing on Vladislava soon. I couldn't care less about being among the first ones down. I just need data, do you understand?"

"I understand," Gorbovsky said. "Indeed so. You, as I recall, are a biologist."

"Yes. Besides that, I passed the cosmonaut-pilot courses and graduated with honors. You gave me my examinations, sir. But of course you don't remember me. I'm a biologist first and last, and I don't want to wait any more. Quippa promised to take me with him. But he made two landing attempts and then gave up. Then Sterling came. There was a real daredevil. But he didn't take me along either. He didn't have the chance—he went for a landing on the second run, and he didn't come back."

"He was an idiot," said Gorbovsky, looking at the ceiling. "On a planet like this you have to make at least ten runs. What did you say his name was? Sterling?"

"Sterling," Sidorov answered.

"An idiot," declared Gorbovsky. "A brainless idiot."

Falkenstein looked at Sidorov's face and muttered, "Well, there we have it. We've got ourselves a hero here."

"Speak Russian," Gorbovsky said sternly.

"What for? He knows Japanese."

Sidorov flushed. "Yes," he said. "I know it. Only I'm no hero. Sterling—there's a hero. But I'm a biologist, and I need data."

"How much data did you get from Sterling?" asked Falkenstein.

"From Sterling? None," said Sidorov. "He got killed, after all."

"So why are you so thrilled with him?"

Sidorov shrugged. He did not understand these strange people. They were very strange people—Gorbovsky, Falkenstein, and probably their friends too. To call the remarkable daredevil Sterling a brainless idiot. . . . He remembered Sterling—tall, broad-shouldered, with a booming carefree laugh and sure gestures. And how Sterling had said to Bader, "The careful ones stay on Earth, August. It's a qualification for the job, August!" and snapped his sturdy fingers. Brainless idiot. . . .

Okay, thought Sidorov, *that's their business. But what should I do? Sit back again with folded hands and radio Earth that our allotment of cyberscouts have burned up in the atmosphere; that the scheduled attempt to land hasn't succeeded; that the scheduled detachment of explorer spacers refused to take me along on a search run; that I argued myself blue in the face with Bader again and he still insists he won't trust me with a ship, and that he's expelling me from "the little corner of the universe entrusted to his care" for "systematic impertinence"? And once again kind old Rudolf Kruetzer in Leningrad, shaking his head under his academic skullcap, will put forward his intuitive notions in favor of the existence of life in systems of blue stars, and that mad dog Gadzhibekov will roar on about his experimental conclusions denying the possibility of life in the systems of blue stars; and again Rudolf Kruetzer will tell everyone about the same eighteen bacteria caught by Quippa's expedition in the atmosphere of the planet Vladislava; and Gadzhibekov will deny any link whatsoever between these eighteen bacteria and the atmosphere of Vladis-*

lava, alluding with full justification to the difficulty of identification given the actual conditions of the experiment in question. And once again the Academy of Biology will leave open the question of the existence of life in the systems of blue stars. But there is life, there is, is, is, and we only need to reach out to it. Reach out to Vladislava, a planet of the blue star EN 17.

Gorbovsky looked at Sidorov and said affectionately, "When all is said and done, why is it so necessary to come with us? We have our own biologist—Percy Dickson, a wonderful scientist. He's a little crazy but he'll get you samples, whatever sort you like, and in any quantity."

"Eh," Sidorov said, and waved his hand.

"Honestly," said Gorbovsky. "You wouldn't like it at all if you did come along. And so everything will be all right. We'll land and get you everything you need. Just give us instructions."

"And you'll do everything backward," said Sidorov. "Quippa asked for instructions too, and then brought back two containers full of penicillium. An ordinary terrestrial mold. You yourself don't know the working conditions on Vladislava. You won't be in the mood for my instructions there."

"You've got a point," sighed Gorbovsky. "We don't know the conditions. You'll have to wait a little longer, Comrade Sidorov."

Falkenstein nodded in satisfaction.

"All right," said Sidorov. His eyes were almost closed. "Then at least take the instructions."

"Absolutely," said Gorbovsky. "Immediately."

In the course of the next forty cycles, Gorbovsky made sixteen search runs. He was using an excellent impulse craft which Bader had supplied him, the *Skiff-Aleph*. He did the first five runs by himself, testing Vladislava's exosphere at the poles, at the equator, at different latitudes. Finally he selected the north polar region and started taking Falkenstein with him. Time after time they plunged into the atmosphere of the orange-black planet, and time after time they jumped back out like corks from water. But each time they plunged deeper.

Bader assigned three observatories to the work of the Assault-men. They continually kept Gorbovsky informed about the movements of weather fronts in Vladislava's atmosphere. The production of atomic hydrogen—the fuel for the *Skiff-Aleph*—began on Bader's order: the fuel expenditure had turned out to be enormous, beyond expectations. The research into the chemical composition of the atmosphere by means of bomb probes with meson emitters was curtailed.

Falkenstein and Gorbovsky would return from a run exhausted, worn to shreds, and they would greedily rush to a meal, after which Gorbovsky would force his way to the nearest sofa and lie there for a long time, amusing his friends with various maxims.

Sidorov, on Gorbovsky's invitation, remained on the *Tariel*. He was allowed to place trap containers for biosamples, and an automatic biological laboratory, in the *Skiff-Aleph*'s test-equipment slots. In the course of this he cut into the domain of Ryu, the atmosphere physicist. But Sidorov had little to show for his efforts—the containers came back empty, the recordings of the autolab did not yield to decipherment. The influence on the instruments of the wild atmosphere's magnetic fields fluctuated chaotically, and the autolab required human direction. When he came out of the airlock, Gorbovsky would first of all see Sidorov's gleaming skull and would wordlessly clap his hand to his forehead. Once he said to Sidorov, "The thing is, Mikhail, that all biology flies out of my head at the one-hundred-twenty-kilometer mark. It's simply knocked out. It's very dangerous there. Just sneeze, and you're dead."

Sometimes Gorbovsky took Dickson with him. After each such run the long-haired biologist rested in bed. At Sidorov's timid request that Dickson look after the instruments, he answered straight out that he did not plan on worrying about any side issues. "There's just not enough time, kid."

None of them is planning on worrying about side issues, Sidorov thought bitterly. *Gorbovsky and Falkenstein are looking for a city, Falkenstein and Ryu are studying the atmosphere, and Dickson is observing the godlike pulses of all three of them. And they put off the landing, put it off, put it off.... Why don't they hurry? Can they really not care?*

It seemed to Sidorov that he would never understand these strange creatures called Assaultmen. Everyone in the whole huge world knew of the Assaultmen and was proud of them. It was considered an honor just to be the personal friend of an Assaultman. But now it turned out that no one knew clearly what an Assaultman was. On the one hand, it was something incredibly daring—on the other, something shamefully cautious; they kept coming back. They always died natural deaths.

They said, "An Assaultman is one who prudently waits for the exact moment when he can afford to be imprudent." They said, "An Assaultman stops being an Assaultman when he gets killed." They said, "An Assaultman goes places that machines don't come back from." They also said, "You can say, 'He lived and died a biologist.' But you have to say, 'He lived an Assaultman and died a biologist.'" All these sayings were very emotional, but they explained absolutely nothing. Many outstanding scientists and explorers were Assaultmen. There was a time when Sidorov had been thrilled by the Assaultmen too. But it was one thing to be thrilled sitting at a school desk, and quite another to see Gorbovsky crawl like a tortoise over miles that could be covered in a single risky but lightning-fast swoop.

When he returned from the sixteenth run, Gorbovsky declared that he intended to move on to the exploration of the last and most complex part of the path to the surface of Vladislava. "There are twenty-five kilometers of an unknown layer left before the surface," he said, blinking his sleepy eyes and gazing over their heads. "Those are very dangerous miles, and I will move with particular caution. Falkenstein and I will make at least another ten or fifteen runs. If, of course, Director Bader will furnish us with the fuel."

"Director Bader will furnish you with the fuel," Bader said majestically. "You need not have the least doubt about that, Leonid."

"Wonderful!" said Gorbovsky. "The fact is that I will be extremely cautious, and for that reason I feel justified in taking Sidorov with me."

Sidorov jumped up. Everyone looked at him.

"Well, so you've waited it out, kid," said Dickson.

"Yes. We have to give a new boy a chance," said Bader.

Waseda only smiled, shaking his handsome head. And even Falkenstein remained silent, although he was displeased. Falkenstein did not like heroes.

"It's the thing to do," Gorbovsky said. He stepped back and, without looking behind him, sat down with enviable precision on the sofa. "Let the new boy go." He smiled and lay down. "Get your containers ready, Mikhail—we're taking you along."

Sidorov tore himself from the spot and ran out of the wardroom. When he had left, Falkenstein said, "Bad move."

"Don't be selfish, Mark," Gorbovsky drawled lazily. "The kid has been sitting here for a year already. And all he needs is to collect some bacteria from the atmosphere."

Falkenstein shook his head and said, "It's a bad move. He's a hero."

"That's nothing," Gorbovsky said. "I remember him now—the cadets called him Athos. Besides, I read a little book of his. He's a good biologist and he won't act up. There was a time when I was a hero too. And you. And Ryu. Right, Ryu?"

"Right, captain," Waseda said.

Gorbovsky narrowed his eyes and rubbed his shoulder. "It aches," he said in a plaintive voice. "Such a horrible turn. And against the wind at that. How's your knee, Mark?"

Falkenstein raised his leg and flexed it several times. Everyone followed his movements attentively. " 'Oh, that this too, too solid flesh would melt,' " he said in a drawl.

"I'll give you a massage right now," Dickson said, and got up ponderously.

The *Tariel* moved along a meridional orbit, passing over Vladislava's north pole every three and a half hours. Toward the end of the cycle, the landing craft, with Gorbovsky, Falkenstein, and Sidorov aboard, separated from the starship and dropped down, into the very center of a black spiral funnel that slowly twisted inside the orange haze covering Vladislava's north pole.

At first everyone was silent. Then Gorbovsky said, "They must have landed at the north pole."

"Who?" asked Sidorov.

"Them," Gorbovsky explained. "And if they built their city anywhere, then it's right at the north pole."

"In the place where the north pole was back then," Falkenstein said.

"Yes, of course, there. Like on Mars."

Sidorov tensely watched an orange kernel and black spots on

the screen fly headlong from some sort of weather center. Then this motion slowed down. The *Skiff-Aleph* was braking. Now they were descending vertically.

"But they could have landed at the south pole too," said Falkenstein.

"They could have," Gorbovsky agreed.

If Gorbovsky did not find the extraterrestrials' settlement at the north pole, Sidorov thought, he would dawdle around the south pole just as methodically, and then, if he found nothing at the south pole, he would crawl over the whole planet, until he did find something. He even began to pity Gorbovsky and his colleagues. Especially his colleagues.

"Mikhail," Gorbovsky suddenly called.

"Yes?" Sidorov called back.

"Mikhail, did you ever see elves dancing on the green?"

"Elves?" asked Sidorov in surprise.

He looked back. Gorbovsky was sitting turned half toward him, staring at him with a wicked look in his eyes. Falkenstein sat with his back to Sidorov.

"Elves?" asked Sidorov. "What elves?"

"With wings. You know, like this. . . ." Gorbovsky took one hand off the control keys and moved his fingers vaguely. "You haven't? A pity. I haven't either. Nor Mark nor anyone else that I know of. But it would be interesting to watch, wouldn't it?"

"Undoubtedly," Sidorov said dryly.

"Leonid," said Falkenstein. "Why didn't they dismantle the shells of their stations?"

"They didn't need to," said Gorbovsky.

"It's uneconomical," said Falkenstein.

"So they were uneconomical."

"Wastrel explorers," Falkenstein said, and fell silent.

The craft shook.

"It's got us, Mark," Gorbovsky said in an unfamiliar voice.

The craft began to shake horribly. It was impossible to imagine that they could endure such violent shaking. The *Skiff-Aleph* was entering the atmosphere, where wild horizontal currents roared, dragging long black stripes of crystalline dust after them; where the radar was blinded; where lightning of unimaginable force flashed in the thick orange fog. Here powerful, completely inexplicable surges of magnetic fields deflected instruments and broke up the plasma cord in a photon rocket's reactor. Photon rockets were no good here, but neither were things pleasant on the first-line atomic intrasystem craft *Skiff-Aleph.*

But it was quiet in the control room. Gorbovsky, lashed to his seat by straps, writhed in front of the control panel. Black hair fell into his eyes, and at every shock he bared his teeth. The shocks continued without interruption, and he looked as if he were laughing. But it was not laughter. Sidorov had never dreamed that Gorbovsky could look like that—not merely strange, but somehow alien. Gorbovsky was like a devil. Falkenstein was like a devil too. His legs spread apart, he hung over the atmosphere traps, jerking his stretched-out neck. It was surprisingly quiet. But the needles of the instruments, the green zigzags and spots on the fluorescent screens, the black and orange spots on the periscope screen—everything rushed about, circled around in a merry dance, and the deck swayed from side to side like a shortened pendulum, and the ceiling jerked, fell, and jumped up again.

"The cybernavigator," Falkenstein croaked hoarsely.

"Too early," Gorbovsky said, and once again bared his teeth. "We're getting carried away. There's a lot of dust."

"Damn it, it's too early," said Gorbovsky. "I'm going for the pole."

Sidorov did not hear Falkenstein's answer, because the autolab had started working. The indicator light flashed, and under the transparent plastic plate, the recording tape had started inching along. "Ha!" shouted Sidorov. There was protein outside. Living protoplasm. There was a lot of it, and with every second there was more. "What's going on?" Sidorov said then. The width of the tape was not sufficient for the recorder, and the instrument automatically switched over to the zero level. Then the indicator light died out, and the tape stopped. Sidorov gave a growl, tore off the factory seal, and dug into the instrument's mechanism with both hands. He knew this instrument well. He himself had taken part in its construction and he could not imagine what had gone wrong. Under great strain, trying to keep his balance, Sidorov groped at the block of printed circuits. They could fracture from shocks. He had completely forgotten about that. They could have fractured twenty times over during the previous runs. *Just as long as they haven't fractured,* he thought. *Just as long as they're still intact.*

The ship shook unbearably, and Sidorov banged his forehead several times against a plastic panel. Once he banged the bridge of his nose, and for a while was completely blinded by tears. Evidently the circuit blocks were intact. Then the *Skiff-Aleph* turned sharply over on its side.

Sidorov was thrown from his seat. He flew across the control room, clenching in both arms fragments of panel torn out by the anchors. He did not even realize at first what had happened. Then he realized, but could not believe it.

"Should have strapped in," said Falkenstein. "Some pilot."

Sidorov managed to crawl back to his seat on hands and knees along the dancing deck. He fastened the straps and stared dully at the smashed interior of the instrument.

The craft lurched as if it had run into a wall. His dry mouth gaping, Sidorov swallowed air. It was very quiet in the control room, except for Falkenstein's wheezing—his throat had filled with blood. "The cybernavigator," he said. At that moment the walls again shuddered. Gorbovsky remained silent.

"There's no fuel feed," said Falkenstein, unexpectedly calmly.

"I see," said Gorbovsky. "Do your job."

"Not a drop. We're falling. It's jammed."

"I'm turning on the emergency tank, last one. Altitude forty-five kilometers . . . Sidorov!"

"Yes," Sidorov said, and started coughing.

"Your containers are filling up." Gorbovsky turned his long face with the dry flashing eyes toward him. Sidorov had never seen such an expression on him while he was lying on the sofa. "The compressors are working. You're in luck, Athos!"

"In real luck," said Sidorov.

Now they were hit from below. Something crunched inside Sidorov, and his mouth filled with bitter-tasting saliva.

"The fuel's coming through!" shouted Falkenstein.

"Fine—wonderful! But man your own station, for God's sake. Sidorov! Hey, Mikhail!"

"Yes," Sidorov said hoarsely, without unclenching his teeth.

"Do you have a reserve rig?"

"Um," said Sidorov. He was thinking poorly now.

"Um what?" shouted Gorbovsky. "Yes or no?"

"No," said Sidorov.

"Some pilot," said Falkenstein. "Some hero."

Sidorov gnashed his teeth and started looking at the periscope screen. Turbid orange stripes raced from right to left across the screen. It was so frightening and so sickening to look at it that Sidorov shut his eyes.

"They landed here!" shouted Gorbovsky. "The city is there, I know it!"

Something in the control room chimed delicately during the frightful reeling silence, and suddenly Falkenstein roared out in a heavy broken bass:

> The whirlwind thunders forth its rage
> The sky explodes in red;
> A blinding firestorm blocks your way
> But if you should turn back this day
> Then who would go on ahead?

I would go on, thought Sidorov. *Fool, jackass. I should've waited for Gorbovsky to decide on a landing. Not enough patience. If he had gone for a landing today, I wouldn't give a damn about the autolab.*

And Falkenstein roared,

> The smiles like frost, the looks that stray
> Your night thoughts in your bed;
> The Assaultman funked it, people say,
> But had you not come back that day,
> Then who would go on ahead?

"Altitude twenty-one kilometers!" shouted Gorbovsky. "I'm switching over to horizontal."

Now come the endless minutes of horizontal flight, thought Sidorov. *The ghastly minutes of horizontal flight. Minute after minute of jerks and nausea, until they've enjoyed their explorations to the full. And I'll sit here like a blind man, with my stupid smashed machine.*

The craft lurched. The blow was very strong, enough to cause a momentary vision blackout. Then Sidorov, gasping for breath, saw Gorbovsky smash his face into the control board, and Falkenstein stretch out his arms, fly over the couch, and slowly, as if in a dream, come to rest on the deck. He remained there, face down. A piece of strap, broken in two places, slid over his back evenly, like an autumn leaf. For a few seconds the craft moved by inertia, and Sidorov, seizing the clasp of his straps, felt that everything was falling. But then his body became heavy once again.

Finally he unfastened the clasp and stood up on legs of cotton. He looked at the instruments. The needle of the altimeter was climbing upward, the yellow zigzags of the monitoring system rushed about in blue hops, leaving behind foggy traces which slowly faded out. The cybernavigator was heading the craft away from Vladislava. Sidorov jumped over Falkenstein and went up to the board. Gorbovsky was lying with his head on the control keys. Sidorov looked back at Falkenstein. He was already sitting up, propping himself up on the deck. His eyes were closed. Then Sidorov carefully lifted up Gorbovsky and laid him on the back of the seat. *To hell with the autolab,* he thought. He turned off the cybernavigator and rested his fingers on the sticky keys. The *Skiff-Aleph* began to swing about, and suddenly dropped a hundred yards. Sidorov smiled. He heard Falkenstein wheeze angrily behind him, "Don't you dare!"

But he didn't even turn around.

"You're a good pilot, and you made a good landing. And in my opinion you're an excellent biologist," said Gorbovsky. His face was all bandaged. "Excellent. A real go-getter. Isn't that so, Mark?"

Falkenstein nodded, and, parting his lips, he said, "Undoubtedly. He made a good landing. But he wasn't the one who raised ship again."

"You see," Gorbovsky said with great feeling, "I read your monograph on protozoa—it's superb. But we have come to the parting of the ways."

Sidorov swallowed with difficulty and said, "Why?"

Gorbovsky looked at Falkenstein, then at Bader. "He doesn't understand."

Falkenstein nodded. He was not looking at Sidorov. Bader also nodded, and looked at Sidorov with a sort of vague pity.

"Well? And?" Sidorov asked defiantly.

"You're too fond of excitement," Gorbovsky said softly. "You know, *Sturm und Drang,* as Director Bader would say."

"Storm and stress," Bader translated pompously.

"Precisely," said Gorbovsky. "Entirely too fond. And we can't have that. It's a *rotten* character trait. It's deeply ingrained. And you don't even understand."

"My lab was smashed," said Sidorov. "I couldn't do anything else."

Gorbovsky sighed and looked at Falkenstein. Falkenstein said with disgust, "Let's go, Leonid."

"I couldn't do anything else," Sidorov repeated stubbornly.

"You should have done something else. Something quite different," said Gorbovsky. He turned and started down the corridor.

Sidorov stood in the middle of the corridor and watched the three of them leave, Bader and Falkenstein each supporting Gorbovsky by an arm. Then he looked at his own hand and saw red drops on the fingers. He started for the med section, leaning against the wall because he was swaying from side to side. *I wanted to do what was right*, he thought. *I mean, that was the most important thing, landing. And I brought back the containers of microfauna. I know that's very valuable. It's valuable for Gorbovsky too: after all, sooner or later he himself will have to land and carry out a sortie across Vladislava. And the bacteria will kill him if I don't neutralize them. I did what I had to. On Vladislava, on a planet of a blue star, there is life. Of course I did what I had to.* He whispered several times, "I did what I had to." But he felt that it wasn't quite so. He had first felt this down there, down below, when they were standing by the spaceship, waist deep in seething petroleum, with geysers on the horizon rising up in enormous columns, and Gorbovsky had asked him, "Well, what do you intend to do now, Mikhail?" and Falkenstein had said something in an unfamiliar language and had climbed back into the spaceship. He had felt it again when the *Skiff-Aleph* had forced her way off the surface of the fearsome planet for the third time, and once again had flopped down into the oily mud, struck back by a blow of the storm. And he felt it now.

"I wanted to do what was right," he said indistinctly to Dickson, who was helping him lie down on the examining table.

"What?" said Dickson.

"I had to land," Sidorov said.

"Lie down," said Dickson. He muttered, "Primordial enthusiasm. . . ."

Sidorov saw a large white pear-shape coming down from the ceiling. The pear-shape hung quite close, over his very face. Dark spots swam before his eyes, his ears rang, and suddenly Falkenstein started singing in a heavy bass,

> But had you not come back that day,
> Then who would go on ahead?

"Anybody at all," Sidorov said stubbornly with closed eyes. "Anyone would go on ahead."

Dickson stood by, and watched the cybersurgeon's delicate shining needle enter the mutilated arm. *There's sure enough blood!* thought Dickson. *Oceans and oceans. Gorbovsky barely got them out of there in time. Another half hour, and the kid would never again be making excuses. Well, Gorbovsky always comes back in time. That's the way it ought to be. Assaultmen ought to come back, or else they wouldn't be Assaultmen. And once upon a time, every Assaultman was like Athos here.*

Deep Search

THE cabin was rated for one person, and now it was too crowded. Akiko sat to Kondratev's right, on the casing of the sonar set. To keep out of the way, she squeezed herself against the wall, bracing her feet against the base of the control panel. Of course she was uncomfortable sitting like that, but the seat in front of the panel was the operator's station. Belov was uncomfortable too. He was squatting beneath the hatch, from time to time stretching his numbed legs carefully by turns, first the right, then the left. He would stretch out his right leg, kick Akiko in the back, sigh, and in his low-pitched voice apologize in English, "Beg your pardon." Akiko and Belov were trainees. Oceanographer trainees had to resign themselves to discomfort in the one-man minisubs of the Oceanic Guard.

Except for Belov's sighs and the usual rumble of superheated steam in the reactor, it was quiet in the cabin. Quiet, cramped, and dark. Occasionally shrimp knocked against the spectrolite porthole and rushed off in fright in a cloud of luminous slime. It was like small, soundless pink explosions. As if someone were shooting tiny bullets. During the flashes you could catch glimpses of Akiko's flashing eyes and serious face.

Akiko watched the screen. She had squeezed sideways to the wall and started looking from the very beginning, although she knew that they would have to search a long time, perhaps all night. The screen was under the porthole, in the center of the control board, and in order to see it she had to crane her neck. But she watched it fixedly and silently. It was her first deep-water search.

She was a free-style swimming champion. She had narrow hips and broad muscular shoulders. Kondratev liked to look at her, and he felt like finding some pretext to turn on the light. In order to inspect the hatch fastener one last time before descent, for instance. But Kondratev did not turn on the light. He simply remembered Akiko: slender and angular like a teenager, with broad muscular shoulders, wearing loose shorts and a linen jacket with rolled-up sleeves.

A fat, bright blip appeared on the screen. Akiko's shoulder squeezed up to Kondratev's. He sensed that she was craning her neck in order to see better what was happening on the screen. He could tell this by the odor of perfume—and in addition, he smelled the barely noticeable odor of salt water. Akiko always smelled of salt water: she spent two-thirds of her time in it.

Kondratev said, "Sharks. At four hundred meters."

The blip trembled, broke into tiny spots, and disappeared. Akiko moved away. She did not yet know how to read the sonar signals. Belov did, since he had already spent a year's apprenticeship on the *Kunashir*, but he sat in back and could not see the screen. He said, "Sharks are nasty customers." Then he made a clumsy movement and said, "Beg your pardon, Akiko-san."

There was no need to speak English, since Akiko had studied in Khabarovsk for five years and understood Russian perfectly well.

"You didn't have to eat so much," Kondratev said angrily. "You didn't have to drink. You know what happens."

"All we had was roast duck for two," said Belov. "And two glasses of wine apiece. I couldn't say no. We hadn't seen each other in ages, and his flight leaves this evening. Has already left, probably. Just two glasses. . . . Does it really smell?"

"It smells."

This is rotten, thought Belov. He stuck out his lower lip, blew out softly, and sucked in through his nose. "All I smell is perfume," he said.

Idiot, thought Kondratev.

Akiko said guiltily, "I didn't know it would be so strong, or I wouldn't have used it."

"There's nothing wrong with perfume," Belov said. "It's nice."

Taking him along was a bad move, thought Kondratev.

Belov banged the top of his head against the hatch fastener and hissed in pain.

"What?" asked Kondratev.

Belov sighed, sat down tailor-fashion, and raised an arm, feeling the hatch fastener over his head. The fastener was cold, with sharp, rough corners. It fastened the heavy hatch cover to the hatchway. Over the hatch cover was water. A hundred meters of water to the surface.

"Kondratev," said Belov.

"Yes?"

"Listen, Kondratev, why are we running submerged? Let's surface and open the hatch: fresh air and all that."

"It's wind force five up there," Kondratev answered.

Yes, thought Belov, *a wind force of five, choppy water, so an open hatch would flood. But still, a hundred meters of water over your head is uncomfortable. Fifty-five fathoms. Three hundred thirty feet. Soon the dive will begin, and it'll be two hundred meters, three, five. Maybe down to a kilometer or even two. Pushing my way in here was a bad move,* Belov thought. *I should have stayed on the* Kunashir *and written an article.*

Still another shrimp knocked against the porthole. Like a tiny pink explosion. Belov stared into the darkness, where for an instant the silhouette of Kondratev's close-cropped head had appeared.

Such things, of course, never came into Kondratev's mind. Kondratev was quite different, not like your average person. In the first place, he was from the last century. In the second place, he had nerves of iron. As much iron as in the damned hatch fastener. In the third place, he did not give a damn for the unknown mysteries of the deep. He was immersed in methods of precise calculation of head of livestock, and in the variation of protein content per hectare of plankton field. He was worried about the predator that had been killing young whales. Sixteen young whales in the quarter, and all the very best, as if by choice. The pride of the Pacific whale-herders.

"Kondratev!"

"Yes?"

"Don't be angry."

"I'm not angry," Kondratev said angrily. "Where did you get that idea?"

"I thought you were angry. When do we start the dive?"

"Soon."

Thunk . . . thunk-thunk-thunk-thunk. . . . A whole school of shrimp. Just like the fireworks at New Year's. Belov yawned convulsively and hurriedly slammed his mouth shut. That was what he would do—keep his mouth shut tight the whole mission. "Akiko-san," he said in English, "how do you feel?"

"Fine, thank you," Akiko answered politely in Russian. From her voice it was clear that she had not turned around. *She's angry too,* Belov decided. *That's because she's in love with Kondratev. Kondratev's angry, so she is too. She looks up at Kondratev and never calls him anything but "Comrade Captain." She respects him very highly, she practically worships him. Yes, she's in love with him up to her ears, that's clear to everyone. Probably even to Kondratev. Only so far it isn't clear to her herself. Poor thing, she's really had rotten luck. A man with nerves of iron, muscles of steel, and a face of bronze. That Kondratev is a monumental man. Literally. A Buddha-man. A living monument to himself. And to his century. And to the whole heroic past.*

At 2:00 A.M., Kondratev turned on the cabin light and got out the chart. The submarine hung over the center of a depression eight nautical miles southwest of the drifting *Kunashir.* Kondratev tapped his fingernails absentmindedly on the chart and announced, "We're beginning the dive."

"At last," muttered Belov.

"Will we descend vertically, Comrade Captain?" asked Akiko.

"We're not in a bathyscaphe," Kondratev said dryly. "We'll go down in a spiral."

He did not himself know why he said it dryly. Perhaps because he had glimpsed Akiko again. He thought he had remembered her well, but it turned out that in the few hours of darkness he had endowed her with the features of other women who were not like her at all. Women whom he had liked before. Colleagues at work, actresses from various films. In the light these features disappeared, and she seemed more slender, more angular, darker than he had imagined. She was like a small teenage boy. She sat peacefully beside him, with a lowered glance, her hands resting on her bare knees. *Strange,* he thought. *She never used perfume before, so far as I noticed.*

He turned off the light and headed the submarine into the depths. The sub's nose slanted sharply, and Belov braced himself with his knees against the back of the chair. Now, over Kondratev's shoulder, he saw the illuminated dials and the sonar screen in the upper part of the panel. Trembling sparks flared up and died out on the screen: probably blips of deep-sea fish still too far away for identification. Belov ran his eyes over the dials, looking for the depth indicator. The bathymeter was at the far left. The red needle was slowly crawling to the 200-meter mark. Then it would just as slowly crawl to the 300 mark, then 400. . . . Under the submarine was an abyssal chasm, and the minisub was a tiny mote in an inconceivable mass of water. Belov suddenly felt as if something were interfering with his breathing. The darkness in the cabin became thicker and more unrelenting, like the cold salt water outside. *It's begun,* Belov thought. He took a deep breath and held it. Then he narrowed his eyes, grabbed the back of the chair with both hands, and began to count to himself. When colored spots started swimming before his narrowed eyes he exhaled noisily and ran his hand across his forehead. The hand got wet.

The red needle crossed the 200 mark. The sight was both beautiful and ominous: the red needle and green numbers in the darkness. A ruby needle and emerald numbers: 200, 300 . . . 1000 . . . 3000 . . . 5000. . . . *I can't understand at all why I became an oceanographer. Why not a metallurgist or gardener? Ghastly stupidity. Out of every hundred people only one gets depth sickness. But this one-out-of-a-hundred is an oceanographer, because he likes to study cephalopods. He's simply crazy out of his head about cephalopods. Cephalopods, damn them! Why don't I study something else? Say rabbits. Or earthworms,*

Nice, fat earthworms in the wet soil under a hot sun. No darkness, no horror of a saltwater grave. Just earth and sun. He said loudly, "Kondratev!"

"Yes?"

"Listen, Kondratev, did you ever get the urge to study earthworms?"

Kondratev bent over and groped into the darkness. Something clicked with a ringing sound, and an icy stream of oxygen hit Belov's face. He breathed in greedily, yawning and choking. "Enough," he said finally. "Thanks."

Kondratev turned off the oxygen. No, of course he wouldn't give a damn about earthworms. The red needle crawled past the 300 mark. Belov called once more, "Kondratev?"

"Yes?"

"Are you sure it's a giant squid?"

"I don't understand."

"That a giant squid is what has been getting the whales?"

"It's probably a squid."

"But it could be grampuses?"

"Could be."

"Or a sperm whale?"

"It could be a sperm whale. But a sperm whale usually attacks females. There were plenty of females in the herd. And grampuses attack stragglers."

"No, it's *ika*," Akiko said in a small voice. "*O-ika.*"

O-ika was the giant deep-sea squid. Fierce and quick as lightning. It had a powerful taut body, ten strong arms, and cruel, intelligent eyes. It would rush at a whale from below and instantly gnaw out its insides. Then it would force the carcass down to the bottom. Not even a shark, not even the hungriest, would dare to come close to it. It dug into the silt and feasted at leisure. If a submarine of the Oceanic Guard should catch up to it, it would not give way. It would accept battle, and sharks would gather to pick up the lumps of meat. Giant-squid meat was tough as rubber, but the sharks didn't care.

"Yes," said Belov. "Probably it's a giant squid."

"Probably," said Kondratev. *It doesn't matter whether it's a squid or not,* he thought. *Creatures even more fearsome than the giant squid could have set up housekeeping in depressions like this one. You have to find them and destroy them, for once they taste whale they'll never leave you alone.* Then he thought that if they should meet something really unknown, the trainees would doubtless hang all over his shoulders and demand that he let them "investigate." Trainees always got the idea that a working submarine was a research bathyscaphe.

Four hundred meters.

It was very stuffy in the cabin. The ionizers weren't correcting it. Kondratev heard Belov's heavy breathing behind his back. On the other hand he couldn't hear Akiko at all; you would think she wasn't there. Kondratev let a little more oxygen into the cabin. Then he glanced at the compass. A strong current was swinging the submarine away from its course.

"Belov," Kondratev said, "make a note: warm current, depth four hundred forty meters, direction south-southwest, speed two meters per second."

Belov flicked the dictaphone switch with a squeak, and muttered something in a low voice.

"A regular Gulf Stream," said Kondratev. "A little Gulf Stream."

"Temperature?" Belov asked in a weak voice.

"Twenty-four degrees Celsius."

Akiko said timidly, "A curious temperature. Unusual."

"It would be very quaint if there's a volcano somewhere under us," Belov moaned. "Have you ever tasted giant-squid soup, Akiko-san?" he asked. He started in English and finished in Russian.

"Watch it," said Kondratev. "I'm going to leave the current. Hang onto something."

"Easier said than done," muttered Belov.

"Aye, aye, Comrade Captain," said Akiko.

You can hang onto me, Kondratev wanted to suggest to her, but he was too shy. He rolled the submarine sharply over to the port side, and plunged almost straight down.

"*Ufff,*" grunted Belov. He let go of the dictaphone, which hit Kondratev in the back of the head. Then Kondratev felt Akiko's fingers grip his shoulder—grip and slide off. "Grab onto my shoulders," he ordered.

At that instant she almost fell face first onto the edge of the control panel. He barely managed to catch her arm, and she hit her face against his elbow. "Excuse me," she said.

"*Ufff*, easy there," moaned Belov. "Take it easy, Kondratev!"

It felt like an elevator coming to a sharp stop. Kondratev took his head away from the board, fumbled to his right, and encountered Akiko's downy hair.

"Did you hurt yourself?" he asked.

"No, sir. Thank you for asking."

He bent down and caught hold of her by the arm. "Thank you," she repeated. "Thank you. I can manage myself."

He let go of her and glanced at the bathymeter. Six hundred fifty . . . six hundred fifty-five . . . six hundred sixty.

"Take it easy, Kondratev," Belov pleaded in a weak voice. "Enough already."

Six hundred eighty meters. Three hundred seventy-two fathoms. Two thousand two hundred thirty feet. Kondratev leveled off. Belov hiccuped loudly and pushed away from the back of the seat.

"That's it," Kondratev announced, and turned on the light.

Akiko hid her nose with her hand; tears were running down her cheeks. "Eyes are sparking," she said, smiling with difficulty.

"I'm sorry, Akiko-san," Kondratev said. He felt guilty. There had been no need for such a sharp dive. It was just that he had gotten tired of the endless spiral descent. He wiped sweat from his forehead and looked back. Belov sat hunched up, bare to the waist, holding his crumpled shirt near his mouth. His face was damp and gray, his eyes red.

"Roast duck," said Kondratev. "Remember, Belov."

"I'll remember. Let me have some more oxygen."

"No. You'll poison yourself." Kondratev felt like saying a few more words about wine, but he restrained himself and turned out the light. The submarine again moved in a spiral and everyone, even Belov, kept silent for a long time. Seven hundred meters, seven hundred fifty, eight hundred. . . .

"There it is," Akiko whispered.

A hazy narrow spot was moving unhurriedly across the screen. The creature was still too far away—so far it was impossible to identify. It could be a giant squid, a sperm whale, a food whale away from the herd, a large whale shark, or some unknown animal. There were still many animals either unknown or little known to humans in the deep. The Oceanic Guard had reports of enormous long-legged and long-tailed turtles, of sea serpents, of deep-sea spiders that nested in the chasms to the south of the Bonin Islands, of sea gnats—little predatory fish that swarmed in herds of many thousands at a depth of a mile or a mile and a quarter and wiped out everything in their path. So far there had been neither the opportunity nor any special need to verify these reports.

Kondratev quietly swung the submarine to keep the creature in its field of vision.

"Let's get a little closer to it," Belov asked. "Get closer!" He breathed noisily in Kondratev's ear. The submarine slowly began the approach.

Kondratev turned on the sight, and crossed threads of light flashed onto the screen. The narrow spot was swimming near the crosshairs.

"Wait," said Belov. "There's no hurry, Kondratev."

Kondratev got annoyed. He bent over, felt under his legs for the dictaphone, and poked it over his shoulder into the darkness.

"What's going on?" asked Belov, displeased.

"The dictaphone," Kondratev said. "Make a note: depth eight hundred meters, target sighted."

"We've got time."

"Let me," said Akiko.

"Beg your pardon." Belov gave a cough. "Kondratev! Don't even think of shooting it, Kondratev. We've got to have a look first."

"So look," said Kondratev.

The distance between the submarine and the animal lessened. Now it was clearly a giant squid. If it were not for the trainees, Kondratev would not have delayed. A worker of the Oceanic Guard had no business delaying. Not one other sea creature brought as much harm to whaleherding as did the giant squid. It was subject to instant annihilation whenever one encountered a submarine—the squid's blip would move within the crosshairs of the screen, and then the submarine would launch torpedoes. Two torpedoes. Sometimes three, to be certain. The torpedoes would dart along the ultrasonic beam and explode next to the target. And at the sound of the explosion, sharks would move in from all sides.

Kondratev took his finger off the torpedo launch switch with regret. "Look," he repeated.

But there was not yet anything to look at. The limit of clear vision in the clearest ocean water did not exceed eighty or a hundred feet, and only the sonar allowed them to locate targets at distances of up to a third of a mile.

"I wish it would show up," Belov said excitedly.

"Don't be in such a hurry."

The minisubs of the Oceanic Guard were intended to guard plankton crops from whales, and to guard whales from sea predators. The submarines were not intended for research purposes. They were too noisy. If the squid did not feel like closer acquaintance with the submarine, it would move off before they could turn the searchlights on and look it over. To pursue it would be useless—giant cephalopods were capable of a speed twice that of the quickest minisub. Kondratev was relying only on the amazing fearlessness and cruelty of the squid, which sometimes would incite it into skirmishes with fierce sperm whales and herds of grampuses.

"Careful, careful," Belov repeated tenderly and imploringly.

"Want some oxygen?" Kondratev asked savagely.

Akiko softly touched him on the shoulder. She had been standing bent over the screen for several minutes, her hair tickling Kondratev's ear and cheek.

"*Ika* sees us," she said.

Belov shouted, "Don't shoot!"

The spot on the screen—now it was big and round—moved downward fairly rapidly. Kondratev smiled, pleased. The squid was coming out under the submarine in its attack position. It had no thought of fleeing. Instead, the squid was offering battle.

"Don't let it get away," whispered Belov.

Akiko said, "*Ika* is getting away."

The trainees did not yet understand what was going on. Kondratev began to lower the nose of the submarine. The squid's blip once again flashed in the crosshairs. He had only to push the release to blow the vermin to shreds.

"Don't shoot," Belov repeated. "Just don't shoot."

I wonder what happened to his depth sickness, thought Kondratev. He said, "The squid will be under us now. I'm going to stand the sub on its bow. Get ready."

"Aye, aye, Comrade Captain," said Akiko.

Without speaking a word, Belov began moving energetically, getting himself settled. The submarine slowly rotated. The blip on the screen grew larger, and took on the form of a many-pointed star with winking rays. The submarine hung motionless nose down.

Evidently the squid was puzzled by the strange behavior of its intended victim. But it only delayed a few seconds. Then it moved to the attack. Rapidly and surely, as it must have done thousands of times before in its unimaginably long life.

The blip on the screen swelled and filled the whole screen.

Kondratev immediately turned on all the searchlights, two on the hatch side and one fixed to the bottom. The light was very bright. The transparent water seemed yellow-green. Akiko sighed briefly. Kondratev looked at her out of the corner of his eye for a moment. She was squatting over the porthole, hanging onto the edge of the control panel with one hand. A bare, scratched knee was sticking out from under her arm.

"Look," Belov said hoarsely. "Look, there it is! Just look at it!"

At first the shining haze beyond the porthole was motionless. Then some sort of shadows began to stir in it. Something long and supple showed briefly, and after a second they could see the squid. Or rather they could see a broad white body, two unwavering eyes in its lower part, and under the eyes, like a monstrous mustache, two bundles of thick, waving tentacles. In an instant all this moved over the porthole and blocked off the light from the searchlights. The submarine rocked strongly, and something repulsive-sounding, like a knife on glass, began to scrape over the plating.

"There you are," said Kondratev. "Have you enjoyed your fill?"

"It's enormous!" Belov breathed reverently. "Akiko-san, did you see how enormous it is?"

"*O-ika,*" whispered Akiko.

Belov said, "I have never come across a record of such an enormous specimen. I would estimate the distance between the eyes as something over two meters. What do you think, Kondratev?"

"About that."

"And you, Akiko-san?"

"One and one half to two meters," Akiko answered after a silence.

"Which with the usual proportions would give us . . ." Belov started counting on his fingers. "Would give us a body of at least thirty meters, and a weight—"

"Listen," Kondratev interrupted impatiently. "Have you looked enough?"

Belov said, "No, wait. We've got to tear away from it somehow and photograph it whole."

The submarine rocked again, and once again the repulsive screech of horny jaws on metal could be heard.

"We're not a whale, dearie," Kondratev muttered gloatingly, and said aloud, "It won't leave us voluntarily now, and it'd crawl over the submarine for at least two hours, no less. So now I'll shake it off, and it'll fall under the jet of superheated water from the turbines. Then we'll quickly turn around, photograph it, and shoot it. All right?"

The submarine began to rock violently. It was obvious that the squid was turning nasty, was trying to bend the submarine in two. For several seconds one of the squid's arms showed in the porthole—a violet hose as fat as a telephone pole, studded with greedily waving suckers. Black hooks sticking out of the suckers kicked against the spectrolite.

"What a beauty," Belov cooed. "Listen, Kondratev, can't we surface with it?"

Kondratev threw back his head and, narrowing his eyes, looked up at Belov. "Surface?" he said. "Maybe. He won't unlatch from us now. How much did you say he could weigh?"

"About seventy metric tons," Belov said uncertainly.

Kondratev whistled and once again turned to the board.

"But that's in air," Belov added hurriedly. "In water—"

"Still no less than ten tons," said Kondratev. "We couldn't make it. Get ready—we're going to rotate."

Akiko hurriedly squatted down, without taking her eyes from the porthole. She was afraid of missing something interesting.

If it weren't for the trainees, Kondratev thought, *I would have finished with this vermin long ago, and would be looking for its relatives.* He did not doubt that somewhere on the bottom of the depression were hiding the children, grandchildren, and great-grandchildren of the monster—potential, and perhaps already actual, pirates on the whale migration lanes.

The submarine rotated into horizontal position.

"It's stuffy," muttered Belov.

"Hang on tighter," said Kondratev. "Ready? Here we go!" He turned the speed handle as far as it would turn. Full speed, thirty knots. The turbines howled piercingly. Behind, something banged, and they heard a muffled yelp. *Poor Belov,* thought Kondratev. He dropped the speed and swung the helm about. The submarine went around in a semicircle and again pointed toward the squid.

"Now look," said Kondratev.

The squid hung twenty yards in front of the submarine's bow —pale, strangely flat, with drooping, writhing tentacles and a drooping body. It looked like a spider burned by a match. Its eyes were squinting thoughtfully off below and to one side, as if it were mulling something over. Kondratev had never seen a live squid so close, and he examined it with curiosity and loathing. It really was an unusually large specimen. Perhaps one of the largest in the world. But at that moment nothing about it gave the impression of a powerful and fearsome predator. For some reason Kondratev recalled the bundles of softened whale intestines in the enormous steeping vats of the whale-butchering complex in Petropavlovsk.

Several minutes went by. Belov lay with his stomach pressing on Kondratev's shoulders, and aimed the whirring movie camera. Akiko muttered something into the dictaphone in Japanese without taking her eyes off the squid. Kondratev's neck started to ache, and furthermore he was afraid that the squid would regain consciousness and would clear out, or else would throw itself on the submarine again, and then they would have to start over from the beginning.

"Aren't you about done yet?" inquired Kondratev.

"And how!" Belov answered strongly but irrelevantly.

The squid came to. A rippling shudder went through its arms.

The enormous eyes, the size of soccer balls, turned like hinges in sockets, and stared at the light from the searchlights. Then the arms stretched out ramrod straight, and contracted again, and the pale violet skin filled with dark color. The squid was scalded, stunned, but it was preparing for another pounce. No, the giant squid was not leaving. It was not even considering leaving.

"Well?" Kondratev asked impatiently.

"Okay," Belov said with dissatisfaction. "You can do it."

"Get off of me," said Kondratev.

Belov got off and rested his chin on Kondratev's right shoulder. He had obviously forgotten about depth sickness. Kondratev glanced at the screen, then laid a finger on the release lever. "Too close," he muttered. "Oh, well. Fire one!" The submarine shuddered. "Fire two!" The submarine shuddered again. The squid was slowly opening its arms when the two pyroxilyn torpedoes exploded one after the other below its eyes. Two dull flashes and two enormous peals of thunder: boo-oom, boo-oom. A black cloud obscured the squid and then the submarine was thrown on its stern; it turned over on its port side and began to dance about in place.

When the agitation had ceased, the searchlight illuminated a gray-brown heaving mass from which spinning, formless, billowing shreds tumbled into the abyss. Some were still twisting and twitching in the beams of light, rushing into the yellow-green thickness of dusty twilight. Then they disappeared into the dark. On the sonar screen, one after another, four, five, seven blips had already appeared—unhurried, biding their time.

"Sharks," said Kondratev. "There they are."

"Sharks are nasty customers," Belov said hoarsely. "But this squid . . . It's a shame—such a specimen! You're a barbarian, Kondratev. What if it was intelligent?"

Kondratev remained silent and turned on the light. Akiko was sitting hunched up to the wall, with her head tilted over on her shoulder. Her eyes were closed, her mouth half-open. Her forehead, cheeks, neck, and bare arms and legs gleamed with sweat. The dictaphone lay under her feet. Kondratev picked it up. Akiko opened her eyes and smiled with embarrassment.

"We'll start back now," Kondratev said. He thought, *Tomorrow night I'll dive down here and finish off the rest.*

"It's very stuffy, Comrade Captain," said Akiko.

"You said it!" Kondratev replied angrily. "Cognac and perfume and. . . ."

Akiko lowered her head.

"Well, never mind," said Kondratev. "We'll come back tomorrow. Belov!"

Belov did not answer. Kondratev turned around and saw that Belov had raised his arms and was groping at the hatch fastener. "What are you doing, Belov?" Kondratev asked calmly.

Belov turned his gray face toward him and said, "It's stuffy in here. We have to open up."

Kondratev punched him in the chest and he fell over backwards, his Adam's apple thrust out sharply. Kondratev hurriedly opened up the oxygen valve, then got up, and, stepping over Belov, inspected the fastener. It was all right. Then Kondratev poked Belov under a rib with a finger. Akiko watched him with tear-filled eyes.

"Comrade Belov?" she asked.

"Roast duck," Kondratev said angrily. "And depth sickness to boot."

Belov sighed and sat up. His eyes were bleary, and he squinted at Kondratev and Akiko and asked, "What happened, people?"

"You practically drowned us, glutton," said Kondratev.

He lifted the nose of the submarine toward the vertical and began to ascend. The *Kunashir* must already have arrived at the rendezvous point. It was becoming impossible to breathe in the cabin. Oh, well—it would all soon be over. When the light was on in the cabin, the bathymeter needle looked pink, the numbers white. Six hundred meters, five hundred eighty, five fifty. . . .

"Comrade Captain," said Akiko, "permission to ask a question?"

"Granted."

"Was it just luck that we found *ika* so quickly?"

"It found us. It must have been trailing us for ten kilometers, looking us over. Squids are always like that."

"Kondratev," moaned Belov, "can't we go a little faster?"

"No," said Kondratev. "Be patient."

Why doesn't it do anything to him? thought Belov. *Can he really be made of iron? Or do you get used to it? Good lord, if I could just see the*

*sky. Just so I see the sky, and I'll never go on another deep-water search.
Just so the photos come out. I'm tired. But he's not tired at all. He's sitting
there practically upside down, and it doesn't do anything to him. And for
me, just one look at the way he's sitting is enough to make me sick to my
stomach.*

Three hundred meters.

"Kondratev," Belov said again. "What are you doing tomorrow?"

Kondratev answered, "Han Chol and Valtsev are arriving tomorrow morning with their submarines—in the evening we'll
comb the depression and finish off the rest."

Tomorrow evening Kondratev was going down into that grave
again. And he could say that calmly, with pleasure.

"Akiko-san."

"Yes, Comrade Belov?"

"What are you going to do tomorrow?" he asked in English.

Kondratev glanced at the bathymeter. Two hundred meters.

Akiko sighed. "I don't know," she said.

They fell silent. They remained silent until the minisub had
surfaced.

"Open the hatch," Kondratev said.

The submarine rocked on a small wave. Belov raised his arms,
turned the catch of the hatch fastener, and pushed on the hatch
cover.

The weather had changed. There was no more wind, nor storm
clouds. The stars were small and bright, and a sliver of moon
hung in the sky. Small shining waves lazily swept the ocean.
They splashed and murmured at the hatch turret. Belov scrambled out first. Akiko and Kondratev climbed after him. Belov
said, "Nice. It's nice."

Akiko also said, "Nice."

Kondratev too affirmed that it was nice, and added, after some
thought, "Just wonderful."

"Permission to go swimming, Comrade Captain," said Akiko.

"Swim, please," Kondratev conceded politely, and turned
around.

Akiko stripped down to her swimming suit, laid her clothes on
the edge of the hatch, and stuck a foot in the water. Her red suit
looked almost black, and her arms and legs unnaturally white.
She raised her arms and slipped noiselessly into the water.

"I think I'll go in too," said Belov. He undressed and climbed into the ocean. The water was warm. Belov swam to the stern and said, "It's wonderful. You were right, Kondratev."

Then he remembered the violet tentacle as thick as a telephone pole and he hurriedly scrambled back onto the submarine deck. Going over to the hatch on which Kondratev was sitting, he said, "The water is as warm as soup. You should have a dip."

They sat silently while Akiko splashed in the water. The black spot of her head bobbed against a background of shining waves.

"Tomorrow we'll finish them all off," Kondratev said. "All of them, however many are left. We've got to hurry. The whales will be arriving in a week."

Belov sighed and did not answer.

Akiko swam up and grasped the edge of the hatch. "Comrade Captain, may I go with you again tomorrow?" she asked with desperate audacity.

Kondratev said slowly, "Of course you can."

"Thank you, Comrade Captain."

To the south, over the horizon, the beam of a searchlight rose up, jabbing into the sky. It was the signal from the *Kunashir*.

"Let's go," said Kondratev, getting up. "Come on out, Akiko-san."

He took her by the arm and easily lifted her from the water.

Belov said gloomily, "I'll see how the film came out. If it's bad, I'll come down with you too."

"But no cognac," said Kondratev.

"And no perfume," added Akiko.

"Anyhow, I'll ask Han Chol," said Belov. "Three's a crowd in one of these cabins."

★

★

The Mystery of the Hind Leg

"I didn't like your first book," said Parncalas. "There is nothing in it to stir the imagination of the serious person."

They were sitting in lounge chairs under a faded hot awning on the veranda of Cold Creek Post—Jean Parncalas, biotechnician of the Gibson Reserve, and Evgeny Slavin, correspondent for the European Information Center. On the low table between the lounge chairs stood a sweating five-liter siphon bottle. Cold Creek Post was on the top of a hill, and an excellent view of the hot, blue-green savanna of western Australia opened up from the veranda.

"A book should always rouse the imagination," Parncalas continued. "Otherwise it is not a real book, but merely a rotten textbook. In essence, we could put it thus: the purpose of a book is to arouse the imagination of the reader. True, your first book was intended to fulfill another, no less important function as well, namely to bring to us the viewpoint of a man of your heroic era. I expected a great deal from that book, but alas, it is obvious that in the course of the work you lost that very point of view. You are too impressionable, Evgeny *mon ami!*"

"It's simpler than that, Jean," Evgeny said lazily. "Much simpler, *mon ami.* I had a great horror of appearing before the human race as a sort of Campanella in reverse. But anyhow, you're quite correct. It was a mediocre book."

He leaned over in the lounge chair and filled a tall narrow glass with foaming coconut milk from the siphon bottle. The glass instantly started sweating.

"Yes," said Parncalas, "you had a great horror of being Campanella in reverse. You were in too much of a hurry to change your psychology, Evgeny. You wanted very much to stop being an alien here. And that was wrong. You should have remained an alien a little longer: you could have seen much that we do not notice. And isn't that the most important task of any writer—to notice things that others do not see? That is, rousing the imagination and making people think?"

"Perhaps."

They fell silent. Profound quiet reigned all around, the drowsy quiet of the savanna at noon. Cicadas chirred, vying with one another. A slight breeze rose up, rustling the grass. Piercing sounds arrived from far off—the cries of emus. Evgeny suddenly sat up and craned his neck. "What's that?" he asked.

Past the post, darting through the high grass, rushed a strange machine—a long vertical pole, evidently on wheels, with a sparkling revolving disk on the end. The machine looked extremely ridiculous. Bobbing and swinging, it went off toward the south.

Parncalas raised his head and looked. "Ah," he said. "I forgot to tell you. That's one of the monsters."

"What monsters?"

"No one knows," Parncalas said calmly.

Evgeny jumped up and ran over to the railing. The tall, ridiculous pole was quickly receding, swaying from side to side, and in a minute it had disappeared from view. He turned to Parncalas.

"What do you mean nobody knows?" he asked.

Parncalas drank his coconut milk. "No one knows," he repeated, wiping his mouth. "It's a very amusing story—you'll like it. They first appeared two weeks ago—these poles on one wheel

and the crawling disks. You often see them in the savanna between Cold Creek and Rollins, and the day before yesterday one
pole got as far as the main street of Gibson. My emus trampled
one disk. I saw it—a big scrapheap of bad plastic and the remains
of a radio installation on perfectly disgusting-looking ceramic.
Like a schoolchild's model. We got in touch with the people at
Gibson, but no one there knew anything. And, it became clear,
no one anywhere knows anything."

Parncalas again raised the glass to his lips.

"You're discussing this surprisingly calmly, Jean *mon ami*,"
Evgeny said impatiently. Pictures, were forming in his imagination, one more fantastic than the next.

Parncalas smiled. "Sit down, Evgeny. There is no reason to be
alarmed. The monsters haven't hurt anyone—even the emus and
kangaroos aren't afraid of them—and anyhow, you didn't let me
finish: the comrades in Jakoi are already investigating. They—
Where are you going?"

Evgeny was hastily making ready. Into his pockets he stuffed
dictaphone cartridges, microbook cases, and his tattered note-
books. "Jakoi—that's the Australian cybernetic center, right?" he
said. "They've built some interesting computer there, haven't
they?"

"Yes, the CODD computer," Parncalas said in an offended
tone. He was very disappointed that Slavin was leaving so soon.
It was pleasant to converse with the correspondent—he very
much liked listening.

"Why CODD?"

"Collector of Dispersed Data. A mechanical archaeologist, I've
heard."

Evgeny stopped. "So these monsters could be from there?"

"I already told you—no one knows," Parncalas said crossly.
"No one knows anything. Not in Jakoi, not in Gibson, not in the
whole world. . . . At least stay for supper, Evgeny."

"No, thank you—I'm in a big hurry. Well, *mon cher* Jean, thank
you for the hospitality. We'll see each other again." Evgeny
drained his glass in one gulp, nodded cheerfully, and, jumping
over the railing, ran down the hill to his pterocar.

The scientific settlement of Jakoi stood in the shade of monsterous black acacias with crowns forty or fifty yards in diameter. A

little way off, on the shore of a deep lake with clear, dark blue water, the ruins of some ancient settler's farm gleamed white. The rectangle of the landing pad stood out clearly between the settlement and the ruins. There were no vehicles on the pad, and no people either.

But the pterocar did not need a landing pad, and Evgeny flew around the acacias looking for a place closer to the settlement. A third of a mile from the settlement he suddenly noticed unusual activity. At first it seemed to him that there was a game of rugby on. A heap of intertwined black and white human bodies rolled and heaved in the grass. Up from the heap echoed heated cries. *Wonderful!* thought Evgeny. *Well played!* At that instant the pile broke up, exposing something round, black, and shiny, and one of the players spun like a top off to one side, and fell. He remained lying, contorted, holding his arms to his stomach. *Or no,* thought Evgeny, *it's no game after all.* Another three people darted out from under the acacia branches, throwing off their jackets on the run. Evgeny quickly headed for a landing.

As he jumped out of the pterocar, the man who had been twisted up with pain was already sitting up. Holding his stomach as before, he was shouting loudly, "Watch the hind leg! Hey! Watch the hind leg!"

Evgeny ran past him at a trot. Out of the heap of swarming bodies came shouts in Russian and English:

"Get the legs down! Push the legs to the ground!"

"The antennas! Don't break the antennas!"

"Help, guys! It's digging in!"

"Hold onto it, damn it!"

"Hey, Percy, let go of my head!"

"It's digging in!"

Into Evgeny's head flashed the thought, *They've caught some sort of lizard,* but here he caught sight of the hind leg. It was black, shiny, with sharp notches, like the leg of an enormous beetle, and it was clawing its way over the ground, leaving deep furrows behind it. There were also many other legs there—black, brown, and white, and also fidgeting, jerking, and dragging—but all these were ordinary human legs. Spellbound, Evgeny watched the hind leg for several seconds. Time after time it contracted, digging deep into the earth, and then with effort it straightened out again, and each time the shouting crowd moved another five feet or so.

"Ha!" Evgeny shouted in a blood-curdling voice, and, with both hands, he seized the hind leg by a joint and pulled it toward him.

A distinct crunch rang out. The leg tore off with unexpected ease, and Evgeny fell backward.

"Don't you dare break it!" thundered a wrathful voice. "Get that idiot out of here!"

Evgeny lay there for a while, holding the leg in his embrace, and then he slowly got up.

"A little more! Just a little bit, Joe!" boomed the same voice. "Let go of my arm. . . . Ha! Ha! . . . Now we've got you, my pretty!"

Something gave forth a plaintive ringing sound, and then silence set in. The heap of bodies froze, and only a heavy, intermittent breathing could be heard. Then everyone at once started talking and laughing, getting up, wiping their sweaty faces. A large, motionless black mound remained in the torn-up grass.

Someone said in a disillusioned voice, "The same thing again!"

"A tortoise! A septipede!"

"You've really got yourself dug in, you bad girl!"

"A little more and it would've gotten clean away."

"Yes, it gave us a hard time."

"Where's the hind leg?"

All glances turned to Evgeny. He said boldly, "The hind leg is here. It tore off. I never thought it would come off so easily."

They surrounded him, examining him with curiosity. An enormous half-naked fellow, with a shock of tousled red hair on his head, and with a ruddy orange beard, extended a powerful, scratched hand. "Give it here, will you?"

In the other hand this brawny lad carried a fragment of shiny wire. Evgeny happily handed over the leg. "I'm Evgeny Slavin," he said. "Correspondent for the European Information Center. I flew out because they told me things were interesting here."

The redhead flexed the black toggle lever of a leg several times, with a thoughtful expression. The leg gave a cheep. "I'm Pavel Rudak, deputy director of the CODD project," said the lad. "And these"—he poked the lever in the direction of the others—"these are other servants of the Great CODD. You can meet them later, after they've taken the tortoise away."

"Is it worth the bother?" asked a small curly-headed Australian aborigine. "We already have two just like it. Let it sit here."

"The other two are similar, but not exactly the same, Tappi," said Rudak. "The hind leg on this one has only one joint."

"Is that so?" Tappi grabbed the hind leg from Rudak and flexed it several times too. "Yes, you're right. Too bad it's broken off."

"I didn't know," said Evgeny.

But no one was listening to him any longer. Everyone had gathered around Tappi, and then they moved in a group to the black mound in the grass, and bent over it. Rudak and Evgeny were left by themselves.

"What's this about a septipede?" asked Zhenya.

"It's one of the monsters of the Great CODD," Rudak answered.

"Ah," said Evgeny, disappointed. "So they are your monsters after all."

"It's not so simple, Comrade Slavin, not so simple. I didn't say they were our monsters, I said they were the monsters of the Great CODD." He bent over, felt around in the grass, and picked up several pebbles. "And we go hunting for them. Within the last ten days, all we've done is go hunting. Anyway, it must be said that you've made a most timely appearance, Comrade Correspondent." He began very accurately dropping the pebbles on the unhappy tortoise, which was being dragged back to the settlement. The pebbles banged resonantly against its hard armor.

"Paul Rudak!" shouted one of the draggers. "Our burden is heavy! Where are thy strong arms?"

"O thoughtless ones!" exclaimed Rudak. "My strong arms are carrying the hind leg! Tappi, where did you put it?"

"In the grass! Look in the grass, Paul!"

"Let me carry the hind leg," said Evgeny. "I broke it off, so I should be the one to carry it."

"Go ahead," Rudak conceded cheerfully. "I'll help the others."

In two bounds he caught up to the "thoughtless ones," pushed them aside, crawled under the tortoise, grunted, and lifted it on his back. "Catch me if you can!" he thundered in a strained voice, and he started to run at a gallop toward the settlement.

The thoughtless ones rushed after him, whooping. Evgeny grabbed the hind leg, balanced it across the back of his neck like a yoke, and started jogging after them. The leg was serrated, and fairly heavy.

"I'm taking bets for the hind leg," proclaimed Pavel Rudak from the doorway of the laboratory. "I'll even bet my own hind leg that our correspondent is tormented by thirst!"

Evgeny, who was sitting by the laboratory wall, sighed quietly, and fanned himself with somebody's straw hat. His neck burned. "You win," he moaned.

"Where are the thoughtless servants? How dare they abandon such an honored guest? It's an affront to the entire European Information Center!"

"Your thoughtless servants are worshiping the hind leg in the building across the way," answered Evgeny, getting up. "They asked me to wait here for a little while. They said you would be back in a minute. That was just half an hour ago."

"Disgraceful!" Rudak said with some embarrassment. "Let's go, Comrade Slavin. I'll try to make amends for their crimes. I'll slake your thirst and throw open unto you the hatches of the coolers."

"Get to it!"

Rudak took him by the arm and brought him at an angle across the street, to a tidy white cottage. It was clean and cool there. Rudak sat him down at the table, placed in front of him a glass, a decanter, and a bucket of ice, and set about playing host. "There's no delivery line here," he boomed. "We do the cooking ourselves. In cyberkitchens."

"A UKM-207?" asked Evgeny.

"No, I have an American system."

Evgeny did not eat. He drank and watched Rudak eating. Rudak cleaned his plate, emptied his jug, and admonished, "You don't have to look at me that way. That's yesterday's supper, today's breakfast, and today's dinner."

Evgeny stealthily emptied the very last out of the jugs and thought, *And today's supper.*

"You're in luck, correspondent," Rudak continued. "Things really are interesting around here nowadays. They will be even more interesting tomorrow, when Professor Lomba, the director of the CODD project, gets back."

"I've seen Professor Lomba," said Evgeny.

Rudak stopped eating and quickly asked, "When?"

"Early this morning, in Gibson. He was consulting an acquaintance of mine. Only I didn't know he was the director of the CODD project."

Rudak lowered his eyes and once again set to eating. "What did you think of him?" he inquired after a moment.

"How should I put it . . .?" said Evgeny. "He seemed gloomy more than anything."

"Mmm, yes," drawled Rudak. He pushed the plate away. "This evening will be very interesting." He sighed. "Well, Comrade Slavin, please ask your questions."

Evgeny hurriedly loaded the dictaphone. "First of all," he said, "what is the Great CODD?"

"One moment." Rudak leaned against the back of his armchair and put his hands behind his head. "First I must ask you something. What sort of education have you had?"

"I graduated from the medical institute, the institute of journalism, and the training courses for a spaceflight surgeon."

"And all that was a century and a half ago," Rudak elaborated. "And nothing else?"

"I've traveled over the whole Planet as a correspondent, an old newshound. My field of scientific interest is comparative linguistics."

"So," said Rudak. "And you haven't heard anything about Komatsuwara's seven principles?"

"Nothing."

"Nor, of course, about the algebra of information fields?"

"No."

"Nor about the fundamental theorem of information dissipation?"

Evgeny kept silent. Rudak thought a moment and said, "All right. The court understands everything. We will do all we can. Just listen very carefully, and if I get carried away, grab me by the hind leg."

This is what Evgeny understood: The Collector of Dispersed Data was intended primarily for the collection of dispersed data. This, to be sure, was clear enough from the name. "Dispersed data" meant traces of all events and phenomena dispersed in space and time. Komatsuwara's first principle (the only one he could understand) stated that nothing in nature, and even more in society, ever disappeared without a trace—everything left evidence. The overwhelming majority of these traces were to be found in the form of extremely dispersed data. In the last analysis, they had the form of energy of one sort or another, and the collection problem was much complicated by the fact that over millions of years the original forms underwent repeated changes. In other words, the traces were laid one upon another, mixed up, and often were erased by traces of subsequent events and phenomena. It was theoretically possible to find and restore any trace—the trace left by the collision of a quantum of light with a molecule in the hide of a brontosaurus, or the trace of a brontosaurus tooth on a tree fern. The Great CODD had been built for the searching out, the sorting, and the comparing of these traces, and for their transformation into the original forms of data—for instance, into images.

Evgeny picked up only an extremely murky impression of how the Great CODD worked. First he imagined billions upon billions of cybernetic protozoan microinformants, which would wander in clouds throughout the whole world, climbing to the very stars, collecting dispersed traces of the distant past and dragging them to some immense mechanical memory storehouse. Then his imagination sketched for him a web of wires embracing the whole Planet, stretching between gigantic towers which were scattered in hundreds over islands and continents from pole to pole. In short, he didn't understand a thing, but did not ask again: he decided that sometime he would listen to the dictaphone tape a few times at leisure, with the corresponding books before his eyes, and then he would understand it all. But then, when Rudak began to discuss the results of his work, Evgeny forgot even about the monsters.

"We have managed to get some very interesting pictures and even entire episodes," Rudak said. "Of course, the overwhelming majority of materials are waste—hundreds and thousands of frames superimposed one upon another, and the data filter simply breaks down when it attempts to separate them. But still we've been able to see something. We have witnessed the flash of a supernova near the sun one hundred million years ago. We have seen the struggles of dinosaurs and episodes of the Battle of Poitiers, the starships of alien visitors to Earth, and something else strange, incomprehensible, to which we so far have nothing corresponding or even analogous."

"Would it be possible to have a look?" Evgeny asked with a quiver.

"Of course. But let's return to this afternoon's topic."

The Great CODD was not only a collector of dispersed data. It was an unusually complicated and highly independent logical-analytical computer. Its levels held, besides billions of memory cells and logic elements, besides every possible information transformer and filter, its own workships, which it controlled itself. It could even build onto itself, creating new elements and models, and developing its own data. This opened up wide possibilities for its use beyond its primary purpose. At present, for example, it was carrying out all calculations for the Australian economic sphere, was being used to solve many problems in general cybernetics, and was performing functions of precise diagnostics, having for this purpose branches in all the major cities of the Planet and on some off-planet bases. Besides all this, the Great CODD undertook "fortune telling."

The Congolese Auguste Lomba, the present director for the CODD project and one-time student of Komatsuwara, had programmed several problems related to the prediction of the behavior of a living organism. CODD had coped with problems of invertebrate behavior determination fairly easily, and two years before, Lomba had programmed and fed to the machine a problem of extraordinary complexity.

"The problem received the title of 'Buridan's sheep.' The biological code was taken from a young merino sheep, by the Casparo-Karpov method, at a moment when the sheep was between two feeding troughs full of mixed fodder. This code, along with additional data about sheep in general, was fed into CODD. The machine was required: a) to predict which trough the merino would choose, and b) to give the psychophysiological basis for this choice."

"But what about free will?" Evgeny asked.

"That's exactly what we want to find out about," answered Rudak. "Perhaps it just doesn't exist." He was silent for a bit. "In the control experiment the sheep chose the right trough. Actually, the problem came down to the question of why. For two years the machine just thought. Then it began building models. Effector machines often solve problems through models. Like the time CODD solved a problem about earthworms—it built such a superb model that we swiped CODD's idea and started building subterrenes. Amazing devices."

Rudak fell into thought. Evgeny started fidgeting impatiently in his chair.

"Are you uncomfortable?" inquired Rudak.

"Not at all, it's just that it was quite fascinating."

"Ah, you found it fascinating too? Now then, how can I put it without breaking the spell?"

He's covering something up, Evgeny thought. He said, "I must have seen one of those models you're talking about. A sort of pole with a mirror. Only it could hardly be a model of a sheep. Not even one of Buridan's."

"That's the point," Rudak said with a sigh. "No one believes that it's a model of a sheep. Papa Lomba, for instance, wouldn't believe it. He gathered all the materials on the programming and went off to the center to verify them." Rudak sighed again. "He's due back this evening."

"And what exactly is the problem?" asked Evgeny.

"The problem is that CODD is making poles on wheels and seven-legged beetles. And sometimes those sort of flat disks that don't have legs, don't have arms, but do have gyroscopes. And no one can see what that has to do with sheep."

"And actually," Evgeny said pensively, "why should a sheep have that many legs?"

Rudak looked at him suspiciously. "Precisely—why?" he said with unnatural enthusiasm.

They looked at each other silently for some time. *He's covering something up. Oh, that beard is a slippery one!* Evgeny thought.

Gracefully, and without the help of his arms, Rudak stood up using only one leg. "And now let's go, Comrade Slavin, and I'll introduce you to the manager of the film library."

"One more question," Evgeny said while reloading the dictaphone. "Where is your Great CODD located?"

"You're sitting on it. It's underground, twenty-eight levels, six hectares. The brain, the workshops, the energy generators, everything. And now stand up and let's go."

CODD's film library was at the other end of the settlement, in a low studio. On the roof of the building gleamed the gridded panels of a stereocinerama projector. Immediately beyond the studio began the savanna.

The studio smelled of ozone and sour milk. The manager of the film library sat at a table and studied through a binocular microscope a splendid photo of the hind-leg joint. The librarian was a pretty Tahitian woman of about twenty-five.

"Hello, girl," Rudak rumbled tenderly.

The librarian tore herself away from the microscope, and a smile blossomed. "Hello, Paul," she said.

"This is Comrade Slavin, correspondent for the European Center," said Rudak. "Treat him with respect. Show him frames two-sixty-seven, three-fifteen, and seven-five-one-two."

"If it wouldn't be too much trouble, of course," Evgeny put in gallantly.

The librarian looked very much like Sheila. "With pleasure," said the librarian. "But is Comrade Slavin mentally prepared?"

"Uh . . . how about it, Comrade Slavin, are you prepared?"

"Completely," Evgeny answered with certainty.

"Then I'll leave you," said Rudak. "The monsters await me." He turned the doorknob and left. They could hear him shouting to the whole settlement, "Akitada! Did the equipment come?" The answer was not audible.

The librarian sighed and said, "Take a folding chair, Comrade Slavin, and let's go."

Evgeny went out, and sat down by the studio wall. The librarian efficiently estimated the height of the sun, calculated something, her lips moving and returned to the studio. "Frame two-sixty-seven," she announced through the open window.

The sunlight disappeared. Evgeny saw a dark-violet night sky with bright, unfamiliar stars. Low strips of clouds stretched over the horizon, and the dark silhouettes of strange trees, something like palms and something like giant sprouts of cauliflower, slowly appeared. Reflections of the stars trembled in black water. Then, over the clouds, a white patch began to glow. It burned brighter and brighter; weird shadows crept along the black oily surface, and suddenly from beyond the horizon a blinding white, pulsating luminary exploded and rushed in jerks across the sky, extinguishing the stars. A gray mist began rushing between the trunks of the strange trees, irridescent sparks flashed, and then everything disappeared. Once again the sunlit savanna lay in front of Evgeny.

"After that, there's solid static," said the librarian.

"What was it?" asked Evgeny. He expected something big.

"The rising of a supernova. More than a hundred million years ago. It gave rise to the dinosaurs. Frame three-fifteen coming up. This is our pride and joy. Fifty million years later."

Once again the savanna disappeared. Evgeny saw a gray water-covered plain. Everywhere the pulpy stalks of some sort of vegetation stuck up out of the water. A long gray animal shuffled over the plain, knee-deep in water. Evgeny could not at first make out where the animal's head was. A wet cylindrical-shaped trunk plastered with green grass tapered evenly at both ends and merged into a long flexible neck and tail. Then Evgeny examined the tiny flat head with its lipless toadlike mouth. There was something of the chicken about the habits of the monster—with every step it ducked its head into the water, and immediately jerked it up again, quickly grinding some sort of greenery in its teeth.

"Diplodocus," said the librarian. "Twenty-four meters long."

Then Evgeny caught sight of another monster. It was crawling alongside the first one with a snakelike motion, leaving a stripe of muddied water behind it. At one point it barely turned aside from the pillar-shaped feet of the diplodocus, and for a minute Evgeny saw an enormous, pale, tooth-filled mouth. *Something's going to happen*, he thought. It was much more interesting than the flash of a supernova. The diplodocus, evidently, had no suspicion of the presence of its toothy companion, or else it simply did not consider it worthy of any attention. But the other beast, maneuvering adroitly under the diplodocus's legs, approached closer to its head, then jumped out of the water in a jerk, instantly bit off the head, and dived.

Evgeny closed his mouth, his teeth chattering. The picture was unusually bright and distinct. The diplodocus stopped for a second, raised its decapitated neck high and . . . walked on, just as evenly dipping the bleeding stump into the turbid water. Only after several paces did its front legs buckle. The hind legs continued walking, and the enormous tail waved unconcernedly from side to side. The neck shot upward to the sky one last time, and then helplessly flopped down into the water. The front part of the body began to collapse on its side, but the hind part continued to move forward. Then the hind legs collapsed too, and instantly dozens of snarling toothy mouths surfaced in the turbid foaming water and darted forward.

"Wow!" said Evgeny, wiping away sweat. "What a sight!"

"A typical scene of predatory dinosaurs hunting a large diplodocus," the librarian said in a businesslike tone. "They ate each other all the time. Almost all the data which we receive from that epoch is uninterrupted predation. But how did you like the quality of the image, Comrade Slavin?"

"Excellent quality," said Evgeny. "Except for some reason it's always blinking."

Above the tops of the acacias, a pot-bellied six-engined craft thundered by. The librarian ran out of the studio. "The equipment!" she shouted. "Let's go, Comrade Slavin—that's the equipment coming in."

"But please!" yelped Evgeny. "What about the rest? You promised to show me another one!"

"You don't want to see it, believe me," the librarian said with conviction. She hurriedly folded up the chair. "I don't know what got into Paul's head. Number seven-five-one-two is the slaughter in Constantinople. Fifteenth century. The image quality is excellent, but it's such an unpleasant scene. Really, Comrade Slavin, you don't want to see it. Let's go watch Paul catch the monsters instead."

The enormous six-rotored helicopter had landed near the place where Evgeny had left his pterocar, and the unloading of equipment was in full swing. Platforms on high wheels, loaded with dull yellow boxes, rolled out of the opened holds. They took the boxes to the foot of one of the acacias, where in the space between two mighty roots the indefatigable Rudak supervised their assembly. His stentorian voice rang out far across the evening savanna.

The film librarian excused herself and ran off somewhere. Evgeny began walking in uncertain circles around Rudak. Curiosity was getting the better of him. The platforms on high wheels rolled up, unloaded, and departed, and the "servants of CODD" —guys and girls—put the yellow boxes in place and screwed them together, and soon the contours of an enormous angular construction had taken form under the acacia. Rudak rushed off somewhere into its bowels, humming, whistling, and emitting booming shouts. It was noisy and cheerful.

"Strong and Joy, get busy with the intravisors!"

"Dum-didi-dum-didi-dum-dum! Whoever's there, hand me the contact thingie."

"The feeders! Where did the damn feeders get to?"

"Ooh-la-la! Farther to the right! That's good."

"Frost, get me out of this mess!"

Someone innocently poked Evgeny in the side, and he was asked to move out of the way. At last the enormous helicopter was unloaded, and it began to roar, stirring up a wind and shreds of grass, and moved off from under the acacia over to the landing pad. Rudak crawled out from under the assembly on hands and knees, got up, brushed his hands, and said, "Well, we can get started. Stations, everyone." He jumped up on the platform where a small control panel was set up. The platform creaked. "Pray for us, Great CODD," yelled Rudak.

"Stanislav hasn't come back yet!" someone shouted.

"That spells trouble!" Rudak said, and climbed down from the platform.

"Does Professor Lomba know about all this?" a slim maiden with a boyish hair cut asked timidly.

"Professor Lomba will find out," Rudak said grandly. "But just where is Stanislav?"

The ground in the clearing in front of the acacias bulged and cracked. Evgeny jumped a full yard. It seemed to him that the pale, tooth-filled maw of a dinosaur was poking up from the grass.

"At last!" said Rudak. "I had already started worrying—his oxygen ran out a minute ago. Or two minutes, actually."

A ringed metallic body half a yard thick drew itself out of the ground slowly and clumsily, like a giant earthworm. It kept crawling and crawling, and it was still unclear how many rings might yet be hidden underground, when its front part started turning rapidly, screwed itself off, and fell into the grass. A damp, scarlet face with a wide-gaping mouth stuck out of the black aperture.

"Aha!" Rudak roared. "Took you long enough, Stanislav!"

The face hung over the edge, spat, and declared in a strong voice, "It's got a whole damn arsenal down there. Entire armadas of crawling disks. Get me out of this thing."

The ringed worm kept crawling and crawling out of the ground, and rays of the red setting sun played on its metal sides.

"Let's get going," Rudak declared, and again climbed onto the platform. He smoothed his beard out on the left and on the right, made faces at the girls who had crowded below, and with a pianist's gesture lay his hands on the board. The board blazed with indicator lights.

Then everything in the clearing went quiet. Evgeny, picking up his movie camera, noted worriedly that several people had scrambled into an acacia and were sitting on the branches, while the girls crowded more closely toward the platform. Just in case, Evgeny moved closer himself.

"Strong and Joy, get ready!" Rudak thundered.

"Ready!" two voices shouted.

"I'll start warbling on the main frequency. You sing on the flanks. And let's have a lot of noise."

Evgeny expected everyone to begin singing and drumming, but it got even quieter. A minute went by.

"Turn up the voltage," Rudak ordered softly.

Another minute went by. The sun set, and the brighter stars appeared in the sky. Somewhere an emu cried sleepily. A girl standing next to Evgeny sighed heavily. Suddenly there was movement up above, on the acacia branch, and someone's voice, trembling with excitement, shouted, "There they are! There, in the clearing! You're looking in the wrong direction!"

Evgeny did not understand where he ought to look, nor did he know who "they" might be, or what one might expect of them. He picked up the movie camera and moved back a little more, crowding the girls toward the platform, and suddenly he saw them. At first he thought it was an illusion, that it was simply spots swimming before his tired eyes. The black starlit savanna began to stir. Indistinct gray shadows rose up on it, unspeaking and ominous; the grass rustled, something squeaked, and he could hear a solid tapping, jingling, crackling. In an instant the quiet was filled with deep indistinct rustlings.

"Light!" bellowed Rudak. "The enemy cometh!"

A joyful howl rang out from the acacia. Dry leaves and twigs rained down. In the same instant a blinding light flashed over the clearing.

Over the savanna marched the army of the Great CODD. Marched to surrender. Evgeny had never seen such a parade of mechanical monsters in his life. Obviously the servants of the Great CODD were seeing them for the first time too. Homeric laughter shook the acacia. The designers, those experienced warriors in the cause of mechanical perfection, were enraged. They toppled from the branch in bunches, and dashed into the clearing.

"No, look. You just look!"

"The seventeenth century! Watt's linkage!"

"Where's Robinson? Robinson, were you the one who figured that CODD was smarter than you?"

"Let's hear it for Robinson! Yea, Robinson!"

"Guys, get a load of these wheels! They won't even make it all the way to us!"

"Guys! Guys! Look! A steam engine!"

"Author! Author!"

Horrible scarecrows moved into the clearing. Lopsided steam-tricycles. Dishlike rattling contrivances that sparked and gave off a burning smell. The familiar tortoises, furiously kicking their famous single hind legs. Spider-shaped mechanisms on extremely long wire legs on which, now and then, they lowered themselves to the ground. In back, mournfully wobbling, came the poles on wheels with the wilted mirrors on the tips. All these dragged themselves onward, limping, pushing, knocking, breaking down on the way, and emitting steam and sparks. Evgeny aimed the movie camera like a zombie.

"I'm not a servant any longer!" yelled someone in the acacia.
"Me neither!"

"Look at those hind legs!"

The front ranks of mechanical monsters reached the clearing
and stopped. The ones in back piled into them and they all
collapsed into a heap, tangling up, their outlandish articulations
spread wide. Above, the poles on wheels toppled over with a
dull thud, breaking in two. One wheel, its springs ringing,
rolled up to the platform, circled around, and fell down at
Evgeny's feet. Then Evgeny looked at Rudak. Rudak was standing on the platform, his hands resting against his sides. His
beard was waving.

"There we are, guys," he said. "I give all this to you for pillage
and looting. Now we'll find out how and why they tick—probably."

The conquerers threw themselves upon the defeated army.

"You can't really mean the Great CODD built all this to study
the behavior of Buridan's sheep, can you?" Evgeny asked in horror.

"And why not?" said Rudak. "It could very well be. It probably
is." He winked with unusual slyness. "Anyhow, it's certainly
clear that something is out of kilter here."

Two strapping designers dragged a small metal beetle by its
rear leg. Just opposite the platform the leg broke off, and the
designers fell into the grass.

"Monsters," muttered Rudak.

"I already told you it wasn't fastened on well," said Evgeny.

A sharp elderly voice roared through the merry noise: "Just
what is going on here?"

Silence set in instantly. "Oh, boy," Rudak said in a whisper,
and climbed down from the platform.

It seemed to Evgeny that Rudak had suddenly shriveled.

An old gray-haired black in a white lab coat approached the
platform, limping. Evgeny recognized him—it was Professor
Lomba. "Where is my Paul?" he asked in an ominously affection-
ate voice. "Children, who can tell me where my deputy is?"

Rudak remained silent. Lomba walked straight toward him.
Rudak stepped backward, knocked his back against the platform,
and stopped.

"So, Paul my dear boy, just what's going on here?" Lomba asked, looming close.

Rudak answered sheepishly, "We seized control from CODD —and rounded up all the monsters into one pile."

"The monsters, eh?" Lomba said tersely. "An important problem! Where does the seventh leg come from? An important problem, my children! A very important problem!"

Suddenly he grabbed Rudak by the beard and dragged him through the crowd, which opened in his path, to the middle of the clearing. "Look at him, children!" he shouted ceremoniously. "We are astounded! We rack our brains! We fall into despair! We imagine that CODD has outsmarted us!" With each "we" he pulled Rudak's beard, as if ringing a bell. Rudak's head swung submissively.

"What happened, teacher?" a girl asked timidly. From her face it was obvious that she felt very sorry for Rudak.

"What happened, my dear little girl?" Lomba at last let go of Rudak. "Old Lomba goes to the center. He drags the best specialists away from their work. And what does he find out? Oh, the shame! What does he find out, you redheaded villain?" He again grabbed Rudak by the beard, and Evgeny hurriedly aimed his camera. "They're laughing at old Lomba! Old Lomba has become the laughingstock of every last cyberneticist! They're already telling jokes about old Lomba!" He let go of the beard and stuck a bony fist in Rudak's broad chest. "I'll get you! How many legs does an ordinary Australian merino sheep have? Or perhaps you've forgotten?"

Evgeny suddenly noticed that upon these words a few young men started moving back with the clear intention of losing themselves in the crowd.

"Don't let the programmers get away," Lomba ordered without turning his head.

There was a noise in the crowd, and the young men were pushed into the center of the circle.

"What do these intellectual pirates do?" inquired Lomba, turning sharply towards them. "They indicate in the program that a sheep has seven legs."

The crowd began to grow noisy.

"They deprive the sheep of a cerebellum."

Laughter—approving, as it seemed to Evgeny—spread through the crowd.

"Poor, nice, well-meaning CODD!" Lomba raised his arms to the heavens. "It piles absurdity upon absurdity! Could it suppose that its red-bearded hooligan of a master would give it a problem about a five-sided triangle?"

Rudak muttered miserably, "I won't do it again. Honest I won't."

The crowd, laughing, thrashed the programmers on their resonant backs.

Evgeny spent the night at Rudak's. Rudak bedded him down in the study, then went back to the acacias, brushing his beard carefully. An enormous orange moon, gridded with the gray squares of D-spaceports, looked into the open window. Evgeny looked at it and laughed happily, going over the events of the day in his mind.

He very much liked days like this, ones that did not go by for nothing—days when he had managed to meet new, good or merry or simply nice people. People like thoughtful Parncalas, or magnificent Rudak, or Lomba the Thunderer. *I'll have to write about this,* he thought. *Absolutely! About how intelligent young men, at their own risk, inserted a notoriously nonsensical program into an unusually complicated and capable machine, to see how the machine would react. And how it reacted, carefully trying to create a consistent model of a sheep with seven legs and no cerebellum. And how an army of these monster-models marched over the warm black savanna in order to surrender to a red-bearded intellectual pirate. And how the intellectual pirate got pulled by the beard—not for the first time nor, probably, for the last. Because he's very interested in problems involving five-sided triangles and square spheres . . . which are detrimental to the dignity of an honest, well-intentioned computer. It could come out all right—a story about intellectual hooliganism.*

Evgeny fell asleep and woke up at dawn. Dishes were quietly crashing in the dining room, and a discussion in low tones was under way:

"Now everything's going smooth as silk—Papa Lomba has calmed down and gotten interested."

"As well he should! Such neat data on the theory of machine error!"

"But still, guys, CODD turned out to be fairly simpleminded. I expected more inventiveness."

Someone suddenly laughed and said, "A seven-legged sheep without the least sign of an organ of balance! Poor CODD!"

"Quiet—you'll wake the correspondent!"

After a long pause, when Evgeny had already begun to drowse, someone suddenly said with regret, "It's a shame that it's all over already. It was interesting! O seven-legged sheep! We've seen the last of thy mystery and it's a crying shame."

Candles Before the Control Board

At midnight it started to rain. The highway got slick and Zvantsev reduced speed. It was unusually dark and bleak—the glow of city lights had disappeared behind the black hills—and it seemed to Zvantsev as if his car were going through a desert. The white beam of the headlights danced ahead on the rough wet concrete. There were no cars going the other way. Zvantsev had seen the last one before he turned onto the highway leading to the Institute. Half a mile before the gate was a housing development, and Zvantsev saw that despite the late hour almost all the windows were lit up, and the veranda of a large cafe by the road was full of people. It seemed to Zvantsev that they were keeping quiet, waiting for something.

Akiko looked back. "They're all watching us," she said.

Zvantsev did not answer.

"They must think we're doctors."

"Probably," said Zvantsev.

It was the last village with lights. Beyond the gate began damp darkness.

"There should be an appliance factory somewhere around here," said Zvantsev. "Did you notice it?"

"No, sir."

"You never notice anything."

"You're the one driving, sir. If I were driving I would notice everything."

"Somehow I doubt that," said Zvantsev. He braked sharply, and the car skidded. It slipped sideways across the screeching concrete. The headlights illuminated a signpost. The sign had no light, and it looked faded: NOVOSIBIRSK INSTITUTE OF BIOLOGICAL CODING—21 KM. A warped plywood board with a clumsily written notice was nailed under the sign: ATTENTION! TURN ON ALL NEUTRALIZERS. REDUCE SPEED. ROADBLOCK AHEAD. And the same thing in French and English. The letters were large, with black blotches.

"Uh-huh," muttered Zvantsev. He bent under the wheel and turned on the neutralizers.

"What kind of roadblock?" asked Akiko.

"I don't know what kind," said Zvantsev, "but it's clear you should have stayed in town."

"No," said Akiko.

When the car had started moving again, she asked cautiously, "Do you think they'll let us through, sir?"

"I don't think they'll let *you* through."

"Then I'll wait," Akiko said calmly.

The car glided slowly and noiselessly over the highway. Zvantsev, still looking forward, said, "Still, I wish they would let you through."

"So do I," said Akiko. "I want very much to say good-by to him. . . ."

Zvantsev silently watched the road.

"We've rarely seen each other lately," Akiko continued. "But I love him very much. I don't know anyone else like him. I never loved even my father the way I love him. I even cried. . . ."

Yes, she cried, thought Zvantsev. *The ocean was blue-black, the sky was dark blue, and his face was blue and swollen when Kondratev and I led him carefully toward the convertiplane. The scorching coral sand*

*crunched underfoot, and it was hard for him to walk, and he almost hung
in our arms, but he wouldn't let us carry him. His eyes were closed, and
he mumbled guiltily, "Gokuro-sama, gokuro-sama. . . ." The oceanog-
raphers went behind and to one side, but Akiko walked right next to
Sergei, holding out the shabby white cap famous over the whole ocean with
both her hands, like a tray, and crying bitterly. That was the first and
most serious attack of the disease—six years ago on a nameless islet fifteen
nautical miles to the west of Octopus Reef.*

". . . I've known him for twenty years. Since I was a child. I
very much wish to say good-by to him."

The gridded arch of a microweather installation swam up out
of the damp darkness and passed overhead. There were no lights
at the weather station. *The installation's not working,* Zvantsev
thought. *That's why we're getting this crap from the sky.* He looked
sidelong at Akiko. She was sitting with her legs drawn up on the
seat, looking straight ahead. Lights from the dashboard dials fell
on her face.

"What's going on here?" said Zvantsev. "Some sort of quiet
zone?"

"I don't know," said Akiko. She turned, trying to make herself
more comfortable, poked her knee against Zvantsev's side, and
suddenly froze, staring at him with eyes shimmering in the semi-
darkness.

"What's the matter?" he asked.

"Perhaps he is already. . . ."

"Nonsense," said Zvantsev.

"And everyone has gone to the Institute. . . ."

"Nonsense," Zvantsev said decisively. "Rubbish."

An uneven red light burned far ahead. It was weak and flickering, like a small star on a turbulent night. Just in case, Zvantsev
again reduced speed. Now the car was moving very slowly, and
they could hear the patter of rain. Three figures in shiny wet rain
capes appeared in the headlight beam, standing in the middle of
the highway. In front of them, a substantial-sized log lay across
the road. The one standing on the right was holding a large
smoking torch overhead, and slowly waving it from side to side.
Zvantsev moved the car up a little closer and stopped. *So here's the
roadblock,* he thought. The man with the torch shouted something
indistinct into the patter of the rain, and all three started quickly

toward the car, moving clumsily in their enormous wet rain capes. The man with the torch once again shouted something, contorting his mouth angrily. Zvantsev turned off the headlights and opened the door. "The engine!" shouted the man. He came up close. "Turn off the engine, for God's sake!"

Zvantsev turned off the engine and got out onto the highway, into the drizzle. "I'm Zvantsev, the oceanographer," he said. "I'm on my way to see Academician Okada."

"Put out the dome light in the car!" said the man. "And quickly, please!"

Zvantsev turned, but the light in the passenger compartment was already out.

"Who's that with you?" the man with the torch asked.

"My colleague," Zvantsev answered shortly. "Oceanographer Kondrateva."

The three figures in the rain capes remained silent.

"Can we go on?"

"I'm Mikhailov, technician," said the man with the torch. "I was sent to meet you and tell you that it's impossible to see Academician Okada."

"I'll speak about that with Professor Casparo," said Zvantsev. "Take me to him."

"Professor Casparo is very busy. We would not like him to be disturbed."

Zvantsev would have liked to ask who "we" were, but he restrained himself, because Mikhailov had the vague monotonous voice of a man who is dead tired.

"I have news of the highest importance for the Academician," said Zvantsev. "Take me to Casparo."

The three remained silent, and the uneven red light played over their faces. The faces were wet, pinched.

"Well?" Zvantsev said impatiently. Suddenly he realized that Mikhailov was asleep. The hand with the torch trembled and dipped lower and lower. Mikhailov's eyes were closed.

"Tolya," one of his companions said quietly, poking him in the shoulder.

Mikhailov came to himself, waved the torch, and fixed his swollen eyes on Zvantsev. "What?" he asked hoarsely. "Ah, you want to see the Academician. It's impossible to see Academician

Okada. The whole area of the Institute is closed. Please, go away."

"I have news of the highest importance for Academician Okada," Zvantsev repeated patiently. "I am Oceanographer Zvantsev, and in the car is Oceanographer Kondrateva. We're bringing important news."

"I'm Technician Mikhailov," the man with the torch said again. "It's impossible to see Okada now. He will be dead in the next six hours or so, and we may not make it." His lips were barely moving. "Professor Casparo is very busy and has requested not to be disturbed. Please, go away."

He suddenly turned to his companions. "Give me another two tablets," he said despairingly.

Zvantsev stood in the rain and thought about what else he could say to this man who was falling asleep on his feet. Mikhailov stood sideways to him and threw back his head and swallowed something. Then Mikhailov said, "Thanks, guys, I'm dead on my feet. It's still raining here, and cool, and back there we're just falling off our feet, one after another, getting up again, and collapsing again. . . . Then we carry them off. . . ." He was still speaking indistinctly.

"Oh, well. It's the last night."

"Yes, and the ninth one," said Mikhailov.

"The tenth."

"Is it really the tenth? My head is like mush." Mikhailov turned to Zvantsev. "Excuse me, comrade . . ."

"Zvantsev, oceanographer," Zvantsev said for the third time. "Comrade Mikhailov, you simply have to let us through. We've just flown in from the Philippines. We're bringing information to the Academician, very important scientific information. He has been waiting for it all his life. You see, I've known him thirty years. I can tell better than you whether he should die without hearing this. It's extremely important information."

Akiko got out of the car and stood beside him. The technician was silent, shivering with cold underneath his rain cape. "Well, all right," he said at last. "Only there are too many of you." That was how he said it: "too many." "Only one of you should go."

"Very well," said Zvantsev.

"But if you ask me it won't do any good," Mikhailov said.

"Casparo won't let you see the Academician. The Academician is in isolation. You could ruin the whole experiment if you break the isolation, and then. . . ."

"I will speak with Casparo myself," Zvantsev interrupted. "Take me to him."

"All right," said the technician. "Let's go."

Zvantsev looked back at Akiko. There were many large and small drops on her face. She said, "Go on, sir." Then she turned to the men in the rain capes. "Somebody give him a rain cape, and get in the car yourself. Park the car crosswise across the road."

They gave Zvantsev a rain cape. Akiko wanted to go back to the car and turn it around, but Mikhailov said that the engine should not be turned on. He got up and lit the way with his awkward smoking torch, while they shoved the car around and positioned it across the road manually. Then the full complement of the roadblock crew got into the passenger compartment. Zvantsev peered inside. Akiko had sat down again, curling up, in the front seat. Mikhailov's companions were already asleep, leaning their heads on one another.

"Tell him . . ." said Akiko.

"Yes, of course."

"Tell him we'll be waiting."

"Right," said Zvantsev. "I'll tell him."

"Well, go."

"Sayonara, Aki-tyan."

"Go on. . . ."

Zvantsev carefully closed the door and went up to the technician. "Let's go."

"Let's go," the technician responded in a quite new, very brisk voice. "We'll walk fast—we've got to cover seven kilometers."

They started off, taking broad steps over the rough wet concrete.

"What are you doing out there?" asked the technician.

" 'Out there'?"

"Well, out there . . . in the outside world. We haven't heard anything in two weeks. What's going on in the Council? How is the Big Shaft project coming?"

"There are a lot of volunteers," said Zvantsev. "But not

enough annihilators. Not enough cooling units. The Council is planning on transferring thirty percent of energy to the project. Practically all the specialists on deep penetration have been called back from Venus."

"A good move," said the technician. "There's nothing for them to do on Venus now. Who did they choose to head up the project?"

"I haven't the vaguest idea," Zvantsev said angrily.

"Not Sterner?"

"I don't know."

They were silent for a bit.

"Real junk, right?" said the technician.

"What?"

"These torches are real junk, right? What crap! Can you smell how it stinks?"

Zvantsev sniffed and stepped two paces to the side. "Yes," he said. The torch reeked of oil. "Why are you using them?" he asked.

"It was Casparo's order. No electrical appliances, no electric lights. We're trying to keep interference down to a minimum. Do you smoke, by the way?"

"Yes."

The technician stopped. "Give me your lighter," he said. "And your radiophone. You do have a radiophone?"

"I do."

"Give them to me." Mikhailov took the lighter and radiophone, removed their batteries, and threw these into a ditch. "I'm sorry, but it's necessary. For twenty kilometers around not one electrical appliance is turned on."

"So that's what's going on," said Zvantsev.

"Yes. We've plundered all the apiaries around Novosibirsk to make beeswax candles. Have you heard about those?"

"No."

They again started walking quickly in the steady rain.

"The candles are junk too, but at least they're better than torches. Or woodsplints—have you heard about those?"

"No," said Zvantsev.

"There's an old song, 'Light My Fire.' I had always thought the metaphor involved some sort of generator."

"Now I understand why it's raining," Zvantsev said after a silence. "That is, I understand why the microweather installations are shut down."

"No, no," said the technician. "The microweather stations are one thing, but the rain is being driven to us specially from Wind Ridge. There's a continental installation there."

"What's it for?" Zvantsev asked.

"To shield us from direct solar illumination."

"What about discharges from the clouds?"

"The clouds arrive electrically neutral—they are discharged along the way. And in general, the experiment has turned out to be on a much grander scale than we had thought at first. We've got all the biocoding specialists gathered here. From the whole world. Five hundred people. And that's still too few. And the whole Northern Ural region is working for us."

"And so far everything's going all right?" Zvantsev asked.

The technician was silent.

"Can you hear me?" Zvantsev asked.

"I can't give you an answer," Mikhailov said reluctantly. "We hope everything is going as it should. The principle has been verified, but this is the first experiment with a human being. One hundred twenty trillion megabits of information, and a mistake in any one bit can distort a good deal."

Mikhailov fell silent, and they walked a long time without saying a word. Zvantsev did not notice at first that they were walking through a village. The village was empty. The dull walls of the cottages shone weakly, and the windows were dark. Here and there, open garage doors showed black behind lacy wet hedges.

The technician forgot about Zvantsev. *Another six hours and it will be all over,* he thought. *I'll go home and collapse into bed. The Great Experiment will be over. The great Okada will die and become immortal. Oh, how beautiful! But until the time has come, no one will even know whether the experiment was a success. Not even Casparo himself. The great Casparo, the great Okada, the Great Experiment! The Great Encoding.* Mikhailov shook his head—the familiar heaviness was once again crawling onto his eyes, clouding his brain. *No, you've got to think. Valerio Casparo said that we've got to start thinking now. Everyone should think, even the technicians, even though we don't know enough. But*

Casparo said that everyone must think. Valerio Casparo, or Valerii Konstantinovich Kasparo, in the vulgar tongue. It's funny, how he works and works, and suddenly he says to the whole hall, "Enough. Let's sit for a while, staring stupidly ahead!" He picked up that phrase from something he read. If you ask him about something during that time, he says, "Young man, you see to it yourself. Don't bother me while I'm sitting here, staring stupidly ahead." I'm thinking about the wrong thing again. So: first off we'll state the problem. Given: that a complex of physiological neuronic states (to put it more simply, a living brain) is hard-coded according to the third Casparo-Kaprov system onto a crystalline quasibiomass. With the proper isolation, a hard code on a crystalline quasibiomass will be preserved with a normal noise level for quite a long time—the relaxation time for the code is on the order of twelve thousand years. Time enough. Required: to find a means of transferring the biomass code onto a living brain, that is to say onto a complex of physiological functioning neurons in the null state. Of course, for this we also need a living brain in the null state, but for such a business people always have been found and will be found—me, for example. . . . But they still wouldn't permit it. Casparo won't even hear of a living brain. There's an eccentric for you. So now you sit and wait for the guys in Leningrad to build an artificial one. So. In short, we have encoded Okada's brain onto a crystalline biomass. We have the number for Okada's brain, the number for Okada's thoughts, the number for his ego. And now we have to find a means of transferring the numbers to another brain. Let it be an artificial one. Then Okada will be reborn. The enciphered ego Okada will once again become a real, acting ego. Question: how is this to be done? How? . . . It would be nice to figure it out right now and make the old man happy. Casparo has been thinking about this for a quarter of a century. Run up to him sopping wet like Archimedes, and shout, "Eureka!" Mikhailov stumbled and almost dropped the torch.

"What's the matter?" asked Zvantsev. "Are you falling asleep again?"

Mikhailov looked at him. Zvantsev walked on, his hood raised, his arms stuck under the rain cape. In the red, flickering light his face seemed drawn and hard. "No," said Mikhailov. "I'm thinking. I'm not sleeping."

Some sort of dark hulk loomed ahead. They walked quickly, and soon caught up to a large truck that was slowly crawling along the highway. At first Zvantsev did not realize that the truck was moving with its engine turned off. Two good-sized camels were pulling it.

"Hey, Saka!" shouted the technician.

The door of the cab opened a bit, a head stuck out, fixed shining eyes on them, and disappeared again. "What can I do for you?" asked a voice from the cab.

"Let me have a candy bar," Mikhailov said.

"Get it yourself—I don't feel like getting out. It's wet."

"So I'll get it myself," Mikhailov said briskly, and disappeared somewhere along with the torch.

It got very dark. Zvantsev walked alongside the truck, matching his pace to that of the camels, which were barely moving. "Can't they go a little faster?" he muttered.

"They don't want to, the scoundrels," came the voice from the cab. "I've tried thrashing them with a stick, but they only spit at me." The voice was silent for a bit and then added, "Just four kilometers an hour. And they spit all over my rain cape." The driver sighed deeply and suddenly yelled, "Hey, you weird critters! Giddap! Giddap! Or whatever they say where you come from."

The camels snorted distainfully.

"You should move over to the side," advised the driver. "Though I guess they're not going to do anything right now."

The air smelled of oil, and Mikhailov again appeared alongside. His torch smoked and crackled. "Let's go," he said. "It's close now."

They easily passed the camel team, and soon low, dark structures appeared along the sides of the road. Peering ahead in the darkness, Zvantsev made out an enormous building—a black rift in the black sky. Here and there in the windows, yellow flames flickered weakly.

"Look," Mikhailov said in a whisper. "Do you see the buildings by the sides of the road?"

"So?" Zvantsev whispered back.

"That's where the quasibiomass is. This is where he'll be kept."

"Who?"

"Well, the brain, then," Mikhailov whispered. "His brain!"

They suddenly turned and came out right at the entrance to the Institute building. Mikhailov swung open the heavy door. "Go on in," he said. "Just don't make any noise, please."

It was dark, cold, and strange-smelling in the hall. In the middle of a large table winked several fat, guttering candles, along with dishes and a large soup pot. The dishes were dirty. Dried-out pieces of bread lay in a basket. The candlelight provided only poor illumination. Zvantsev took several steps, and brushed his rain cape against a chair. The chair fell over with a crash.

"Yike!" someone shouted from behind. "Tolya, is that you?"

"Yes, it's me," Mikhailov said.

Zvantsev looked around. A reddish form occupied a corner of the hall, and when Mikhailov went over there with his torch, Zvantsev saw a girl with a pale face. She was lying on a sofa, wrapped up in something black.

"Did you bring something scrumptious?" the girl asked.

"Saka is bringing it," Mikhailov answered. "Would you like a chocolate bar?"

"Please."

Mikhailov started digging into the folds of his rain cape, waving his torch.

"Go spell Zina," the girl said. "She can sleep in here. The boys are sleeping in Room Twelve now. Is it still raining outside?"

"Yes."

"Good. There's not much to go now."

"Here's your candy bar," said Mikhailov. "I'm going. This comrade is here to see the Academician."

"To see who?"

"The Academician."

The girl whistled softly.

Zvantsev walked across the hall and looked back impatiently. Mikhailov came after him, and the girl sat down on the couch and unwrapped the candy bar. By the candlelight Zvantsev could only make out her small, pale face and a strange silvery lab coat with a hood. Mikhailov threw off his rain cape, and Zvantsev saw that he also wore a long silvery coat. In the uncertain light of the torch he looked like a ghost.

"Comrade Zvantsev," he said, "wait here for a little bit. I'll go bring you a lab coat. Only, in the meantime, don't take off your rain cape."

"All right," Zvantsev said, and sat down on a chair.

Casparo's study was dark and cold. The rain pattered on. Mikhailov had left, saying that he would call Casparo. He had taken the torch, and there were no candles in the study. At first Zvantsev sat in the visitors' chair in front of the large empty desk. Then he got up, went over to the window, and started looking out into the night, leaning his forehead against the cold glass. Casparo did not come.

It's going to be very difficult without Okada, Zvantsev thought. *He could have lasted another twenty years—we should have taken better care of him. We should have stopped him from going on deep-water searches a long time ago. If a man is over a hundred, and has spent sixty of those years at a depth of five hundred fathoms . . . then he gets blue palsy, damn him!*

Zvantsev stepped back from the window, went over to the door, and looked out into the corridor. Candles burned sparsely along the long corridor walls. From somewhere came a voice repeating something over and over with the steadiness of a metronome. Zvantsev listened closely, but he could not make out a single word. Then long white figures glided out of the reddish twilight at the end of the corridor, and slipped past noiselessly, as if swimming in air. Zvantsev saw drawn dark faces under the peaks of the silvery hoods.

"Are you hungry?" one said.

"No. Sleepy."

"I think I'll go eat."

"No, no. Sleep. First sleep."

They spoke softly, but he could hear them a long way down the corridor.

"Jean almost screwed up her section. Casparo grabbed her arm just in time."

"What a mess!"

"Yeah. You should've seen his face."

"What a mess, what a mess! Which section?"

"One twenty-six oh three. Approximately. Aural associations."

"Oh boy, oh boy, oh boy."

"Casparo sent her off to get some sleep. She's sitting in Room Sixteen, crying."

The two people in white disappeared. Zvantsev could hear

them talking as they went down the staircase, but he no longer could make out the words. He closed the door and returned to the chair.

So, some Jean had almost screwed up the aural association center. Disgraceful! Casparo had grabbed her by the arm. But what if he hadn't grabbed her? Zvantsev folded his arms and closed his eyes. He knew almost nothing about the Great Experiment. He knew only that it *was* a great experiment, that it was the most complicated thing that science had ever come up against. To encode the distribution of excitations in each of billions of brain cells, to encode the linkages between the excitations, the linkages between the linkages. The smallest mistake threatened irrevocable distortions. . . . A girl had almost annihilated a whole section. . . . Zvantsev remembered that it was section number 12603, and he became afraid. Even if the probability of a mistake or distortion during the transfer of the code was very small. . . . Twelve thousand sections, trillions of units of information. Casparo still hadn't come.

Zvantsev went out into the corridor again. He moved from candle to candle, toward the strange monotonous voice. Then he caught sight of a wide-open door, and the voice became quite loud. Beyond the door was an enormous hall, winking with hundreds of flames. Zvantsev saw panels with dials stretching along the walls. Several hundred people were sitting along the walls in front of the panels. They all wore white. The air in the hall was hot and heavy, and smelled of hot wax. Zvantsev realized that the ventilation and air-conditioning system was shut off. He went into the hall and looked around. He was searching for Casparo, but even if Casparo was here, it was impossible to pick him out among the hundreds of people in identical silvery coats with hoods pulled low.

"Section one eighty-seven twenty-two filled," said a voice. It was unnaturally quiet in the hall—there was only that voice and the rustle of many movements. Zvantsev spied a table with several armchairs in the center of the hall. He went over to the table.

"Section one eighty-seven twenty-three filled."

A broad-shouldered man with his head propped up by his arms was sitting in one of the chairs opposite Zvantsev. He was sleeping, and he sighed heavily in his sleep.

"Section one eighty-seven twenty-four filled."

Zvantsev looked at his watch. It was exactly 3:00 A.M. He saw a man in white come into the hall and disappear somewhere into the gloom, where nothing could be seen except the winking flames.

"Section one eighty-seven twenty-five filled."

A man with a candle came over to the table, stood the candle in a puddle of wax, and sat down. He laid a folder full of papers on the table, turned over one page, and immediately fell asleep. Zvantsev watched his head sink lower and lower and at last come to rest on the papers.

"Section one eighty-seven twenty-six filled."

Zvantsev once again glanced at his watch. It had taken little more than ninety seconds to fill two sections. The Great Encoding had been going on for ten days, and fewer than twenty thousand sections were full.

"Section one eighty-seven twenty-seven filled."

And so on for ten days. Someone's strong hand came to rest on Zvantsev's shoulder. "Why aren't you sleeping?"

Zvantsev lifted his head and saw a round, tired face under a hood. Zvantsev recognized it.

"Get to sleep. Right now."

"Professor Casparo," Zvantsev said, getting up.

"Get to sleep, get to sleep. . . ." Casparo looked him in the eye. "Or if you can't sleep, relieve somebody."

He walked quickly to one side, stopped, and again peered fixedly at Zvantsev. "I don't recognize you," he said. "But it doesn't matter—get to sleep!"

He turned his back and quickly walked along the rows of people sitting before the control boards. Zvantsev heard his harsh receding voice: "A half unit. Pay a little more attention, Leonid, half a unit. . . . Good . . . fine . . . also good. . . . A unit, Johnson, watch it more carefully. . . . Good . . . also good . . ."

Zvantsev got up and walked behind him, trying not to let him out of sight. Suddenly Casparo shouted, "Comrades! Everything is going beautifully! Just be a little more attentive! Everything's going very well. Just watch the stabilizers, and everything will be fine!"

Zvantsev bumped into a long table at which several people

were sleeping. No one turned around, and none of the sleepers raised his head. Casparo had disappeared. Then Zvantsev walked at random along a yellow chain of flames in front of the control boards.

"Section one eighty-seven nine zero filled," said a new, fresh voice.

Zvantsev realized that he was lost, and now did not know where the exit was, nor where Casparo had disappeared to. He sat on an overturned chair, his elbows resting on his knees, his chin propped on his hands, and stared at a winking candle in front of him. The candle was slowly guttering.

"Section one eighty-seven ninety-eight.... Eighty-seven ninety-nine.... Eighty-eight zero zero.... Filled.... Filled."

"*Aaaugh!*" Someone shouted loudly, frightfully. Zvantsev jumped up. He saw that no one had turned around, but even so, everyone at once froze, their backs tensed. Twenty paces away, by one of the technicians' chairs, a tall man was standing clutching his head and shouting, "Back! Back! *Aaaugh!*"

Casparo appeared from somewhere and darted toward the board, walking at a headlong pace. It was quiet in the hall except for the sputtering of wax.

"I'm sorry!" the tall man said. "I'm sorry . . . sorry . . ," he repeated.

Casparo straightened up and shouted, "Listen to me! Sections one eighty-seven ninety-six, eighty-seven ninety-seven, eighty-seven ninety-eight, eighty-seven ninety-nine, eighty-eight zero zero! Re-tape! Do it over!"

Zvantsev saw hundreds of people in white simultaneously raise their right hands and make some adjustment on their boards. The candle flames began to flicker.

"I'm sorry, I'm sorry," the man repeated.

Casparo clapped him on the back. "Get to sleep, Henry," he said. "Get to sleep right away. Calm down, it's no big deal."

The man walked along the boards, repeating the same thing: "I'm sorry, I'm sorry." No one turned around. Someone else already sat at his station.

"Section one eighty-seven ninety-six filled," said the fresh voice.

Casparo stood a while, then slowly, stooping far over, he

started walking past Zvantsev. Zvantsev moved toward him, and suddenly caught sight of his face. He stopped and let Casparo pass. Casparo went up to a small separate board, sank heavily into a chair, and sat there for several seconds. Then he roused himself, and, collapsing forward, pushed his face into the large eyepiece of a periscope which extended down through the floor.

Zvantsev stood nearby, near the long table, with his gaze fixed on the tired, hunched back. He could still see Casparo's face as it had looked in the flickering candlelight. He remembered that Casparo was no longer young either, only, say, five or six years younger than Okada. He thought, *How many years has he lost in these ten days? There will be a reckoning for this, and soon!*

Two people walked up to Casparo. Instead of a hood, one of them wore a round, transparent helmet, which gleamed dimly in the candlelight. "We won't make it," the man in the helmet said quietly. He spoke to Casparo's back.

"How long?" Casparo asked without turning around.

"Clinical death in two hours. Plus or minus twenty minutes."

Casparo turned around. "But he looks good. . . . See for yourself." He tapped the eyepiece with a finger.

The man in the helmet shook his head.

"Paralysis of the nerves," the second one said very quietly. He looked back, ran his bulging eyes over Zvantsev, and, bending over toward Casparo, said something in his ear.

Zvantsev recognized him. It was Professor Ivan Krasnov.

"Very well," said Casparo. "We'll do it this way." The two turned together and quickly disappeared into the darkness.

Zvantsev groped for a chair, sat down, and closed his eyes. *It's over*, he thought. *They won't make it. He'll die. He'll die completely.*

"Section one nine zero zero two filled," said the voice. "Section one nine zero zero three filled. . . . Section one nine zero zero four . . ."

Zvantsev did not know anything about the encoding of nerve linkages. He imagined Okada lying on a table under a deathly white light, with a fine needle crawling slowly over the convolutions of his exposed brain, and that the code impulses were put down character after character on a long tape. Zvantsev understood perfectly well that in reality it wasn't done like that at all, but his imagination kept sketching him the same picture: the shining needle crawling over the brain, and, recorded on an endless tape, the mysterious signs signifying memory, habits, associations, experience. . . . And from somewhere death was creeping up, destroying cell after cell, linkage after linkage, and they had to outrace it.

Zvantsev knew almost nothing about the encoding of nerve linkages. But he did know that the boundaries of the brain areas that carried out separate thought processes were still unknown. That the Great Encoding was possible only under conditions of the most extreme isolation and with the most precise registration of all irregular fields. Hence the candles and torches, and the camels on the highway, the empty villages, and the black windows of the microweather installation, and the halting of the moving roads. Zvantsev knew that a means of monitoring the encoding that did not distort it had not yet been found. That Casparo worked half-blind and anyhow was encoding things which, perhaps, were not at all what should be encoded. But Zvantsev also knew that the Great Encoding was the road toward the immortality of the human ego, because a person wasn't arms and legs. A person was memory, habits, associations, a brain. A *brain*.

"Section one ninety-two sixteen filled. . . ."

Zvantsev opened his eyes, got up, and went over to Casparo. Casparo was sitting looking straight ahead.

"Professor Casparo," said Zvantsev, "I am Zvantsev, the oceanographer. I must speak to Academician Okada."

Casparo raised his eyes and looked up at Zvantsev for a long time. His eyes were dull, half-closed. "That is impossible," he said.

They looked at each other silently for some time.

"Academician Okada has been waiting for this information all his life," Zvantsev said quietly.

Casparo did not answer. He turned his eyes away and once again stared straight ahead. Zvantsev looked around. Darkness. Candle flames. White silvery hooded coats.

"Section one ninety-two ninety-two filled," said the voice.

Casparo got up and said, "That's it. The end."

And Zvantsev saw a small red lamp winking on the board by

the eyepiece of the periscope. *The light,* he thought. *So it's over.*

"Section one ninety-two ninety-four filled. . . ."

Out of the darkness a small girl in a fluttering lab coat came running at top speed. She darted straight to Casparo, knocking Zvantsev out of the way.

"Sir," she said despairingly, "there's only one free section left."

"We won't need any more," Casparo said. He got up and ran into Zvantsev. "Who are you?" he asked tiredly.

"I'm Zvantsev, the oceanographer," Zvantsev said quietly. "I had wanted to speak to Academician Okada."

"That is impossible," Casparo said, "Academician Okada is dead."

He bent over the board and turned four switches, one after another. A blinding light flashed on under the ceiling of the enormous hall.

It was already light when Zvantsev went down into the lobby. The grayish light of a foggy morning poured into the enormous windows, but there was a feeling that any moment now the sun would burn through, and the day would be clear. There was no one in the lobby. A crumpled coverlet lay on the sofa. Several candles were burning down on the table between jars and dishes of food. Zvantsev looked back at the staircase. Voices sounded from above. Mikhailov, who had promised to go with Zvantsev, was somewhere up there.

Zvantsev went over to the sofa and sat down. Three young men came down the staircase. One went up to the table and started wolfing down food with his bare hands. He moved plates around, dropped a soft-drink bottle, grabbed it, and started drinking. The second was sleeping as he walked, scarcely moving his eyes. The third, holding the sleeper back by the shoulders, was saying enthusiastically, "Casparo told Krasnov. That's all he said. And right away the old man collapsed right onto the board. We grabbed him and took him to the study, and Serezhka Kruglov was already sleeping there. So we laid the two of them together."

"I can't believe it," the first one said indistinctly—he was still chewing. "Did we really have time for so much?"

"Damn it, how many times do I have to tell you! Ninety-eight percent. And some tenths—I don't remember exactly."

"Really ninety-eight percent?"

"I see you're zonked out altogether. You don't understand what people are saying to you."

"I understand all right, but I don't believe it." The one who was eating suddenly sat down and grabbed a jar of preserves. "I can't believe it. Things seemed to be going quite poorly."

"Guys," muttered the sleepy one. "Let's go, huh? I've plain had it."

All three suddenly made a great commotion and left. More and more people were coming down the staircase. Sleepy ones, barely dragging their legs. Excited ones, with bulging eyes and voices hoarse from long silence.

It doesn't look like a funeral, Zvantsev thought. He knew that Okada was dead, but he didn't believe it. It seemed as if the Academician had simply fallen asleep, except that no one knew yet how to wake him. No matter—they would find out. *Ninety-eight percent,* he thought. *Not bad at all.* It was very strange, but he did not feel the grief of loss. There was no mourning. He felt only something on the order of dissatisfaction, thinking that he would have to wait, perhaps for a long time, for Okada to return. As had happened before, when Okada had gone away to the mainland for an extended stay.

Mikhailov touched him on the shoulder. He was wearing neither rain cape nor lab coat. "Let's go, Comrade Zvantsev."

Zvantsev got up and walked after him toward the doorway. The heavy double doors opened by themselves, easily and silently.

The sun had not yet come up, but it was light, and the clouds were rapidly disappearing from the blue-gray sky. Zvantsev saw low cream-colored buildings, streets sprinkled with red fallen leaves running between them. People were coming out of the Institute and dispersing among the streets in groups of twos or threes.

Someone shouted, "The fellows from Kostroma are relaxing in building six, floors two and three!"

Small, many-legged litter robots moved along the streets in sparse files. They left behind them dry, gray, clean concrete.

"Would you like a candy bar?" asked Mikhailov.

Zvantsev shook his head. They walked toward the highway between rows of squat yellow buildings that lacked doors and windows.

There were many buildings—a whole street of them. These were the blocks with the quasibiomass, the repository of Okada's brain—twenty thousand sections of biomass, twenty squat buildings, each with a frontage of thirty meters, each extending six levels underground.

"Not bad for a start," said Mikhailov. "But we can't go on like this. Twenty buildings for one person is too much. If so much space were assigned to each of us. . . ." He laughed and threw the candy wrapper onto the pavement.

Who knows? thought Zvantsev. *Maybe one suitcase will be enough for you. And for me too.* The litter robot, its long legs tapping on the pavement, toddled unhurriedly over to the discarded wrapper.

"Hey, Saka!" Mikhailov shouted suddenly. A truck drew up to them and stopped, and their driver with the flashing eyes stuck his head out of the cab. They all climbed in. "Where are your camels?" Mikhailov asked.

"They're grazing somewhere," the driver said. "I've had enough of them. They spat at me again while I was unharnessing them."

Mikhailov was already asleep, with his head on Zvantsev's shoulder.

The driver, small and dark-eyed, drove the heavy truck fast, and sang quietly, almost without moving his lips. It was some old, half-forgotten song. At first Zvantsev listened, and then suddenly he caught sight of helicopters moving low over the highway. There were six of them. The quiet zone, so recently dead, was now teeming with life. The moving roads had started up. People were hurrying to their homes. The microweather installations had started working, as had the traffic lights on the highway. Someone was already tearing off the plywood sheet with the rough lettering. The radio would be announcing that the Great Encoding had been completed and had gone satisfactorily. The helicopters must be carrying in a press group. They would stereocast an image of the squat yellow buildings and the burned-out candles before the powered-down control boards to the whole world. And someone, of course, would creep in to wake up Casparo, and they would grab the interloper by the seat of his pants, and in the heat of the moment maybe even give him a sound thrashing. And the whole world soon would know that human beings would soon become eternal. Not humanity, but human beings, each individual human being, each personality. Well, perhaps at first only the best ones. . . . Zvantsev looked at the driver. "Comrade," Zvantsev said, smiling, "do you want to live forever?"

"Yes," answered the driver, also smiling. "And I will live forever."

"I want to too," said Zvantsev.

Natural Science in the Spirit World

KOCHIN, the lab assistant, tiptoed up to the door and looked into the bedroom. The esper was sleeping. He was fairly elderly, and his face was very unhappy. He was lying on his side with his hand under his cheek. When Kochin opened the door, the esper made a smacking sound and said distinctly, "I haven't got my sleep in yet. Leave me alone."

Kochin went up to the bed and touched him on the shoulder. "It's time, Comrade Peters. Please get up."

Peters opened bleary eyes. "Just another half hour," he said plaintively.

Kochin, distressed, shook his head. "It's impossible, Comrade Peters. If you oversleep. . . ."

"Right," the esper said with a sigh. "I'll be dull." He sat up and stretched. "You know what I just dreamed about, George? I dreamed that I was at home on the farm, on the Yukon. My son had just come back from Venus and I was showing him the beaver preserve. Do you know about my beavers, George? They're just like people."

The esper climbed out of bed and started doing his exercises. Peters's son had died two years before on Venus, Kochin knew, and Peters missed his wife very much. He didn't trust his young assistant on the farm and worried a great deal about the beavers. He was very melancholy and bored here, and he didn't like the work he was doing at all.

"Never mind!" said Peters, rotating his hairy torso energetically. "You don't have to pity me, Georgie boy! I understand— if I have to I have to, and there's nothing to be done about it."

Kochin flushed painfully. He'd never learn how to behave in the presence of an esper, it seemed. Some sort of awkwardness always came up.

"You're a good boy, Georgie," Peters said warmly. "Usually people don't like having their thoughts read. That's why we espers prefer solitude, and then when we do show up in civilization we try to run on at the mouth a little more—if we're quiet, people get the idea we're hard at work. One young cockerel here is always repeating some sort of mathematical formulas in his head when I'm around. So what happens? I don't understand a single formula, but on the other hand, I sense clearly that he's mortally afraid of my guessing his tender feeling toward a certain young individual." Peters grabbed a towel and started for the bathroom.

Kochin hurriedly wiped cold perspiration from his forehead. *Thank God I'm not in love with anybody!* he thought untruthfully. *Katya might be offended. These espers are really fine people! I wonder whether he can pick up anything through the bathroom door? Of course we get him good and annoyed with our experiments, but then again he won't stay here long. . . . A young cockerel—that's Petya Bystrov, of course. I wonder who is the object of his affection.*

"I'll never tell," declared Peters, appearing at the bathroom door. He pulled on a knit shirt. "Okay, Georgie, I'm ready. Where to today? The torture chamber again?"

"Right," said Kochin. "The same as always. Maybe you'd like some breakfast? You still have fifteen minutes."

"No," said Peters. "I get dull from food too. Just give me some glucose." He unbuttoned his sleeve. Kochin got a flat box of activated glucose out of his pocket, took out one ampule, and pressed its sucker against the swollen vein on Peters's arm. When the glucose had penetrated, Peters knocked the empty ampule off with a snap, and rolled his sleeve down. "Well, let's go suffer," he said with a sigh.

The Institute for Space Physics had been built about twenty years before on Kotlin Island in the Gulf of Finland. The old Krondstadt base had been completely demolished; there remained only the gray, moss-covered walls of the ancient forts and, in the park of the science town, the golden monument to those who had taken part in the Great Revolution. An artificial archipelago on which were located the rocketports, airports, energy receivers, and energy stations of the Institute had been created to the west of Kotlin Island. The islands furthest west in the archipelago were occupied by what were called the "loud" laboratories—from time to time explosions thundered there, and they had fires. Theoretical work and "quiet" experiments were conducted in the long, flat buildings of the Institute itself, on Kotlin Island.

The Institute worked on the leading edge of science. The range of work was extremely broad. Problems of gravity. Deritrinitation. Questions of new physical axiomatics. The theory of discrete space. And very many more specialized problems. Fairly often the Institute took on for research problems which seemed, and which in the last analysis turned out to be, hopelessly complicated and inaccessible. The experimental approach to these problems often demanded monstrous expenditures of energy. Time after time the leadership of the Institute disturbed the World Council with monotonous requests for an hour's worth, two hours' worth, and sometimes even a day's worth of the energy of the Planet. In clear weather Leningraders could see on the horizon the shiny spheres of the gigantic energy receivers erected on the most distant islands of the "Kotlin Achipelago." Some wit on the Resources Committee had called these energy receivers "Danaidian barrels," claiming that the energy of the Planet vanished there as if into a bottomless barrel, without visible result; and many on the Council waxed wroth on the subject of the Institute's activities, but they gave the energy unfailingly, because they considered that humanity was rich and could permit itself some expenditure on the problems of the day after tomorrow. Even at the height of work on the Big Shaft, which was digging toward the center of the Planet.

Four years earlier a group of Institute members had carried out an experiment having the aim of measuring the energy expended during sigma-deritrinitation. On the border of the Solar System, far beyond the orbit of Transpluto, a pair of drone spaceships were driven up to relativistic velocities and brought to a collision at a relative speed of 295 thousand kilometers per second, over ninety-eight percent of lightspeed. The explosion was terrific; the mass of both starships was turned almost entirely into radiation. The starships disappeared in a blinding flash, leaving after them a thin cloud of metallic vapor. On finishing their measurements, the researchers discovered an energy deficit: a part of the energy, relatively very small, but perfectly detectable, had "disappeared." On the qualitative side, the result of the experiment had been nothing to write home about. According to the theory of sigma deritrinitation, a certain part of the energy was, after all, supposed to disappear at a given point in space, in order to ooze out in some form in regions perhaps quite removed from the place of the experiment. This, indeed, was the very essence of the sigma-D-principle, and something similar had happened in its time in the case of the famous *Taimyr*. But on the quantitative side the energy deficit exceeded the predicted quantity. Part of the energy had "disappeared" to parts unknown. Two concepts had been enlisted to explain this contradiction of the conservation laws. One was the hypothesis that the energy had gotten away in an as-yet-unknown form, for example in some sort of field unknown to science for which instruments for detection and registration did not yet exist. The other was the theory of interpenetrating spaces.

The theory of interpenetrating spaces had been worked out long before this experiment. This theory regarded the world as a perhaps infinite aggregate of interpenetrating spaces with quite various physical properties. It was this difference in properties that permitted spaces to coexist physically, with no noticeable interaction with each other. It was an abstract theory, and had not led to experimentally verifiable concrete equations. However, it followed from the theory that various forms of matter possess differing abilities to penetrate from one space into a neighboring one. It was proven as well that the penetration procedes the more easily the greater the energy concentration. The concentration of the energy of the electromagnetic field was enormous in the experiment with the spacecraft. This led to the proposal that the energy "leakage" could be explained as an energy transfer from our space to some neighboring space. There were few data, but the idea was so attractive that it immediately found adherents in the Institute.

Experimental work on the theory of interpenetrating spaces had been undertaken by members of the Department of the Physics of Discrete Space. They immediately turned away from the cumbersome, dangerous, and not very precise experiments connected with the swallowing up and excretion of enormous energies. Anyhow, such experiments left open the question of unknown fields. Consequently it was planned to carry out research on spatial penetrability on the most varied fields: gravitational, electromagnetic, nuclear. But the trump card and main hope was the brilliant idea of one of the members who had noticed a remarkable similarity between the psychodynamic field of the human brain and the hypothetical "linkage field," whose general mathematical description had been established by the theory of interpenetrating spaces at a time when researchers in psychodynamics had not yet even possessed a mathematical apparatus. The hypothetical "linkage field" was a field which, according to the theory, had the maximum ability to penetrate from one space into the next. Sufficiently accurate artificial receivers for the "psychodynamic field" (and accordingly also for the "linkage field") did not exist, and so it was up to the espers.

There were ten billion people on the Planet, and a total of one hundred twenty-two registered espers. The espers read thoughts. The mystery of this unusual ability was still apparently very far from solution. It was clear only that the espers were surprisingly sensitive to the psychodynamic radiation of the human brain and that this sensitivity was innate. Some espers could detect and decipher the thoughts of a person thousands upon thousands of kilometers away. Some received psychodynamic signals only over a distance of a few paces. The parapsychologists argued over whether the espers were the first signs heralding the appearance on the evolutionary ladder of a new kind of human being, or whether this was simply an atavism, the remnant of a mysterious sixth sense that had once helped our ancestors to orient themselves in the dense primeval forest. The more powerful espers worked in the long-distance communication stations, augmenting the usual radio link with distant expeditions. Many espers worked as doctors. And many worked in fields unrelated to thought-reading.

However that might be, the workers of the Institute for the Physics of Space hoped that the espers would be able to simply "hear" the linkage field. This would be remarkable confirmation of the theory of interpenetrating spaces. The best espers on the Planet had gathered at Kotlin Island at the invitation of the Institute. The plan of the experiment was simple. If a linkage field between neighboring spaces existed, then, according to the theory, it should be very similar to the psychodynamic field of a human brain and should accordingly be picked up by the espers. If an esper were isolated in a special chamber shielded from the outside world (including human thoughts) by a thick layer of mesomatter, then there would be left in that room only the gravitational field of the Earth, which made no difference to the psychodynamic field, and the hypothetical linkage field coming from the neighboring spaces. Of course, such an experimental arrangement was far from ideal. Only a positive result would be decisive. A negative result indicated nothing—it neither confirmed nor rejected the theory. But so far it was the only chance. The espers were stimulated with neutrino radiation, which increased the sensitivity of the brain; were placed in the chambers; and were left to "listen."

Peters and Kochin walked unhurriedly down the main street of the science town. The morning was foggy and grayish. The sun had not yet risen, but far, far ahead the gridded towers of the energy receivers reflected a pink light at an enormous height. Peters walked with his hands clasped behind his back, and sang in an undertone a ditty in English about *"Johnny coming down to Highlow, poor old man."* Kochin, with a look of independence, walked alongside and tried not to think about anything. Near one of the cottages Peters suddenly ceased singing and stopped. "We have to wait," he said.

"Why?" asked Kochin.

"Sieverson is asking me to wait up." Peters nodded in the direction of the cottage. "He's putting on his overcoat."

One-two-three / Pioneers are we, Kochin thought. *Two espers— that's twice as . . . five times five is eleven—or something like that.* "Is Sieverson really by himself? Doesn't he have a guide?"

"Five times five is twenty-five," Peters said querulously. "And I don't know why Sieverson wasn't assigned a guide."

Sieverson appeared at the door of the cottage. "Don't swear, young man," he said to Kochin sternly. "When we were your age we were more polite."

"Now, now, Sieverson old chap," said Peters. "You yourself know you don't think that. . . . Thank you, I slept very well. And you know, I dreamed about beavers. And that my Harry had come back from Venus."

Sieverson came down to the sidewalk and took Peters's arm. "Let's go," he said. "Beavers—I've felt like a beaver myself these past few days. You, at least, have dreams, but I—did I tell you that I've just had a granddaughter born, Peters? . . . Oh, I did tell you. Well, I can't see her even in a dream, because I haven't seen her even once in real life. And I feel ashamed, Peters. To spend my old age on nonsense like this. . . . Of course it's nonsense— don't you contradict me."

Kochin trudged behind the pair of venerable espers and repeated to himself, *The integral from zero to infinity of e to the minus-x- squared power, radical pi over two. . . . A circle is a geometric locus of points equidistant. . . .*

Old Sieverson grumbled, "I'm a doctor, and in my village I know everyone unto the seventh generation backward and forward, and everyone knows me. I've listened to people's thoughts all my life. Every day I've been able to be of help to someone because I heard his thoughts. Now I'm ashamed and stifled. Ashamed and stifled from sitting in total loneliness in these stupid casemates and listening to—what?—the whisperings of ghosts! The whisperings of imaginary spirits springing from someone's delirious imagination! Don't you contradict me, Peters! I'm twice as old as you!"

The unwritten code of the espers forbade them to converse mentally in the presence of a non-esper. Kochin was a non-esper, and he was present. He repeated to himself, *The mathematical expectation of a sum of random quantities is equal to the sum of their mathematical expectations. . . . Or to put it another way . . . uh, the sum of their mathematical expectations . . . mathematical expectations. . . .*

"They drag us away from our regular work," Sieverson continued grumbling. "They drive us into this gray fog. Don't argue, Peters, they do drive us! They drove me! I couldn't refuse when they asked me, but nothing prevents me from looking upon this request as an attack on my person. . . . Don't argue, Peters, I'm older than you! Never in my life have I had cause to regret being an esper. . . . Oh, you have had cause? Well, that's your business. Of course beavers don't need an esper. But people, sick and suffering people, *they* need—"

"Hold on, old chap," said Peters. "As you see, even healthy people need espers. Healthy but suffering—"

"Who is healthy here?" exclaimed Sieverson. "These physicists, or should I say alchemists? Why do you think I haven't left up to now? I can't very well disappoint them, damn them all! No, young man—" He broke off and turned to Kochin. "There are few people like me. Espers so old and so experienced! And you can stop muttering your abracadabra—I can hear perfectly well what you are sending. Peters, don't defend the young whippersnapper, I know what I'm saying! I'm older than all of you put together!"

Sixty-two times twenty-one, Kochin, red and damp from spite, thought stubbornly. *Is . . . is . . . Six times two . . . You're lying, old man, you couldn't be that old. And anyhow . . . "Through the heavens at midnight an angel did fly . . ." Who wrote that? Lermontov.*

The harsh voice of the loudspeaker rang out over the town: "Attention, comrades! We are relaying a warning from the local microweather station. From nine-twenty to ten-oh-five there will be an average-sized rainfall over the western end of Kotlin Island. The western boundary of the rain zone is the extreme edge of the park."

"You're foresighted, Sieverson," said Peters. "You wore your overcoat."

"I'm not foresighted," muttered Sieverson. "I simply picked

up the decision from the weathermen this morning at six o'clock, when they were talking it over."

Wow! Kochin thought excitedly.

"You're a very strong esper," Peters said with great respect.

"Nonsense!" Sieverson retorted. "Twenty kilometers. You would have caught that thought too, but you were sleeping. I, on the other hand, am afflicted with insomnia on this fogbound island."

When they came out to the edge of the town, a third esper caught up to them. A young one, of very presentable appearance, with a cold, self-assured face. He was draped out picturesquely in a modish gold toga. Petya Bystrov was with him.

While the espers exchanged silent greetings, Petya Bystrov, after glancing furtively at them, ran a hand over his throat and said with his lips only, "Eh, I'm having a rough time."

Kochin spread his hands.

At first the espers walked silently.

Kochin and Bystrov, their heads hanging, followed several paces behind. Suddenly Sieverson yelled in a cracked falsetto, "Please speak aloud, McCullough! Please speak with words in the presence of young people who are non-espers!"

"Sieverson, old chap!" said Peters, looking at him reproachfully.

McCullough waved the skirt of his toga ostentatiously and said in a haughty tone, "Well, I can repeat it in words too! I have nothing to hide. I can't pick up anything in those stupid chambers. There's nothing to be picked up there. I'm telling you, there's simply *nothing* to be picked up there."

"That's no concern of yours, young man!" screamed Sieverson. "I'm older than you and nonetheless I sit there without one murmur of complaint, and will continue to sit there as long as the scientists require! And if the scientists ask us to sit there, they have a reason for it."

"Sieverson, old chap!" said Peters.

"Yes, of course it's more boring than hanging around on street corners wrapped up in a hideous gold bathrobe and eavesdropping on other people's thoughts! And then doing party tricks for the girls! Don't argue with me, McCullough, you *do* do that!"

McCullough wilted, and for some time they all walked silently.

Then Peters said, "Unfortunately, McCullough is right. Not in eavesdropping on others' thoughts, of course—but I can't pick anything up in the chamber either. Neither can you, Sieverson old chap. I'm afraid that the experiment will end up a failure."

Sieverson muttered something inaudible.

The heavy slab of titanium steel covered on two sides with a shiny layer of mesomatter slowly descended; and Peters was left alone. He sat down in an armchair in front of a small, empty table, and prepared to be bored for ten straight hours. In accordance with the conditions of the experiment, neither reading nor writing was permitted. You had to sit and "listen" to the silence. The silence was total. The mesoshield did not let a single thought in from outside, and here, in this chamber, for the first time in his life Peters experienced a surprisingly unpleasant feeling of deafness. Probably the designers of this chamber had not suspected how favorable for the experiment this silence was. A "deaf" esper strained to listen, trying to catch even a whisper of a signal, whether he wanted to or not. Moreover, the designers had not known what suffering it cost an esper used to the constant clamor of human thoughts to spend ten hours in the deaf chamber. Peters called it the torture chamber, and many espers had picked up the term.

I have already sat here for one hundred ten hours, thought Peters. *At the end of today it will be a hundred twenty. And nothing. No trace of the notorious "linkage field" which our poor physicists think about so much. And a hundred-some hours is a good many. Just what are they expecting? A hundred espers, each of whom has sat in one of these things for about a hundred hours—that's ten thousand hours. Ten thousand hours down the drain. The poor, poor physicists! And the poor, poor espers! And my poor, poor beavers! Pete Ballantine is a greenhorn, a kid, out of school for only a few days. I know in my bones that he's late with the feedings. Probably a week and a half late. I'll have to send another radiogram this evening. But he's stubborn as a mule, he doesn't want to hear anything about the special conditions of the Yukon. And Winter is a greenhorn too, and wishy-washy.*

Peters turned nasty. *And Eugene is a green, self-satisfied fool. You have to love the beavers! They need love! You have to love them with your whole heart! So that they themselves will climb up onto the bank for you and poke their noses into your hand. They have such nice cute faces. And these "fur breeders" have only got problems on their minds. Fur breeding! How to get two pelts from one beaver! And then make it grow a third! Oh, if only I had my Harry with me. . . . Harry, my boy, how hard it is without you! If you only knew!*

I remember how he came up to me . . . when was it? In January—no, February—of one nineteen. He came up and said that he had volunteered for Venus. He said, "I'm sorry, Pa, but that's where they need us now." After that he came back twice—in one twenty-one and in one twenty-five. The old beavers remembered him, and he remembered every last one of them. He always told me that he came back because he had gotten homesick, but I knew that he had come back for medical treatment. Ah, Harry, Harry, we could get all our good beavers together and set up a fine farm now, on Venus. That's possible today. They're taking many different animals there now. . . . But you didn't live to see it, my boy.

Peters got out his handkerchief, wiped his eyes, stood up, and started pacing the room. *This damned nonsensical cage. . . . Are they going to keep us here much longer?* He thought that by now all hundred espers must be stirring in their individual cages. Old loud Sieverson, who contrived to be peevish and kindly at the same time. And that self-satisfied fool McCullough. Where did people like McCullough come from? Probably you found them only among the espers. And all because telepathy, whatever you thought of it, was an abnormality. At least for now. Fortunately, people like McCullough were rare even among espers. Among professional espers they were nonexistent. Take, for example, that Yura Rusakov, the long-distance esper. On the long-distance stations there were many professional espers, but they said that Yura Rusakov was the strongest of them all, the strongest esper in the world. He could even pick up direction. That was a very rare talent. He had been an esper since earliest childhood and from earliest childhood he had known it. And still he was a jolly, good boy. He had been well brought up—he hadn't been treated from infancy like a genius and prodigy. The most frightful thing for a child was loving parents. But this one had been brought up in school, and he was a really nice kid. They said he had cried when he received the last message from the *Explorer.* After the accident there had been only one person left alive on the *Explorer,* the young midshipman Walter Saronian. A very, very talented young man, evidently. And one with a will of iron. Wounded, dying, he had started searching for the cause of the accident—and had found it!

Peters came to alertness. Some extraneous, barely noticable, inaudible nuance had, it seemed, crept into his consciousness. No. It was only the echo off the walls. He wondered what *it* would be like if it existed. Georgie-boy had affirmed that theoretically it should be received as noise. But naturally he couldn't explain what kind of noise, and when he tried, he either quickly slipped into mathematics or else put forward uncertain analogies to broken radio sets. The physicists knew theoretically what kind of noise, but they had no sensory notion of it, while the espers, not understanding the theory, perhaps were hearing this noise twenty times a day without suspecting it. *What a pity there's not one single esper physicist! Perhaps that Yura Rusakov will become the first. He or one of the kids at the long-distance stations. It's a good thing we instinctively distinguish our thoughts from those of others and can only accidentally take an echo for an outside signal.*

Peters sat down and stretched out his legs. Still, the physicists had thought up a funny business—catching spirits from another world. It was natural science in the spirit world. He looked at his watch. Only thirty minutes had passed. *Well, spirits are spirits. Let's listen.*

At precisely seventeen hundred hours, Peters went up to the door. The heavy slab of titanium steel lifted, and into his consciousness rushed a whirlwind of excited alien thoughts. As always, he saw the strained, expectant faces of the physicists, and as always, he shook his head No. He was unbearably sorry for these young, bright fellows—many times he had imagined how wonderful it would be if right from the threshold he could smile and say, "Linkage fields do exist—I picked up your linkage field for you." But what were you going to do if the linkage field either did not exist or was beyond the ability of espers? "Nothing," he said aloud, and stepped into the corridor.

"Too bad," one of the physicists said disappointedly. He always said "too bad."

Peters went up to him and laid his hand on his shoulder.

"Listen," he said, "perhaps this is enough? Perhaps you've made some sort of mistake?"

The physicist forced a smile. "Come now, Comrade Peters!" he said. "The experiments have hardly begun. We didn't expect anything else at first. We'll strengthen the stimulator . . . yes, the stimulator. If only you would agree to continue . . ."

"We must gather a large statistical sample," said the other physicist. "Only then can we draw any conclusions. We're very much counting on you, Comrade Peters, on you personally and on your colleagues."

"All right," said Peters. "Of course." He saw very well that they were no longer counting on anything. They were just hoping for a miracle. But the miracle could happen. Anything could happen.

Pilgrims and Wayfarers

THE water deep down wasn't all that cold, but still I was frozen. I sat on the bottom just under the precipice and for a whole hour I kept cautiously turning my head, peering into the turbid greenish twilight. I had to sit motionless, for septipods are alert and suspicious creatures. The slightest sound, any quick movement, can frighten them, and then they hie off and return only at night; and it's not a good idea to tangle with them at night.

An eel would stir under my feet and swim back and forth a dozen times or so, and then a pompous striped perch would come back once again. And every time, it stopped and goggled at me with its empty round eyes. It had only to swim off, and a school of silvery minnows would appear and start grazing over my head. My knees and shoulders were thoroughly stiff with cold, and I was worried that Mashka might get tired of just waiting for me, and instead come into the water to find me and rescue me. Finally I had so vividly imagined her sitting alone at the edge of the

244 · THE PLANET WITH ALL THE CONVENIENCES

water, and waiting, and being afraid, and wanting to dive in and look for me, that I was about ready to come out. But just then, the septipod finally emerged from a thicket of seaweed twenty paces to the right.

It was a fairly large specimen. It had appeared instantly and noiselessly, like a ghost, with its round gray torso out in front. A whitish mantle pulsed softly, weakly, and automatically, taking in water and pushing it out, and the septipod rocked lightly from side to side as it moved. The tips of its tucked-up tentacles, like long strips of old rags, trailed after it, and the slit of its barely opened eyes gleamed dimly in the twilight. It swam slowly, as they all did during the daytime, in a strange eerie torpor, going who knew where or why. Probably the darkest, most primitive instincts moved them, perhaps the same instincts that direct the motion of amoebas.

Very slowly and steadily I raised the tag gun and pointed the barrel, aiming for the swollen back. A silvery minnow suddenly darted forth and disappeared, and I thought that the eyelid over the enormous glazed eye trembled. I pulled the trigger and immediately pushed up from the bottom, getting away from the caustic ink. When I looked around again, the septipod was no longer in sight. There was just a thick blue-black cloud that was spreading through the water, obscuring the bottom. I darted toward the surface and started swimming toward shore.

The day was hot and clear, and a bluish steamy haze hung over the water. The sky was empty and white, except for motionless blue-gray piles of clouds that rose up over the forest like castle towers.

A strange man in brightly colored swimming trunks, was sitting in the grass in front of our tent, a headband stretched across his forehead. He was tanned and though not muscular, somehow improbably sinewy, as if he were tied together with rope under his skin. It was immediately apparent that this was an impossibly strong man. My Mashka, long-legged, dark, with a shock of sun-bleached hair falling over sharp vertebrae, wearing a navy blue bathingsuit, was standing in front of him. No, she wasn't sitting by the water pining for her daddy—she was energetically telling something to this wiry stranger, gesturing at full blast. I was a bit miffed that she hadn't even noticed my arrival. But the stranger noticed. He quickly turned his head, took a good look, and, with a smile, brandished an open hand. Mashka turned around and yelled happily, "Ah, there you are, Daddy!"

I climbed onto the grass, took off my mask, and wiped my face. The stranger was examining me smilingly.

"How many did you tag?" Mashka asked in a businesslike voice.

"One." I had a cramp in my jaw.

"Oh, Daddy," Mashka said. She helped me take off the aquastat, and then I stretched out in the grass. "Yesterday he tagged two," Mashka explained, "and four the day before that. If it's going to go this way, we'd better move right on to another lake." She took a towel and started drying my back. "You're like a fresh-frozen goose," she declared. "This is Leonid Andreevich Gorbovsky. He's an astroarchaeologist. And this, Leonid, is my daddy. His name is Stanislav Ivanov."

The sinewy Leonid Gorbovsky nodded, smiling. "You're frozen," he said. "Up here it's very nice—the sun, the grass. . . ."

"He'll be all right in a minute," said Mashka, drying me with all her might. "He's usually quite a merry old soul—he's just chilled through."

It was clear that she had just been talking a lot about me, and was now using all her power to save face for me. Well, let her save it. I didn't have enough time to bother with that myself—my teeth were chattering.

"Mashka and I have been very worried about you," Gorbovsky said. "We even wanted to dive after you, but I don't know how. You probably can't imagine a man who hasn't had occasion to go diving even once in his work." He lay down on his back, turned over onto his side, and leaned on one arm. "Tomorrow I'm shipping out," he said confidingly. "I don't know when I'll have another chance to lie down on the grass by a lake and have the opportunity to go diving with an aquastat."

"Please, go ahead," I suggested.

He looked carefully at the aquastat, then touched it. "Certainly," he said, and lay down on his back. He put his hands behind his head and looked at me, slowly blinking his sparse lashes. There was something unfailingly winning about him. I couldn't even say what exactly. Perhaps the eyes—trusting and a little sad. Or the fact that the way one of his ears stuck out from under the headband was somehow very amusing. After he had inspected me to his satisfaction, he turned his eyes and stared at a blue dragonfly swaying on a blade of grass. His lips gently puckered out in a whistle. "A dragonfly!" he said. "A little dragonfly. Blue . . . like the lake . . . a beauty. It sits so primly and looks around to see who to gobble up." He stretched out his arm, but the dragonfly let go of the blade of grass and flew off in an arc into the reeds. He followed it with his eyes, and then lay down again. "How complicated it all is, people," he said. Mashka immediately sat down and fastened her round eyes upon him. "I mean, this dragonfly—perfect, elegant, pleased with everything! It's eaten a fly, it's reproduced, and then it's time to die. Simple, elegant, rational. And you don't have spiritual turmoil, pangs of love, self-awareness, or bother about the meaning of life."

"A machine," Mashka said suddenly. "A boring old robot!"

That was my Mashka! I almost laughed, but held myself back; but I must have snorted, for she looked at me with displeasure.

"Boring," Gorbovsky agreed. "Precisely. And now imagine, comrades, a dragonfly colored a venomous yellow-green, with red crossbars, a wingspan of seven meters, and a vile black slime on its mandibles. Can you imagine?" He raised his brows and looked at us. "I see you can't. Well, I ran from them in panic, even though I had a gun. So you ask yourself, what have they got in common, these two boring robots?"

"This green one," I said, "it must have been on another planet?"

"Undoubtedly."

"Pandora?"

"Precisely. Pandora," he said.

"What *do* they have in common?"

"That is the question. What?"

"Well, that's clear enough," I said. "An identical level of information processing. Reactions on the level of instinct."

He sighed. "Words," he said. "Now, don't get angry, but it's just words. That doesn't help me. I have to search for evidence of intelligence in the universe, and I don't even know what intelligence is. And they tell me about various levels of information processing. I know that the level is different in me and in the dragonfly, but that's all intuition. You tell me: say I've found a termite mound. Is that evidence of intelligence, or not? On Mars and Vladislava we've found buildings with no windows, with no doors. Is that evidence of intelligence? What am I looking for? Ruins? Inscriptions? A rusty nail? A heptagonal nut? How do I know what sort of traces they leave? Suppose their aim in life is to annihilate atmosphere everywhere they find it. Or to build rings around planets. Or to hybridize life. Or to create life. Maybe this dragonfly itself is a self-replicating cybernetic apparatus released since time immemorial. To say nothing of the bearers of intelligence themselves. I mean, you can walk past a slimy monster grunting in a puddle twenty times and only turn your nose away. And the monster looks at you with its fine yellow eyes and thinks, 'Curious. Undoubtedly a new species. I'll have to come back here with an expedition and catch a specimen or two.' " He shaded his eyes with his hand and started humming a song. Mashka devoured him with her eyes and waited. I waited too, and thought sympathetically that it's no fun working when the problem hasn't been stated clearly. No fun at all. You stumble around in the dark and you have no joy or even satisfaction in your work. I'd heard about these astroarchaeologists. I could never take them seriously. No one takes them seriously.

"But there is intelligent life in the universe," Gorbovsky said suddenly. "That's beyond doubt. But it isn't the way we think. It's not what we're expecting. And we're looking in the wrong places. Or in the wrong way. And we simply don't know what we're looking for."

There you are, I thought. *The wrong thing, in the wrong place, in the wrong way.... That's simply frivolous, comrades. Pure childishness.*

"Take for example the Voice of the Void," he continued. "Have you heard of it? Probably not. Fifty years ago it was written up, but no one mentions it any more. Because, you see, there has been no progress, and if there's no progress, then of course there can't be any Voice either. After all, we have a whole flock of these birds—they don't know much about science, out of laziness or a poor education, but they know by hearsay that man is almighty. Almighty. But he can't decode the Voice of the Void. Good heavens, for shame, that can't be, we won't permit it! This cheap anthropocentrism. . . ."

"And what is the Voice of the Void?" Mashka asked quietly.

"There's a certain curious phenomenon. In certain directions in space. If you turn the shipboard receiver to autotuning, sooner or later it tunes in on a strange broadcast. You hear a cool, calm voice repeating the same words over and over in an unknown language. They've been picking it up for years, and for years it's repeated the same thing. I've heard it, and lots of other people have heard it, but only a few will talk about it. It's not very pleasant to recall. I mean, here you are, and the distance to Earth is unimaginable. The ether is empty—not even any real static, just weak whispers. And suddenly you hear this voice. And you're on watch, alone. Everyone is asleep, it's quiet, scary, and here comes this voice. Believe me, it's not pleasant at all. There are recordings of the voice. A lot of people have racked their brains trying to decipher them and many are still racking them, but if you ask me it's hopeless. There are other mysteries too. Spacers could tell a good deal, but they don't like to. . . ." He was silent for a bit, then added with a certain sad insistency, "You've got to understand that. It's not a simple matter. We don't even know what to expect. They could meet us at any minute. Face to face. And, you understand, they could turn out to be immeasurably superior to us. Completely unlike us, and immeasurably superior to boot. You hear talk of collisions and conflicts, about all sorts of different understandings of humaneness and good, but that's not what I'm afraid of. What I'm afraid of is the unparalleled humiliation of the human race, of a gigantic psychological shock. We're so proud, after all. We've created such a wonderful world, we know so much, we've fought our way out into the wide universe, and there we discover and study and explore—what? For them, the universe is simply home. They've lived in it for millions of years, as we've lived on Earth, and they're just surprised at us: where did these things out among the stars come from?"

He suddenly fell silent and got up with a jerk, listening intently. I even trembled.

"It's thunder," Mashka said quietly. She was staring at him with her mouth half open. "Thunder. There'll be a storm."

He was still listening intently, sweeping his eyes across the sky. "No, it's not thunder," he said at last, and sat down again. "It's a liner. There, see?"

Against a background of blue-gray clouds a gleaming streak flashed and fell. And again the sky thundered weakly.

"So sit down now, and wait," he said incomprehensibly. He looked at me, smiling, and there was sadness and strained expectation in his eyes. Then it all disappeared and his eyes became trusting as before. "And what are you working on, Comrade Stanislav Ivanov?" he asked.

I concluded that he wanted to change the subject, and I started telling him about septipods. That they belonged to the subclass of dibranchiates of the class of cephalopod mollusks, and represented a special, previously unknown tribe of the order of octopods. They were characterized by the reduction of the third left arm (the one symmetrical with the hetocotylized third right arm), by three rows of suckers on the arms, by the complete absence of a coelom, by an unusually powerful development of the venous heart, by a concentration of the central nervous system that was the maximum for all cephalopods, and by certain other less significant characteristics. The first of the septipods had been discovered recently, when individual specimens appeared off the eastern and southeastern coasts of Asia. And after a year they began to be found in the lower courses of major rivers —the Mekong, the Yangtze, the Huang Ho, and the Amur—and also in lakes like this one, fairly distant from the coastline. And that was surprising, because usually cephalopods were stenohalines to the nth degree, and they avoided even Arctic waters with their reduced salinity. And they almost never came out on dry land. But a fact was a fact: the septipods felt fine in fresh water and came out on land. They climbed into boats and onto bridges, and recently two had been discovered in the forest about thirty kilometers from here.

Mashka was not listening to me. I had already told her all this. She went into the tent, brought out a radio, and switched on the autotuning. Evidently she couldn't wait any longer to catch the Voice of the Void.

But Gorbovsky listened very attentively. "Were those two still alive?" he asked.

"No, they were found dead. There's an animal preserve here in the forest. Wild boars had trampled the septipods and half eaten them. But they had still been alive thirty kilometers from water! Their mantle cavities were filled with wet algae. Obviously in this way the septipods created a certain reserve of water for journeys over dry land. The algae were from a lake. The septipods had undoubtedly walked from these very lakes farther to the south, into the heart of dry land. It should also be noted that all the specimens caught up to this point have been adult males. Not one female, not one young. Probably females and young can't live in fresh water or come out on land.

"All this is very interesting," I continued. "As a rule marine animals change their way of life sharply only during periods of reproduction. Then instinct forces them to go off to some quite unusual places. But reproduction has nothing to do with it here. Here there is some other instinct at work, perhaps one still more ancient and powerful. Right now the important thing for us is to follow the migratory path. So here I spend ten hours a day at this lake, under water. Today I've tagged one so far. If I'm lucky, by evening I'll tag another one or two. At night they become unusually active and grab anything that gets close to them. There have even been instances of attacks on people. But only at night."

Mashka had turned the volume of the radio all the way up, and was enjoying the powerful sounds.

"A little quieter, Mashka," I requested.

She turned it down.

"So you tag them," said Gorbovsky. "Fascinating. With what?"

"Ultrasonic generators." I pulled a charge from the tag gun and displayed the ampule. "Little bullets like this. Inside is a generator with a range under water of thirty kilometers."

He cautiously took the ampule and examined it attentively. His face became sad and old. "Clever," he muttered. "Simple and clever." He turned the ampule all around in his fingers as if feeling it, then lay it in front of me on the grass and got up. His movements had become slow and uncertain. He stepped over to his clothes and scattered them, found his trousers, and then froze, holding them in front of him.

I watched him, feeling a vague disquiet. Mashka held the tag gun at the ready, in order to explain how it was used, and she watched Gorbovsky too. The corners of her lips sank dolefully. I had noticed long ago that this often happened with her: the expression on her face became the same as that of the person she was observing.

Gorbovsky suddenly started speaking very softly, and with a certain mocking quality in his voice: "Honestly, it's fascinating. What a precise analogy. They stayed in the depths for ages, and now they've risen up and entered an alien, hostile world. And what drives them? An ancient, dark instinct, you say? Or an information-processing capacity which had risen up to the level of unquenchable curiosity? After all, it would be better for it to stay home, in salt water, but something draws it . . . draws it to the shore." He roused himself and started pulling on his trousers. These were old-fashioned, long. He hopped on one leg as he put them on. "Really, Stanislav, you have to think that these are very complex cephalopods, eh?"

"In their way, of course," I agreed.

He was not listening. He turned toward the radio set and was staring at it. Mashka and I stared too. Powerful, discordant signals, like the interference from an X-ray installation, were coming from the set. Mashka put down the tag gun. "On six point oh eight meters," she said distractedly. "Some sort of service station, or what?"

Gorbovsky listened closely to the signals, with his eyes closed and his head leaning to one side. "No, it's not a service station," he said. "It's me."

"What?"

"It's me. Me—Leonid Andreevich Gorbovsky."

"H-how can—?"

He gave a mirthless laugh. "How indeed? I would very much like to know how." He pulled on his shirt. "How can it be that three pilots and their ship, on return from a flight to EN 101 and EN 2657, have become sources of radio waves of wavelength six point oh eight three meters?"

Mashka and I, naturally, remained silent. Gorbovsky fell silent too, while he fastened his sandals.

"Doctors examined us. Physicists examined us." He got up and brushed sand and grass from his pants. "All of them came to the same conclusion: it's impossible. You could die laughing, to see the surprise on their faces. But honestly, it was no laughing matter to us. Tolya Obozov refused leave and shipped out for Pandora. He said he preferred to do his broadcasting a little farther from Earth. Falkenstein went off to an underwater station to work. So here I am alone, wandering and broadcasting. And I'm always expecting something. Anticipating it and fearing it. Fearing, but anticipating. Do you understand me?"

"I don't know," I said, and glanced sidelong at Mashka.

"You're right," he said. He took the receiver and pressed it thoughtfully to his protruding ear. "And no one knows. It's been a whole month already. It doesn't weaken, and it never stops. *Whee-waa . . . whee-waa . . .* day and night. Whether we're happy or sad. Whether we're full or hungry, working or loafing. *Whee-waa . . .* But the emission from the *Tariel* is falling off. The *Tariel* is my ship. They laid her up, just in case. Her emissions are jamming the controls of some sort of equipment on Venus, so they keep sending inquiries from there, keep getting annoyed. Tomorrow I'm taking her a little farther out." He straightened up and slapped his thighs with his long arms. "Well, time I left. Good-by. Good luck. Good-by, little Mashka. Don't rack your brains over this. It's a very complicated problem, honestly."

He raised his open hand, bowed, and started off—tall, angular. We watched him go. He stopped near the tent and said, "You know, you should be a bit more delicate with these septipods. Otherwise you just tag and tag, and it, the one with the tag, has all the hassle."

And he left. I lay on my stomach for a long while and then looked at Mashka. She was still watching him. It was clear that Leonid Andreevich Gorbovsky had made an impression on her. But not on me. His notions about how the bearers of intelligence in the universe could turn out to be immeasurably superior to us had not moved me at all. So let them be. If you asked me, the more superior they were, the less chance we would have of meeting up with them along the way. It was like fishing for roach, where a wide-mesh net was useless. And as for pride, humiliation, shock —well, we would probably live through it. I myself would somehow live through it. And if we were discovering and were exploring for ourselves a universe they had tamed long ago, well, what of it? It wasn't tame from our point of view! Anyhow, for us they were just a part of nature that we had to discover and explore, even should they be three times superior to us—to us they were part of the environment! Although, of course, if, say, they had tagged me the way I would tag a septipod. . . .

I glanced at my watch and sat up hurriedly. It was time to get back to work. I noted down the number of the last ampule. I checked the aquastat. I ducked into the tent, found my ultrasonic rangefinder, and put it in the pocket of my swim trunks.

"Give me a hand, Mashka," I said, and started to strap on the aquastat.

Mashka was still sitting in front of the radio, listening to the unfading *"whee-waa."* She helped me put on the aquastat, and together we went into the water. Under water I turned on the rangefinder. Signals rang out. My tagged septipods were wandering all over the lake in their sleep. We looked knowingly at one another, and surfaced. Mashka spat, pushed her wet hair back from her forehead, and said, "There's a difference between an interstellar ship and wet slime in a gill bag."

I told her to return to shore and I dove again. No, in Gorbovsky's place I wouldn't be so worried. All this was too frivolous, like all that astroarchaeology of his. Traces of ideas! Psychological shock! There wouldn't be any shock. Probably we wouldn't even notice each other. They could hardly find us all that interesting.

The Planet with All the Conveniences

Ryu stood up to his waist in lush green grass and watched the helicopter land. Silver and dark-green shock waves from the rotors' backwash swept over the grass. It seemed to him that the helicopter was taking its time about landing, and he shifted impatiently from foot to foot. It was very hot and close. The small, white sun was high, and moist heat rose up from the grass. The rotors started squealing more loudly, and the helicopter turned sideways to Ryu, then instantly dropped four or five feet and sank into the grass at the top of the hill. Ryu ran up the slope.

The engine went quiet, the rotors turned more slowly, then stopped. Several people got out of the helicopter. The first was a lanky man in a jacket with rolled-up sleeves. He wore no helmet, and his sun-bleached hair stuck out on end over his long brown face. Ryu recognized him: it was Pathfinder Gennady Komov, the leader of the group. "Hello, landlord," Komov said gaily, extending his hand. *"Konnichi-wa!"*

"*Konnichi-wa*, Pathfinders," said Ryu. "Welcome to Leonida."
He held out his hand too, but they had to cross another ten
paces to make contact.

"I'm very, very glad to see you," said Ryu, smiling widely.
"Did you get lonely?"

"And how! Alone on a whole planet."

Behind Komov's back someone said, "Damn!" and something
dropped noisily into the grass.

"That's Boris Fokin," Komov said without turning around.
"An archaeologist equipped with full autodescent."

"At least when there's such lush grass," Boris Fokin said, getting up. He had a small red mustache, a freckled nose, and a white
filmiplast helmet, now knocked aslant. He wiped his green-
smeared hands on his pants and introduced himself. "Fokin.
Pathfinder archaeologist."

"Welcome, Fokin," said Ryu.

"And this is Tatyana Palei, archaeological engineer," said
Komov.

Ryu pulled himself together and inclined his head politely.
The archaeological engineer had outrageous gray eyes and blinding white teeth. The archaeological engineer's hand was strong
and rough. The archaeological engineer's coverall draped itself
with devastating elegance.

"Just call me Tanya," said the archaeological engineer.

"Ryu Waseda," said Ryu. "Ryu is the given name, and Waseda
is the surname."

"Mboga," said Komov. "Biologist and hunter."

"Where?" asked Ryu. "Oh, forgive me. A thousand apologies."

"Never mind, Comrade Waseda," said Mboga. "Pleased to
meet you."

Mboga was a pigmy from the Congo, and only his black head,
wrapped tightly in a white kerchief, could be seen over the grass.
The steel-blue barrel of a carbine stuck up next to his head.

"This is Tora-Hunter," Tanya said.

Ryu had to bend down to shake Tora-Hunter's hand. Now he
knew who Mboga was. Tora-Hunter Mboga, member of the
Commission on the Preservation of the Wildlife of Alien Planets.
The biologist who had discovered the "battery of life" on Pandora. The zoopsychologist who had tamed the monstrous Mar-

tian *sora-tobu hiru,* the "flying leeches." Ryu was embarrassed by his faux pas.

"I see that you don't carry a weapon, Comrade Waseda," said Mboga.

"I do have a pistol," Ryu said. "But not a very heavy one."

"I understand." Mboga nodded encouragingly and looked about. "We did end up setting the prairie on fire," he said softly.

Ryu turned around. A flat plain covered with lush shining grass stretched from the hill to the very horizon. Two miles from the hill the grass was on fire, kindled by the landing boat's reactor. Thick puffs of white smoke sailed through the whitish sky. The boat could be seen dimly through the smoke—a dark egg on three widespread struts. A wide burned-out patch around the boat showed black.

"It will soon go out," said Ryu. "It's very damp here. Let's go —I'll show you your estate."

He took Komov by the arm and led him past the helicopter to the other side of the hill. The others followed. Ryu looked back several times, nodding at them with a smile.

Komov said in vexation, "It's always a bad show when you spoil things with your landing."

"The fire will soon go out," Ryu repeated.

He heard Fokin behind him, fussing over the archaeological engineer. "Careful, Tanya girl, there's a tussock here."

"I see it," the archeological engineer answered. "Watch your own step."

"Here is your estate," said Ryu.

A broad, calm river crossed the green plain. In a river bend gleamed a corrugated roof. "That's my lab," said Ryu. To the right of the laboratory, streams of red and black smoke rose up into the sky. "They're building a storehouse there," Ryu said. They could see silhouettes of some sort rushing about in the smoke. For an instant there appeared an enormous clumsy machine on caterpillar treads—a mother robot—and then something flashed in the smoke, a peal of rolling thunder rang out, and the smoke began to pour more thickly. "And there's the city," said Ryu. It was rather more than a kilometer from the base to the city. From the hill the buildings looked like squat gray bricks. Sixteen flat gray bricks, sticking up out of the green grass.

"Yes," said Fokin. "A very unusual layout."

Komov nodded silently. This city was quite unlike the others. Before the discovery of Leonida, the Pathfinders—the workers of the Commission for the Research of the Evidence of the Activity of Extraterrestrial Intelligence in Outer Space—had come across only two cities—the empty city on Mars and the empty city on Vladislava. Obviously the same architect had designed both—cylindrical buildings descending many levels underground, made of shining silicones arranged in concentric rings. But this city on Leonida was entirely different—two rows of gray boxes made of porous limestone.

"Were you there after Gorbovsky?" asked Komov.

"No," answered Ryu. "Not even once. Actually, I had no time. After all, I'm not an archaeologist—I'm an atmosphere physicist. And then, Gorbovsky had asked me not to go there."

A boom! boom! came from the construction site. Red puffs of smoke flew up in thick clouds. Through them the smooth walls of the storehouse could already be made out. The mother robot came out of the smoke into the grass. Next to her hopped black cyberbuilders like praying mantises. Then the cybers formed a chain and ran off to the river.

"Where are they going?" Fokin asked curiously.

"Swimming," said Tanya.

"They're leveling an obstruction," Ryu explained. "The storehouse is almost ready. Now the whole cybernetic system is retuning. They'll build a hangar and a water system."

"A water system!" exclaimed Fokin.

"Still, it would have been better to have moved the base a little farther from the city," Komov said doubtfully.

"This is how Gorbovsky laid it out," said Ryu. "It's not a good idea to get too far from base."

"Also true," Komov agreed. "But I wouldn't want the cybers wrecking the city."

"Come now! I never let them near it."

"A planet with all the conveniences," said Mboga.

"Yes indeed!" Ryu confirmed happily. "The river, the air, the greenery, and no mosquitoes, no harmful insects."

"All the conveniences indeed," Mboga repeated.

"Is it possible to go swimming?" asked Tanya.

Ryu looked at the river. It was greenish and turbid, but it was a real river with real water. Leonida was the first planet that had turned out to have real water and breathable air. "I think so," said Ryu. "I haven't tried it myself, though. There hasn't been time."

"We'll swim every day," said Tanya.

"I'll say!" shouted Fokin. "Every day! Three times a day! All we'll do is go swimming!"

"Okay," said Komov. "What's that?" He pointed to a ridge of low hills on the horizon.

"I don't know," said Ryu. "No one has been there yet. Falkenstein got sick all of a sudden, and Gorbovsky had to leave. He only had time to unload the equipment for me, and then he shipped out."

For some time everyone stood silently, looking at the hills on the horizon. Then Komov said, "In three days or so I'm going to fly along the river myself."

"If there are any more traces," said Fokin, "then undoubtedly we'd find them along the river."

"Probably," Ryu agreed politely. "Now let's go to my place."

Komov looked back at the helicopter.

"Never mind, let it stay," said Ryu. "The hippopotamuses don't climb hills."

"Hippopotamuses?" said Mboga.

"That's what I call them. They look like hippopotamuses from far off, and I've never seen them close up." They started down the hill. "On the other side of the river the grass is very tall, so I've only seen their backs."

Mboga walked next to Ryu with a light gliding step. The grass seemed to flow around him.

"On the other hand there are birds up here," Ryu continued. "They're very large and sometimes they fly very low. One almost grabbed my radar set."

Komov, without slowing down, looked into the sky, shading his eyes with a hand. "By the way," he said. "I should send a radiogram to the *Sunflower*. May I use your communicator?"

"By all means," said Ryu. "You know, Percy Dickson wanted to shoot one. A bird, I mean. But Gorbovsky wouldn't let him."

"Why not?" asked Mboga.

"I don't know," said Ryu. "But he was dreadfully angry; he even wanted to take everyone's weapons away."

"He did take them away from us," Fokin said. "There was a great flap at the Council. If you ask me, it became very ugly, Gorbovsky simply ladled out his authority on top of everyone."

"Except Tora-Hunter," noted Tanya.

"Yes, I took a gun," Mboga said. "But I understand Gorbovsky. You don't feel like shooting here."

"Still, Gorbovsky is a peculiar man," declared Fokin.

"Possibly," said Ryu with restraint.

They approached the low circle of the door to the spacious laboratory dome. Over the dome three gridwork radar dishes turned in various directions.

"You can pitch your tents here," said Ryu. "And if you need it, I'll give you a team of cybers, and they'll build you something more substantial."

Komov looked at the dome, looked at the puffs of red and black smoke behind the laboratory, and then looked back at the gray roofs of the city and said guiltily, "You know, Ryu, I'm afraid we'll be in your way here. Wouldn't it be better if we got settled in the city? Eh?"

"Besides, there's a smell of burning here," added Tanya. "And I'm afraid of the cybers."

"I'm afraid of the cybers too," Fokin said decisively.

Offended, Ryu shrugged his shoulders. "As you like," he said. "I think it's very nice here myself."

"Tell you what," said Tanya. "We'll put up the tents and you can move in with us. You'll like it, you'll see."

"Hmm," said Ryu. "Maybe . . . But for now you're all invited to my place."

The archaeologists stooped down and walked toward the low door. Mboga went last, and he did not even have to bow his head.

Ryu hesitated at the threshold. He looked back and saw the trampled ground, the yellowed crushed grass, the dismal pile of lithoplast, and he thought that somehow there really was a smell of burning here.

The city consisted of a single street, very broad, overgrown with thick grass. The street extended almost due north and south, and stopped close to the river. Komov decided to make camp in the center of the city. The setting up started at around 3:00 P.M.

local time (a day on Leonida was twenty-seven hours some minutes).

The heat seemed to grow worse as the afternoon wore on. There was no breeze, and warm air shimmered over the gray parallelepipeds of buildings. It was a bit cooler only in the southern part of the city, near the river. There was a smell of, in Fokin's words, hay and "a touch of chlorella plantation."

Komov took Mboga and Ryu, who had offered his help, got in the helicopter, and set off for the boat to get equipment and provisions, while Tanya and Fokin surveyed the city. There was relatively little equipment, and Komov transferred it in two trips. When he had come back the first time, Fokin, while helping with the unloading, had stated somewhat pompously that all the buildings in the city were quite similar in size.

"Very interesting," Ryu said politely.

This showed, Fokin stated, that all the buildings had one and the same function. "All we have to do is establish what," he added as an afterthought.

When the helicopter returned the second time, Komov saw that Tanya and Fokin had set up a high pole and had raised over the city the unofficial flag of the Pathfinders—a white field with a stylized depiction of a heptagonal nut. A long time ago, almost a century back, one prominent spaceman and fervent opponent of the study of the evidence of extraterrestrial intelligence in outer space had once said heatedly that the only evidence that he was ready to consider irrefutable would be a wheel on an axle, a diagram of the Pythagorean theorem carved onto a cliffside, or a heptagonal nut. The Pathfinders had accepted the challenge and had emblazoned their flag with a depiction of a heptagonal nut.

Komov saluted the flag gladly. Much fuel had been burned and many parsecs had been traveled since the flag had been created. It had first flown over the circular streets of the empty city on Mars. At that time the fantastic hypothesis that both the city and the Martian satellites could have a natural origin had still had currency. At that time even the most daring Pathfinders merely considered the city and the satellites to be the sole remains of a mysterious vanished Martian civilization. And many parsecs had to be traveled, and much ground had to be dug, before only one hypothesis remained unrefuted: the empty cities and the abandoned satellites had been built by visitors from an unknown distant planetary system. But this city on Leonida . . .

Komov got the last pack out of the helicopter cabin, jumped into the grass, and slammed the door shut. Ryu went up to him, and said while rolling down his sleeves, "And now I must leave you, Gennady. I have a sounding in twenty minutes."

"Of course," said Komov. "Thank you, Ryu. Come have supper with us."

Ryu looked at his watch and said, "Thank you, but I can't guarantee it."

Mboga, leaning his carbine against the wall of the nearest building, inflated a tent right in the middle of the street. He watched Ryu leave and then smiled at Komov, parting the gray lips on his small wrinkled face. "This is verily a planet with all the conveniences, Gennady," he said. "Here we walk around weaponless, pitch tents right on the grass. And this . . ." He nodded in the direction of Fokin and Tanya. The Pathfinder archaeologist and the archaeological engineer, having trampled down the grass around them, were fussing over the autolab in the shade of a building. The archaeological engineer wore shorts and a silk sleeveless blouse. Her heavy shoes adorned the roof of the building, and her coverall lay next to the packs. Fokin, wearing gym shorts, was tearing off his sweat-drenched jacket.

"Good grief," Tanya was saying. "How did you connect the batteries?"

"In a minute, in a minute, Tanya," Fokin answered vaguely.

"No," said Komov. "This isn't Pandora." He dragged a second tent out of the pack and set about fitting the rotary pump to it. *No, this isn't Pandora*, he thought. On Pandora they had forced their way through murky jungles wearing heavy-duty spacesuits, carrying cumbersome disintegrators with the safety catches off. It squished underfoot, and with every step multilegged vermin ran every whichway, while overhead two blood-red suns shone dimly through the tangle of sticky branches. And it was not only Pandora! On every planet with an atmosphere the Pathfinders and the Assaultmen moved with the greatest caution, driving before them columns of robot scouts, self-propelled biolabs, toxicanalyzers, condensed clouds of universal virophages. Immediately after landing, a ship's captain was required to burn out a safety zone with thermite. It was considered an enormous crime to return to a ship without a preliminary, very careful disinfection and disinfestation. Invisible monsters more terrible than the plague or leprosy lay in wait for the unwary. It had happened only thirty years back.

It could happen even now on Leonida, the planet with all the conveniences. There were microfauna here too, and very abundant they were. But thirty years ago, small Doctor Mboga had found the "battery of life" on fierce Pandora, and Professor Karpenko on Earth had discovered bioblockading. One injection a day. You could even get by with one a week. Komov wiped his damp face and started undoing his jacket.

When the sun had sunk toward the west and the sky in the east had turned from a whitish color to dark violet, they sat down to supper. The camp was ready. Three tents crossed the street, and the packs and boxes of equipment were neatly stacked along the wall of one of the buildings. Fokin, sighing, had cooked supper. Everyone was hungry, and consequently they did not wait for Ryu. From the camp they could see that Ryu was sitting on the roof of his laboratory, doing something with the antennas.

"Never mind—we'll leave some for him," Tanya promised.

"Go ahead," said Fokin, starting to eat his boiled veal. "He'll get hungry and he'll come."

"You picked the wrong place to put the helicopter, Gennady," said Tanya. "It blocks off the whole view of the river."

Everyone looked at the helicopter. It really did destroy the view.

"You get a fine river view from the roof," Komov said calmly.

"No, really," said Fokin, who was sitting with his back to the river. "There's nothing tasteful around here to look at."

"What do you mean nothing?" Komov said as calmly as before. "What about the veal?" He lay down on his back and started looking at the sky.

"Here's what I'm thinking about," Fokin retorted, wiping his mustache with a napkin. "How will we dig into these graves?" He tapped his finger against the nearest building. "Shall we go under, or cut into the wall?"

"That's not quite the problem," Komov said lazily. "How did the owners get in?—*that's* the problem. Did they cut into the walls too?"

Fokin looked thoughtfully at Komov and asked, "And what in fact do you know about the owners? Maybe they didn't need to get in there."

"Uh-huh," said Tanya. "A new architectural principle. Somebody sat down on the grass, put walls and a ceiling around himself, and . . . and. . . ."

"And went away," Mboga finished.

"Well, suppose they really are tombs?" Fokin insisted.

Everyone discussed this proposal for some time.

"Tatyana, what do the analyses say?" asked Komov.

"Limestone," said Tanya. "Calcium carbonate. Plus many impurities, of course. You know what it's like? Coral reefs. And the more so, since the building is made out of a single piece."

"A monolith of natural origin."

"Here we go again with that natural business!" cried Fokin. "It's a scientific law: you have only to find new evidence of aliens, and immediately people appear to declare that it's a natural formation."

"It's a natural proposition," said Komov.

"Tomorrow we'll put together the intravisor and have a look," Tanya promised. "The main thing is that this limestone has nothing in common with the stuff that the city on Mars is built from. Or the amberine of the city on Vladislava."

"So someone else is wandering among the planets," said Komov. "It would be nice if this time they left us something a little more substantial."

"If we could just find a library," moaned Fokin. "Or some sort of machinery!"

They fell silent. Mboga got out a short pipe, and started filling it. He squatted, looking pensively over the tents into the bright sky. Under the white kerchief, his small face had a look of complete peace and satisfaction.

"It's peaceful," said Tanya.

Boom! Bang! Rat-tat-tat! came from the direction of the base.

"The devil!" muttered Fokin. "What in hell do we need that for?"

Mboga blew a smoke ring, and, watching it rise, said softly, "I understand, Boris. For the first time in my life I myself feel no joy in hearing our machines at work on an alien planet."

"It's somehow not alien, that's the thing," said Tanya.

A large black beetle flew in from somewhere or other, buzzing noisily, circled over the Pathfinders twice, and left. Fokin sniffed softly, and buried his nose in his bent elbow. Tanya got up and went into the tent. Komov got up too and stretched happily. It was so quiet and nice around that he was completely nonplussed when Mboga suddenly jumped up on his feet as if shot from a gun, and then froze, with his face turned toward the river. Komov turned his head in that direction too.

Some sort of enormous black hulk was moving toward the camp. The helicopter partly hid it, but they could see it sway as it walked, and could see the evening sun gleam on its moist shiny sides, which were puffed out like the belly of a hippopotamus. The hulk moved fairly rapidly, brushing aside the grass, and Komov saw with horror that the helicopter was swaying and had slowly started to tip over. Between the wall of a building and the belly of the helicopter a massive low forehead with two enormous bulges stuck out. Komov saw two small dull eyes, staring, as it seemed, straight at him. "Look out!" he yelled.

The helicopter tipped over, propping itself up in the grass on its rotor vanes. The monster kept moving toward the camp. It was no less than ten feet tall. Its striped sides rose and fell evenly, and they could hear measured, noisy breathing.

Behind Komov's back, Mboga cocked the carbine with a click. Then Komov came to himself and backed toward the tent. Fokin scrambled quickly back on all fours, overtaking him. The monster was already just twenty paces away.

"Can you manage to break camp?" Mboga asked quickly.

"No," answered Komov.

"Then I'm going to fire," said Mboga.

"Wait a moment," said Komov. He stepped forward, waved his arm, and shouted "Stop!"

For an instant the mountain of meat on the hoof did stop. The knobby forehead suddenly lifted up, and a mouth as capacious as a helicopter cabin, stuffed with green grass cud, gaped open.

"Gennady!" cried Tanya. "Get back at once!"

The monster emitted a prolonged screeching sound and moved forward even faster.

"Stop!" Komov shouted again, but now without much enthusiasm. "Evidently it's herbivorous," he stated, and moved back toward the tents.

He looked back. Mboga was standing with his carbine at his shoulder, and Tanya was already covering her ears. Next to Tanya stood Fokin, with a pack on his back. "Are you going to shoot at it today or not?" Fokin yelled in a strained voice. "It'll make off with the intravisor or—"

Ka-thwak! Mboga's semiautomatic hunting carbine was a .64 caliber, and the kinetic energy of the bullet at a distance of ten paces equaled nine tons. The bullet landed in the very center of the forehead between the two bulges. The monster sat down hard on its rear. *Ka-thwak!* The second bullet turned the monster over on its back. Its short fat legs moved convulsively through the air. A *"kh-h-a-a-a"* came from the thick grass. The black belly rose and fell, and then all was quiet. Mboga put the carbine down. "Let's go have a look," he said.

The monster was no smaller in size than an adult African elephant, but it more resembled a gigantic hippopotamus.

"Red blood," said Fokin. "And what is this?" The monster lay on its side, and along its belly extended three rows of soft protuberances the size of a fist. A shiny thick liquid oozed from the growths. Mboga suddenly inhaled noisily, took a drop of liquid on the tip of a finger, and tasted it.

"Yuck!" said Fonin.

The same expression appeared on all their faces.

"Honey," said Mboga.

"You don't say!" exclaimed Komov. He hesitated, then also extended a finger. Tanya and Fokin watched his movements with disgust. "Real honey!" he exclaimed. "Lime-blossom honey!"

"Doctor Dickson had said that there are many saccharides in this grass," said Mboga.

"A honey monster," said Fokin. "Pity we did him in."

"We!" exclaimed Tanya. "Good grief, go put away the intravisor."

"Well, okay," said Komov. "What do we do now? It's hot here, and with a carcass like this next to the camp . . ."

"I'll take care of it," said Mboga. "Drag the tents twenty paces or so down the street. I'll make all the measurements, look it over, and then annihilate it."

"How?" asked Tanya.

"With a disintegrator. I have a disintegrator. And you, Tanya, get away from here. I am now going to embark on some very unappetizing work."

They heard footsteps, and Ryu jumped out from behind the tent with a large automatic pistol. "What happened?" he asked, panting.

"We killed one of your hippopotamuses," Fokin explained pompously.

Ryu quickly looked everyone over and immediately relaxed. He stuck his pistol in his belt. "Did it charge?" he asked.

"Not exactly," Komov answered confusedly. "If you ask me, it was simply out for a stroll, but we have to stop it."

Ryu looked at the overturned helicopter and nodded.

"Can't we eat it?" Fokin shouted from the tent.

Mboga said slowly, "It looks like somebody has already tried eating it."

Komov and Ryu went over to him. With his fingers, Mboga was feeling broad, deep, straight scars on the loin parts of the animal. "Powerful fangs did that," said Mboga. "Ones sharp as knives. Someone took off slices of five or six kilos each with one swipe."

"Some sort of horror," Ryu said very sincerely.

A strange, prolonged cry sounded high in the sky. Everyone looked up.

"There they are!" said Ryu.

Large light-gray birds like eagles rushed headlong down on the city. One behind another, they dropped from an enormous altitude. Just over the humans' heads they spread broad, soft wings and darted upward just as violently, pouring waves of warm air over the humans. They were enormous birds, larger than terrestrial condors or even the flying dragons of Pandora.

"Meat eaters!" Ryu said excitedly. He started to draw the pistol from his belt, but Mboga seized him firmly by the arm.

The birds rushed over the city and off into the violet evening sky to the west. When the last of them had disappeared, the same disturbing prolonged cry sounded.

"I was ready to fire," Ryu said with relief.

"I know," said Mboga. "But it seemed to me. . . ." He stopped.

"Yes," said Komov. "It seemed that way to me too."

Upon consideration, Komov ordered the tents to be moved not merely twenty paces, but onto the flat roof of one of the buildings. The buildings were low—only seven feet or so high—so it was not difficult to climb on top of them. Tanya and Fokin put the packs with the most valuable instruments on the roof of the next building over. The helicopter was not damaged. Komov took it up and landed it neatly on the roof of a third building.

Mboga spent the whole night under the floodlights, examining the monster's carcass. Then at dawn the street filled with a shrill hissing sound, a large cloud of white steam flew up over the city, and a shortlived orange glow flashed out. Fokin, who had never before seen an organic disintegrator at work, dashed out of a tent wearing only shorts, but all he saw was Mboga, who was unhurriedly cleaning a flood light, and an enormous cloud of fine gray dust over blackened grass. All that remained of the honey monster was its ugly head, expertly prepared, coated with transparent plastic, and destined for the Capetown Museum of Exozoology.

Fokin wished Mboga a good morning and was about to go back into the tent and finish his sleep, when he ran into Komov.

"Where are you going?" Komov inquired.

"To get dressed, of course," Fokin replied with dignity. The morning was fresh and clear, except for scattered white clouds which floated unmoving in the violet sky to the south. Komov jumped down onto the grass and set off to fix breakfast. He planned on fixing fried eggs, but he couldn't find the butter.

"Boris," he called, "where's the butter?"

Fokin was standing on the roof in a strange pose—he was doing Yoga exercises.

"I have no idea," he said haughtily.

"You did the cooking yesterday evening."

"Uh . . . yes. So the butter is where it was last evening."

"And where was it last evening?" Komov asked with restraint.

Fokin, with a displeased look, disengaged his head from under his right knee. "How should I know?" he said. "We restacked all the boxes afterward."

Komov sighed, and started patiently examining box after box. There was no butter. Then he went over to the building and dragged Fokin down by a leg. "Where's the butter?" he asked.

Fokin had just opened his mouth to reply when Tanya came around the corner, wearing a sleeveless blouse and shorts. Her hair was wet.

"Morning, boys," she said.

"Morning, Tanya my sweet," said Fokin. "You haven't by any chance seen the box of butter?"

"Where have you been?" Komov asked fiercely.

"Swimming," said Tanya.

"What do you mean you've been swimming?" said Komov. "Who gave you permission?"

Tanya unfastened from her belt an electric hacker in a plastic sheath, and threw it onto the boxes. "Gennady, old dear," she said, "there aren't any crocodiles here. The water is wonderful and the bottom is grassy."

"You haven't seen the butter?" Komov asked.

"No, I haven't—but has anybody seen my shoes?"

"I have," said Fonin. "They're on the other roof."

"No, they're not."

All three turned around and looked at the roof. The shoes were gone. Komov looked at Mboga. He was lying on the grass in the shade, sleeping soundly, with his small fists under his cheek.

"Come now!" said Tanya. "What would he do with my shoes?"

"Or the butter," added Fokin.

"Perhaps they were in his way," muttered Komov. "Well, all right. I'll cook something without butter."

"And without shoes."

"All right, all right," said Komov. "Go work on the intravisor. You too, Tanya. Try to get it put together as soon as possible."

Ryu came to breakfast. Before him he herded a large black machine on six hemomechanical legs. The machine left behind it a broad swath through the grass, stretching all the way back to the base. Ryu scrambled up to the roof and sat at the table, while the machine stopped in the middle of the street below.

"Tell me, Ryu," said Komov. "Did anything ever get lost on you back at the base?"

"Like what?" asked Ryu.

"Well, say you leave something outside overnight, and you can't find it in the morning."

"Not that I know of." Ryu shrugged. "Sometimes little things get lost—bits of rubbish, pieces of wire, scraps of lithoplast. But I think my cybers pick up that sort of trash. They're very economical little comrades, and they can find a use for anything."

"Could they find a use for my shoes?" asked Tanya.

Ryu laughed. "I don't know," he said. "I hardly think so."

"And could they find a use for a box of butter?" asked Fokin.

Ryu stopped laughing. "You've lost your butter?" he asked.

"And a pair of shoes."

"No," said Ryu. "The cybers don't go into the city."

Deftly as a lizard, Mboga climbed onto the roof. "Good morning," he said. "I'm late."

Tanya poured him his coffee. Mboga always breakfasted on one cup of coffee.

"So, we've been robbed," he said, smiling.

"Meaning it wasn't you?" asked Fokin.

"No, it wasn't me. But last night the birds we saw yesterday flew over the city twice."

"And so much for the shoes," said Fokin. "Somewhere I—"

"I haven't lost anything in two months," said Ryu. "Of course, I keep everything in the dome. And then, I have the cybers. And smoke and noise all the time."

"Okay," said Fokin, getting up. "Let's get to work, Tanya girl. Imagine, a pair of shoes!"

They left, and Komov started gathering up the dishes.

"I'll post a guard around you this evening," said Ryu.

"As you like," Mboga said thoughtfully. "But I'd prefer doing it myself at first. Gennady, I'm going to bed right now, and tonight I'll set up a little ambush."

"Very well, Doctor Mboga," Komov said reluctantly.

"Then I'll come too," said Ryu.

"Do that," Mboga agreed. "But no cybers, please."

From the next roof came an outburst of indignation. "Good grief, I asked you to put the packs down in order of assembly!"

"I did! That *is* how I put them!"

"You call this order of assembly? E-7, A-2, B-16 . . . then E again!"

"Tanya my sweet! Honest! Comrades!" Fokin called across the street in a wounded voice. "Who mixed up the packs?"

"Look!" shouted Tanya. "Pack E-9 is gone completely!"

Mboga said quietly, "Messieurs, we're also missing a sheet."

"What?" said Komov. He was pale. "Search everywhere!" he shouted, jumping from the roof and running toward Fokin and Tanya. Mboga watched him go and then started looking to the south, across the river. He could hear Komov say on the next roof, "What exactly is missing?"

"The HFG," Tanya answered.

"So what are you standing there jabbering for? Put together a new one."

"That will take two days," Tanya said angrily.

"Then what do you suggest?"

"We'll have to cut," said Fokin. Then silence reigned on the roof.

"Ryu, look," Mboga said suddenly. He stood up and, shading his eyes from the sun, looked across the river.

Ryu turned around. Across the river the green plain was dotted with black spots—hippopotamus backs, and there were very many of them. Ryu had never imagined that there could be so many. The spots were slowly moving south.

"I think they're going away," Mboga said.

Komov decided to spend the night under the open sky. He dragged his cot out of the tent and lay down on the roof, his hands behind his head. The sky was blue-black, and a large greenish-orange disk with fuzzy edges—Palmyra, the moon of Leonida—crawled slowly up from the eastern horizon. Muffled drawn-out cries, no doubt those of the birds, came from the dark plain across the river. Brief flashes of sheet lightning appeared over the base, and something gnashed and crackled softly.

We'll have to put up a fence, thought Komov. *Enclose the city with an electric fence, and run through a fairly weak current. But then, if it's the birds, a fence won't help. And it probably is the birds. A huge critter like that wouldn't have any trouble at all in dragging off a pack. It could probably even carry off a person. After all, on Pandora once a flying dragon grabbed a man in a heavy-duty spacesuit, and that was maybe one-hundred-fifty kilos. That's the way things are going. First shoes, then a pack . . . and the whole expedition has only one carbine. Why was Gorbovsky so set against weapons? Of course we should have opened fire then—at least to scare them away. Why wouldn't the doctor fire? Because it "seemed" to him . . . and I wouldn't have fired myself, because it had "seemed" to me too. And just exactly what had it seemed to me?* Komov wiped his forehead, wet from nervousness, vigorously with his hand. *Enormous birds, beautiful birds, and how they flew! What noise-less, effortless, perfect flight! Well, even hunters sometimes pity the game, and I'm no hunter.*

A bright white little spot among the twinkling stars slowly went past the zenith. Komov got up on his elbows and watched it. It was the *Sunflower*—a kilometer-long super-long-range Assault starship. It was now orbiting Leonida at a distance of two megameters. They had only to send a distress signal, and help would come from there. But should they send a distress signal? They had lost one pair of shoes, a pack, and something had "seemed" to the chief. . . .

The little white spot grew dim and vanished. The *Sunflower* had gone off into Leonida's shadow. Komov lay down again and put his hands behind his head. *Aren't there just too many conveniences?* he thought. *Warm green plains, sweet-scented air, an idyllic river with no crocodiles . . . Maybe this is only a smokescreen that some sort of unknown forces are operating behind? Or is everything much simpler? Say Tanya lost her shoes somewhere in the grass. And everyone knows Fokin is a muddler—the lost packs could be lying somewhere under a pile of excavator parts. I mean, today he was running around all day from pile to pile, glancing around on the sly.*

Komov must have dozed off. When he awoke again, Palmyra was high in the sky. From the tent where Fokin was sleeping came smacking and snoring sounds. There was whispering on the next roof:

". . . As soon as the cable broke, off we flew, leaving Saburo below. He chased after us and shouted for us to stop, then named me captain and *ordered* me to stop. Of course right away I started steering for the relay mast. We tied up to it and hung there for the whole night. And the whole time we shouted at each other, arguing over whether Saburo should go find Teacher or not. Saburo could go, but wouldn't, and we would, but couldn't. Finally in the morning they saw us and got us down."

"Well, I was a quiet girl. And I was always scared of any sort of machinery. I'm still afraid of cybers."

"There's no reason to be afraid of cybers, Tanya. Cybers are gentle."

"I don't like them. I don't like the way they're sort of animate and inanimate at the same time."

Komov turned over on his side and looked. Tanya and Ryu were sitting crosslegged on the next roof. *Ah, the lovebirds,* thought Komov. *Tomorrow they'll be yawning all day.* "Tanya," he said in a low voice, "it's time to go to sleep."

"I'm not sleepy," said Tanya. "We were walking along the bank." Ryu started to move off in embarrassment. "It's nice by the river. The moonlight, and the fish jumping. . . ."

Ryu said, "Hey, where's Doctor Mboga?"

"He's at work," said Komov.

"Really!" Tanya said happily. "Ryu, let's go find Doctor Mboga!"

She's hopeless, Komov thought, and rolled over onto his other side. The whispering on the roof continued. Komov got up decisively, took his cot, and went back into the tent. It was very noisy there—Fokin was sleeping with all his might. *You muddler, you muddler,* Komov thought as he settled himself in. *Such a night for romance. But you grew your mustache and thought it was in the bag.* He wrapped himself up in a sheet and fell asleep instantly.

A muffled roar tossed him on the cot. It was dark in the tent. *Ka-thwack! Ka-thwack!* thundered two more shots. "The devil!" Fokin yelled in the darkness. "Who's there?" Komov heard a short harelike cry and a triumphant yell, "Ha! Come here, come with me!" Komov tangled himself up in the sheet and could not get up. He heard a muffled blow, Fokin's "Ow!", and then something small and dark showed for an instant, and disappeared through the light triangle of the doorway of the tent. Komov darted after it. Fokin did too, and they bumped heads violently. Komov clenched his teeth and at last flung himself outside. The other roof was empty. Looking around, Komov saw Mboga running through the grass down the street toward the river, and Riu and Tanya following on his heels, stumbling. And Komov noticed something else—someone was running far ahead of Mboga, parting the grass before him—was running much faster than

Mboga. Mboga stopped, pointed his carbine straight up with one arm, and fired again. The wake in the grass swerved to one side and disappeared around the corner of the last building. After a second a bird, white in the moonlight, gracefully spread wide its enormous wings, and rose up from that spot.

"Shoot!" yelled Fokin.

He was already dashing down the street, stumbling at every fifth step. Mboga stood motionless, with his carbine lowered, and, craning his neck, watched the bird. It made an even, noiseless circle over the city, gaining altitude, and flew off to the south. In a moment it had disappeared. Then Komov saw more birds flying very low over the base—three, four, five—five enormous white birds shot upward over the cybers' workplace, and disappeared.

Komov got down from the roof. The dead parallelepipeds of the buildings threw dense black shadows onto the grass. The grass looked silver. Something jingled underfoot. Komov bent over. A cartridge-case gleamed in the grass. Komov crossed over the distorted shadow of the helicopter, and heard voices. Mboga, Fokin, Ryu, and Tanya were walking unhurriedly toward him.

"I had him in my hands!" Fokin said excitedly. "But he knocked me on the head and tore away. If he hadn't slugged me, I never would have let him go! He was soft and warm, like a child. And naked."

"We almost caught him too," said Tanya. "But he turned into a bird and flew away."

"Come now!" scoffed Fokin. "Turned into a bird. . . ."

"No, really," Ryu insisted. "He rounded the corner, and right away a bird flew up."

"So?" said Fokin. "He flushed a bird, and you stood there with your mouths gaping."

"A coincidence," said Mboga.

Komov went up to them, and they stopped.

"What exactly happened?" asked Komov.

"I had caught him," declared Fokin, "but he knocked me over the head."

"I heard that," said Komov. "How did it all start?"

"I was sitting on the packs, in ambush," said Mboga. "I saw someone creeping through the grass right in the middle of the street. I wanted to catch him, and I moved toward him, but he saw me and turned back. I saw I couldn't catch him, and fired into the air. I'm very sorry, Gennady, but I think I frightened them off."

Silence reigned. Then Fokin asked doubtfully, "Exactly why are you sorry, Doctor Mboga?"

Mboga did not answer at once. Everyone waited. "There were at least two of them," he finally said. "I discovered one, and the other was in the tent with you. But when I ran past the helicopter . . . well, look for yourselves," he concluded unexpectedly. "You'll have to examine it. Probably I'm wrong." Silently Mboga started walking toward the camp. The others, exchanging glances, moved after him. Mboga stopped near the building on which the helicopter was sitting. "Somewhere around here," he said.

Fokin and Tanya quickly crawled into the dark shadow under the wall. Ryu and Komov looked down expectantly at Mboga. He was thinking.

"There's nothing here," Fokin snapped.

"Just what did I see?" muttered Mboga. "Just what did I see?"

Fokin, irritated, moved away from the wall. The black shadow of the rotor vane crept across his face.

"Aha!" Mboga said loudly. "A strange shadow!"

He threw down the carbine and with a running jump he leapt onto the wall. "Please!" he said from the roof.

On the roof, beyond the helicopter fuselage, as if in a shop window, the things were neatly arranged—the butter, pack number E-9, the shoes, a neatly folded sheet, a pocket microelectrometer in a plastic case, four neutron batteries, a ball of dried vitriplast, and a pair of sunglasses.

"Here are my shoes," said Tanya. "And my sunglasses. I dropped them into the river yesterday."

"Ye-es," Fokin said, and looked around carefully.

Komov seemed to come to himself. "Ryu!" he quickly shouted. "I have to get hold of the *Sunflower* immediately. Fokin, Tanya, make a photograph of this display! I'll be back in half an hour."

He jumped off the roof and started walking quickly, then broke into a run, heading down the street toward the base. Ryu followed him without saying anything.

"What's going on?" yelled Fokin.

Mboga squatted down, got out his small pipe, puffed at it unhurriedly, and said, "They're people, Boris. Even animals can steal things, but only people can bring back what they have stolen."

Fokin moved back and sat on the wheel of the helicopter.

Komov returned alone. He seemed very excited, and in a high-pitched metallic voice he ordered them to break camp immediately. Fokin started showering him with questions. He demanded explanations. Then Komov recited in the same metallic voice: "By order of the captain of the starship *Sunflower:* Within three hours the meteorological base and laboratory, and the archeological camp will be dismantled; all cybernetic systems will be shut down; and all personnel, including Atmosphere Physicist Waseda, will return on board the *Sunflower.*" Fokin submitted out of sheer surprise and set to work with unusual diligence.

In two hours the helicopter made eight trips, and the cargo robots trampled down a broad road through the grass from the base to the boat. Of the base, only empty construction sites remained—all three systems of construction robots had been herded inside the storehouse and completely deprogrammed.

At six o'clock in the morning local time, when the east had begun to glow with the green dawn, the exhausted humans gathered by the boat, and here, at last, Fokin lost patience.

"Well, all right," he began in an irate hoarse whisper. "You relayed us orders, Gennady, and we have carried them out honestly. But I would like to find out at last how come we're leaving here! Why?" he yelped suddenly in a falsetto, picturesquely throwing up his hands. Everyone jumped, and Mboga dropped the pipe from his teeth. "Why? We look for Brothers in Reason for three hundred years, and run off with our tails between our legs as soon as we've discovered them? The best minds of humanity—"

"Good grief," said Tanya, and Fokin shut up.

"I don't understand a thing," he said then in a hoarse whisper.

"Do you think, Boris, that we are capable of representing the best minds of humanity?" asked Mboga.

Komov muttered gloomily, "We've sure messed things up

here! We burned out a whole field, trampled crops, shot guns. And around the base!" He waved his hand.

"But how could we know?" Ryu said guiltily.

"Yes," said Mboga. "We made many mistakes. But I hope they've understood us. They're civilized enough for that."

"What sort of a civilization is this!" said Fokin. "Where are the machines? Where are the tools? Where are the cities?"

"Shut up, Boris," said Komov. " 'Machines, cities'—just open your eyes! Do we know how to fly on birds? Have we bred animals that produce honey? Has our last mosquito been long exterminated? 'Machines.' . . ."

"A biological civilization," said Mboga.

"What?" asked Fokin.

"A biological civilization. Not machines, but selection, genetics, animal training. Who knows what forces they've mastered? And who can say whose civilization is superior?"

"Imagine, Boris," said Tanya.

Fokin twirled his mustache furiously.

"And we're clearing out," said Komov, "because none of us has the right to take upon himself the responsibility of first contact." *Oh, am I sorry to leave!* he thought. *I don't want to go—I want to search them out, to meet them, to talk, to see what they're like. Can this really have happened at last? Not some brainless lizards, not some sort of leeches, but a real human race. A whole world, a whole history. . . . Did you have wars and revolutions? Which did you get first, steam or electricity? And what is the meaning of life? And might I perhaps have something to read? The first essay in the comparative history of intelligent species. And we have to go. Oh boy, oh boy, do I ever feel like staying! But on Earth there has already for fifty years been a Commission on Contacts, which for all those years has been studying the comparative psychology of fish and ants, and arguing over in what language to say the first "uh." Only now you can't laugh at them any more. I wonder whether any of them had foreseen the possibility of a biological civilization. Probably. What haven't they foreseen?*

"Gorbovsky is a man of phenomenal penetration," said Mboga.

"Yes," said Tanya. "It's frightening to think what old Boris could have done if he'd had a gun."

"Why single me out?" Fokin said angrily. "What about you? Who was it that went swimming with a hacker?"

"We're all a fine bunch," Ryu said with a sigh.

Komov looked at his watch. "Takeoff in twenty minutes," he announced. "Stations, please."

Mboga hesitated in the airlock and looked back. The white star EN 23 had already risen over the green plain. It smelled of moist grass, warm earth, fresh honey. "Yes," said Mboga. "Really a planet with all the conveniences. Why did we ever think nature could have created anything like it?"

PART FOUR: *What You Will Be Like*

Defeat

"You're going to the island of Shumshu," Fischer announced.

"Where is that?" Sidorov asked gloomily.

"The northern Kurils. Your flight leaves today at twenty-two thirty. A combined cargo-passenger run from Novosibirsk to Port Provideniya."

They planned on testing embryomechs under varied conditions. Mostly the Institute did work for spacemen, and consequently thirty research groups out of forty-seven had been sent to the Moon and to various planets. The remaining seventeen were to work on Earth.

"All right," Sidorov said slowly. He had hoped that they would assign him a space group, even if only a lunar one. It seemed to him that he had a good chance, for it had been a long time since he had felt as well as he had recently. He was in excellent shape, and had continued to hope up to the last minute. But for some reason Fischer had decided otherwise, and Sidorov couldn't even talk to him man to man, since some glum-faced strangers were sitting in the office. *So this is how I'm going to grow old,* thought Sidorov. "All right," he repeated calmly.

"Severokurilsk already knows," Fischer said. "The exact site of the experiment will be decided in Baikovo."

"Where's that?"

"On the island of Shumshu. It's Shumshu's administrative center." Fischer hooked his fingers together and started looking out the window. "Sermus is staying on Earth too," he said. "He's going to the Sahara."

Sidorov was silent.

"So," said Fischer. "I have already assigned you some assistants. You'll have two of them. Good kids."

"Greenhorns."

"They'll manage," Fischer said quickly. "They've had good preparation. Good kids, I tell you. One of them, incidentally, has been an Assaultman like you."

"Fine," Sidorov said indifferently. "Is that it?"

"That's it. You can start off, and good luck. Your cargo and your people are in One-sixteen."

Sidorov started walking toward the door. Fischer hesitated, then called after him, "And come back soon, Kamerad. I have an interesting topic for you."

Sidorov closed the door behind him and stood there a moment. Laboratory 116 was five stories below, he remembered, so he headed for the elevator.

An Egg—a polished sphere half as high as a man—was standing in the righthand corner of the laboratory, and two people were sitting in the left corner. They stood up when Sidorov came in. Sidorov stopped and looked them over. They were both about twenty-five, no older. One was tall, blond, with an ugly red face. The other was a little shorter, a dark, handsome, Spanish type, wearing a suede jacket and heavy climbing boots. Sidorov stuck his hands into his pockets, stood on tiptoes, and came down again on his heels. *Greenhorns,* he thought, and suddenly felt the attack of irritation so strong that he surprised himself. "Hello," he said. "My name is Sidorov."

The dark one showed white teeth. "We know, sir." He stopped smiling and introduced himself: "Kuzma Sorochinsky."

"Galtsev, Viktor," said the blond one.

I wonder which of them was the Assaultman, thought Sidorov. *Probably the Spanish-looking one, Sorochinsky.* He asked, "Which of you was the Assaultman?"

"I was," answered the blond Galtsev.

"Disciplinary?" asked Sidorov.

"Yes," said Galtsev. "Disciplinary." He looked Sidorov in the eye. Galtsev had baby-blue eyes and fluffy, feminine lashes. Somehow they did not fit in with his coarse red face.

"Well," said Sidorov, "an Assaultman is supposed to be disciplined. Any person is supposed to be disciplined. But that's water under the bridge. What can you do, Galtsev?"

"I'm a biologist," Galtsev said. "A specialist in nematodes."

"Right," Sidorov said, and turned to Sorochinsky. "And you?"

"Gastronomical engineer," Sorochinsky reported loudly, again showing his white teeth.

Marvelous, thought Sidorov. *A worm specialist and a pastry cook. An undisciplined Assaultman and a suede jacket. Good kids. Especially this excuse for an Assaultman. Thank you, Comrade Fischer, you always take such good care of me.* Sidorov imagined Fischer carefully and carpingly picking the off-planet groups out of two thousand volunteers, then looking at the clock, looking at the lists, and saying to himself, "Sidorov's group. The Kurils. Athos is efficient, experienced. Three people will be quite enough for him. Two, even. It's hardly the Hot Plateau on Mercury, after all. We'll give him this Sorochinsky and this Galtsev. All the better, Galtsev has been an Assaultman too."

"You've been briefed for this work?" asked Sidorov.

"Yes," said Galtsev.

"I'll say we have, sir," said Sorochinsky. "We've got it coming out our ears!"

Sidorov went over to the Egg and touched its cold, polished surface. Then he asked, "Do you know what this is? You, Galtsev."

Galtsev raised his eyes to the ceiling, thought a bit, and said in a monotone, "Embryomechanical device EM-8. Embryomech Model Eight. An autonomous self-developing mechanized system including: FMC program control—the Fischer mechanochromosome; a system of organs of perception and action; a digestive system; and a power system. The EM-8 is an embryome-chanical device which is capable under any conditions of convert-ing any raw material into any structure given in its program. The EM-8 is intended—"

"You," Sidorov said to Sorochinsky.

Sorochinsky rattled off, "The present prototype of the EM-8 is intended for tests under terrestrial conditions. The program is standard program number sixty-four: the conversion of the embryo into an airtight residential dome for six persons, with hall and oxygen filtration."

Sidorov looked out the window and asked, "Weight?"

"Approximately one hundred and fifty kilos."

General assistants for experimental groups could really get by without knowing any of this.

"Fine," said Sidorov. "Now I'll tell you what you don't know. In the first place, the Egg costs nineteen thousand man-hours of skilled labor. In the second place, it really does weigh all of one hundred and fifty kilos, and you will haul it yourselves to where we need it."

Galtsev nodded. Sorochinsky said, "Of course, sir."

"Wonderful," said Sidorov. "You can start right now. Roll it to the elevator and go down to the lobby. Then go to the store-room and take out the recording apparatus. Then you can go about your own business. Be at the airport with all the cargo by ten o'clock P.M. Try not to be late."

He turned and left. From behind came a heavy thud. Sidorov's group had started carrying out its first order.

At dawn a cargo-passenger stratoplane dropped a pterocar with the group over the Second Kuril Strait. Very elegantly, Galtsev brought the pterocar out of its dive, looked around, looked at the map, looked at the compass, and immediately found his way to Baikovo—several rings of two-story buildings made of red and white lithoplast, stretching in a semicircle around a small but deep bay. The pterocar, wrenching its tough wings, landed on the embankment. An early passerby, a teenage boy in a striped sailor undershirt and canvas pants, told them where the adminis-tration building was. There the current administrator of the island, an elderly round-shouldered Ainu who was a senior agronomist, welcomed them and invited them to breakfast. After he had heard Sidorov out, he offered him a choice of several low knolls on the northern shore. He spoke Russian fairly clearly, although sometimes he hesitated in the middle of a word, as if unsure where the accent went.

"The northern shore is fairly far off," he said, "and there are no good roads going there. But you have a ptero . . . car. And then, I can't suggest anything closer for you. I don't understand experiments very well. But the greater part of the island is taken up by melon fields, seedbeds, and so forth. Schoolchil . . . dren are working everywhere now, and I can't take unneces . . . sary risks."

"There is no risk," Sorochinsky said flippantly. "No risk whatsoever."

Sidorov remembered how once he had sat on a fire escape for a whole hour, getting away from a plastic vampire that needed protoplasm in order to put the finishing touches on itself. But then it hadn't been the Egg that time. "Thank you," he said. "The northern shore will suit us very well."

"Yes," said the Ainu. "There are no melon fields or seedbeds there. Only birches. And somewhere there's an archaeo . . . logical project."

"Archaeological?" Sorochinsky said with surprise.

"Thank you," said Sidorov. "I think we'll set off right away."

"First you will have breakfast," the Ainu reminded them politely.

They breakfasted silently. As they were leaving the Ainu said, "If you need something, don't—how do you say it?—hes . . . itate to call on me."

"Thank you. We won't—how do you say it?—hes . . . itate one bit," Sorochinsky assured him.

Sidorov glared at him, and once in the pterocar said, "If you pull something like that again, punk, I'll throw you off the island."

"I'm sorry," said Sorochinsky, turning beet red. The flush made his smooth, dark face still more handsome.

In truth on the northern shore there were neither melon fields nor seedbeds, only birches. Kuril birches grow "lying down," creeping across the ground, and their wet gnarled trunks and branches form a flat, impenetrable tangle. From the air a Kuril birch thicket looks like an inoffensive green meadow, perfectly suitable for the landing of a fairly light craft. Neither Galtsev, who was driving the pterocar, nor Sidorov nor Sorochinsky had any conception of Kuril birches. Sidorov pointed out a round knoll and said, "There." Sorochinsky looked at him timidly and said, "A good place." Galtsev lowered the landing gear and steered the pterocar to a landing right in the middle of a broad green field at the foot of the round knoll.

The car's wings stood still, and in a minute the pterocar had come crackling nose first into the sparse verdure of the Kuril birches. Sidorov heard the crackling, saw a million varicolored stars, and lost consciousness.

Then he opened his eyes and first of all saw a hand. It was large, tanned, and its freshly scratched fingers seemed to be playing over the keyboard on the control panel, rather uncertainly.

The hand disappeared, and a dark-red face with blue eyes and feminine eyelashes came into view.

Sidorov wheezed and tried to sit up. His right side hurt badly, and his forehead smarted. He touched his forehead, then brought his fingers over before his eyes. The fingers were bloody. He looked at Galtsev, who was wiping his smashed mouth with a handkerchief.

"A masterly landing," said Sidorov. "You bring joy to my heart, nematologist."

Galtsev was silent. He pressed the crumpled handkerchief to his lips, and his face was motionless. Sorochinsky's high trembling voice said, "It's not his fault, sir."

Sidorov slowly turned his head and looked at Sorochinsky.

"Honest, it's not his fault," Sorochinsky repeated, and moved away. "You just look where we landed."

Sidorov opened the door a bit, stuck his head outside, and stared for several seconds at the uprooted, broken trunks which were caught in the landing gear. He extended an arm, plucked a few hard glossy leaves, crumpled them in his fingers, and tasted them with his tongue. The leaves were tart and bitter. Sidorov spat and asked, without looking at Galtsev, "Is the car in one piece?"

"Yes," Galtsev answered through his handkerchief.

"What happened? Tooth knocked out?"

"Right," said Galtsev. "Knocked clean out."

"You'll live," promised Sidorov. "You can put this down as my fault. Try to lift the car to the knoll."

It wasn't easy to pull free of the thicket, but at last Galtsev landed the pterocar on top of the round knoll. Sidorov, rubbing his right side, got out and looked around. From here the island looked uninhabited, and flat as a table. The knoll was bare and rusty from volcanic slag. To the east crept thickets of Kuril birches, and to the south stretched the rectangles of melon fields. It was about four and a half miles to the western shore. Beyond it, pale violet mountain peaks jutted up into a lilac-colored haze, and still farther off, to the right, a strange triangular cloud with sharp edges hung motionless in the blue sky. The northern shore was much closer. It descended steeply into the sea. An awkward gray tower—probably an ancient defensive emplacement—jutted up over a cliff. Near the tower a tent showed white, and small human figures moved about. Evidently these were the archaeologists of whom the administrator had spoken. Sidorov sniffed. He smelled salt water and warm rocks. And it was very quiet. He could not even hear the surf.

A good spot, he thought. *We'll leave the Egg here, put the movie cameras and so forth on the slopes, and pitch camp below, in the melon fields. The watermelons must still be green here.* Then he thought about the archaeologists. *They're about three miles off, but still we should warn them, so they won't be surprised when the embryomech starts developing.*

Sidorov called over Galtsev and Sorochinsky and said, "We'll do the test here. This seems to be a good place. The raw materials are just what we need—lava, tuff. So step to it!"

Galtsev and Sorochinsky went over to the pterocar and opened up the trunk. Sunglints burst forth. Sorochinsky crawled inside and grunted a bit, and in one sudden heave he rolled the Egg out onto the ground. Making crunching sounds on the slag, the Egg rolled a few paces and stopped. Galtsev barely had time to jump out of its way. "Careful," he said quietly. "You'll strain yourself."

Sorochinsky hopped out and said in a gruff voice, "Never mind —we're used to it."

Sidorov walked around the Egg, and tried shoving it. The Egg didn't even rock. "Wonderful," he said. "Now the movie cameras."

They fussed about for a long time setting up the movie cameras: an infrared one, a stereo camera, another that registered temperature, a fourth with a wide-angle lens.

It was already around twelve when Sidorov carefully blotted his sweaty forehead with a sleeve and got the plastic case with the activator out of his pocket. Galtsev and Sorochinsky started moving back, looking over his shoulders. Sidorov unhurriedly dropped the activator into his palm—it was a small shiny tube with a sucker on one end and a red ribbed button on the other. "Let's get started," he said aloud. He went up to the Egg and stuck the sucker to the polished metal. He waited a second, then pressed the red button with his thumb.

Without taking his eyes off the Egg he stepped back a pace. Now nothing less than a direct hit from a rocket rifle could halt the processes that had begun under the gleaming shell. The embryomech had begun to adjust itself to the field conditions. They did not know how long this would take. But when the adjustment was finished, the embryo would begin development.

Sidorov glanced at his watch. It was five after twelve. With an effort he unstuck the activator from the surface of the Egg, returned it to its case, and put it in his pocket. Then he looked at Galtsev and Sorochinsky. They were standing behind his back and watching the Egg silently. Sidorov touched the gleaming surface one last time and said, "Let's go."

He ordered the observation post to be set up between the knoll and the melon field. The Egg could easily be seen from there— a silvery ball on the rust-colored slope under the dark-blue sky. Sidorov sent Sorochinsky over to the archaeologists, then sat down in the grass in the shade of the pterocar. Galtsev was already dozing, sheltered from the sun by the wing. Sidorov sucked on a fruit drop, looking sometimes at the top of the knoll, sometimes at the strange triangular cloud in the west. Finally he got out the binoculars. As he expected, the triangular cloud turned out to be the snowy peak of a mountain, perhaps a volcano. Through the binoculars he could see the narrow shadows of thawed patches, and could even make out snow patches lower than the uneven white edge of the main mass. Sidorov put down the binoculars and began to think about the embryo. It would probably hatch from the Egg at night. This was good, because daylight usually interfered with the operation of the movie cameras. Then he thought that Sermus had probably thrown a fit with Fischer, but had nonetheless started off for the Sahara. Then he thought that Mishima was now loading at the spaceport in Kirghizia, and once again he felt an aching pain in his right side. "Not getting any younger," he muttered and glanced sidelong at Galtsev. Galtsev lay face down, with his hand under his head.

Sorochinsky returned in an hour and a half. He was shirtless, his smooth, dark skin shiny with sweat. He was carrying his foppish suede jacket and his shirt under his arm. He squatted down in front of Sidorov and, teeth agleam, related that the archaeologists thanked them for the warning and found the test very interesting, that there were four of them, that schoolchildren from Baikovo and Severokurilsk were helping them, that they were excavating underground Japanese fortifications from the middle of the century before last, and, finally, that their leader was a "ve-ry nice girl."

Sidorov thanked him for this fascinating report and asked him to see about dinner, then sat down in the shade of the pterocar and, nibbling a blade of grass, squinted at the distant white cone. Sorochinsky woke up Galtsev, and they wandered off to the side, talking softly.

"I'll make the soup, and you do the main dish, Viktor," said Sorochinsky.

"We've got some chicken somewhere," Galtsev said in a sleepy voice.

"Here's the chicken," said Sorochinsky. "The archaeologists are fun. One has let his beard grow—not a bit of bare skin left on his face. They're excavating Japanese fortifications from the forties of the century before last. There was an underground fortress here. The guy with the beard gave me a pistol cartridge. Look!"

Galtsev muttered with displeasure, "Please, don't shove it at me—it's rusty."

The odor of soup wafted up.

"That leader of theirs," Sorochinsky continued. "What a nice girl! Blonde and slender—except she's got fat legs. She sat me down in the pillbox and had me look through the embrasure. She says they could cover the whole northern shore from there."

"Well?" asked Galtsev. "Did they really shoot from there?"

"Who knows? Probably. I was mostly looking at her. Then she and I started measuring the thickness of the ceiling."

"So you were measuring for two hours?"

"Uh-huh. Then I realized she had the same last name as the guy with the beard, and I cleared out. But let me tell you, it's really filthy in those casemates. It's dark, and there's mold on the walls. Where's the bread?"

"Here," said Galtsev. "Maybe she's just the guy with the beard's sister?"

"Could be. How's the Egg coming?"

"No action."

"Well, all right," said Sorochinsky. "Comrade Sidorov, dinner's ready."

Sorochinsky talked a lot as he ate. First he explained that the Japanese word for pillbox, *tochka*, derived from the Russian *ognevaya tochka*, "firing point," while the Russian word for pillbox, *dot*, though assumed by the ignorant to be an acronym for *dolgovremennaya ognevaya tochka*, "permanent firing point," must really come from the English "dot," which meant "point." Then he began a very long discourse on pillboxes, casemates, embrasures, and density of fire per square meter, so that Sidorov ate quickly, refused any fruit for desert, and left Galtsev to watch the Egg. He got into the pterocar and began to drowse. It was surprisingly quiet, except that Sorochinsky, while washing the dishes in a stream, would every so often break out singing. Galtsev was sitting with the field glasses, his eyes glued to the top of the knoll.

When Sidorov awoke, the sun was setting, a dark-violet twilight was crawling up from the south, and it had gotten chilly. The mountains to the west had turned black, and now the cone of the distant volcano hung over the horizon as a gray shadow. The Egg on the hilltop shone with a scarlet flame. A blue-gray haze had crawled over the melon fields. Galtsev was sitting in the same pose listening to Sorochinsky.

"In Astrakhan," Sorochinsky was saying, "I once had 'Shah's rose,' a watermelon of rare beauty. It has the taste of pineapple."

Galtsev coughed.

Sidorov sat for a few moments without moving. He remembered the time he and Captain Gennady had eaten watermelons on Venita. The planetological station had gotten a whole shipload of watermelons from Earth. So they ate watermelon, ate their way into the crunchy pulp, the juice running down their cheeks, and then they shot the slippery black seeds at each other.

". . . lip-smacking good, and I say it as a gastronome."

"Quiet," said Galtsev. "You'll wake up Athos."

Sidorov arranged himself more comfortably, laying his chin on the back of the seat in front of him and closing his eyes. It was warm and a bit stuffy in the pterocar—the passenger compartment was slow to cool.

"Did you ever ship out with Athos?" Sorochinsky asked.

"No," said Galtsev.

"I feel sorry for him. And I envy him at the same time. He's lived through a life such as I'll never have. I and most other people. But still, it's all behind him now."

"Why exactly is it all behind now?" asked Galtsev. "He's just stopped spacing."

"A bird with its wings clipped. . . ." Sorochinsky fell silent for a moment. "Anyhow, the time of the Assaultmen is over," he said unexpectedly.

"Nonsense," Galtsev answered calmly.

Sidorov heard Sorochinsky start moving around. "No, it's not nonsense," Sorochinsky said. "There it is, the Egg. They're going to build them by the hundreds and drop them on unexplored and dangerous worlds. And each Egg will build a laboratory, a spaceport, a starship. It'll develop mine shafts and pits. It'll catch your nematodes and study them. And the Assaultmen will just gather data and skim off the cream."

"Nonsense," Galtsev repeated. "A laboratory or a mine shaft is one thing—but an airtight dome for six people?"

"What bothers you—the airtight part?"

"No—the six people who'll be under it."

"It doesn't matter," Sorochinsky said stubbornly. "It's still the end of the Assaultmen. A dome for people is only the beginning. They'll send automatic ships ahead to drop the Eggs, and then when everything is ready the people will come."

He began to talk about the prospects of embryomechanics, paraphrasing Fischer's famous report. *A lot of people are talking about it,* thought Sidorov. *And all that is true.* But when the first drone intrasystem craft had been tested, there had also been much talk about how all spacemen would have to do was skim off the cream. And when Akimov and Sermus had launched the first cyberscout system, Sidorov had even been on the point of giving up space. That had been thirty years before, and since that time more than once had had to jump into hell behind swarms of robots gone haywire, and to do what they could not. *A greenhorn,* he thought again about Sorochinsky. *And a blabbermouth.*

When Galtsev had said "Nonsense" for the fourth time, Sidorov got out of the car. Sorochinsky shut his mouth and jumped up at the sight of him. He had half an unripe watermelon, with a knife sticking out of it, in his hands. Galtsev continued sitting with his legs crossed.

"Would you like a watermelon, sir?" asked Sorochinsky.

Sidorov shook his head and, with his hands in his pockets, started looking at the top of the knoll. The red reflections from the polished surface of the Egg were dimming before his eyes. It was getting dark fast. A bright star suddenly rose out of the darkness, and slowly crawled through the black-blue sky.

"Satellite Eight," said Galtsev.

"No," Sorochinsky corrected with assurance. "That's Satellite Seventeen. Or no—the Mirror Satellite."

Sidorov, who knew that it was Satellite Eight, sighed and started walking toward the knoll. He was utterly fed up with Sorochinsky, and anyhow he had to inspect the movie cameras.

On the way back, he saw a fire. The irrepressible Sorochinsky had built a campfire and was now standing in a picturesque pose, waving his arms. ". . . the end is only a means," Sidorov heard. "Happiness consists not in happiness itself, but in the pursuit of happiness."

"Somewhere I've read that," said Galtsev.

Me too, thought Sidorov. *Many times. Should I order Sorochinsky to go to bed?* He looked at his watch. The luminous hands showed midnight. It was quite dark.

The Egg burst at 2:53 A.M. The night was moonless. Sidorov had been drowsing, sitting by the fire, with his right side turned toward the flame. Redfaced Galtsev was nodding nearby, and on the other side of the fire Sorochinsky was reading a newspaper, leafing through the pages. And then the Egg burst, with a sharp, piercing sound like that of an extrusion machine spitting out a finished part. Then the hilltop glowed briefly with an orange light. Sidorov looked at his watch and got up. The hilltop stood out fairly sharply against a background of starry sky. When his eyes, blinded by the campfire, had adjusted to the darkness, he saw many weak orangeish flames, slowly shifting around the place where the Egg had been.

"It's begun," Sorochinsky said in an ominous whisper. "It's begun! Viktor, wake up, it's begun!"

"Maybe you'll finally shut up now?" Galtsev snapped back. He also whispered.

Of the three, only Sidorov really knew what was going on on the hilltop. The embryomech had spent the first ten hours after activation adjusting to its surroundings. Then the adjustment process had ended, and the embryo had begun to develop. Everything in the Egg that was not needed for development had been cannibalized for the alteration and strengthening of the working organs, the effectors. Then the shell was broken open, and the embryo started to nourish itself on the feed at its feet.

The flames got bigger and bigger, and they moved faster and faster. They could hear a buzzing and a shrill gnashing—the effectors were biting into the ground and pulverizing chunks of tuff. Flash, flash! Clouds of bright smoke noiselessly detached themselves from the hilltop and swam off into the starry sky. An uncertain, trembling reflection lit up the strange, ponderously turning shapes for a second, and then everything disappeared again.

"Shall we go a little closer?" asked Sorochinsky.

Sidorov did not answer. He was remembering how the first embryomech, the ancestor of the Egg, had been tested. At that time, several years before, Sidorov had been a complete newcomer to embryomechanics. The "embryo" had been spread throughout a spacious tent near the Institute—eighteen boxes of it, like safes, along the walls—and in the middle there had been an enormous pile of cement. The effector and digestive systems were buried in the cement pile. Fischer had waved a hand and someone closed a knife switch. They had sat in the tent until late in the evening, forgetting about everything in the world. The pile of cement melted away, and by evening the features of a standard lithoplast three-room house, with steam heating and autonomous electrohousekeeping, had risen out of the steam and smoke. It was exactly like the factory model, except that in the bathroom a ceramic cube, the "stomach," was left, along with the complicated articulations of the effectors. Fischer had looked the house over, tapped the effectors with his foot, and said, "Enough of this fooling around. It's time to make an Egg."

That was the first time the word had been spoken. Then had come a lot of work, many successes, and many more failures. The embryo had learned to adjust itself, to adapt to sharp changes of environment, to renew itself. It had learned to develop into a house, an excavator, a rocket. It had learned not to smash up when it fell into a chasm, not to malfunction while floating on waves of molten metal, not to fear absolute zero. . . . *No*, thought Sidorov, *it's a good thing that I stayed on Earth.*

The clouds of bright smoke flew off the hilltop faster and faster. The cracking, scraping, and buzzing merged into an uninterrupted jangling noise. The wandering red flames were forming chains, and the chains were twisting into queer moving lines. A pink glow settled over them, and he could already make out something enormous and bulging, rocking like a ship on waves.

Sidorov again looked at his watch. It was five to four. Obviously the lava and tuff had turned out to be eminently suitable material—the dome was rising much faster than it had on cement. He wondered what would come next. The mechanism built the dome from the top down, as the effectors dug deeper and deeper into the knoll. To keep the dome from ending up underground, the embryo would have to resort either to driving piles for support, or to moving the dome to one side of the pit dug by the effectors. Sidorov imagined the white-hot edge of the dome, to which the effectors' scoops were molding more and more bits of lithoplast heated to malleability.

For a minute the hilltop was plunged into darkness. The din ceased, and only a vague buzzing could be heard. The embryo was readjusting the work of the energy system.

"Sorochinsky," said Sidorov.

"Here!"

"Get over to the thermocamera and shove it up a little closer. But don't climb the knoll."

"Yes, sir."

Sidorov heard him ask Galtsev for the flashlight in a whisper, and then a yellow circle of light bobbed over the gravel and disappeared.

The noise started again. The pink glow reappeared on the hilltop. Sidorov thought that the black dome had moved a little, but he was not sure about it. He thought with vexation that he should have sent Sorochinsky to the thermocamera right away, as soon as the embryo had burst from the Egg.

Then something gave a deafening roar. The hilltop blazed up in red. A crimson bolt of lightning slowly crawled down the black slope, then disappeared. The pink glow turned yellow and bright, and was immediately obscured by thick smoke. A thundering blow struck his ears, and with horror Sidorov saw an enormous shadow which had risen up in the smoke and flames which shrouded the hilltop. Something massive and unwieldy, reflecting a lustrous brilliance, started rocking on thin shaky legs. Another blow thundered out, and another glowing bolt of lightning zigzagged down the slope. The ground trembled, and the shadow which had appeared in the smoky glow collapsed.

Sidorov started running along the knoll. Inside it, something crashed and cracked, waves of hot air shimmered at his feet, and in the red, dancing light Sidorov saw the movie cameras—the sole witnesses of what was happening on the hilltop—starting to fall, taking lumps of lava with them. He stumbled over one camera. It wobbled, spreading wide the bent legs of the stand. He moved more slowly then, and hot gravel rained down the slope toward him. It quieted down above, but something still smouldered in the darkness there. Then another blow resounded, and Sidorov saw a weak yellow flash.

The hilltop smelled of hot smoke plus something unfamiliar and acrid. Sidorov stopped on the edge of an enormous pit with perpendicular edges. In the pit a nearly finished dome—the air-tight dome for six people, with hall and oxygen filtration—was lying on its side. Molten slag glimmered in the pit. Against this background he could see the torn-off hemomechanical tentacles of the embryo waving weakly and helplessly. Out of the pit came hot acrid smells.

"What can the matter be?" Sorochinsky asked in a whining voice.

Sidorov raised his head and saw Sorochinsky on hands and knees at the very edge of the crater.

"I'll huff, and I'll puff, and I'll blow your house down," Sorochinsky said mournfully. "I'll huff, and I'll—"

"Shut up," Sidorov said quietly. He sat down on the edge of the pit and started to work his way down.

"Don't," said Galtsev. "It's dangerous."

"Shut up," Sidorov repeated. He had to find out fast what had happened here. The developmental work on the Egg, the most perfect machine created by human beings, could not be interfered with. It was the most perfect machine, the most intelligent machine. . . .

The intense heat singed his face. Sidorov squinted and crawled down past the red-hot edge of the newborn dome. He looked around below. He caught sight of fallen concrete arches, rusty blackened reinforcement bars, a broad dark passageway which led somewhere into the depths of the knoll. Something turned ponderously underfoot. Sidorov bent over. He did not at once realize what this gray metal stump was, but when he did, he understood everything. It was an artillery shell.

The knoll was hollow. Two hundred years ago some bunch of bastards had built a dark, concrete-lined chamber inside it. They had stuffed this chamber full of artillery shells. The mechanism erecting the supporting piles for the dome had broken into the vault. The crumbling concrete had not been able to bear the weight of the dome. The piles had slipped into it as if into quicksand. Then the machine had started flooding the concrete with molten lithoplast. The poor embryomech could not know that there was an ammunition dump here. It couldn't even know what an artillery shell was, because the people who had given life to its program had themselves forgotten what artillery shells were. It seemed that the shells were charged with TNT. The TNT had degraded over two hundred years, but not completely. Not in all the shells. And all of them that could explode, had started exploding. And the mechanism had been turned into a junkheap.

Pebbles showered down from above. Sidorov looked up and saw Galtsev descending toward him. Sorochinsky was coming down the opposite wall.

"Where are you going?" Sidorov asked.

Sorochinsky answered in a small voice, "We want to help, sir."

"I don't need help."

"We only . . ." Sorochinsky began, and hesitated.

A crack opened up along the wall behind Sidorov.

"Look out!" yelled Sorochinsky.

Sidorov stepped to the side, tripped over the shell, and fell. He landed face down and immediately turned over on his back. The dome rocked, and ponderously collapsed, burying its scorching-hot edge deep into the black ground. The ground trembled. Hot air lashed Sidorov's face.

A white haze hung over the knoll, where the dome, sticking up out of the crater, shone dimly. Something was still smouldering there, and from time to time it gave off muffled crackling sounds. Galtsev, his eyes red, was sitting with his arms around his knees, looking at the knoll too. His arms were wound with bandages and the entire left half of his face was black with dirt and soot. He had not yet washed it off, although the sun had risen long ago. Sorochinsky was sleeping by the campfire, the suede jacket covering his head.

Sidorov lay down on his back and placed his hands under his head. He didn't want to look at the knoll, at the white haze, at Galtsev's fierce-looking face. It was very pleasant lying there and staring into the blue, blue sky. You could look into that sky for hours. He had known that when he was an Assaultman, when he had jumped for the north pole of Vladislava, when he had stormed Belinda, when he had sat alone in a smashed boat on Transpluto. There was no sky at all there, just a black starry void and one blinding star—the Sun. He had thought then that he would give the last minutes of his life if only he could see a blue sky once more. On Earth that feeling had quickly been forgotten. It had been that way even before, when for years at a time he had not seen blue sky, and each second of those years could have been his last. But it did not befit an Assaultman to think about death. Though on the other hand you had to think a lot about possible defeats. Gorbovsky had once said that death is worse than any defeat, even the most shattering. Defeat was always really only an accident, a setback which you could surmount. You had to surmount it. Only the dead couldn't fight on. But no, the dead *could* fight on, and even inflict a defeat.

Sidorov lifted himself up a little and looked at Galtsev, and wanted to ask him what he thought about all this. Galtsev had also been an Assaultman. True, he had been a bad Assaultman. And probably he thought that there was nothing in the world worse than defeat.

Galtsev turned his head slowly, moved his lips, and said suddenly, "Your eyes are red, sir."

"Yours too," said Sidorov. He should get in touch with Fischer and tell him everything that had happened. He got up and, walking slowly over the grass, headed for the pterocar. He walked with his head back, and looked at the sky. You could stare at the sky for hours—it was so blue and so astonishingly beautiful. The sky you came back to be under.

The Meeting

ALEKSANDR Kostylin stood in front of his enormous desk and examined the slick, glossy photographs.

"Hello, Lin," the Hunter said to him.

Kostylin raised a high-browed bald head and shouted in English, "Ah! Home is the sailor, home from the sea!"

"And the hunter home from the hill," the Hunter finished. They hugged each other.

"What have you got to delight me this time?" Kostylin asked in a businesslike tone. "Are you in from Yaila?"

"Right. Straight from the Thousand Swamps." The Hunter sat down in an armchair and stretched out his legs. "And you're getting fatter and balder, Lin. Sedentary life will be the death of you. Next time I'll take you with me."

Kostylin touched his potbelly worriedly. "Yes," he said. "Terrible. Getting old and fat. The old soldiers are fading away. So, did you bring me anything interesting?"

299]

"Not really, Lin. Nothing much. Ten two-headed snakes, a few new species of polyvalved mollusks. What have you got there?" He reached out a hand and took the packet of photographs from the desk.

"Some greenhorn brought that in. You know him?"

"No." The Hunter examined the photographs. "Not bad. It's Pandora, of course."

"Right. Pandora. The giant crayspider. A very large specimen."

"Yes," said the Hunter, looking at the ultrasonic carbine propped for scale against the bare yellow paunch of the crayspider. "A pretty good specimen for a beginner. But I've seen bigger. How many times did he fire?"

"He says twice. Hit the main nerve center both times."

"He should have fired an anesthetic needle. The lad got a little riled up." With a smile, the Hunter examined the photograph where the excited greenhorn trampled the dead monster. "Well, okay. How are things with you at home?"

Kostylin waved a hand. "Chock full of matrimony. All the girls are getting married. Marta got hitched to a hydrologist."

"Which Marta?" asked the Hunter. "The granddaughter?"

"Great-granddaughter, Pol! Great-granddaughter!"

"Yes, we're getting old." The Hunter laid the photographs on the table and got up. "Well, I'm off."

"Again?" Kostylin said in vexation. "Isn't enough enough?"

"No, Lin. I have to do it. We'll meet in the usual place afterward." The Hunter nodded to Lin and left. He went down to the park and headed for the pavilions. As usual, there were many people at the museum. People walked along lanes planted with orange Venusian palms, crowded around the terrariums, and over the pools of transparent water.

Children romped in the high grass between the trees—they were playing Martian hide-and-seek. The Hunter stopped to watch. It was a very absorbing game. A long time ago the first mimicrodons—large, melancholic lizards ideally suited to sharp changes in their living conditions—had been brought from Mars to Earth. They possessed an unusually well-developed ability to change their skin color, and had the run of the museum park. Small children amused themselves by hunting for them—this required no little sharp-sightedness and agility—and then dragged them from place to place so they could watch the mimicrodons change color. The lizards were large and heavy; the little kids dragged them by the scruffs of their necks. The mimicrodons put up no resistance. They seemed to like it.

The Hunter passed an enormous transparent covering, under which the terrarium "Meadow from the Planet Ruzhen" was located. There, in pale blue grass, the funny rambas—giant, amazingly varicolored insects a little like terrestrial grasshoppers —jumped and fought. The Hunter remembered how, twenty years earlier, he had first gone hunting on Ruzhen. He had stayed in ambush for three days, waiting for something, and the enormous iridescent rambas had hopped around him and sat on the barrel of his carbine. There were always a lot of people around the "Meadow," because the rambas were very funny and very pretty.

Near the entrance to the central pavilion, the Hunter stopped by a railing surrounding a deep round tank, almost a well. In the tank, in water illuminated by violet light, a long hairy animal circled tirelessly—it was an ichthyotherion, the only warmblooded animal to breathe with gills. The ichthyotherion moved constantly—it had swum in those circles one year ago, and five years ago, and forty years ago, when the Hunter had first seen it. The famous Sallier had captured the animal with enormous difficulty. Now Sallier was long dead, and his body reposed somewhere in the jungles of Pandora, while his ichthyotherion still circled and circled in the violet water of the tank.

The Hunter stopped again in the lobby of the main pavilion and sat down in a soft armchair in the corner. The whole center of the bright hall was taken up by a stuffed flying leech—*sora-tobu hiru* (Martian Wildlife, Solar System, Carbon Cycle, Type—Polychordate, Class—Pneumatoderm, Order, Genus, Species— *sora-tobu hiru*). The flying leech was one of the oldest exhibits of the Capetown Museum of Exozoology. This loathsome monster had been holding its maw, like a multijawed power shovel, agape in the face of everyone who had come into the pavilion for a century and a half. Thirty feet long, covered with shiny hard hair, eyeless, noseless. The former master of Mars.

Yes, those were the times on Mars, thought the Hunter. *Times you won't forget. Half a century ago these monsters had been almost completely exterminated. Then suddenly they started multiplying again, and started preying on the lines of communication between the Martian bases, just like in the old days. That was when the famous global hunt was organized. I bumped along in a crawler and couldn't see a thing through the dust clouds the crawler treads had raised. Yellow sand tanks crammed with volunteers were darting along to my left and my right. Just after one tank came out onto a dune, it suddenly overturned, and people spilled out of it every whichway—and just then we came out of the dust, and Elmer grabbed my shoulder and started yelling, and pointing ahead. And I saw leeches, hundreds of leeches, whirling on the saline flat in the low place between the dunes. I started firing, and other people began shooting too, and all the while Elmer was fooling with his homemade rocket launcher, and he just couldn't get it working. Everyone was shouting and swearing at him, even threatening him, but no one could move away from his carbine. The ring of hunters closed up, and we already could see the flashes of fire from the crawlers on the other side, and right then Elmer shoved the rusty pipe of his cannon between me and the driver, and there was a terrible roar and thunder, and I collapsed onto the floor of the crawler, blinded and deafened. Thick black smoke covered the saline flat, all the vehicles stopped, and the people stopped shooting and only yelled and waved their carbines. In five minutes Elmer had used up his ammunition supply, and the crawlers pushed on across the flat, and we started wiping out anything that remained alive after Elmer's rockets. The leeches darted between the vehicles, or got crushed under the tracks, and I kept shooting and shooting and shooting—I was young then, and I really liked shooting. Unfortunately I was always an excellent shot—I never missed. And unfortunately I didn't confine my shooting to Mars and to disgusting predators. It would have been better if I had never seen a carbine in my life.*

He got up, went around the stuffed flying leech, and plodded along the galleries. Obviously he looked bad, for many people were stopping and staring at him anxiously. Finally one girl went up to him and timidly asked whether there was something she could do.

"Come now, my girl," said the Hunter. He forced himself to smile, and he stuck two fingers in his chest pocket and drew out a beauty of a shell from Yaila. "This is for you," he said. "I brought it from quite a way off."

She smiled faintly and took the shell. "You look very bad," she said.

"I'm no longer young, child," said the Hunter. "We old people rarely look good. Too much wear on the soul."

Probably the girl didn't understand him, but then he did not want her to. He stared over her head and went on. Only now he threw back his shoulders and tried to hold himself erect, so that people would not stare at him any more.

All I need is to have little girls feeling sorry for me, he thought. *I've come completely unstuck. Probably I shouldn't come back to Earth any more. Probably I should stay on Yaila forever, settle on the edge of the Thousand Swamps and set out traps for ruby eels. No one knows the Thousand Swamps better than I, and that would be just the place for me. There's a lot there to keep a hunter who won't fire a gun busy.*

He stopped. He always stopped here. In an elongated glass case, on pieces of gray sandstone, stood a wrinkled, unprepossessing, grayish stuffed lizard, with its three pairs of rough legs spread wide. The gray hexapod evoked no emotions from the uninformed visitors. Few of them knew the wrinkled hexapod's wonderful story. But the Hunter knew it, and when he stopped here he always felt a certain superstitious thrill at the mighty power of life. This lizard had been killed ten parsecs from the sun, its body had been prepared, and the dry stuffed carcass had stood for two years on this pedestal. Then one fine day, before the eyes of the museum visitors, ten tiny quick-moving hexapods had crawled from the wrinkled gray hide of their parent. They had immediately died in Earth's atmosphere, burned up from an excess of oxygen, but the commotion had been frightful, and the zoologists did not know to this day how such a thing could have happened. Life was indeed the only thing in existence that merited worship. . . .

The Hunter wandered through the galleries, switching from pavilion to pavilion. The bright African sun—the good, hot sun of Earth—shone down on beasts born under other suns hundreds of billions of miles away, beasts now sealed in vitriplast. Almost all of them were familiar to the Hunter—he had seen them many times, and not only in the museum. Sometimes he stopped in front of new exhibits, and read the strange names of the strange animals, and the familiar names of the hunters. "Maltese sword," "speckled zo," "great ch'i-ling," "lesser ch'i-ling," "webbed capuchin," "black scarecrow," "queen swan" . . . Simon Kreutzer, Vladimir Babkin, Bruno Bellar, Nicholas Drew, Jean Sallier fils. He knew them all and was now the oldest of them, although not the most successful. He rejoiced to learn that Sallier fils had at last bagged a scaly cryptobranchiate, that Vladimir Babkin had gotten a live glider slug back to Earth, and that Bruno Bellar had at last shot that hooknose with the white webbing that he had been hunting on Pandora for several years.

In this way he arrived at Pavilion Ten, where there were many of his own trophies. Here he stopped at almost every exhibit, remembering and relishing. *Here's the flying carpet, also known as the falling leaf. I tracked it for four days. That was on Ruzhen, where it rains so seldom, where the distinguished zoologist Ludwig Porta died so long ago. The flying carpet moves very quickly and has very acute hearing. You can't hunt it in a vehicle—it has to be tracked day and night, by searching out faint, oily traces on the leaves of trees. I tracked this one down once, and since that time no one else has, and Sallier père used to get on his high horse and say that it was a lucky accident.* The Hunter ran his finger with pride across the letters cut into the descriptive plaque: "Acquired and Prepared by Hunter P. Gnedykh." *I fired four times and didn't miss once, but it was still alive when it collapsed on the ground, breaking branches off of the green tree trunks. That was back when I still carried a gun.*

And there's the eyeless monster from the heavy-water swamps of Vladislava. Eyeless and formless. No one had any idea what form to give it when they mounted it for exhibit, and so finally they did it to match the best photograph. I chased it through the swamp to the edge, where several pitfalls were set up, and it fell into one and roared for a long time there and it took two bucketsful of beta-novocaine to put it to sleep. That was fairly recently, ten years ago, and by then I wouldn't use a gun. Pleased to meet you again, monster.

The farther the Hunter went into the galleries of Pavilion Ten, the slower his steps became. Because he didn't want to go farther. Because he couldn't go farther. Because the most important meeting was coming up. And with every step he felt more keenly the familiar melancholy sense of helplessness. The round white eyes were already staring at him out of the clear plastic case. . . .

As usual, he went up to the small exhibit with his head bowed, and first of all he read the notation on the descriptive plaque, which he already knew by heart: "Wildlife of the Planet Crookes, System of EN 92, Carbon Cycle, Type—Monochordate, Class, Order, Genus, Species—*Quadrabrachium tridactylus*. Acquired by Hunter P. Gnedykh, Prepared by Doctor A. Kostylin." Then he raised his eyes.

Under the transparent plastic cover, on a polished slanting plate, lay a head—strongly flattened in the vertical plane, bare and black, with a flat, oval face. The skin on the face was smooth as a drumhead, and there were no teeth, no mouth, no nose apertures. There were only eyes. Round, white, with small black pupils, and remarkably widely spaced. The right eye was slightly damaged, and this gave a strange expression to its dead gaze. Lin was a superb taxidermist—the threefinger had had exactly that expression when the Hunter first bent over it in the fog. That had been long ago.

Seventeen years ago. *Why did it happen?* thought the Hunter. *I hadn't even planned on going hunting there. Crookes had said that there was no life there, except bacteria and land crabs. And still, when Sanders asked me to take a look around the area, I grabbed my carbine.*

Fog hung over the rocky screes. A small red sun—the red dwarf EN 92—was rising, and the fog looked reddish. Rocks crunched under the rover's soft treads, and low crags swam out of the fog one after another. Then something started rustling on the crest on the top of one of the crags, and the Hunter stopped his vehicle. It was impossible to get a good look at the animal at this distance. Furthermore, the fog and the murky illumination lowered the visibility. But the Hunter had an experienced eye. Some sort of large vertebrate was of course stealing along the crest of the crag, and the Hunter was glad that he had brought his carbine along after all. *We'll show up old Crookes*, he thought gaily. He raised the hatch, stuck the barrel of his carbine out carefully, and started to aim. At a moment when the fog had gotten a little thinner and the hunched-up silhouette of the animal showed up distinctly against a background of reddish sky, the Hunter fired. Immediately a blinding violet flash rose up from the place where the animal had been. Something made a loud crash, and a long hissing sound could be heard. Then clouds of gray smoke rose up over the crest and mixed with the fog.

The Hunter was greatly surprised. He remembered loading the carbine with anesthetic needles, and the last thing you would expect from them would be an explosion like this one. He climbed out of the rover and started looking for his kill. He found it where he had expected, under the crag on the rocky scree. It really was a four-legged or four-armed animal, the size of a large Great Dane. It was frightfully burned and mutilated, and the Hunter was amazed by what horrible effect an ordinary anesthetic needle had had. It was hard even to imagine the original appearance of the animal. Only the forepart of the head—a flattened oval, covered with smooth black skin, with lifeless white eyes—remained relatively intact.

On Earth, Kostylin had gotten busy with the trophy. After a week he told the Hunter that the trophy was badly damaged and was of no special interest, save, perhaps, as a proof of the existence of higher forms of animal life in the systems of red dwarfs —and he advised him to be a little more careful with thermite cartridges in future.

"You would almost think you'd fired at it out of fright," Kostylin said in irritation, "as if it had attacked you."

"But I remember perfectly well that I shot a needle," the Hunter objected.

"And I see perfectly well that you hit it in the backbone with a thermite bullet," Lin answered.

The Hunter shrugged and did not argue. He wondered, of course, what could have caused such an explosion, but after all it was not really all that important.

Yes, it seemed quite unimportant then, the Hunter thought. He still stood there, and kept looking at the flat head of the threefinger. *I laughed a little at Crookes, argued a bit with Lin, and forgot everything. And then came doubt, and with it, grief.*

Crookes organized two major expeditions. He covered an enormous area on the planet that bore his name. And he did not find one animal there larger than a land crab the size of a little finger. Then, in the southern hemisphere, on a rocky plateau, he discovered a landing pad of unknown origin—a round plot of fused basalt about twenty meters in diameter. At first this find had aroused much interest, but then it had been discovered that Sanders's starship had landed somewhere in that area two years before for emergency repairs, and the find was forgotten. Forgotten by everyone except the Hunter. Because by that time doubts had already formed in the Hunter's mind.

The Hunter had once heard a story, in the Spacers' Club in Leningrad, about how an engineer had almost gotten burned alive on the planet Crookes. He had climbed out of the ship with a defective oxygen tank. There was a leak in it, and the Crookesian atmosphere was saturated with light hydrocarbons that react violently with free oxygen. Fortunately, they had managed to tear the burning tank off the poor fellow, and he had escaped with only minor burns. As the Hunter had listened to this story, a violet flash over a black hillcrest appeared before his eyes.

When a strange landing pad had been discovered on Crookes, doubts turned into horrible certainty. The Hunter had run to Kostylin. "What have I killed?" he shouted. "Was it an animal or a person? Lin, what have I killed?"

Kostylin listened to him, his eyes turning bloodshot, and then shouted, "Sit down! Cut the hysterics—you're like a whining old woman! Where do you get off talking to me this way? Do you think that I, Aleksandr Kostylin, can't tell the difference between an intelligent being and an animal?"

"But the landing site!"

"You yourself landed on that mesa with Sanders."

"The flash! I hit his oxygen tank!"

"You shouldn't have fired thermite bullets in a hydrocarbon atmosphere."

"Have it your way, but Crookes still didn't find even one more threefinger! I know it was an alien spacer!"

"Hysterical old woman!" yelled Lin. "It could be they won't find one more threefinger on Crookes for another century! It's an enormous planet, filled with caves like a giant Swiss cheese! You simply lucked out, you idiot, and then you didn't manage to follow it through, so you ended up bringing me charred bones instead of an animal!"

The Hunter clenched his hands so that his knuckles cracked. "No, Lin, I didn't bring you an animal," he muttered. "I brought you an alien spacer."

How many words you wasted, Lin old fellow! How many times you tried to convince me! How many times I thought that doubt had departed forever, that I could breathe easy again and not know myself a murderer. Could be like other people. Like the children playing Martian hide-and-seek. But you can't kill doubt with casuistry.

He lay his hands on the case and pressed his face to the clear plastic. "What are you?" he asked with sad yearning.

Lin saw him from afar, and, as always, he was unbearably pained by the sight of a man once so daring and cheerful, now so fearfully broken by his own conscience. But he pretended that everything was wonderful, like the wonderful sunny Capetown day. Clicking his heels noisily, Lin went up to the Hunter, put his hand on his shoulder, and exclaimed in a deliberately cheery voice, "The meeting is over! I could eat a horse, Polly, so we'll go to my place now and have a glorious dinner! Marta has made real Afrikaner oxtail soup in your honor today. Come on, Hunter, the soup awaits us!"

"Let's go," the Hunter said quietly.

"I already phoned home. Everyone is aching to see you and hear your stories."

The Hunter nodded and walked slowly toward the exit. Lin looked at his stooped back and turned to the exhibit. His eyes met the dead white eyes behind the clear pane. Did you have your talk? Lin asked silently.

Yes.

You didn't tell him anything?

No.

Lin looked at the descriptive plaque. "*Quadrabrachium tridactylus.* Acquired by Hunter P. Gnedykh. Prepared by Doctor A. Kostylin." He looked at the Hunter again and quickly, stealthily, after *Quadrabrachium tridactylus*, with his little finger he traced the word "*sapiens.*" Of course not one stroke remained on the plaque, but even so Lin hurriedly erased it with his palm.

It was a burden on Doctor Aleksandr Kostylin too. He knew for sure, had known from the very first.

What You Will Be Like

THE ocean was mirror smooth. The water by the shore was so calm that the dark fibers of seaweed that usually swayed on the bottom, hung motionless.

Kondratev steered the minisub into the cove, brought it right up to shore, and announced, "We're here."

The passengers began to stir.

"Where's my camera?" asked Slavin.

"I'm lying on it," Gorbovsky answered in a weak voice. "Which, I might add, is very uncomfortable. Can I get out?"

Kondratev threw open the hatch, and everyone caught sight of the clear blue sky. Gorbovsky climbed out first. He took some uncertain steps along the rocks, stopped, and poked at a dry mat of driftwood with his foot. "How nice it is here!" he exclaimed. "How soft! May I lie down?"

"You may," said Slavin. He also got out of the hatch and stretched happily.

Gorbovsky lay down immediately.

Kondratev dropped anchor. "I personally don't advise lying on driftwood. There are always thousands of sand fleas there."

Slavin, spreading his legs exaggeratedly wide, started the movie camera chattering. "Smile!" he said sternly.

Kondratev smiled.

"Wonderful!" shouted Slavin, sinking down on one knee.

"I don't quite understand about fleas," came Gorbovsky's voice. "What do they do, Sergei, just hop? Or can they bite you?"

"Yes, they can bite you," Kondratev answered. "Quit waving that camera at me, Evgeny! Go gather some driftwood and make a fire." He climbed into the hatchway and got a bucket.

Slavin squatted down and started digging briskly into the driftwood with two hands, picking out the larger pieces. Gorbovsky watched him with interest.

"Still, Sergei, I don't quite understand about the fleas."

"They burrow into the skin," Kondratev explained, rinsing the pail out with industrial alcohol. "And they multiply there."

"Oh," said Gorbovsky, turning over on his back. "That's terrible."

Kondratev filled the pail with fresh water from the tank on the submarine, and jumped onto the shore. Without talking, he deftly gathered driftwood, lit a fire, hung the pail over it, and got a line, hooks, and a box of bait out of his voluminous pockets. Slavin came up with a handful of wood chips.

"Look after the fire," Kondratev directed. "I'll catch some perch. I'll be back in an instant." Jumping from stone to stone, he headed toward a large moss-covered rock sticking out of the water twenty paces from the shore, moved around a bit on it, and then settled down. The morning was quiet—the sun, just coming above the horizon, shone straight into the cove, blinding him. Slavin sat down tailor-fashion by the fire and started feeding in chips.

"Amazing creatures, human beings," Gorbovsky said suddenly. "Follow their history for the past ten thousand years. What an amazing development has been achieved by the productive sector, for instance. How the scope of scholarship has broadened! And new fields and new professions crop up every year. For instance, I recently met a certain comrade, a very important specialist, who teaches children how to walk. And this specialist told me that there is a very complicated theory behind this work."

"What's his name?" Slavin asked lazily.

"Elena something. I've forgotten her last name. But that's not the point. What I mean is that here we have the sciences and the means of production always developing, while our amusements, our means of recreation, are the same as in ancient Rome. If I get tired of being a spacer, I can be a biologist, a builder, an agronomist—lots of things. But suppose I get tired of lying around, then what is there to do? Watch a movie, read a book, listen to music, or watch other people running. In stadiums. And that's it! And that's how it always has been—spectacles and games. In short, all our amusements come down in the last analysis to the gratification of a few sensory organs. And not even all of them, you'll note. So far no one has, say, figured out how to amuse oneself gratifying the organs of touch and smell."

"There's the thing!" said Slavin. "We have public spectacles, so why not public tactiles? And public, uh, olfactiles?"

Gorbovsky chortled quietly. "Precisely," he said. "Olfactiles. And there will be, Evgeny! There inevitably will be, some day!"

"But seriously, it's all what you should expect, Leonid. A human being strives in the last analysis not so much for the perception itself as for the processing of these perceptions. He strives to gratify not so much the elementary sensory organs as his chief organ of perception, the brain."

Slavin picked out some more chips of driftwood and threw them onto the fire. "My father told me that in his time someone had prophesied the extinction of the human race under conditions of material abundance. Machines would do everything, no one would have to work for his bread and butter, and people would become parasites. The human race would be overrun with drones. But the fact is that working is much more interesting than resting. A drone would just get bored."

"I knew a drone once," Gorbovsky said seriously. "But the girls didn't like him at all and he just became extinct as a result of natural selection. But I still think that the history of amusements is not yet over, I mean amusement in the ancient sense of the word. And we absolutely will have to have some sort of olfactiles. I can easily imagine—"

"Forty thousand people in the stadium," put in Slavin, "and all sniff as one. The 'Roses in Ketchup Symphony.' And the critics —with enormous noses—will write, 'In the third movement, with an impressive dissonance, into the tender odor of two rose petals bursts the brisk fragrance of a fresh onion.' "

When Kondratev returned with a string of fresh fish, the spacer and the writer were guffawing in front of a dying fire.

"What's so funny?" Kondratev inquired curiously.

"It's just *joie de vivre*, Sergei," Slavin answered. "Why don't you ornament your own life with some merry jape?"

"All right," said Kondratev. "Right now I'll clean the fish, and you take the guts and stick them over under that rock. I always bury them there."

"The 'Gravestone Symphony,' " said Gorbovsky. "First movement, *allegro ma non troppo.* "

Slavin's face grew long, and he fell silent, staring glumly at the fatal rock. Kondratev took a flounder, slapped it down on a flat stone, and took out a knife. Gorbovsky followed his every movement with absorption. Kondratev cut off the flounder's head slantwise in one blow, deftly stuck his hand under the skin, and swiftly skinned the flounder whole, as if he were peeling off a glove. He threw the skin and the intestines over to Slavin.

"Leonid," Kondratev said, "fetch the salt, please." Without saying a word, Gorbovsky got up and climbed into the submarine. Kondratev quickly dressed the flounder and started in on a perch. The pile of fish intestines in front of Slavin grew.

"And just where is the salt?" called Gorbovsky from the hatch.

"In the provisions box," Kondratev shouted back. "On the right."

"And she won't start off?" Gorbovsky asked cautiously.

"Who is 'she'?"

"The sub. The control board is what is on the right down here."

"To the right of the board is a box," said Kondratev.

They could hear Gorbovsky moving around in the cabin.

"I found it," he said happily. "Should I bring all of it? There must be over five kilos of the stuff."

Kondratev raised up his head. "What do you mean, five kilos? There should be a little packet."

After a minute's pause, Gorbovsky said, "Yes, you're right.

Coming up." He got out of the hatch, holding the packet of salt in one hand. His hands were covered with flour.

Putting the packet down near Kondratev, he groaned, "Ah, universal entropy!" He was preparing to lie down when Kondratev said, "And now, Leonid, fetch a bay leaf, please."

"Why?" Gorbovsky asked with great astonishment. "Do you mean that three mature, nay, elderly people, three old men, cannot get along without bay leaf? With their enormous experience, with their endurance—"

"Oh, come now," said Kondratev. "I promised you that you would have some proper relaxation, Leonid, but I didn't mean you could fall asleep on me. We can't have this! The bay leaf, on the double!"

Gorbovsky fetched the bay leaf, and then fetched the pepper and sundry other spices, and then, on another trip, the bread. In token of protest, along with the bread he dragged out a heavy oxygen tank and said venomously, "I brought this at the same time. Just in case you needed it."

"Many thanks," said Kondratev. "I don't. Take it back."

Gorbovsky dragged the tank back with curses. When he returned, he did not even try to lie down. He stood next to Kondratev and watched him cook fish soup. Meanwhile, the gloomy correspondent for the European Information Center, with the help of two bits of driftwood, was burying the fish intestines under the "gravestone."

The soup was boiling. From it wafted a stunning aroma, seasoned with the odor of smoke. Kondratev took a spoon, tasted, and considered.

"Well?" asked Gorbovsky.

"A pinch more salt," Kondratev answered. "And perhaps some pepper, eh?"

"Perhaps," said Gorbovsky, his mouth watering.

"Yes," Kondratev said firmly. "Salt and pepper."

Slavin finished interring the fish guts, put the stone on top, and went off to wash his hands. The water was warm and clear. He could see small yellow-gray fish scurrying among the seaweeds. Slavin sat down on a rock and looked around. A shining wall of ocean rose up beyond the cove. Blue peaks on the neighboring island hung motionless over the horizon. Everything was deep blue, shining, and motionless, except for large black and white birds which sailed over the rocks in the cove without crying out. A fresh salt odor came from the water. "A wonderful planet, Earth," he said aloud.

"It's ready!" Kondratev announced. "We will now have fish soup. Leonid, be a good lad and bring the bowls, please."

"Okay," said Gorbovsky. "And I'll bring the spoons while I'm at it."

They sat down around the steaming pail, and Kondratev dished out the fish soup. For some time they ate silently. Then Gorbovsky said, "I just love fish soup. And it's so seldom that I get a chance to eat it."

"There's still half a bucket left," Kondratev said.

"Ah, Sergei!" Gorbovsky said with a sigh. "I can't eat enough to hold me for two years."

"So there won't be fish soup on Tagora," said Kondratev.

Gorbovsky sighed again. "Quite possibly not. Although Tagora isn't Pandora, of course, so there's still hope. If only the Commission lets us go fishing."

"Why wouldn't they?"

"Those are stern and harsh men on the Commission. Like Gennady Komov. He's sure to not even let me lie down. He will demand that all my actions coincide with the interests of the aboriginal population of the planet. And how should I know what their interests are?"

"You are an incredible whiner, Leonid," Slavin said. "Taking you on the Contact Commission was a terrible mistake. Can you see it, Sergei—Leonid, our anthropocentrist par excellence, representing the human race to the civilization of another world!"

"And why not?" Kondratev said judiciously. "I greatly respect Comrade Gorbovsky."

"I respect him too," said Gorbovsky.

"Oh, I even respect him myself," said Slavin. "But I don't like the first question he's planning to ask the Tagorans."

"What question?" asked Kondratev, surprised.

"The very first: 'Could I perhaps lie down?' "

Kondratev snorted into his soup spoon, and Gorbovsky looked reproachfully at Slavin.

"Ah, Evgeny!" he said. "How can you joke like that? Here you are laughing, while I'm shaking in my shoes, because the first contact with a newly discovered civilization is a historic occasion, and the slightest blunder could bring harm down on our descendants. And our descendants, I must say to you, trust us implicitly."

Kondratev stopped eating and looked at him,

"No, no," Gorbovsky said hurriedly. "I can't vouch for our descendants as a whole, of course, but take Petr Petrovich—he expressed himself quite explicitly on the question of his trust in us."

"And whose descendant is this Petr Petrovich?" asked Kondratev.

"I can't tell you any more than that. It's clear from his patronymic, however, that he is the direct descendant of someone named Petr. We didn't discuss it with him, you see. Would you like me to tell you about what we did discuss with him?"

"Hmm," said Kondratev. "What about washing the dishes?"

"No, I will not. It's now or never. People should lie down for a while after a meal."

"Right!" exclaimed Slavin, turning over on his side. "Go ahead and tell us, Leonid."

And Gorbovsky began to tell them. "We were traveling on the *Tariel* to EN 6—an easy flight and not a very interesting one— taking Percy Dickson and seventy-seven tons of fine food to the astronomers there, and then the concentrator blew up on us. God alone knows why—these things happen sometimes even now. We hung in space two parsecs from the nearest base and quietly began to prepare for entry into the next world, because without the plasma concentrator you can't even think about anything else. In this spot, as in any other, there were two ways out: open the hatches immediately, or first eat the seventy-seven tons of the astronomers' groceries and then open the hatches. Mark Falkenstein and I held a meeting over Percy Dickson in the wardroom, and started making up our minds. Dickson had it easy—he had been conked on the head and was still unconscious. Falkenstein and I quickly came to the conclusion that there was no need to hurry. It was the greatest task that we had ever set ourselves— the two of us (there was no hope for Dickson) would annihilate seventy-seven tons of provisions. We could stretch it out for thirty years, anyhow, and after that would be time enough for opening the hatches if we had to. The water and oxygen regeneration systems were in perfect shape, and we were moving with a velocity of two hundred fifty thousand kilometers per second, and we still had the prospect of seeing all sorts of unknown worlds before we got around to the Next One.

"I want to make sure you understand our situation—it was two parsecs to the nearest inhabited point, and there was hopeless void around us, and on board there were two of us alive and one half-dead—three people, note; precisely three, and I say that as ship's captain. And then the door opens, and into the wardroom walks a fourth. At first we weren't even surprised. Falkenstein asked rather impolitely, 'What are you doing here?' And then suddenly it sank in, and we jumped up and stared at him. And he stared at us. Average height, thin, pleasant face, didn't have all that frizzy hair that, say, Dickson has got. Only his eyes were unusual—they had the look of a pediatrician's. And another thing—he was dressed like a spacer during a mission, but his jacket buttoned from right to left. Like a woman's. Or, according to rumor, like the Devil's. That surprised me most of all. And while we were looking at each other, I blinked, and looked again, and now his jacket buttoned the proper way. So I sat down.

" 'Hello,' said the stranger. 'My name is Petr Petrovich. And I know your names, so let's not waste time on that. Instead we'll see how Doctor Percy Dickson is doing.' He shoved Falkenstein aside rather unceremoniously and sat down next to Dickson. 'Excuse me,' I say, 'but are you a doctor?' 'Yes,' he says, 'you could say that.' And he starts undoing the bandage around Dickson's head. Laughing and joking, you know, like a kid undoing a candy wrapper. A chill actually ran across my skin. I looked at Falkenstein—he's turned pale and is just opening and shutting his mouth. Meanwhile, Petr Petrovich had taken off the bandage and exposed the wound. The wound, I should tell you, was horrible, but Petr Petrovich kept his cool. He spread his fingers wide and started massaging Dickson's skull. And, can you imagine, the wound closed up! Right before our eyes. There was no trace of it left. Dickson turned over on his right side and started snoring as if nothing had happened to him.

" 'Let him get his sleep now,' says Petr Petrovich. 'And meanwhile you and I will go see what things are like in the engine room.' And he took us to the engine room. We walked after him like sheep. Except that, in contradistinction to sheep, we didn't even bleat. As you can imagine, we were simply speechless. We hadn't gotten any words ready for such an encounter. Petr Petrovich opens the hatch to the reactor and crawls right into the concentration chamber. Falkenstein gave a cry, and I shouted, 'Be careful! Radiation!' He looked at us thoughtfully, then said, 'Oh, yes, right. Leonid and Mark,' he says, 'you go straight to the control room, and I'll be along in a minute.' And he closed the hatch behind him. Mark and I went to the control room and started pinching each other. We pinched silently, fiercely, cruelly. But neither of us woke up. And two minutes later the instruments come on, and the concentrator board shows the contraption is in a number-one state of readiness. Then Falkenstein stopped pinching and said in a low voice, 'Leonid, do you know how to perform an exorcism?' He had just said that when in came Petr Petrovich. 'Ah,' he says, 'some starship you have here, Leonid. And some coffin. I admire your daring, comrades.' Then he suggests that we sit down and ask him questions.

"I started to think furiously about what would be the smartest question to ask him while Falkenstein, a profoundly practical man, inquired, 'Where are we now?' Petr Petrovich smiled sadly, and at the same instant the walls of the control room became transparent. 'There,' says Petr Petrovich, and he points. 'Right there is our Earth. Four and a half parsecs. And there is EN 6, as you call it. Change course by six-tenths of a second and go straight into deritrinitation. Or maybe,' he says, 'I should throw you right over to EN 6?' Mark answered touchily, 'Thanks just the same, but don't bother, we'd rather do it ourselves.' And he took the bull by the horns and started orienting the ship. Meanwhile I had been thinking about a question, and all the time into my head came something about 'the eternal silence of the infinite spaces.' Petr Petrovich laughed and said, 'Well, all right, you're too shaken up now to ask questions. And I must be on my way. They're expecting me back in those infinite spaces. I think I had better explain briefly.

" 'You see, I am your remote descendant,' he says. 'We, the descendants, very much like to drop in on you, our ancestors, every now and then. To see how things are going, and to show you what you will be like. Ancestors are always curious about what they will be like, and descendants, about how they got that way. But I'll tell you frankly that such excursions are not exactly encouraged. We've got to watch what we're doing with you ancestors. We could goof something up and turn history head over heels. And sometimes it's very hard to refrain from intervening in your affairs. It's all right to intervene the way I'm doing now. Or like another friend of mine. He ended up in one of the battles near Kursk and took it upon himself to repel a German tank attack. He got himself killed, chopped into kindling. Terrible even to think about. Of course he didn't repel the attack by himself, so nobody noticed. And another colleague of mine tried to wipe out the army of Genghis Khan. They hardly even slowed down. . . . Well, that's it, more or less. I've got to go now—they're probably worrying about me already.'

"Here I yelled out, 'Wait, one question! So you people are omnipotent now?' He looked at me with a sort of kindly condescension and said, 'Oh, come now, Leonid. We can do a few things, but there's still enough work left for hundreds of millions of years. For instance,' he says, 'not long ago one of our children accidentally grew up spoiled. We brought him up—brought him up, and gave up on him. Threw up our hands and sent him off to put out galaxies. There are,' he says, 'ten too many in the next megasystem over. And you, comrades,' he says, 'are on the right track. We like you. We believe in you,' he says. 'Just remember: if you are what you plan on being, then we'll become what we are. And what you, accordingly, will be.' And he waved and left. And that's the end of my tale."

Gorbovsky propped himself up on his elbows and looked around at his audience. Kondratev was drowsing, basking in the sun.

Slavin lay on his back, staring thoughtfully at the sky. " 'We get up out of bed for the future,' " he slowly recited. " 'We mend blankets for the future. We marshal our thoughts for the future. We gather strength for the future. . . . We will hear the approaching footsteps of the element of fire, but we will already be prepared to loose waves upon the flame.' "

Gorbovsky listened to the end and said, "That has to do with the content. But what about the form?"

"A good beginning," Slavin said professionally, "but it turned sour toward the end. Is it really so difficult to think of something besides that spoiled child of yours?"

"Yes, it's difficult," Gorbovsky said.

Slavin turned over on his stomach. "You know, Leonid," he said, "Lenin's idea about the development of the human race in spirals has always struck me. From the primitive communism of the destitute, through hunger, blood, and wars, through insane injustices, to the communism of endless material and spiritual wealth. I strongly suspect that this is just theory for you, but I come from a time when the turn of the spiral was not yet completed. It was only in movies, but I did see rockets setting fire to villages, people in flames, covered with napalm. Do you know what napalm is? Or a grafter—do you know about that? You see, the human race began with communism and it returned to communism, and with this return a new turn of the spiral begins, a completely fantastic one."

Kondratev suddenly opened his eyes, stretched, and sat up. "Philosophers," he said. "A bunch of Aristotles. Let's hurry up and wash the dishes, and then go swimming, and I'll show you the Golden Grotto. You haven't seen anything like it, you many-traveled old men."

MOSCOW-LENINGRAD, 1960–1966